The Marquess Returns

Jane Maguire

The Marquess Returns

Copyright © 2024 Jane Maguire

Cover design by Holly Perret

ISBN: 978-1-7382727-2-3

www.janemaguireauthor.com

Also by Jane Maguire

The Inconveniently Wed series

Book 1: **Secrets and a Scandal**

Book 2: **Rumors and a Rake**

Book 3: **Longing for a Lady**

The Rockliffe Dynasty series

Book 1: **A Study in Desire**

Book 2: **A Duke Once Lost**

Book 3: **The Marquess Returns**

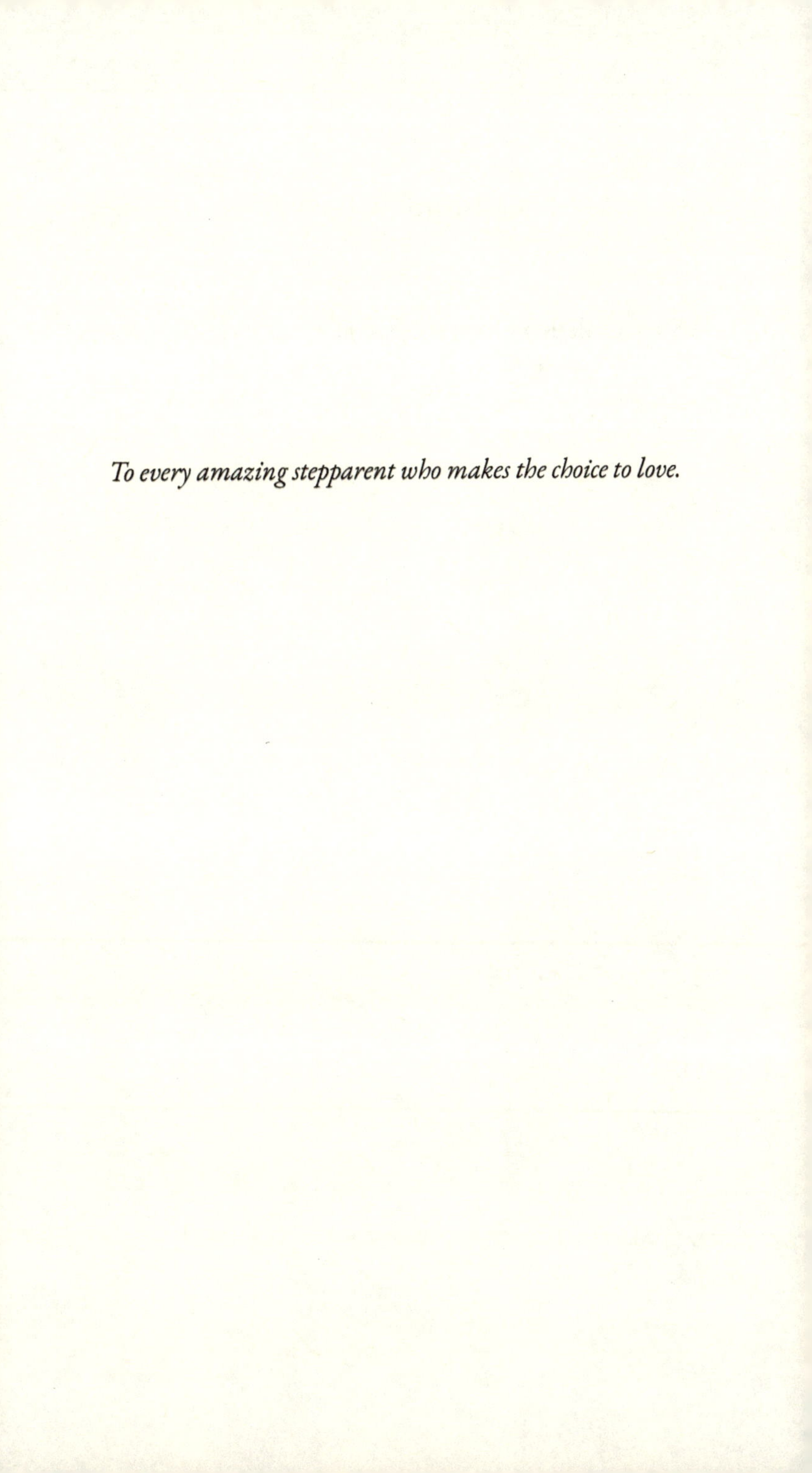

To every amazing stepparent who makes the choice to love.

Content Advisory

This book deals with the subjects of infertility and childbirth trauma. Reader discretion is advised.

The Marquess Returns

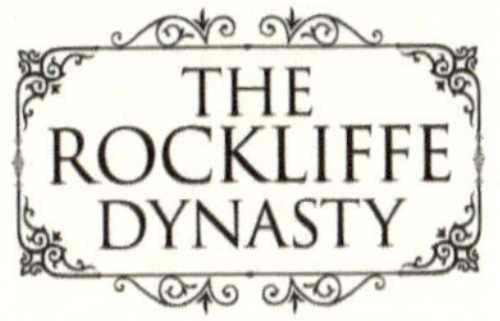

By Jane Maguire

Prologue

July 1798

Few sentences beginning with the words *I dare you* ever led to a course of action that was sensible and wise, and this was proving no exception.

With a frown, Miss Phoebe Windham wriggled her foot until her slipper came free from the patch of mud she'd carelessly trod upon, flicking away sludgy brown drops. That brief obstacle behind her, she hiked up her skirts, sparing her hem further abuse as she continued traipsing through the wood.

No, not sensible and wise at all. However, she didn't intend to let that stop her. Not on an afternoon such as this, when the sun blazed high in the sky, casting muggy heat over her surroundings.

She'd tried to keep herself occupied with worthwhile pursuits during the earlier part of the day. Writing a few letters. Practicing the pianoforte. Mending a pair of stockings. Yet as the air in the vicarage had grown more oppressive, leaving her aunt and uncle fanning themselves listlessly in the sitting room and the younger children scattering to places unknown, she and her eldest cousin, Clara, had become idle. A situation that tended to lead to frivolity.

Like her, Clara was a girl of eighteen, eager to have a companion in a place that could prove, as she claimed, exceptionally dull. Phoebe couldn't abide dullness, either. A lack of occupation gave her too much time to think about all she'd lost. Of how much her circumstances had changed.

And so, she and Clara had begun playing a game. Something to take away the worst of the tedium. *I dare you ...* The phrase they took turns uttering, watching with a mixture of awe and amusement as they each performed the tasks assigned by the other. *I dare you to climb to the top of the apple tree. I dare you to sneak the bottle of currant wine out of the kitchen.*

The latest challenge of Clara's invention, though, was in a class of its own. *I dare you to go to Beaumont Manor and swim in Lord Rockliffe's lake.*

Phoebe quickened her pace, keeping her eyes to the ground so she didn't have another puddle mishap—for it seemed the blistering sun hadn't yet managed to dry up the remnants of yesterday's rain in places such as this, where the thick tree canopy provided ample shade. It didn't help that the area had no proper path, only a topsy-turvy mixture of roots and underbrush. Then again, why would there be anything more? People likely had little cause to come this way, to the far corners of the Rockliffe estate. Likewise, she and Clara shouldn't be here, either. They were trespassers.

But whatever trepidation that knowledge caused, she tried to push it away as she kept up her steady footsteps, Clara right behind her. The challenge had been issued, and she refused to forfeit in favor of returning to boredom and overbearing sultriness at the vicarage.

"I think ... I think we're almost there," Clara huffed after a period where the lone sound that passed between them was the rustle of their feet against leaves and grass.

Phoebe turned to glance at her red-cheeked cousin, then diverted her gaze in the direction of Clara's finger, which pointed straight ahead. Sure enough, the oak trees seemed to be thinning, and beyond the sturdy trunks were glimpses of manicured grass and a hint of glimmering water.

The lengthy walk in such weather had left her just as winded as Clara, with beads of perspiration dampening her hair and coating her skin. Yet the sight beyond the trees beckoned, giving her a sudden burst of energy, and she dashed forward, leaving the panting Clara behind.

All at once, she reached the edge of the clearing and pressed her palm to the tree trunk behind her for support, letting out a short gasp. Prior to this point, Beaumont Manor—home of the elusive and supposedly cantankerous Marquess of Rockliffe— had been nothing more than a stately house in the distance, visible when her walks led her up the hill just outside the village. Now, she was immersed in the heart of it, standing atop a slope that traveled down to a sprawling lake of crystalline blue. To the side of the shore closest to her stood a Doric temple, crafted of the same pale stone as the house, and across from that, on the opposite end of the lake, was a footbridge, leading up to a vast lawn. The expanse of lush grass, dotted with shrubs, hedges, and more towering trees, eventually reached the house's massive terrace, where the marquess himself could stand and survey the majesty of the land he owned.

That had been her first protest when Clara issued the challenge. *I cannot. What if someone looks out and catches me?* A possibility that seemed even more likely now that she'd laid eyes on the back side of Beaumont Manor, with its rows of gleaming, full-length windows to give its occupants a perfect view of the lake.

However, Clara had dismissed her worries, assuring her that the family hadn't yet returned from their Season in London. Which Phoebe knew for a fact wasn't entirely true. Perhaps the incident from last week hadn't made an impression on Clara, but for Phoebe, it was a different story.

She pushed a damp strand of hair off her forehead, reliving the memory yet again. The thundering hooves that had come up behind them as she and Clara strolled into the village early one morning. The magnificent black gelding kicking up piles of dust as it raced past. And the rider atop him, clad in matching black, with powerful thighs that held tight to the horse's flanks and strong, commanding arms that flicked the reins.

That's the marquess, Clara had hissed excitedly in her ear as the dusty clouds settled around them, leaving Phoebe blinking in surprise at the figure who was already halfway up the road. When Clara had described the dour Marquess of Rockliffe after Phoebe first arrived in Bowden, she supposed she'd pictured—well, not *that*. Not someone large and athletic, whose flash of chiseled features contained vestiges of youth.

She'd tried—unsuccessfully, if she were being honest—to put the incident, and the spark it ignited low in her belly, out of her mind, until Clara's dare had warranted speaking of it again. But once more, Clara had met her with assurances. *Oh, the marquess is long gone. It's rare he visits Beaumont Manor at all, and while perhaps some estate business required his attention, I believe he only stayed for a day or two before going back to London. Papa himself said that he left last week.*

And so, Phoebe had begun the trek to Beaumont Manor, out of protests but replete with apprehension that refused to dissolve. However, a challenge was a challenge, and after all her long, somber days, she couldn't deny that a little thrill also went along with it.

Before she could think on the matter any longer, she

pulled her feet out of her mud-caked slippers, letting her stockings sink into the grass. The sensation was blissful, the green blades soft and warm upon her heels, creating a slight tickling sensation. It was nothing, though, compared to how it would feel to jump into the crystal water. To have coolness envelope her overheated body, to float upon its surface as the sun beat down on her.

She reached to her back, fumbling to find the tapes of her hated black bombazine gown. Shedding the stiff, thick garment would be a relief in itself, and when she combined that with a plunge into the lake—heaven. She surveyed the landscape once more, and for the first time, the thrill of what she was doing outweighed the trepidation. If she walked a little more, down to where the lake curved outward and clusters of trees lined the shore, she would be concealed from view even if there did happen to be servants going about the house. In fact, it would be nearly like having her own private swimming area, and maybe she could even entice Clara to jump in with her—

Water erupted from the center of the lake, and an arm broke through the perfect glassy surface.

An arm, and a head, and then another arm, and she stumbled backward, clamping her mouth closed just in time to suppress a shriek. Her hand flew to her bodice, grasping it before the loosened gown had a chance to puddle to the ground. If she had any sense whatsoever, she would grab her slippers and begin a hasty sprint to the safety of the wood.

She didn't do that, though. She was frozen, watching the body—the very male body—glide through the water. Watching as strong arms propelled him toward the opposite shore, and beads of water sparkled against his sun-bronzed skin like diamonds. His head went below the surface, the depths of the lake swallowing him once more. But by that point, she already knew what she'd seen. The sun had caught his drenched hair, making the darkened mass shine with hints of bronze. The same color she'd detected as the man on horseback went galloping by, and the morning light had made the hair beneath his top hat blaze.

Clara was wrong. The Marquess of Rockliffe remained very much in residence.

Grass rustled behind her, and she put up a hand, warning Clara not to come any closer. Neither of them could afford to risk making even the slightest noise until ... until ... Lord, what was she still doing here? Why hadn't she run from the start?

She spared a glance for her discarded slippers upon the ground, calculating the time it would take to grab them and disappear back into the trees. Three seconds? Five seconds? Fast enough that the marquess would still be underwater, none the wiser—

Water splashed up again, this time beside the shore, and the marquess's head and bare shoulders emerged from the lake. Phoebe's breath caught, her heart thundering within her chest. And still, she couldn't move.

Observing him in the seconds-long encounter on the side of the road had been one thing. However, as much as that incident had left her with an unbalanced, fluttery feeling, it couldn't compare to the fire running through her veins from seeing him in the lake. His untamed hair glistened, pouring rivulets down the back of his neck, and his muscles, previously just suggested by his tight riding coat, were on full display. He was rising, beginning to pull himself onto the shore—

Where it became apparent he didn't have on a stitch of clothing.

Her cheeks flamed, and while she'd spent the whole day feeling overheated, her body now seemed on the verge of combustion. This was absurd, terrible, so wrong ... *thrilling*—

The marquess paused in his ascent, and his head whipped around, sending a shower of droplets back into the lake. Even from a distance, she could tell he was squinting against the blinding sunrays. Until all at once, his eyes widened. Locked with hers.

Whatever spell had transfixed her promptly shattered, and though her heart seized, she managed to dip to the ground and snatch up her slippers before bursting back into the trees.

"Wh—?"

Clara formed the beginning of a word, but by that point, Phoebe was grasping her arm, dragging her along as she sprinted through the dense oak wood. She ran with abandon until her lungs ached and one of her stockings ripped across the sole. Only when they reached the meadow bordering the road back to the village—and were safely away from the Rockliffe estate—did she allow herself to collapse into the tall grass, her chest heaving with exertion.

Clara sank down beside her, fighting to catch her breath. Not saying anything but staring, her face contorted with utter perplexity.

"He was there," Phoebe finally managed to choke out once her inhales and exhales became less ragged. "The marquess. *In the lake.*"

"The marquess ..." Clara's voice died out, and suddenly, her bewilderment turned to a look of horrified recognition. "Oh, Phoebe, I am *so* sorry. I don't know how that could have happened, truly."

Phoebe felt her brow shoot up, and she fixed her cousin with a cutting glare. *Why* had she thought listening to Clara was a good idea? *Not that I regret what I saw ...*

The redness in Clara's cheeks spread to her ears, and she rushed to take a few more stuttering breaths. "Like I told you, Papa said he left; I'm certain of it. I really didn't think there was any chance he'd come back. Not until the Season ended and he had the marchioness and the rest of his family with him, at least. Even then, it was doubtful, for there are rumors that he and Lady Rockliffe are estranged ..."

Clara continued to talk, but Phoebe could no longer absorb the words. Not after *marchioness*. Her head spun. Her chest felt like it might explode. And still, a few lingering twinges—drat them, anyway—tugged at the apex of her thighs.

What a little fool she was. Lusting after a man who belonged to someone else. Whom she could never have even if he didn't.

She staggered to her feet, reaching for the fastenings at the back of her dress so she could secure the respectable high-necked bodice back into place. "I forfeit." That probably went without saying, but best she make it *very* clear. "Give me whatever punishment you see fit. Cover my face in soot if it pleases you, but I forfeit."

She crammed her foot, torn stocking and all, into her muddy slipper, glancing around her to seek out the other one—

It wasn't there. Blast, blast, *blast*, she must have dropped it somewhere between here and the wood at Beaumont Manor. In her haste, maybe she hadn't picked it up in the first place.

Well, that wasn't going to stop her now. Squaring her shoulders, she marched over the grass toward the road, ignoring the fatigued ache in her legs. The sooner they got home, the better. If she had any bit of luck left on her side, the day's heat would keep everyone they knew indoors, and Aunt Harriet and Uncle Martin would be too weary to take notice when she and Clara crept through the back door of the vicarage. For how was she to explain how she'd gotten herself in such a state?

"It's my turn," she said when Clara, still breathing heavily, caught up to her, fighting to match her strides. "I dare you to ... to write an anonymous love letter to Matthew Wilkinson."

"Phoebe, really!" Clara's already flushed cheeks reddened

further, and she let out a giggle. "But I suppose a dare is a dare."

Good. Her challenge had hit the mark. Phoebe allowed herself to slow long enough to emit a near-silent sigh of relief. Clara had done no end of talking about Mr. Wilkinson, a visiting solicitor's apprentice, after she'd encountered him at the assembly hall several days prior. Finding the proper words to write him would take the rest of the day if not longer. Long enough that today's incident would be firmly out of mind, and they would never have cause to speak of it again.

That's where Phoebe needed it. Away from Clara's head and, especially, away from her own. No more images of broad shoulders, muscular arms, a dripping torso—

No more.

Her slipper may have remained by the lake. The rest of her needed to move along and not look back.

1

June 1806

Of the two letters Phoebe held clenched within her shaking fists, it was difficult to say which one was worse. Her eyes darted between both pages—one covered with the tidy handwriting of a practiced clerk, the other filled with the overlarge, sloping scrawl of a man in his cups—while her stomach sank down to her half-boots. As different as the letters appeared, they each contained a shock of equal proportions. They each shattered the faint strands of hope she'd developed for the future and promised certain misery.

"That settles it, then." Aunt Harriet, sitting beside her on the under-stuffed sofa cushion, gave a decided nod. "You were presented with a problem, followed by a solution. I'm not certain where the dilemma lies."

Phoebe stared, open-mouthed, at her aunt's sharp features, feeling her face go bloodless and cold. Did Harriet really not see? Not understand?

Of course she didn't. Phoebe sagged against the sofa's arm, fighting back the wretched sting of tears. Aunt Harriet and

Uncle Martin had their own children to worry about. Schooling to pay for. Dowries to provide. If ever they'd felt the slightest bit of affection for the niece who'd been cast upon them, Phoebe had obliterated it years ago with her shameful misdeeds.

She threw aside the letter in her left hand, the neat rows of words beginning to mock her. Cousin Eugenia's solicitor had penned a missive that proved nothing short of courteous. That didn't change the fact that it delivered a crushing blow.

Mrs. Eugenia Colepeper's will had been read, and she bequeathed onto her cousin and longtime companion, Miss Phoebe Windham, her harlequin brooch.

Not the sum at which she'd hinted as Phoebe toiled for a pittance, desperate to place herself back in *someone's* good graces. *You should be grateful I even took you in*, Eugenia had been fond of reminding her during the months when she deferred Phoebe's meager salary or decided not to give it at all. *You have a long road of repentance, but if you can prove yourself obedient and modest, perhaps I'll consider you worthy of a reward in the end.*

Except Phoebe hadn't received a monetary reward. She'd gotten a brooch. One she could hardly even sell, for she knew for a fact that the jewels were paste.

"If I were you, I'd be thanking God for my good fortune." Harriet gave a pointed glance at the letter still within Phoebe's grasp, her tone acrid enough to pull Phoebe from her thoughts. "Second chances such as the one Sir Ambrose is willing to give you do not come along every day. You were fool enough to turn him down the first time, and look where that got you. Now is your chance to set everything right."

The paper started to prick Phoebe's skin, the uncomfortable sensation seeping through her gloves, almost as if by touching his words, she was also touching a piece of Ambrose himself. She tossed the letter on the sofa with the other, trying not to shudder.

Harriet's eyes narrowed, and she let out an impatient huff. "Has Sir Ambrose done something to cause you offense?"

"N-no." Phoebe dragged out the word, struggling with how best to convey her sentiments. She could hardly fault Ambrose for inheriting her father's baronetcy despite her father's deepest wish that the title not fall to *that unmitigated jackass*. Such was the law of primogeniture.

There was no single event that caused her to recoil from the mere mention of Ambrose's name. Rather, it was a combination of little things, which had started the moment he came to overtake her home at Birchby Park close to nine years prior. The way he'd leered at her from across the dinner table or brushed up against her—accidentally, of course, yet it wouldn't stop happening—as she traversed the corridors. His marriage proposal had come soon after, delivered with a grandiose smile, as if he'd done such a favor to his unfortunate displaced cousin that she should be exalting at his feet. Yet Phoebe hadn't considered it a favor or a privilege. Instead, she'd fled from Birchby Park, begging Harriet—her deceased mother's sister in Kent—to take her in.

That decision had come with its own devastating consequences, and the arrangement had been short-lived. Even so, she couldn't regret turning down Ambrose's proposal. Not when, during the rare visits she and Eugenia had taken back to Birchby Park, she'd witnessed the woman he'd gone on to marry cowering in corners, silent and skittish. The servants, too, had seemed to walk on eggshells, while the later the hour grew, the rowdier Ambrose had become.

No, he'd never done anything specific to Phoebe that warranted censure. However, she always wedged a chair against the door when they slept under the same roof, for the possibility hung over her head, ready to come to fruition at any moment. It was a deep-rooted feeling she had, that she'd harbored for all these years and couldn't shake. Ambrose meant trouble, and she needed to stay away.

"No," she repeated, having none of the right words to explain what she so urgently needed her aunt to understand, "but I cannot ..."

She closed her eyes, requiring a moment where the offending letter on the sofa wasn't in plain view. Whoever could have predicted that such an unfortunate mix of circumstances would come to pass? That Ambrose's poor, suffering wife would die. That six months later, his much older sister, Eugenia, would die. That he would take the two events as cause to reissue his past proposal.

"Please, allow me to stay here, just until I make other arrangements." Phoebe began to reach for Harriet's hand before thinking better of it and pressing her palms into her lap. Twisting her skirt within her fingers. "I'll make myself useful in whatever way I can. I could assist with Margaret and Fanny's schooling, or—"

"Absolutely not." Harriet's hand flew to her chest as if Phoebe had just uttered sacrilege. "Margaret and Fanny are impressionable young girls. They require instruction from people of only the highest moral character."

Phoebe bit her lip, trying to keep her cheeks from heating. *Highest moral character.* That's what it always came back to, wasn't it? Aunt Harriet and Uncle Martin had been willing—begrudgingly—to welcome her back to the vicarage when the promise of an inheritance had been involved. With that hope gone, she remained nothing but the sum of her sins. A source of shame. A burden. Specifically, a burden they could wash their hands of, again, if she would only take the opportunity presented to her.

She wouldn't degrade herself by doing more pleading. The firm set of Harriet's mouth told her it was useless. If she couldn't stay here due to the stain she cast onto the household and the risk she posed to her cousins' delicate young minds, she would have to think of another plan.

She dug her fingers into her temple, sensing the beginning of a headache. Could Clara possibly help her? They'd exchanged infrequent letters over the years, although her cousin had almost certainly been warned away from doing so, and Clara hadn't forgotten her even after marrying Mr. Matthew Wilkinson and setting up a household in London. Phoebe didn't want to be a burden on Clara, either, who was now the mother of two small children with a third on the way. Yet if there was any chance Clara would admit her into her home for a time, that Phoebe could help her cousin with the children, or anything else she required—

"Also, don't you even think about bringing Clara into this." Harriet snapped at her like a rabid dog, as if she'd somehow garnered the power to read Phoebe's thoughts. "She doesn't need your influence around her children, either. Heed my words, Phoebe. If you seek to interfere with them, I will never forgive you, nor will I forgive her if she grows foolish enough to allow it."

Phoebe swallowed, although she was unable to get rid of the lump that felt ready to choke her. Aunt Harriet was right; she couldn't march into Clara's life and risk bringing shame upon her cousin or estranging her from her mother. But what else was Phoebe to do? Who else could she turn to?

No one.

The weight of the truth came crashing down upon her shoulders, causing moisture to prick the corners of her eyes once more. "I ..." She locked eyes with Harriet, seeking some sort of guidance forward, but was met with only coldness. To her aunt, the sole problem in play was Phoebe's stubbornness.

Phoebe dropped her gaze to the sofa so she wouldn't betray herself by showing Harriet her tears. Yet the sofa was no better than her flint-faced aunt. Not when staring up at her were the two letters that obliterated everything she'd hoped for the future.

I have nothing.

She pushed herself off the sofa, her feet tangling awkwardly as she stumbled away. She didn't have it in her to remain in the confines of the sitting room any longer, faced with Harriet and the letters. Her tears were about to spill over, for it was far too much to bear, this encounter that had proved fruitless, shattering ...

"I certainly hope your haste is on account of a need to fetch quill and paper so you can inform Sir Ambrose of your acceptance." Harriet's curt remark gave her the briefest pause as it sent another dagger into her chest. However, she shook it off, her legs finding a sudden rush of strength to carry her down the corridor and out the front door of the vicarage.

The glaring sunlight disoriented her the moment she burst into the open air. But what did it matter when there was no safe direction left to go? She ran blindly, over gravel and grass, beneath sunrays whose warmth couldn't permeate her skin, with a single focus: to get away. Where was irrelevant, as long as she achieved distance.

Yet all the while, her pounding footfalls gave a crushing reminder. Her troubles were far too grave to outrun.

2

"What do you mean, *gone*?" Nicholas Prescott, the seventh Marquess of Rockliffe, practically shouted the words while a cavernous pit formed in his stomach.

"Well, she ..." The butler, Barrington, flushed to the roots of his thinning hair, fiddling with the cravat about his neck that appeared unusually dust-stained. "She wasn't in her rooms when Mrs. Connelly brought up her tea, and while I can assure you that we've since done an extensive search of the house and gardens, no one can find her, my lord."

"Damn it!" Nicholas's voice rose another notch, just as his stomach sank even lower. "Why was she not supervised more carefully?"

Rather than wait for another of Barrington's simpering responses, Nicholas brushed past him, marching across the entrance hall's marble tiles and flinging open the door. For all the good that would do. Before him stretched the front drive, surrounded by an expanse of perfectly clipped but vacant grass and shrubs. Of course she wasn't here or someone would have spotted her already.

"Damn." He uttered the oath again, this time under his

breath. From the moment he'd pulled up in front of Beaumont Manor several hours prior, the day had become nothing less than headache-inducing. The house, full of furniture to be rearranged and rooms to be aired, was in disarray. The servants wouldn't stop asking him questions about how he wanted things organized.

But *this* ... this latest development went farther than a mere aggravation. This was beyond bearing.

"Get me a horse." He spun back into the entrance hall, fixing Barrington with a glower that unquestionably meant *now*.

With a brisk tip of his head, the butler vanished, leaving Nicholas alone to release a shuddering breath. Yet no sooner had the man rushed off than Mrs. Connelly, the housekeeper, stepped out of the shadows, looking even more red-faced than Barrington. "I'm so sorry, my lord, for—"

"Keep looking." Nicholas snapped his shoulders upright, pressing his mouth into a tight line. "I want every member of this household to continue searching both the rooms and grounds until she turns up. Have a groom at the ready to come locate me if there are any new developments. I'll ride toward the village in case there's any sign of her there."

"Of course, my lord." Mrs. Connelly bowed her graying head, and if he wasn't mistaken, her eyes shimmered with the threat of unshed tears. "I really am sorry—"

"I don't need apologies." Nicholas turned and threw open the door again, sparing a single glance over his shoulder before rushing outside. "Just find her."

He raced down the steps to a drive that remained infuriatingly empty. Why wasn't his horse here yet? Yes, he'd given the order only moments earlier, but that didn't make his impatience any less profound. Why did everything have to take so long, with each agonizing second feeling more like an hour?

The faint sound of hooves pounding against grass echoed

in the distance, and he pressed his hand to his forehead as a shield against the sun, surveying the landscape until he caught sight of his black gelding, Merlin, bounding up from the direction of the stables.

Rather than wait, he sprinted toward the horse. An action that would save him little time, but doing *something* was far preferable to standing idle while more seconds dragged by.

They met partway across the lawn, and he scarcely gave the startled groom a chance to pull Merlin to a halt and jump to the ground before snatching the reins into his fist and vaulting onto the horse's back.

"If there's anything else you need, my lord." The groom looked up at him hesitantly as Nicholas adjusted himself in the saddle. "I'm sorry about what happ—"

"Get on a horse yourself and search the park."

Nicholas didn't wait for a response before taking off at a gallop toward the drive. He'd been a stranger to the estate for a long time, but he and Merlin became quickly reacquainted, the horse displaying the same speed and agility that had enticed Nicholas to purchase him from Tattersall's in the first place.

Sometime after they raced through the front gates of Beaumont Manor, it occurred to him that if they continued traveling at such a tear, he wouldn't see Emily even if he did happen to pass her. Likewise, maybe he shouldn't have been so hasty back at the house, either. He could have taken a moment to form a cohesive plan. To ensure each member of the staff knew what was expected of them so they could search as efficiently as possible.

However, snapping at others and then rushing off was far easier than leaving time to confront his fear. Not to mention his inadequacy. He could rage at the staff all he wanted, but in the end, this was another link in *his* long chain of failures.

With reluctance, he pulled Merlin back to a canter so he

could examine the surrounding fields, feeling the weight of the situation punch him in the gut as strongly as when Barrington had first broken the news. There was no gentle way to repeat it to himself.

After barely three hours back in Kent, he'd lost his twelve-year-old daughter.

He turned his head from one side of the road to the other, seeking any flickers of motion in the tall grass. Emily couldn't have gone far ... could she? She still had so little strength. Then again, one could never underestimate the power of tenacity. At least he could rest secure in the knowledge that the stagecoach didn't come through the village until later in the day, should she have her sights set on a grand escape. Yet the idea brought little comfort.

Hadn't his mother warned him about this? His fingers tightened around the reins until he felt a crack in his joints. It would be folly, she'd insisted in a voice that garnered no protest, to rush away from London so quickly after their lengthy journey. He should take time to reestablish himself in society before the Season came to an end. To prove that the Prescotts were so much greater than scandal. Besides, the extended stay in London would benefit Emily, too. Give her a chance to rest before another period of upheaval. Allow her to be close to the family's longtime physician should his services be required. Provide Nicholas an opportunity to arrange for a suitable nursemaid or governess, for the sooner Emily regained some order in her life, the better.

If anything, his mother's insistence they stay had made him that much more determined to leave. Society and their gossip could go hang as far as he was concerned. He didn't need the ton gawking at him, just as Emily didn't need more prodding by the physician. All they required was country air and a quiet place to move on from the shambles of the past, where they could try to rebuild a vague sense of normalcy.

Yet as he continued his frantic journey down the road, with not another person in sight, doubt clawed at his insides. The Dowager Marchioness of Rockliffe was the last person on earth from whom he would ever accept advice, but that didn't stop her proclamation from buzzing repeatedly like a gnat that had gotten trapped in his ear: *Emily needs order.*

Had he taken the time to employ a caregiver who could provide that, perhaps she wouldn't have disappeared.

He swallowed the bile that rose in his throat, forcing his tight fingers to unclench. This wasn't the time to get tangled up in regrets. What good did that ever do? He needed to keep a level head, to search systematically. Damn it, he just needed to *find* her.

In the distance, a flutter of white peeked out from behind the sturdy trunk of a lone elm. Nicholas blinked away the dust that stung his eyes, focusing on that inconspicuous spot to the side of the field. The white patch remained, fluttering like a flag in the breeze.

Except not a flag. It was a hair ribbon.

He drove Merlin forward the instant he made the connection, the horse's powerful legs suddenly unable to move fast enough for his liking. They thundered over gravel, veering to the right side of the road and into the field.

Where he suddenly slowed again, his chest seizing and then flooding with relief. *Emmy.* His daughter's thin, muslin-clad frame reclined against the tree trunk, an orange bundle heaped upon her lap. And she wasn't alone. An unfamiliar woman sat beside her, her voluminous black dress a contrast to Emily's white one.

But most pertinently—Emily was *speaking* to her. Not sulking, not uttering sullen, one-word responses, but engaged in a conversation, her voice an indistinct hum that floated toward him on the breeze.

He watched the incongruous scene an instant longer

before pushing on. Merlin's resultant whinny caused Emily's wan face to fly up in surprise, and the stranger beside her adopted an equivalent look of shock as he ground to a stop beside the tree.

He jumped to the grass, his chest burning with the effort of drawing air into his overworked lungs. Ignoring the ache, he rushed forward a couple steps before abruptly halting. Emily still stared at him, although her astonishment had transformed into a tight-lipped glower.

"Emily ..." He managed her name between breaths, although an appropriate speech to follow failed him. The right words didn't seem to exist as far as she was concerned.

She held his gaze a moment longer, her amber eyes containing a hint of challenge. And then, before another sound could cross his lips, she turned her head to the ground, giving him the cut direct as effectively as the most practiced society matrons from Almack's.

So, that's how it was to be. Not that he should feel surprised. His shoulders, temporarily relieved of tension, grew rigid once more.

He brought his eyes down to her lap, where her hand traveled in rhythmic motions over the bundle atop her skirts. A bundle, it would appear, that wasn't an inanimate object but an overlarge tabby cat. Whereas Emily would no longer condescend to look at him, the creature took up glaring in her stead as if it couldn't imagine anything more offensive than his presence.

Which had to be due, at least in part, to his imagination, surely. He frowned, returning the yellow-eyed stare. Emily's disdain had grown familiar, but this was a *cat*, for Christ's sake.

A growl rumbled in the animal's throat, and it bared its teeth, emitting a hiss.

Point taken. He'd antagonized his daughter and an unknown feline alike.

He tightened his hands into fists, fighting the urge to growl in frustration himself and bang his head against the tree trunk. Then again, if he dared get any closer to the tree, the monstrosity of a cat was apt to sink its claws into his leg and not let go.

The grass rustled, and a black-gloved hand reached up to grab one of the low-lying branches. *The woman.* Nicholas had become so caught up with approaching Emily—and the distasteful creature she'd befriended—that the stranger's presence had faded into the background. However, she was very much still here, whispering a few words in his daughter's ear and then using the branch to pull herself to her feet. She brushed the stray bits of grass from her skirts and stepped out of the tree's shade and into the sunlight, bending into a curtsey. "My lord."

He tilted his head, watching as her body stretched back up to its full height. She wore the heavy black clothing of mourning, her dress so stiff and large that the fabric looked ready to consume her. Beyond that, there was nothing particularly remarkable about her. She was neither short nor tall, her features neither plain nor striking. Her tightly knotted hair, uncovered by a bonnet, was an ordinary shade of brown. Her eyes didn't stand out as being one definitive color but rather a combination of muted blue, green, and gray.

And even so, there was something that sparked in his brain, almost like a faint flare of recognition. "Are we acquainted?"

"No, my lord." She answered him at once, and something —either a flush, or the angle at which the sunrays hit her as she shook her head—brightened her cheeks.

She sounded so certain, yet the declaration didn't sit right with him. She'd recognized him, after all. "And what is your name?"

"Miss Phoebe Windham, my lord."

Phoebe Windham. It didn't ring familiar. "Do you live in Bowden, Miss Windham?"

"No." She paused, her fingers going to her sleeve to flick away a blade of grass she'd missed. "I've been but an occasional visitor over the years, imposing on my aunt and uncle's kindness. My uncle is Martin Buxton, the vicar. I believe you and I may have spotted one another in church one time."

No, that wasn't it, either. He'd kept his visits to Beaumont Manor to a minimum over the past decade and his visits to church less frequent still. He remembered the vicar, his wife, and their brood of children well enough, but this woman was an anomaly.

"I was pleased to make the acquaintance of a young lady while I was out on my walk today." She motioned toward Emily, putting his musings to an abrupt end. "We both found the heat a trifle exhausting, I'm afraid, and she was kind enough to come sit with me in the shade. Marigold and I are quite in her debt."

Marigold? The ball of fur readjusted itself in Emily's lap, swishing its giant orange tail across the grass, and it was all he could do to keep from scoffing. What a ridiculous name for such an ornery animal. But it suddenly made little difference, for her speech caused Emily to look up at her new companion, giving her something that nearly resembled a smile. An expression that had been all but nonexistent upon her face over the past months.

A muscle clenched in his chest, the sensation painful but not unwelcome. "And I am in your debt, Miss Windham, for seeing to my daughter."

He heard her quick intake of breath. Followed her gaze as it flitted once more to Emily, still contentedly stroking the cat while ignoring his existence, and back up to him. "Of ... of course."

They both stood unmoving in their positions upon the grass, and however nondescript the color of her eyes, he found he couldn't look away from them. It was high time he got Emily home so they could put this latest upset behind them, yet his mind wouldn't stop turning over questions like he possessed a puzzle in need of solving. Somehow, Miss Windham held the answer, and he couldn't let her go. Not yet.

"And where do you make your home if not in Bowden?" he asked, steering the conversation back to its original path.

"I ..." She was no longer looking quite at him but beyond him, and for the first time, he noticed shadows beneath her eyes. Marks of someone whose worries kept them up late into the night and left them restless the next day. He knew the look well, for it confronted him each time he happened upon a mirror. "I acted as a companion to my late father's cousin in Bath," she said. "Now that she has passed on, I'm not certain where I'll establish myself or seek employment. It happened less than a month ago, and I'm still working out arrangements."

"My condolences." The empty phrase, so often directed his way over the past year, crossed his lips easily. In truth, though, his mind was far from death and sympathy but contemplating another idea entirely. "If you have no place else to go, will you not stay with your family at the vicarage a while?"

It should make no difference to him. However, he found a strange comfort in imagining the woman who made Emily smile residing just a short distance away.

"No." Again, she jumped on the word, her chin making a slight quivering motion. "No, I'm afraid that's impossible. I'll be leaving shortly. Just as I should now take my leave of you and Em—*Lady* Emily and allow you to carry on with your day."

No. How absurd that the word rose in his throat, that the first thing he could think of was enticing her to stay.

Although perhaps not so absurd after all. The question of why Miss Windham, with her giant black dress and ordinary features, tugged at his memory remained a mystery. But as for the rest of the puzzle, a solution was beginning to take shape.

"Come to Beaumont Manor."

Her lips parted, and she made another of those brisk, breathy sounds. "I beg your pardon?"

"I want to speak with you further, Miss Windham. I have a proposition that goes beyond what I wish to discuss in the middle of a field."

Her boots poked out from beneath her heavy black hem, tapping uncertainly against the grass. Her cheeks were coloring again, her gently sloped brows rising in curiosity.

Until all at once, her expression became guarded, and she gave her head a decided shake. "I cannot—"

"Emily." He chanced a step forward, and when the world didn't erupt into chaos, he ducked and took another one so that he and his daughter shared the same shade beneath the tree. If Miss Windham felt disinclined to jump at the invitation, he wasn't above adopting methods of persuasion. "Would you like your new friend to come for tea?"

Emily didn't look at him—not that that came as any great surprise. However, she did tilt her head upward, exactly where he needed it to go: toward Miss Windham. Emily's face had yet to shed the gauntness acquired during her illness, making her eyes stand out against her pale skin like two saucers. Dark, shining, and doleful. Difficult to refuse.

She didn't speak to Miss Windham, either, but she gave an unmistakable little nod. Another hint of a half-smile.

While Miss Windham had horrid taste in pets, she didn't

come across as cantankerous and hard-hearted herself. Indeed, her resolve seemed to crumble in a heartbeat, and she caught her bottom lip between her teeth, a flash of white against pink. *Alluring*.

He diverted his eyes instantly, down to the high neck and long sleeves of her sack-like mourning dress. The picture of solemnity and modesty. *Ah, perhaps that was the problem.* "If you'd like to go home first and fetch a chaperone," he said, "I'll send my carriage to the vicarage to collect you both."

"That won't be necessary." She released her lip, and it was only when she pinched her mouth into a tight line that he realized how plump and rosy it had appeared when she wasn't concealing it. She crossed her hands in front of her, the fingers of one glove drumming against the other in silent deliberation before coming to a halt. And then, he heard it. The softest sigh of acquiescence. "If you and Lady Emily go home on horseback, I'll follow on foot."

"Very well." He made a brusque motion with his chin, solidifying the arrangement before she had a chance to rethink her decision. Then, he turned to the tree trunk, extending a hand to Emily. "Let's go now. As Miss Windham said, she'll follow."

For one hopeful moment, his daughter examined the glove he offered her, and he almost thought he'd done well enough that she would accept it. Yet in the next instant, she was grabbing hold of a low-lying branch just like Miss Windham had done, using it for support as she shakily rose to her feet.

She favored him with a glance when she'd righted herself, alerting him that he hadn't turned invisible, at least. However, there was no warmth in it, only the same note of challenge, daring him to confront her.

The leafy branches blocked out the sun, casting her face in shadows, and his mind flashed backward until suddenly, all he could see was her mother. Not because their appearances were overtly similar, but because there was a parallel in the way they both looked at him. Specifically, in the way Cecilia had looked at him on that night so many years ago as she'd paced the darkened bedchamber, half yelling and half crying, a mixture of outrage and devastation potent enough to set the house ablaze. *You cannot blame me. I never set out to deceive you. This was forced upon us. I didn't choose it!*

White skirts billowed as Emily pivoted into the sunlight, making Cecilia vanish and only a petulant twelve-year-old girl remain. His hand clenched again, and he gave himself a moment to catch his breath and watch her retreat. On an encouraging note, she shuffled over to Merlin and stopped at the horse's side. That much wouldn't be a fight, anyway.

Something brushed against his leg, and his body jerked, his eyes darting downward. That damn demon of a feline, displaced from Emily's lap, had the gall to sidle up to him, leaving a trail of fur across his boots.

He shook his foot, warning it away, and the spurned creature opened its mouth, voicing its displeasure with another aggrieved hiss.

"To hell with you," he muttered, quietly enough that there was no chance of the curse reaching his daughter's ears.

Then, he stepped out from under the shade of the tree, striding over to Emily and Merlin so they could make their way home without delay. Stopping briefly at Miss Windham's side to affirm the plan. "Good day. We'll expect you shortly. Oh, and Miss Windham?"

He forced away a scowl, hating himself for what he was about to say. Realizing it was a necessary evil. "You'd best bring along the cat."

3

W hy, oh *why*, did she have such a penchant for getting herself in trouble?

Phoebe stared at the pattern of scrolling vines covering the Aubusson rug beneath her feet, unable to stop her half-boots from making anxious little taps. Her back was wedged, straight as a riding crop, against the plush velvet sofa, while her fingers gripped its ornately gilded arm.

If her heart didn't skitter so vehemently, perhaps she would laugh at herself and her latest tangle. At the way she'd fled the vicarage seeking some kind of refuge and had instead ended up in a drawing room at Beaumont Manor, awaiting an audience with the marquess.

Her mind raced in circles, taking her back through all the steps that had led her to this point. The arrival of the damnable letters. Her desperate run without a course. And then, the sight that had stopped her in her tracks.

With the way her vision blurred from the glare of sunlight and the sheen of her tears, she'd nearly missed the flash of white rushing in her direction as she bounded through a field, heading north of the village. However, a well-timed blink had pushed the white streak into her awareness, making her realize that just as determinedly as she raced away from Bowden, the streak hurtled toward it.

A streak, she'd determined after another series of blinks, that was actually a girl. That's when Phoebe had halted, bending to catch her breath as her gaze remained on the scene and recognition set in. Not because she'd ever encountered the girl before, but because the closer she came, the more it had become apparent that her dark eyes were red-rimmed and haunted, and her face was drawn. In the unknown girl, Phoebe had seen herself: someone desperately trying to flee a world crumbling around her.

The girl had kept her mouth set in a determined line, as if nothing and no one could stop her. But at the same time, it was impossible to miss the way her thin shoulders sagged with exhaustion, and that her legs jerked unsteadily while she ran, as if she might collapse.

Naturally, Phoebe had called out to her as she passed, trying not to startle at the girl's labored breathing. But fatigue or not, the girl had barely looked at her, seeming resolute in her mission to keep going.

Fortunately, a familiar meow had sounded at that exact moment, the timing of which couldn't have been better. Phoebe alone may have proved insufficient enticement to stop the girl, but the cat's cry made her pause, and her huge, sad eyes followed Phoebe's across the field until they locked upon an orange mass of fur sauntering out from behind the trunk of a lone elm.

Aunt Harriet and Uncle Martin had disdained the large stray tabby that had started loitering around the vicarage, yowling insistently for scraps of food. Phoebe, on the other hand, had taken pity on the creature and given in to its demands, thus earning her a fast friend.

And allowing her a foray into befriending the girl, too.

After Phoebe had uttered a few more gentle words of coaxing, the girl consented to follow her to the tree, where they both sank against the trunk so Phoebe could introduce the cat. *Marigold*, she'd called the animal for the color of her fur.

From there, the girl had revealed little about herself beyond her name, spoken in a low, toneless voice. *Emily*. However, it mattered to Phoebe not a whit, given that Emily, who looked even frailer up close, had been content to sit with her, sucking long mouthfuls of air into her lungs until she'd relaxed enough that her fingers no longer trembled when she stroked Marigold's fur. Eventually, she'd even responded with enthusiasm to Phoebe's stories about the cat, asking to hear more about the mischievous creature's antics. An explanation of whatever had compelled Emily to run, and where her home was, could wait. Phoebe knew full well that these weren't always easy topics to discuss, and she'd had no intention of prodding the girl before she felt ready to divulge the information freely.

Yes, it mattered not a whit until a horse had come thundering down the road and into the field, targeting their peaceful tree. Until a long-ago memory of broad shoulders and hair that glinted auburn in the sun had flashed in her head. Until that memory came to life, except instead of barreling away like a flash, the marquess had stopped to stare at them, making her heart pound out of her chest.

Even then, she'd been slow to make the connection. She'd watched the odd exchange between him and Emily, had answered his questions while hardly knowing what she said. But not until he'd uttered the words—*I am in your debt, Miss Windham, for seeing to my daughter*—had the identity of the girl she'd stumbled upon truly hit her.

What were the chances?

Furthermore, what were the chances that such an

unlikely encounter would end with a request—no, a command—to go to the marquess's home and listen to a *proposition?*

She unclenched her fingers from the sofa arm and reached for her teacup, taking a sip of the lukewarm liquid. She could have said no. *Should* have said no. Yet there was something about the way Emily—*Lady* Emily had nodded and looked up at her with that sad, all-too-familiar expression that made refusal impossible. And something, in turn, about the way Lord Rockliffe had looked at his daughter. So brief Phoebe had nearly missed it, but the unfettered relief that flooded his features when he discovered the girl, before it became masked by his stony exterior, had been clear.

She drained the contents of her cup, although the dryness in her throat didn't dissipate. It had proved disquieting enough to take tea in the drawing room with Lady Emily, Marigold, and the housekeeper, Mrs. Connelly, where not only was there no sign of the marquess, but no one so much as mentioned his name. However, having to sit and wait in silence, now that Mrs. Connelly had declared Lady Emily overtired and whisked her from the room, promising that Lord Rockliffe would be in directly, took her nerves to a whole other level.

She forced her feet to still against the rug, bringing her eyes to the ormolu clock and painted porcelain vases upon the mantel. To the gold-tasseled curtains framing the window beside it. To the terrace doors on the adjacent wall, whose gleaming panes of glass gave a perfect view of the sprawling greenery beyond, and even a little hint of the crystal blue lake—

Oh, *why* had she turned her head that way? And why, despite everything, did the memory of her past sojourn to its shores run through her head as clearly as if it had happened yesterday? She could still see those powerful arms cutting through the water, could still feel the heat that had enveloped her body—

"Miss Windham?"

Phoebe whipped her head around, sending her teacup clattering back to the end table. She should have heard his footsteps approaching from the corridor, should have noticed the door coming open. Except, in her state of distraction, she hadn't, and suddenly, Lord Rockliffe was here, striding across the drawing room and toward the sofa.

"My lord." She pushed herself to her feet, bending into a stiff curtsey and watching his polished black boots approach, one footfall after another.

Ultimately, though, he didn't stop at the sofa but at the wing chair alongside it, lowering himself onto the brocade seat. "Do you require anything else?" He gestured toward the teapot and the empty plate that had formerly contained a stack of millefruit biscuits.

"No, thank you." She swallowed as she dropped herself back to the sofa, the crumbs of the biscuit she'd consumed with Lady Emily sticking in her throat.

"Good. We may as well get right to it, then." He leaned back in his chair, fixing her with an assessing gaze. *Blue.* His eyes were brilliant, peerless blue that seemed to pierce right through her. "You are the vicar's niece, you have worked as a lady's companion, and you are currently seeking a new living situation. Do I have that all correct?"

"You do."

"In that case, might you consider a governess position?"

She opened her mouth to reply, but no sound came out. Was he ... was he really asking what she thought he did?

"I'm offering you one, Miss Windham," he said, swiftly vanquishing any doubt. "Lady Emily and I are newly returned from a voyage abroad, and she requires a governess without delay. I believe you'd be suited to the task."

Of all the things he could have said ... Of all the implications this could have ... "I cannot." She could hardly get the words out fast enough.

"Why?" His eyes narrowed. He was a marquess, after all, clearly not used to having his requests denied.

Yet here she was, denying him. Where was she even to begin with her reasons why? "I ..." She could scarcely hear herself think above the pounding of her heart. "I don't think I'd be well suited at all. I have no experience. No references. You do not *know* me."

For a moment, there was silence, the marquess's long, gloved fingers drumming noiselessly against the leg of his breeches until at last, he deigned to speak again. "Did you go to school, Miss Windham?"

She swallowed again, half-wishing she'd requested more tea after all. Not that it could have fixed the aridity in her throat or made what she had to say work against her any less. "I didn't. My parents hired a governess."

"Well." A muscle in his jaw twitched, and she could almost think him on the verge of smirking. "In that case, I deem you sufficiently qualified."

She pressed her lips together, feeling heat begin to creep up her neck. How was she to make him see? Her education wasn't the problem, nor her upbringing. She was a baronet's daughter, possessing knowledge of languages, writing, drawing, music, and dancing. The issue lay with her past. Her sins.

They require instruction from people of only the highest moral character. Aunt Harriet's affronted words from when Phoebe had dared to suggest herself as a possible teacher for her cousins echoed through her head. *The highest moral character ...* In other words, not her. And if the vicar and his wife considered her so distastefully unsuitable, the marquess would, too, if he only knew the reality of things.

"In truth, Miss Windham, I'm not interested in hiring a

governess with the best references or the most well-honed skills." Lord Rockliffe's shoulders stiffened against the back of his chair, and when he spoke again, his voice came out lower, more deliberate. "My daughter is still recovering from the same fever that killed her mother. At present, I don't care in the least what she learns about subjects like languages or painting. I just want her to have a companion who will make her happy again. Whom she esteems. From what I've witnessed thus far, you'll be equal to the task."

A familiar sting returned to the corners of Phoebe's eyes. Not on her own account this time, but for the pale-faced, motherless girl who'd sat in the grass stroking Marigold, her thin body heaving as she struggled to catch her breath. Her troubles, too, had proved too great to outrun.

Phoebe hadn't known. She'd been back in Bowden for too short a time, and too focused on the difficulties that followed her, to learn the latest news from Beaumont Manor. She'd known nothing about the marquess and his family being away from England. About him becoming a widower. About Emily grieving.

She blinked, forcing her impending tears to retreat. He had that look on his face again, breaking through the measured facade. *Vulnerability.* Her chest ached, and for a moment, her trepidation melted away, making her wish she could lean over and reach for him. That she could then run upstairs and hold the girl she hadn't even known several hours prior in her arms.

But she couldn't, of course, nor could she accept. The tragedy of their situation didn't change anything about the shame of her own.

"As for the matter of your salary." Lord Rockliffe's voice regained its commanding tone, his expression turning closed off once more. "I'm prepared to offer two hundred pounds per annum."

"*Pardon*?" She could feel her eyes go wide and her mouth even wider. Was the sheer overwhelmingness of the day causing her to mishear things? It was an obscene sum, far beyond what a governess could dream.

Yet dream she did; she couldn't help herself. Eugenia had left her nothing, taking Phoebe's plans and crushing them. The amount of money the marquess offered would change everything. Not only could she travel to Suffolk, just as she hoped, but with a year's salary, she could afford to establish herself there. To have a quiet, comfortable home of her own. Her chest clenched anew, the sensation half painful, half hopeful.

Then again, a year was a long time. Three hundred and sixty-five days in which this could also come crashing down around her.

"And what if I'm not to your liking after all?" She pressed her fingertips into the velvet seat cushion, steadying herself before she got carried away. "As I said, my lord, you barely know me. What if, after a period, you or Lady Emily decide I don't suit and would rather engage the services of someone else?" *What if you discover the truth and cast me out, just like everyone else?*

"Ah." His fingers took up drumming again, back and forth over the tan-colored wool that hugged his thigh. "If that's of concern to you, we'll implement a trial period. One month. Paid, of course."

Strains of hope whirred within her, fighting above the endless doubts.

"Fifty pounds," he said. "I think that's a fair sum for the trial. Yours to keep whether you continue with the position or not."

Fifty pounds. She bit down on her lip before her mouth gaped once more. Even that would be more than enough. Enough to travel north. Enough to put Ambrose's proposal firmly out of mind.

Enough to sustain her when the arrangement at Beaumont Manor inevitably fell apart.

And until it did, she would have a home. A purpose. The potential, if his faith in her didn't prove misguided, to make a grief-stricken girl's days a little brighter.

"I want you to start immediately. Today, if possible." His eyes continued to bore into her with their intense, unyielding blue. He didn't seem the sort who possessed an abundance of patience, and he awaited a response. No doubt realized he'd made her an offer that was more than generous.

In turn, she knew there was only one answer left to give. Although with it, she would also need to receive a particular reassurance. "I'll have to go to the vicarage to collect my things. I trust, in the meantime, that you can procure a written contract with the details of our arrangement?"

"Of course." He sprang to his feet so fast that she couldn't be certain whether she detected another flicker of relief upon his face or had merely imagined it. "My secretary will see to the contract, and I'll call for the carriage to take you at once."

She pushed herself upright as well, half-surprised her legs still supported her. She should have anticipated the whirlwind her words would set in motion, but it caught her off guard just the same. Because all of a sudden—and not for the first time that day—her life had changed, spiraling in directions she never could have imagined.

Catapulting her toward *him*.

She tensed, momentarily neglecting to breathe. She'd thought he was about to rush from the room, to solidify their arrangement before she had a chance to change her mind. Except he was still here, standing in front of his chair just as she stood in front of the sofa beside it. Close enough that she could detect the scent of the outdoors on him, along with a hint of sweat that came from exertion. Why did he not move?

Why did he not stop peering at her? And why could she not stop peering back?

She'd always known he was tall and broad-shouldered, but up close, his large stature became so much more pronounced. Every surface of him appeared solid, and were she to place a hand on him, he would undoubtedly feel hot beneath her fingertips—

A growl rumbled beneath the chair, causing her head to dart down just in time to see a flash of orange pop out and swipe at Lord Rockliffe's boot.

He staggered, jerking his foot off the carpet. "What the—"

"Marigold!" she cried as the identity of the covert orange attacker became clear. Had the cat been sitting there waiting this entire time? She hadn't even known Marigold remained in the room, thought for sure she'd slunk away after Lady Emily.

She crouched down, sweeping the delinquent creature out from under the chair and into her arms. "I apol—"

"I'll call for the carriage," he repeated, his boots already back on the floor, striding across the room. And then, just like that, he was gone. Never once looking back.

Leaving her alone in an opulent drawing room holding a perturbed cat while fighting to regain her ability to breathe.

She stared at the empty doorway, her hand sweeping over Marigold's thick fur in an effort to calm them both. Yet she could still smell that masculine scent. Could picture his fingers drumming against his thigh, his blue eyes assessing her.

What had she just agreed to? On one hand, she'd saved herself. Procured the employment she desperately needed. Found a living situation where she'd be welcome instead of a burden. But on the other ...

As if by reflex, her head turned toward the terrace door, giving her another glimpse of the lake beyond.

On the other, she couldn't shake the niggling sense that she wasn't done getting herself into trouble.

4

For someone who'd happened upon the ideal solution to his troubles, Nicholas found himself surprisingly discontent. He took a long swallow from his snifter of brandy, gazing into the flames that warmed his study.

Was everything not as it should be? True to her word, Miss Windham had traveled to the vicarage and returned to Beaumont Manor scarcely two hours later with a small valise in hand. From there, she'd been taken to a bedchamber near Emily's so she could settle herself in, and she and his daughter had eaten an adequate dinner together before Emily retired early for the night.

All information that had been provided to him by Mrs. Connelly as he sat at his solitary dining table eating food he didn't truly taste. Beaumont servants proved the height of efficiency and care—his mother, the dowager marchioness, would accept nothing less—and he could rest assured that the housekeeper would observe how things progressed between Emily and the new governess and report back to him with the latest developments.

As for Miss Windham, assuming his intuition hadn't

steered him wrong, she was just the person he needed to help restore order to his daughter's life. To assist in ways he could not. Miss Windham, along with her damnable cat, would see that Emily was cared for and kept occupied. What more could he ask for than that? *Other than the impossible, such as an undoing of the past two years.*

He finished the contents of his glass, sparing a glance for his pocket watch and then pushing himself out of the wing chair before the fireplace. There were still endless hours before morning, and he'd be damned if he continued to sit here and stew until he became plagued by problems of his own invention.

No doubt the marquess's disused bedchamber would be sufficiently aired by now, with the counterpane turned down for the night and a small fire burning in the grate. However, there was little point in heading there directly when sleep felt like an elusive entity.

He would go to the library first, he decided by the time his footsteps reached the doorway, and rummage through the shelves for something to read. An old, familiar book from his days at Cambridge would provide a suitable, if not entirely effective, distraction from thoughts of runaway daughters. Of fields and cats and governesses. Of contracts.

He gave his head an abrupt shake as he walked down the corridor, wishing the action could clear his mind altogether. After he selected a book, he may need to return to the study for another brandy before going upstairs.

Except suddenly, brandy didn't matter, nor did reading, sleep, nor anything but the sight before him. He'd reached the threshold of the dusky library only to discover it far from empty. Facing away from him, in front of the bookshelf on the opposite wall, stood Miss Windham, illuminated by the glow of a lone candle she'd placed upon the shelf.

Not the same as he'd seen her earlier, though, with her

huge black dress. She'd since changed into her nightclothes, a simple white dressing gown that skirted the floor, hugging the curve of her hips and bottom on the way down. She stood in shadows instead of blazing sunlight, yet so much more of her was revealed.

Not indistinctive, as had been his previous assessment. Not indistinctive at all.

She couldn't have heard him approach, for she didn't turn. She didn't move at all save for one slipper-clad foot, which tapped rapidly against the carpet.

And here he was, staring like a green boy who'd never seen a female pass through his library before.

"Ahem." He took a step forward, his cravat beginning to feel like it had been knotted too tightly about his throat.

Her body jerked, and she sucked in an audible burst of air as she whirled around to face him. "M-my lord." She recovered herself quickly, sinking into a seamless curtsey despite her startlement. However, the flurry of motion wasn't so fast that he missed her shoving a book beneath her arm, concealing it with her billowing sleeve.

"I didn't mean to intrude," she said, her body straightening back to its full height. Her dressing gown revealing the slope of generous breasts. "I thought I might seek out something to read, both for myself and for Lady Emily once we begin our lessons. I hope you have no objection."

"Not at all." He strode into the room, coming up alongside her where she remained by the shelf, candlelight dancing across her face. "Although you may have better luck finding something to suit Emily's interests if you search the schoolroom upstairs. I've been informed that in our absence, my nephews, of an age with Emily, lived at Beaumont Manor for a time along with a tutor, so I imagine they would have left behind some suitable reading material."

She nodded, a hint of color spreading across her cheeks. It

was uncanny how much softer her face looked now that it was framed by a loose braid with a few wavy tendrils left free to dust the pale skin of her throat. "Yes, quite right. I'll look there instead. Goodnight, my l—"

"Wait." He held out a hand, halting her as she moved to exit.

Her throat twitched as she swallowed, her eyes peering up at him, huge and glittering, like those of an animal caught in a trap.

He swallowed, too, for his mouth had gone dry, the snifter of brandy in his study feeling like something he'd consumed days instead of moments ago. It shouldn't matter to him in the least the color of Miss Windham's cheeks and eyes, or whether she wore a shapeless mourning dress or nothing at all.

Then again, *no*. Best not let his thoughts travel down *that* road.

"I have the contract you requested," he said, his voice coming out far too raspy for his liking. Yet that was the whole reason he'd told her to stop, so he may as well get on with it. "If you'll accompany me to my study, you can sign it and make the terms of your employment official."

"Certainly." She gave the sleeve of her dressing gown a subtle adjustment before retrieving her candle, and when he crossed the room, she followed, trailing after him into the corridor.

Which was just as well. Taking care of the task now would save him the trouble of seeking her out in the schoolroom tomorrow and interfering where his presence wasn't wanted. However, his footsteps fell heavily, plodding against the floor almost like a protest.

Ridiculous. His fingers clenched at his own inanity. Why wish for a delay in the inevitable?

"Here." He strode back into the study he'd just vacated, crossing to the vast mahogany desk that occupied the center of the room and taking up the lone piece of parchment he'd left in the corner. "You'd best read through it and ensure the wording is to your liking."

Her dressing gown swished against the floor as she settled beside him, the flames in the fireplace casting the filmy fabric in a new—more revealing—light. She set her candle on the desktop and accepted the proffered document, her brows furrowing as she began to read.

He had no cause to believe she would find fault with it, for he'd included the same terms he'd mentioned verbally. The outlandish salary offered in a moment of desperation. The fifty pounds he'd promised her for a month-long trial. Despite how, the more he thought about it, the more it seemed like his promise lacked foresight.

Yes, he'd bought himself a short-term solution, but thanks to his hastiness, he and Emily could find themselves in the same position again in just thirty days' time. Her alone and anguished. Him failing miserably. And Miss Windham far away, fifty pounds richer.

"Thank you, my lord." After a moment, she glanced up from the document, and the way the firelight caught her eyes solved the mystery of their color. *Gray.* "Everything looks in order."

She returned the parchment to his desktop, reaching for the quill he'd left out and dipping it in the inkpot. Her hips swayed beneath the clinging fabric of her dressing gown as she leaned over, and a faint scent hit his nose, sweet and floral. Almost like they remained back in a field scattered with wildflowers.

It doesn't matter. The only thing that signified was the quill scratching across the parchment, leaving behind her name in a neat scrawl. *Phoebe Windham.* Thus, putting in place an official start to her employment. A beginning to the thirty days.

Whether he'd solved his problems or just set himself up for new ones, he could no longer say.

"And thank you, Miss Windham. That will be all. Goodnight." He spun away, safely out of the clutches of wildflower perfume and dressing gowns. He wanted no more of those things tonight, or talk of contracts. His chair by the fire, on the other hand, looked doubly enticing, especially because his brandy decanter remained on the end table beside it. He'd best have another glass and stop getting ahead of himself.

"My lord?"

He'd nearly made it to his chair and his much-anticipated second nightcap when her hesitant voice called out to him.

He gritted his teeth, making a measured turn back in her direction. At least from this distance, it was impossible to pick up her scent. To notice each subtle motion her body made, each tiny rustle of her dressing gown.

"I thought Lady Emily and I would go on a picnic tomorrow." She took a couple tentative steps toward him, her candle back in hand, illuminating her face with flickering light. "I mentioned it to her, and she seemed amenable. We won't go far. Just to the close side of the, uh, lake. As long as you don't think such an excursion would be too taxing for her."

"No, I don't believe so." He shook his head, giving a silent word of thanks that she stopped where she was, not coming any closer to his chair. "If she wishes to go, then, by all means, take her."

His eyes shifted back to the brandy decanter, and he allowed himself a long, quiet exhale. There was no need to get himself so tangled in knots. Yes, Miss Windham could potentially deem her trial salary sufficient and carry on her way in one month's time. Parallelly, though, she was bound to stay in his employment for the days in the interim. Whatever her plans for afterward, he had the sense he could trust her with

Emily's well-being for as long as she remained in her role as governess.

And if he had someone he could trust in that regard, then there was no need for him to remain skulking about Beaumont Manor, as useless and ornery as the cat who now lived under his roof. He could leave Emily and Miss Windham to their lakeside picnics and remove himself to Foxhill, his hunting box in Northamptonshire. The secluded refuge would take him in, just as it had countless times over the years when the thought of showing himself to anyone felt nigh on unbearable.

"My lord?" Again, that hesitant voice rippled through the study, making the vague shreds of equilibrium he'd recovered vanish into the shadows. He'd thought his answer would appease her, that it would entice her to leave. But damn, her feet were on the move in the wrong direction, leading her to approach his chair. "I wondered if you might like to join us. I understand, of course, that you have duties, but if you could spare even a few moments—"

"I cannot." The frostiness of his words matched the ice hardening within his chest. Upon deciding to hire Miss Windham as a governess, he'd never thought to question her intelligence. However, did she really not see the absurdity of what she proposed? Had she failed to notice the scene in the field wherein his daughter refused to speak to him? Wherein she regarded him with pure disdain, when she condescended to look at him at all. And if that hadn't proved obvious enough to her, did she not wonder at the fact that Emily wished to run away from him?

Miss Windham bit down on her lip—*Christ, not that again*—and her brows drew together, causing the candlelight to pick up faint lines on her forehead. "It wouldn't have to be long. Merely—"

"I said I cannot," he snapped, stalking the remaining

couple steps to the end table and snatching up the decanter. He refilled his snifter with an unsteady hand, then let the amber liquid trickle into his throat. Something he'd intended to do after she departed, but he no longer had the patience to wait.

Good manners dictated that he should offer her a refreshment, but he was hardly in a hospitable mood. Didn't want company. As the burn of brandy spread through him once more, so, too, did a stab of awareness, poking at him like a pin prick. If Miss Windham was newly returned to Bowden and hadn't spent much time there to begin with, perhaps she hadn't heard the story behind his lengthy absence from Beaumont Manor. The reason that he, Cecilia, and Emily had left in the first place. Perhaps she didn't know the rumors surrounding the years of his woeful marriage. Surrounding him.

Well, if that was the case, he had no intention of enlightening her this evening. Someone else was bound to do the job soon enough, and then, she would stop with her misguided overtures.

"Goodnight, Miss Windham." He sank into the wing chair, turning his attention to the weakening fire. His message, he hoped, was blatantly clear: she needed to see herself out and leave him in peace.

He waited for the sound of rustling cotton or slippers gliding across carpet, but there was nothing. Only the pop of flames and pounding of his head, until suddenly, an object hit the floor with a heavy thump.

He twisted his neck, peering over the top of his chair to where Miss Windham was bent over, hurriedly grabbing something off the carpet and shoving it back into her sleeve. *The book*. He'd nearly forgotten about the similar scene in the library where she'd taken the volume she perused and concealed it beneath her arm as if she didn't want him to notice it.

"Goodnight, my lord." She righted herself in an instant, although her eyes were huge, and her voice sounded breathless.

Again, the strangest sensation came over him, just as it had when she'd risen to greet him in the field. A flare of recognition he couldn't place, that made it impossible to look away.

Except in the next moment, she was no longer a frozen figure but a woman in motion, crossing the study at a near run.

And then, just like that, she was gone. Giving him the solitude he wanted.

He dropped his head to the chairback and closed his eyes, trying, not for the first time, to make it all go away. His fingers drummed against the side of the brandy snifter, his nails making clinking noises as they hit the crystal. *Up and down ... all is well ... I am alone now.*

His eyes flew open, another jolt of recognition stabbing his gut. Not for Miss Windham and the way she stood looking at him, wide-eyed, in her nightclothes, but for the book she'd tried to hide like she possessed a clandestine object. Surely, she hadn't ... He was mistaken ...

He cast his half-empty glass to the side and jumped to his feet, a solitary repose in his study suddenly the last thing on his mind. Instead, he grabbed a candelabrum and bolted into the corridor, not stopping until he arrived back at the threshold of the darkened library.

She was no longer there, of course, the space beside the bookshelf where he'd first found her now containing nothing but shadows. It made little difference, for he could still envision the exact spot she'd stood with her dressing gown clinging to her hips, her foot tapping repeatedly against the carpet.

He made it to that spot in several long strides, raising the candelabrum to illuminate the rows of books. The shelf in question was just above his head, forcing him to crane his neck. Rather high for someone of Miss Windham's stature, but if she stood on tiptoes and extended her arm, she could likely manage to reach it.

He started with the far-left corner, his eyes traveling over the leatherbound spines. He may have kept himself away from Beaumont Manor for an exceptionally long time, but some details he didn't forget. Such as the position of certain reading material, deliberately kept far from the ground.

There was a slight gap in the middle of the shelf; he recognized it as soon as he saw it. A place where the book—a distinct crimson volume—that normally occupied that position on the shelf had been removed.

No longer there because in a flash of crimson, Miss Windham had thrust it under her sleeve and run away.

"The minx," he muttered under his breath, reaching up so his fingers tightened around the edge of the shelf, right where the book *should* have rested. Instead, Miss Windham could be up in her bedchamber with it right now, flipping through the pages. His cock stirred as a vivid image burst forth of her lying in bed, one hand holding the book while the other slid over her body, pushing up the billowy folds of her nightclothes—

Jesus. He needed to get ahold of himself.

He tore his hand away from the shelf, marching across the room before abruptly stilling, letting his weight slump against the wall beside the doorway. Where was he going? Brandy no longer seemed a wise idea, and he couldn't shake the sense that if he returned to the study, he wouldn't be able to vanquish the scent of wildflowers.

He pressed his head to the wall, letting out a low groan of frustration. He supposed he could go outdoors and wander about like a ghost haunting the garden. Go upstairs and pace around his bedchamber until the carpet wore thin. There would still be no escape. He possessed a sprawling estate, but there was nowhere he could go, nothing he could do, to make his head stop pounding with wishes that held no reason.

He wanted seclusion. Yet he also couldn't stop glancing toward the doorway, picturing Phoebe Windham's dressing gown brushing against the floor, her wide eyes staring back at him.

He wanted to flee to Foxhill. Yet if he left, he would miss the moment—if it came—that Emily ran about Beaumont Manor again, her laughter filling its halls.

He wanted the past fifteen years to disappear. Yet in erasing them, he would also lose the one thing he never regretted, that held value above all others.

There was no winning. No making sense of it.

And whether that was due to him being miserable, or foxed, or rendered irrational by a blast of ill-placed, ill-timed yearning, he couldn't entirely say.

5

L ord Rockliffe, it appeared, spent his early mornings riding. A fact that presented itself as the sound of pounding hooves drew Phoebe to Lady Emily's bedchamber window that overlooked the stables, and a powerful figure on horseback—one who was becoming all too familiar—slowed to a halt before a waiting groom.

Was the universe taunting her? She swallowed, her pulse quickening as the marquess jumped to the ground, his muscles taut beneath his tan riding breeches. Why did the scene seem determined to keep repeating itself in her view? And why did it continue to affect her? Even when she had half a mind to be angry with him.

Her face heated as memories of the previous night rushed through her head. The feeling of his blue gaze boring into her as she leaned down to sign the contract. The way he'd recoiled from her invitation and whisked himself away like a man haunted.

She should have stayed, explained herself better, tried additional powers of persuasion. Except she couldn't. Not after the library incident had thrown her too off balance to think straight.

Her skin grew hotter still, making it feel like tiny flames shot down her body, searing her with their caress. She hadn't intended any wrongdoing by going to the library late at night and sifting through the bookshelves. On the contrary, after Mrs. Connelly had given her a tour of the house and mentioned in passing that Lady Emily enjoyed reading, Phoebe thought she did right by seeking out a book for her new pupil. Given the hour, she hadn't anticipated encountering anyone, and it provided a good opportunity to choose a book for herself as well, to help pass the time as she lay sleepless in a new bed in a strange house.

Perhaps she had herself to blame for opting to stand on tiptoe to explore books she could barely reach. Yet something about the crimson spine near the center of that high-up shelf had caught her interest, and she'd pulled it down, flipping the book open to a page near the middle.

And had promptly startled, making it jerk beneath her fingertips. The page contained an illustration. A little text, too, but her mind hadn't processed it, remaining trained on the image of the woman who leaned, without a scrap of clothing, against a door, while a man knelt before her, his face buried between her thighs. With a trembling hand, Phoebe had flicked to the next page, and then, to the ones beyond. They were all of the same nature, illustration after illustration of a man and woman twined together in the throes of passion, in positions she couldn't have dreamed.

She should have thrown the book back on the shelf at once and fled to the safety of her bedchamber before more trouble could find her. But she hadn't. Somehow, she couldn't let it go.

With a racing heart, she'd flipped through the pages, moving the book close to her candle so light flickered over the details of each scene. *The woman with her elbows on the floor while the man supported her legs, entering her from behind. The man who reclined on a bed while a woman stood over him, lowering herself onto his arousal.* Her eyes had stayed glued to the images like she'd fallen into a trance, while delicious heat built between her thighs.

Until suddenly, a masculine growl had come from behind her, and it all came crashing down. She'd had no time to think, to do anything but shove the book under her sleeve and pretend she *hadn't* been viewing erotic illustrations on her first night in Lord Rockliffe's employ. The book had stayed with her as she'd signed the contract. As she'd spoken to the marquess. As she'd turned to leave and then dropped it—blast her clumsiness—forcing her to pray harder than she'd ever prayed for anything that he didn't realize the nature of what she concealed. The book remained in her bedchamber even now, buried beneath the stockings in her clothespress, because she didn't know how to return it without the possibility of Lord Rockliffe creeping up on her again. *And because, maybe, I don't want to return it yet.*

"Miss Windham?"

Phoebe's head darted to the side, her body giving a small start. She hadn't heard Emily approach, had thought she was still breaking her fast, but here the girl was, peering out the window alongside her.

With a movement as abrupt as Phoebe's own, Emily turned from the window, bringing her amber gaze to Phoebe. "Are we still going to have a picnic today?"

Phoebe smoothed down her thick black skirt, taking a moment to reorient herself in the room. Sure enough, Emily's teacup and plate now rested empty atop the small table where they'd breakfasted, and Marigold sat in the chair she'd previously occupied, sniffing the crumbs at the edge of the tablecloth.

"Certainly. We'll leave shortly." *The sooner the better.* Phoebe hurried over to the end table, collecting the blanket she'd set aside for the excursion. "Why don't you fetch a favorite book or two to bring along? Or perhaps your watercolors? I'll go down to the kitchens and ask to have a basket prepared."

She offered Emily a smile, and at her nod of agreement, Phoebe departed, putting thoughts of marquesses on horseback—and of certain books—soundly out of mind. With any luck, the time outdoors would do them both good. Perhaps the summer sunshine would bring color back to Emily's wan face, and the fresh air would help Phoebe clear her head. Yes, the picnic involved establishing themselves near *the lake*. But she would forbid herself from thinking of past events in that location. Emily deserved her full attention, and in granting it, Phoebe would be much better off as well.

She proceeded with the best of intentions. And she would have fulfilled them, surely, had the sight that greeted her in the kitchen not been that of a tousled, panting Lord Rockliffe.

He stood at the worktable with his back turned to her, his shoulders heaving from the aftereffects of the ride. He'd doffed his coat, and his shirtsleeves clung to him, revealing the muscular contours beneath. As for the breeches hugging his thighs, the angle at which she stood granted her a particularly advantageous view—

She gave a little jolt and then froze. These were the very things she *wasn't* supposed to think of, and here she was, woolgathering.

Well, no more. Mrs. Hodges, the cook, bustled over to the worktable with a mug and a plate of … preserves, it looked like, to give to the marquess, effectively holding his attention. Perhaps Phoebe could back away slowly without detection, then return at a more opportune time—

"Oh, good morning, Miss Windham." The cheery cook's

eyes fell upon the doorway, making Phoebe's plans for escape vanish like smoke flying up a chimney. "Does Lady Emily require something else for her breakfast?"

"Good morning, Mrs. Hodges. And, uh, no." *Blast*, why did her voice sound like a squeak? She forced herself to step into the kitchen and approach the worktable, and with her eyes resting on the cook—solely on the cook—she cleared her throat. Attempted to look pleasant and even-tempered. "However, if you could pack a few things into a picnic basket for us, I would be much obliged."

Mrs. Hodges was quick to acquiesce, moving to the other end of the kitchen and gathering up items with remarkable efficiency.

Meaning there was naught left for Phoebe to do but acknowledge the other person in the room, who had since spun in her direction with the mug pressed to his lips.

"Good morning, my lord." Thankfully, her voice regained its usual volume, and she successfully bobbed into a swift curtsey. She seemed to be growing skilled in that regard—offering a prompt and respectful greeting while pretending the sight of him didn't affect her. For as long as they lived under the same roof, she'd do well to bolster her skills until her nonchalance was no longer feigned but real.

"Miss Windham." He set the mug back on the worktable and curtly inclined his head, a windswept auburn lock tumbling over his perspiration-sheened forehead. Not that she noticed.

She intended to utter a remark about returning to Lady Emily and use it as reason to abscond. She certainly did *not* intend to take another step closer to the worktable and gawk. However, something had appeared on Lord Rockliffe's face. A white line that stretched above his upper lip.

Her eyes flitted down to the mug upon the worktable, empty but for a thin layer of white that coated the sides and pooled at the bottom. *Milk.* The marquess had just downed a mug of milk, the remnants lingering upon his skin.

She bit down on her lip, pressing her mouth into a tight line, although the corners seemed determined to slant upward despite her best efforts to keep them contained. His terse dismissal from the night before still grated. The thought of the pilfered book in her clothespress continued to make her heart beat faster and her stomach twist in knots. He was standing before her, as large and commanding as ever, close enough that she could smell the freshness of the outdoors on him, along with a heady scent that could only be described as *male.*

And even so. Something about the white mark on his neatly shaven visage proved so incredibly ... funny.

"Do you find something amusing about scones, Miss Windham?" His clipped question pulled her out of yet another daydream, and he grabbed the plate which, now that he mentioned it, appeared to contain a scone beneath the abundant heap of preserves.

"Not in the least," she answered promptly, finding herself the recipient of a potent stare that looked dangerously close to becoming a glower—even if the effect was marred by the blatant white slash above his mouth. She swallowed, attempting to think sobering thoughts, to appear every bit as austere as the marquess himself. Yet her efforts did nothing to stop her errant lips from twitching and an unsolicited rejoinder to push its way to the forefront of her thoughts. "Milk, on the other hand ..."

Oh. Oh, no. She'd just said that aloud, hadn't she? Which was preferable, perhaps, to laughing outright, except now, he frowned at her in silence. Causing the white stripe to dip.

Until all at once, his brows shot up in understanding, his hand rapidly swiping along his mouth. Making his other hand —the one holding the plate—jerk along with it and a splotch of red fly through the air.

And land soundly upon the middle of her bodice.

She peered down, feeling her jaw slacken. Her brow crease. The bombazine was too thick to allow the substance to permeate to her skin, yet it remained upon her gown, plain as day. A sticky red spot containing small pieces of—strawberry, it seemed.

Very slowly, she raised her head, as if she didn't quite remember how to move. Lord Rockliffe was staring at her again, his chin cocked to the side, his blue eyes particularly wide. Their gazes locked, and for a moment, there was only stillness, in which the air between them felt heavy enough to break like a thundercloud releasing a deluge.

Yet suddenly, he snapped his neck upright, his spotless lips compressing into a line. Without a word, he reached for the kitchen towel that lay on the edge of the worktable, holding it out to her with all the solemnity the occasion afforded. However, she didn't miss the spark in his eye. The way his mouth became the one that tried, and failed, not to twitch upward.

She accepted the towel with as much dignity as she could muster, silently dabbing at the stain. As she worked, the weight of his gaze stayed upon her, filled with intensity and poorly concealed mirth. Which, very well, she supposed she deserved. Be that as it may, the sensation built, and finally, she could stand it no longer, blurting out the first thing that came to mind. "That is an obscene amount of preserves."

She eyed his plate, trying to sound cross. In truth, humor spread like a contagion, making genuine displeasure impossible. Indeed, how could she feel perturbed when Lord Rockliffe's features had become noticeably brighter, the tense lines in his forehead fading away?

For a moment, it looked like he would free his lip and give her a true smile. A transformation that would no doubt stay in her memory for days—months—to come.

He didn't smile, though, not really. Rather, the twist of his mouth was … sly. The glint in his eyes knowing. "We all have our indulgences, do we not?"

Oh, Lord. Why did the lilt to his words make her think of things far beyond the realm of food? *Such as explicitly illustrated books.*

No. She refused to let her thoughts meander in that direction again. They were speaking of preserves. *Only* preserves. "I prefer gooseberry, myself," she muttered, glancing down at the small wet patch against her bodice that wouldn't come clean.

He made a sound she would almost call a laugh, his body moving a little closer. Brushing against the folds of her black bombazine. "That could only be because you've never had a Beaumont-grown strawberry. A situation that requires urgent remediation."

The plate containing the untouched scone and mound of preserves appeared beneath her nose. A peace offering, perhaps. And while maybe she should have replied that she would keep to gooseberry, thank you very much, she didn't. She tossed aside the kitchen towel and accepted the plate, their fingers brushing as he transferred it into her grasp.

His palm was scarred, she registered with a start, marked by jagged, pink-white lines. A fact that hadn't been visible beneath his gloves or from afar, that she hadn't noticed after the initial shock of being pelted with preserves. However, she didn't spend any further time studying his hands, or her own, which still tingled from the heat of his skin, the coolness of his signet ring. Instead, she held the plate before her eyes, assessing how best to pick up the scone without making a mess.

Which was looking increasingly like an impossible feat. And so, she simply dove in, her fingertips sinking into preserves as she lifted the scone to her mouth and took a bite.

A mixture of sweet and tart burst onto her tongue, a flavor reminiscent of the height of summer. She'd never eaten preserves to such excess and could suddenly see how he would derive pleasure from it. Although did her pleasure truly come from the indulgence? Or was it amplified by the way his pupils grew large as he watched her? By the way he made a low, barely perceptible sound as she licked a dab of preserves from the edge of her lip.

With a motion that proved not entirely steady, she set the plate back on the worktable, wiping her fingers upon the towel. Now that she'd finished eating, the time had come for her to say something. Unfortunate, given how her head whirled with the effects of sugar. Sugar, or his masculine scent, blue eyes, and the piece of hair that toppled across his brow.

She swallowed again, her throat covered in sweetness. "It's ... oh!"

Something swept along her leg, and she lurched in surprise, her gaze shooting downward and encountering Marigold, who sniffed around the floor at her feet. The cat, despite her size, was so stealthy that one rarely heard her enter a room. And if Marigold was here—

Phoebe jerked her head back up, scanning the kitchen to find Mrs. Hodges standing near the other end of the worktable with the requested basket in hand. Emily hovering in the doorway with two books clutched to her chest. Both staring at the scene in wide-eyed silence.

Phoebe's cheeks heated, and she could only hope their color didn't resemble that of the strawberry preserves. Just as she hoped the strawberry stain upon her dress didn't command attention. Black concealed it well, didn't it?

Whatever the case, it was time to put the incident out of mind. She stepped over Marigold, rushing to take the basket from Mrs. Hodges, the unexpected weight of it making her arm drop.

"Thank you, Mrs. Hodges, you've outdone yourself," she

said, hefting the basket onto the worktable and motioning for Emily to join her as she peeked at its contents.

The girl obliged, her footfalls against the kitchen floor every bit as furtive as Marigold's. However, when she arrived at the worktable, she didn't look in the basket but at her father, fixing him, not for the first time in Phoebe's experience, with an unreadable stare. Letting his sparse *good morning* go unanswered but not looking away.

Phoebe's heart didn't seem to be beating at a normal rhythm, and she couldn't rid herself of the taste of strawberry. But suddenly, none of that mattered. She had a purpose in this house that did *not* involve lusting after Lord Rockliffe, and that purpose—nothing more—required her full concentration.

She replaced the lid over the abundance of fruit, sandwiches, and pastries, then dared to look at the marquess. Even drummed up a half-smile. "There's far more here than two people can eat."

She remembered full well how rapidly he'd dismissed her suggestion last night of joining them for the picnic. Did he not feel differently, though, in the light of day when his daughter stood before him?

However, Emily no longer looked at him but at the floor, her attention on Marigold as the cat wove in and out between her feet. Neither of them the least bit interested in acknowledging the marquess's presence.

As for Lord Rockliffe, his jaw tightened, as if the flashes of lightness upon his countenance had been only an illusion. "Yes. Well, I wish you both a pleasant day." He pushed himself away from the worktable, turning in the direction of the corridor.

Phoebe opened her mouth, her chest swelling with the beginning of a protest. But before she could utter a word, Emily took the lead, tugging on Phoebe's arm to guide her toward the kitchen door that led out to the garden. Leaving the marquess swiftly behind before he had a chance to leave them.

So much for well-practiced manners and nonchalance, for Phoebe didn't even have the presence of mind to issue a farewell. All she knew was that Marigold let out a hiss, and in the next moment, the door banged open, and Emily dragged her out into the sunshine.

Fortunately, Emily didn't take it in her head to run about wildly—they'd both done more than enough of that the day before. But nor did she adopt the languid pace of an invalid, instead moving along the grass with steady, determined strides, her cheeks flushing from the effort.

Phoebe didn't try to engage her in conversation as they walked. She had a feeling such efforts wouldn't be welcome; not to mention, the scene in the kitchen had given her a great deal to reflect upon in silence.

It was the oddest thing. She'd seen the way Emily looked at her father. Yesterday in the field. Just now in the kitchen. Before that in her bedchamber window. Always taking stock of his presence. Likewise, there'd been no mistaking Lord Rockliffe's expression of alarm that changed to relief when he came upon his runaway daughter beneath the tree. Nor could Phoebe forget the sentiments he'd expressed, in a gentler tone than all his other directives, when he offered the governess position. *I just want her to have a companion who will make her happy again.*

Despite how they both possessed a stony exterior, the marquess cared for his daughter deeply, and she returned his affection; Phoebe would stake her life on it. Yet, for whatever reason, Emily shut him down the instant he came too close, and he, in turn, was quick to recoil.

For Phoebe's part, staying out of the marquess's company would make matters much, much easier. However, her own silly sentiments meant nothing compared to those of a young girl grieving her mother and a husband grieving his wife. Having one's life turned upside down could cause a person to act in illogical ways, as she well knew, and she'd felt so certain that if she gave Emily and the marquess just a little push together, they could find comfort in one another as they dealt with their loss.

Instead, her efforts had been met with Lord Rockliffe's immediate dismissal while leaving Emily more flint-faced than ever.

Phoebe kicked a stone with the toe of her half-boot and drew in a long inhale, the air especially fragrant now that they neared a cluster of blooming pink shrubs beside the lake. Had she misjudged something about the situation? Yes, perhaps she had, but that didn't mean she should give up. She still knew so little of Lord Rockliffe and Lady Emily's circumstances prior to their return to England, and if Emily took issue with him for some reason, she wanted to understand what it was.

She waited until they'd spread their blanket beneath the shade of an oak tree and each had a glass of lemonade before she tried broaching the subject. It was imperative she proceed with the utmost caution, for she and Emily were still little more than acquaintances, and she couldn't risk the girl shutting her out just as she did the marquess. However, as Emily reclined against the tree trunk, recovering from the effort of their walk and even smiling a little as she watched Marigold chase a butterfly, Phoebe decided it was as good a time as any.

"Are you happy to be back in England, Lady Emily?" she asked casually, reaching for her glass to refill it with lemonade.

For a moment, she didn't know if she'd receive a response, for Emily didn't acknowledge the question but continued to peer out at their surroundings. The tiny ripples drifting across the lake. Marigold crouching in the grass along the shore. Emily's solemn amber eyes took it all in, and the only part of her that moved was the end of her dark braid fluttering in the breeze. Until out of nowhere, her quiet voice emerged, scarcely distinguishable above the rustle of grass and leaves. "Yes, I'm glad. I didn't want to go to India."

"India?" Phoebe couldn't hold back her surprise. She supposed she hadn't given much thought to their destination, and she certainly hadn't pictured a place that far away. "That's quite a voyage."

"Yes." Emily shifted, not toward Phoebe but to press her cheek against the rough surface of the tree trunk. "We didn't make it to India, though. When Mama got sick, we had to disembark in Saint Helena. I didn't want to go there, either."

"I'm very sorry." Phoebe had far more questions than answers, but those would have to wait. For now, she reached for Emily's hand, and the girl's slender fingers returned the pressure of her own. "I know how difficult that must have been for you and your papa."

"Papa wasn't there. Not at first." Emily stiffened, her fingernails grazing the surface of Phoebe's palm. "It was just Mama, me, and Mr. Mowbray. And given how things turned out, Papa may as well have spared himself a trip and stayed home."

Phoebe felt her mouth gaping, the power of speech temporarily knocked from her body. It was becoming more apparent by the second that the story of Lord Rockliffe, his wife, and their ill-fated journey held depths she hadn't begun to fathom. But what did it matter when, in the midst of it all, there remained a girl harboring a deep-rooted hurt? Phoebe may not realize the details of what happened, but she at least had to take what she *did* know and use it to assuage Emily's misbeliefs. "Of course he wouldn't stay home. I'm sure he was very worried about you when you were ill, and he would never leave you to travel without a guardian—"

"Because he had no choice!"

Phoebe gasped at the sudden burst of vehemence in Emily's voice. "I'm certain he didn't do it out of obligation, but out of care and lo—"

"What do you know about it?" At last, Emily snapped her head away from the tree trunk to look at Phoebe, but her eyes were steely, and her slender chin quivered below her clenched teeth. "You've only been here a day, and you know *nothing*."

Again, Phoebe found herself struggling for words, her body stiff and ill-at-ease. As a governess, she should never permit that sort of rejoinder—her own childhood governess would have rapped her knuckles for far less. However, as she peered wordlessly into Emily's thin, trembling face, she found it difficult to see impudence. All that stood out to her was hurt.

"You're right," Phoebe conceded quietly, all too aware that she rested on shaky ground. "I *do* have very little knowledge of what happened, but—"

"Do you think we could read now, Miss Windham?" Emily cut her off and then sank back against the tree, her eyes appearing sorrowful. Pleading. It was as if in the span of an instant, all the fight had drained from her body.

"Yes." Phoebe stretched across the blanket, retrieving one of the books Emily had set down near the picnic basket. "Yes, of course. Why don't I read aloud?"

What other answer could she give? Lord Rockliffe had hired her to make his daughter happy, and she wanted so much to accomplish that. But how would that happiness become anything but fleeting when Emily kept so much unspoken heartache concealed below the surface?

A small hand fell upon Phoebe's arm as she opened the book, and Emily shuffled forward, nestling herself beside Phoebe and resting her head atop her shoulder.

Phoebe swallowed, pushing down the choking sensation in her throat so she could manage the first word upon the page. "I-Introduction." She had no question she'd done right by putting the outburst behind them, for in doing so, she appeared to have gained Lady Emily's trust and affection. For some reason, the thought made her eyes sting.

That didn't mean this was over, though. She kept reading, line after line, not missing a beat. Her mind, however, was elsewhere.

Her resolution remained unchanged; in fact, it had only grown more pressing. Emily had almost seemed to suggest that her father viewed her as a burden, and Phoebe couldn't let that assumption lie. She *would* find the reason for the distance between Lord Rockliffe and his daughter, and then, she would help bridge the gap.

And if she couldn't speak of it to Emily ...

She chanced a glance upward to the crystalline water lapping at the shore.

If she couldn't speak to Emily, it would seem she needed to have a conversation with the marquess.

6

Nicholas had learned his lesson last night about the pitfalls of wandering the house when the hour grew late. As a result, he planned his actions with greater care this evening, going to the library to select an innocuous book on crop rotation as soon as he rose from the dinner table and retiring to his study after that for a single snifter of brandy. Once he drained the contents of his glass, he gave himself a lone option for where to proceed: bed. He was unlikely to sleep for hours yet, but at least in the sanctuary of his bedchamber, he wouldn't run the risk of being disturbed or having any unexpected encounters.

He climbed the stairs slowly, the brandy he'd consumed far from sufficient to dull the memories of the past day. He'd tried to keep himself busy by becoming reacquainted with estate business, but his land agent oversaw things so seamlessly —with occasional directives from the dowager marchioness, no doubt—that there was nothing requiring his immediate attention.

Meaning his mind stayed focused on places it should not. Why could he not stop drifting back to the early-morning scene in the kitchen where Miss Windham appeared, once again wearing the same high-necked, bulky black dress and severe hair knot? As if the sight of her in billowy white nightclothes, with candlelight creating a soft glow across her skin, had been nothing more than a fantasy. Why did he keep thinking of Emily standing beside her, fixing her saucerlike eyes on him before once again turning away like his existence wasn't worth acknowledgment? And why, despite the fact that his presence clearly wasn't welcome, did he feel like he'd somehow done wrong by refusing Miss Windham's invitation to join them for the picnic?

He reached the top of the stairs and started down the corridor, pressing his fingers to his temple. He'd all but made up his mind: assuming Mrs. Connelly continued relaying a favorable report of how Emily fared with Miss Windham, he would depart for Foxhill at the end of the week. Just five days' time.

And they would all find themselves better off for it.

He turned the corner toward the marquess's rooms, readjusting the book on crop rotation beneath his arm. At Foxhill, there was no library, only a few shelves in the study that held books pertaining to the local flora and fauna. At Foxhill, he wouldn't have to sleep under the same roof as the governess who had ... *enlightened* taste in literature. He wouldn't need to think of her in a bedchamber just a staircase and a few corridors away, flipping through pages, studying illustrations, envisioning things that made her body heat in her solitary bed.

His footsteps quickened until he reached his bedchamber door, and he threw it open, rushing inside—

Only to find himself halting near the threshold, blinking. Surely, his eyes deceived him.

But no. The lamps were lit, and a hearty fire blazed in the grate, filling the room with light. Making it all too clear that the orange lump sitting atop his pillow in the middle of the vast tester bed was *that cat.*

"Marigold," he sneered under his breath, a curse rising in his throat the moment the ridiculous name finished crossing his lips. The cat, however, seemed untroubled by his contempt. Indeed, the detestable creature spared him only the pithiest glance before devoting itself fully to the task he'd so rudely interrupted. Namely, giving its paw a series of licks and then dragging it over its face in a steady cycle.

"Enough!" He charged forward, having just spent the last moment he would *ever* spend lingering at the threshold of his room and gawking at a cat. He reached the side of his bed, flinging out his arm to shoo the thing away.

The cat bared its teeth, bestowing one of its characteristic hisses, while remaining firmly planted atop his bed.

"*Leave.*" He swung his arm again, hisses be damned. "My pillow isn't a bloody bath house."

The cat's paw darted out in a lightning-fast streak, its claws grazing the back of his hand. "Fuck!" His book crashed to the floor as he snatched his hand away, grasping it where tiny beads of blood came to the surface. As for the cat, it resumed its position as coolly as ever, taking extra care to bathe its paw thanks to the effort he'd forced it to extend.

"Ugh!" He snarled his frustration, spinning away from the bed and storming back out of the room. Was nowhere in the house safe anymore? Apparently not, and he didn't have the patience to deal with an aggravated poor excuse for a feline at present.

Well, that settled it, and his careful plans could go hang. He was returning to his study, where he would drink the whole damn decanter of brandy if he felt so inclined.

He trudged down the corridor and toward the stairs, his footfalls too loud, too unmeasured—

And found himself crashing into a warm weight, his arms

shooting out instinctively in a way that pulled the obstacle against his chest.

"Oh!" The weight wriggled within his grasp, and a puff of breath hit his throat as it—as *she*—exclaimed her surprise, leaning back to examine the source of the collision. Allowing him to observe the same thing in return, and for recognition to hit him like a blow to the chest.

He held Miss Windham in his arms. Miss Windham with her overlarge black dress, her tightly knotted hair, and her sweet, crisp scent that made it seem like she'd just come in from traipsing about a sunny meadow. Even with the stiff bombazine, her body was so soft against his. So pliant and *hot*.

He released her abruptly, and she jumped backward, words beginning to tumble from her lips. "I'm so sorry, my lord. I didn't mean to sneak around the corner, nor did I intend to wander where I should not. It's just that I cannot seem to find—"

"*Marigold*?" he finished for her, the absurd name feeling vile against his tongue, making his momentary jolt of pleasure vanish. Her brisk, wordless nod told him all he needed to know. "Come with me."

He spun around again, forced to retrace his path, while Miss Windham's hurried footsteps echoed behind him. Was it too much to ask that he have one blasted night of solitude? Aggravation made him move faster, setting him on a determined march back to his bedchamber. At least Miss Windham being here meant she could take care of the cat problem, after which he'd be free to slam his door, ring for brandy in his room, and not come out until morning.

"Here." They reached his bedchamber in record time, and he clasped her hand to pull her inside, then gestured toward the bed with a flourish. The cat hadn't moved from its position on his pillow, the only difference being that it now licked its ludicrously puffy tail, its tongue running along the mass of orange fur with meticulous strokes. "I believe this is what you're seeking."

Miss Windham's eyes grew huge, and her mouth dropped open in horror, displaying a flash of her own pink tongue. "Marigold!" She bolted forward, giving her hands a single sharp clap. "Get down at once."

The cat paused its intensive licking, giving her an affronted stare. Then, with a plaintive meow, it leaped from the bed, ignoring him and Miss Windham both and sauntering into the corridor. Just like that. No claws, growls, or hisses to be had.

I'll be damned.

"Again, my lord, I sincerely apologize." She turned from the bed, her cheeks flushing as she returned to where he lingered near the door. "I'm really not certain how she got in here."

"Nor am I." He scowled at his crumpled pillowcase, which was apt to give him a mouthful of fur when he lay down his head. Although that problem may prove secondary to how he now possessed a memory of Miss Windham hovering at his bedside. His frown deepened, and he gritted his teeth. "Can the creature not sleep in the barn?"

Miss Windham tilted her head, assessing him with a look that was damn unnerving, like she was *his* governess in the midst of giving him a test. "Of course she can, my lord," she said, her voice level and deliberate, "if that's what you wish. However, Lady Emily was concerned about her disappearance, and while the picnic made her tired enough that she fell asleep regardless, I believe she'll be upset if Marigold isn't there when she wakes."

Patience. He exhaled, trying not to make it sound like a snarl. "Fine. Put the cat in her rooms, then. Just see that it doesn't wander anywhere else it shouldn't." He turned his gaze to the roaring fire. To the chair in the corner that he could pull beside the grate. Those things, along with a bottle of brandy and his tedious book on crop rotation, would be his momentarily. "Goodnight, Miss Windham. Close the door on your way out."

But the door didn't close, nor did her skirts swish across the floorboards to signal her retreat.

"My lord?" The incorrigible woman took a step closer to him, so near that his thoughts became a tangle of wildflower fragrance, fluttering dressing gowns, and illicit books. "Might I speak with you for a moment? We could relocate to your study if you prefer, or—"

"No." He made himself turn and meet her gray gaze—although in this light, her eyes really appeared more blue. *God*. Would the trials of this night never end? "Whatever you wish to say, say it here." *Get it over with quickly so I can shut the door myself and make everything go away.*

"Very well." She smoothed her skirts. Reached up and pressed a strand of hair that dared to come loose back into place. Each second an eternity. "Lady Emily and I enjoyed our picnic today."

He folded his arms, waiting for what came next. He already knew about the success of the picnic, the time they'd spent drawing in the schoolroom afterward, and the dinner they'd proceeded to eat together. Mrs. Connelly kept him well-apprised of the situation. As to why Miss Windham considered her announcement worthy of a nighttime discussion, he couldn't say.

"I thought we would make a habit of it on days when the weather is fine," she said at last, her words tumbling out to break the silence. "The fresh air seems to agree with Lady Emily, and I believe that sunshine and gentle exercise will aid in restoring her strength."

Yes, he hoped so, above anything else. That's why he'd hired Miss Windham, on the assumption she'd know what to do to help. Yet his arms tightened around his chest, the purpose of the conversation still eluding him but filling him with a vague sense of unease. "You are free, Miss Windham, to take Emily on as many picnics as you like." Hadn't he already made that much clear? "You do not need my permission."

"Thank you, my lord, truly. But what I mean to say is ..." She gave another aggravating pause. Squared her shoulders. "I understand if other commitments prevented you from joining us today. However, if you could spare a few minutes to take part in one of our upcoming excursions, we would be much obliged."

His fingers curled around his biceps, his nails sinking through his wool coat to stab the skin beneath. Not this futile discussion again. Had she not taken the hint last night? Had she remained completely blind, even after the scene in the kitchen this morning, to his daughter's fondness for giving him the cut direct?

"Tell me, Miss Windham." The fire blazed, but his tone was frigid. "Has Lady Emily also voiced those sentiments?"

She swallowed, the milky column of her throat growing tight. "No, not exactly, but—"

"I already told you that I cannot." He took a step forward. Inhaled the scent of wildflowers. Tensed his jaw. "I'll soon be taking my leave from Beaumont."

"Excuse me?"

Her open-mouthed surprise caused him to blink. "I'm going to Foxhill," he said. "My hunting box in Northamptonshire. I don't know when I'll return." He waited for the declaration—for the assurance that he would soon be far away from here—to put him at ease, although, if anything, his stomach only became more unsettled.

"You cannot."

"*Excuse* me?" He spit her words back at her, his eyes

narrowing. Surely, his ears deceived him. For it *sounded* like the governess had just presumed to tell him what to do.

Pink splotches flooded her cheeks, and she caught her lip —her plump, blasted alluring lip—between her teeth. "It's ... it's just that ... it's not hunting season."

No, it wasn't, and he didn't hunt, either. Not anymore. However, that had never stopped him on any of the other countless occasions when he'd fled north, and it certainly wouldn't now.

"The timing and purpose of my visit to Foxhill are none of your concern." He pressed his mouth closed. Drew his brows together. Prescotts were known for their ability to deliver a scathing glower that left the recipient quaking in their boots. His mother, especially, but Nicholas didn't do a bad impression of it himself.

He waited for Miss Windham to shrink away. To finally do as he'd commanded and *shut. The. Door.*

She stepped closer, the hem of her giant black skirt brushing along his boot. "It *is* my concern." Her voice was hot, insistent. "It is very much my concern when I believe that your daughter needs you here."

He stayed stock-still even as her words punched him in the gut. She didn't know what she was talking about. She didn't bloody know, and she needed to *stop*.

"I would thank you to remember, Miss Windham, that you are in my employ," he snapped. "As such, *I* make the directives and you follow them. Not the other way around."

"But maybe it should be the other way around"—her eyes flashed, and it would seem he'd been wrong about the color all along, for anger made them glint green—"if you refuse to see reason."

Only the tension in his jaw kept him from gaping. How dare she speak to him that way? Thinking she had the right to interfere and presume. Did she not have a care for her position? He'd hired her and could just as easily fire her if she kept up the insubordination.

Except he couldn't actually, could he? He needed her. More specifically, Emily needed her. Perhaps Miss Windham was aware of how that gave her the upper hand.

His body was both ice and fire. Ice because she wouldn't stop clawing at an open wound. Fire because she stood so close, her chest rapidly rising and falling, her lips pressed in a determined line. *They would be soft*, he decided, were he to run his tongue over them until they yielded. Just as her hair would be long and flowing were she to pull out the pins, and her body would be perfectly contoured were he to tear away the fastenings and let that blasted high-necked dress fall to the floor.

Alarm bells pounded in his head, ringing danger, screaming that he needed to crush this before he was the one crushed.

"Enough." He spun on one foot, the sudden movement causing her to pivot, too, until their positions were reversed, and she staggered, her back pressing against the wall. Cornered, but still not backing down, with her chin raised in defiance.

He leaned in, bending his head so it came close to her ear. "You are walking a *dangerously* thin line," he hissed, her body giving a barely perceptible shiver as his breath hit her skin. "We will not speak on it further, and if you're so determined to engage in conversation, then allow me to ask a question of you."

He pulled his face away so he could stare into eyes that were either blue, gray, or green. He didn't know, only knew they were locked with his. Challenging him, unsettling him, sending an inferno shooting through his veins.

It was time to turn the tables.

"What are you doing with that book you snuck out of my library?"

7

Phoebe was too hot. Her head too fluttery to think straight. Her heart raced, yet concurrently, time seemed to stand still. Lord Rockliffe had asked her a question; she knew that much to be true. But now, there was only an endless stretch of silence as he loomed in front of her, waiting for an answer she didn't know how to give.

"Shall I remind you of the book I'm referring to?" His voice came out low, clipped. "Crimson cover. Richly illustrated interior. Why did you take it? Because you sure as hell didn't intend to read it to Lady Emily."

He knew. Of course he knew. She'd been foolish to delude herself into thinking he didn't, what with the way she'd dropped the book on the floor of his study before scurrying out of sight. Her mind flashed to her clothespress, where the book remained buried beneath her stockings, waiting for her to find a discreet moment to return it. *Or waiting for me to bring it to bed so I can study the pages one after another by the light of a lone flame.* Lord Rockliffe couldn't know the direction of her thoughts. Yet something about the way he looked at her made it seem like he did.

In her frustration—for he was so infuriatingly stubborn—she'd forgotten her place and said things a governess should never say to a marquess. The damage was done, and he'd be well within his right to end her employment. What more did she have to lose by telling the truth?

"I took it because it intrigued me." She didn't look away when she spoke. Didn't try to shrink further into the wall even though his heat felt ready to envelop her. "You said I could borrow from the library for my own reading, did you not? As for that particular volume, I suppose I hid it for fear you wouldn't approve of the subject matter."

"I placed no restrictions on what you could or couldn't take." He leaned in, his face aggravatingly unreadable. His lips perilously close to her ear again. "Why don't you tell me what *you* thought of the subject matter?"

Blood pounded in her ears. Between her legs. What would he say if she told him the illustrations had filled her head as she lay sleepless in bed last night? Except instead of imagining the couple on the page, she'd pictured him. *Herself.*

She swallowed, knowing he was close enough to hear, that he would notice each time her throat twitched. "I found it very ... informative."

His palm came forward, pressing into the wall alongside her head. His body was like a cage, holding her in. And foolish creature she was, she had no desire to escape. "I'm glad to hear it, Miss Windham. And do you feel *informed* enough that you're ready to return it for another?"

"No." The word slipped out on a breath before she could think better of it. Yet she'd come this far with the truth that she may as well keep going. Leave him to do with it what he would. "There are still pages I haven't viewed, and I want to see all of them. Perhaps more than once."

She fought the urge to lower her eyes to the floor, instead

examining his face, waiting for a crease or tic to ripple across his features and show just how much she'd appalled him.

It didn't come. There was only a hot trail of breath against her neck, and then, a single whispered word in the shell of her ear. "Naughty."

She shivered, a frisson of desire shooting straight to her core. He knew the truth, then—that she was wicked, lustful, indecent. The way he said it, though, didn't sound like a condemnation. His mouth lingered, hovering just above the edge of her jaw, and maybe the suggestion of his kiss had rendered her nonsensical, for she could almost think the word contained praise.

She closed her eyes, trying to force the whirl of sensations to abate. Instead, darkness made his exhales feel hotter. The nearness—the largeness—of his body even more glaring. She'd lingered in his bedchamber for the sole purpose of speaking to him and making him see reason. However, reason didn't seem to exist anymore. All she could think of was his bed waiting behind them. His lips. His body positioned atop a horse, his bare limbs gliding through water. Her own body quivering with need as she stood in the dusky library looking at images she wasn't supposed to have.

A finger traced along her lower lip. Took hold of her chin, tilting it upward. She pushed up on her tiptoes to meet him, the movement causing her thigh to connect with hardness in his breeches. She couldn't help the needy little cry that escaped. Now that they'd set this in motion, she was powerless to stop the wanting, the anticipation.

But his lips didn't fall on hers. Instead, they returned to her ear, brushing over the sensitive skin. "Tell me to stop," he murmured, the words heavy and heated. "Tell me you don't want this." His tongue flicked along her earlobe. "Tell me I'm a man out of my fucking head and that I should leave you alone before I ravish you right here against the wall." He grazed her with his teeth, an exhilarating shot of pleasure-pain. "Because I promise you, sweet, I wouldn't even make it as far as the bed."

Her eyes flew open, the air rushing from her lungs. Was he trying to shock her? Scare her away? He succeeded only in sending another wicked thrill coursing through her. In making her think of all the ways they could give each other pleasure.

Because the things her relatives said about her were true. *Shameful. Immoral.* Still accurate after all this time, even when life had thrown her enough hard lessons that she should know better.

She acted on impulse. Let her desires lead her. Got herself into trouble. But it wasn't too late to change that. To make a different choice—a *proper* choice—this time before the consequences of her actions threw her into scandal and shattered her world yet again.

"St—"

She couldn't do it. The protest died on her lips, another phrase rising instead. *Ravish me, right here.* No, it wasn't wise in the least. But how could she turn down what her body craved as much as oxygen?

It was too late. With that suggestion of a syllable, he recoiled instantly, his fingers raking through his disheveled hair. He stared at her, his pupils wide, the blue rings around them blazing. A look of disbelief, confusion, regret, *lust* ...

And then, before she could so much as blink, he was gone, his boots pounding down the corridor. Fading away.

She clung to the door jamb, her legs on the verge of buckling, and fought to catch her breath. Her body throbbed, aching because where she'd once been surrounded by the hardness and heat of him—the promise of everything she desired—she now had nothing.

She squeezed her eyes shut again, trying to make the world stop spinning. Everything had happened so quickly, so unexpectedly, so beyond the realm of probability that she could almost imagine herself tangled up in her sheets, awaking from a dream.

Yet when her eyelids flashed open, the fire roaring in the grate made it impossible to deny that she stood anywhere but Lord Rockliffe's bedchamber.

Alone.

8

"Miss Windham?"

A hand fell upon Phoebe's shoulder, snapping her attention away from the blanket of gray clouds drifting outside the window and back into the schoolroom. She'd been woolgathering again. So much so that she hadn't heard Emily come up behind her.

She pressed her mouth into a small smile, pivoting away from the window and leaving the outside world behind. There was little to look at, in any case, for the perfect, cloudless weather they'd enjoyed for their picnic had been followed by four days of gray skies and rain, keeping most of the household—themselves included—indoors.

Only Lord Rockliffe appeared outside the window from time to time, continuing with his morning ride and returning with his wet clothing stuck to his skin. Those sightings were rare, though, and brief. Just enough to remind her that his presence was fleeting, for to the best of her knowledge, he planned to leave tomorrow, and she still had no idea how to change his mind. Especially when their paths hadn't crossed since the night they'd collided in his bedchamber.

"Miss Windham, I asked if we might go to the village." Emily's head was tilted, her dark brows rising expectantly.

"Oh." Phoebe straightened her spine to steady herself, refusing to remain distracted any longer by the marquess problem. However, as she took in Emily's request, a pit formed in her stomach.

The village. She should have known she couldn't avoid it forever. Her time at Beaumont Manor felt almost like living in another world. However, it didn't change the fact that just a few miles away stood the vicarage where she'd left a vague and succinct note about her departure, knowing her aunt and uncle wouldn't trouble themselves much regarding her whereabouts if it meant she no longer darkened their doorstep. They'd be operating under the assumption, though, that she'd gone much farther than the Rockliffe estate. If one of her cousins should spot her—if anyone who recognized her should report what they'd seen—God only knew what her relations would say. Or what gossip could travel back to Lord Rockliffe's ears.

"Look, it's no longer raining, just cloudy." Emily ambled forward to take the place Phoebe had vacated, pressing her finger to the glass. "Please? I'd like a new ribbon for my bonnet."

Phoebe folded her hands together, letting out a silent sigh. What grounds did she have for refusal beyond her own incessant worrying? "Yes, I suppose we can," she said, trying not to let her hesitancy show. If Emily felt up to and took interest in going, there was really no other answer to give.

The resulting smile Phoebe received helped work out some of the knots in her stomach. She'd done right by giving her assent, and the change of scene would do them both good, she told herself as she went downstairs to ensure they could make use of the carriage. Perhaps it would give her a fresh perspective on how to manage Lord Rockliffe that moping by a rain-streaked window could not.

Besides, encountering a relative or acquaintance on High Street wasn't a certainty. Her uncle mostly kept to the church and vicarage, her aunt far preferred paying calls to shopping, and her cousins were apt to be either home at their lessons or rambling about the fields.

By the time they arrived at the haberdasher's, she almost felt good about the excursion. The shopkeeper was delighted to serve Lady Emily and her new governess, and Emily went through the ribbons with care, eventually selecting one in yellow silk that provided a striking contrast with her ebony hair.

Had they ended the outing there, Phoebe would have considered it a success. However, when they exited the haberdasher, Emily ignored the waiting carriage and continued to the shop next door, moving with surprising speed. "They always sold the best sugar plums here." She pointed toward the large window, a half-smile upon her face. "Could we get some?"

Of course, Phoebe didn't think to say no. Emily, with her sunny yellow ribbon in hand, had a certain brightness in her eyes. Even a hint of color in her cheeks. As if, for the time being, she'd managed to shed the heavy cloak of grief and illness and become just a lighthearted girl enjoying a shopping trip.

Phoebe took her arm, leading her toward the entrance without delay. If sugar plums would make Emily happy, she'd gladly procure a whole barrel of them. Yet before she could take hold of the door handle, it swung open from the inside, making them both stumble backward.

"Phoebe?"

She blinked, holding tight to Emily as she regained her

bearings, taking in a scene that didn't seem quite real. "Margaret?"

Somewhere between Beaumont Manor and the haberdashery, she'd convinced herself she had nothing to worry about in coming to Bowden, that all her fretting about gossiping villagers was the result of an overactive imagination. But here stood her cousin Margaret, a girl of fourteen who squinted at the sight in front of her, sharing Phoebe's disbelief.

Phoebe managed to dip her chin in greeting, forcing herself to take a quick breath as her pulse quickened. It was too soon to let her fears spiral out of control. After all, Margaret was an agreeable girl; if Phoebe simply asked her to keep their encounter to herself, she may very well oblige.

A hope that lasted a single second longer, until another figure, thin and severe, stepped through the doorway behind Margaret. "Phoebe?" Unlike Margaret, who'd called her name in surprise, Aunt Harriet spoke it like an accusation, her hand flying to her fichu in affront. "What on e—"

The question dissipated before Harriet finished it, and her narrowed eyes widened as she absorbed the identity of the girl clinging to Phoebe's arm. "Why ... why, Lady Emily. How nice to see you again." Harriet managed an appropriate curtsey, nudging Margaret to follow suit, although she couldn't mask the bewilderment in her voice. Due to the passage of time and the effects of illness, Emily had no doubt changed a great deal since she'd last appeared in Bowden, her frame becoming simultaneously taller and gaunter.

"Mrs. Buxton." Emily's greeting was little more than a whisper, and the eagerness had disappeared from her face.

Phoebe shifted uncomfortably, wishing beyond anything that she could reverse the last few minutes, just long enough so she and Emily remained safely in the haberdashery until after Aunt Harriet and Margaret walked away from the sweet shop.

She'd wanted so much to give Emily the carefree morning she deserved, filled with ribbons and all the sugar plums she could eat. Instead, tension hung heavy in the air, mixed with a moment of awkward silence as they all did nothing but stare.

Phoebe's fault. Because her wrongs couldn't be shed that easily. The past would keep following her and interfering, taking anything she tried to rebuild and threatening to topple it.

"Phoebe, I need to speak with you." Harriet's clipped tone was the first to cut into the quiet, and she stepped forward, placing a commanding hand on Phoebe's free arm. "Privately. *Urgently.*"

Phoebe spared a longing glance for the Rockliffe carriage, waiting on the road like a sanctuary. After a few uttered excuses and words of farewell, she and Emily could escape within its confines and be on their way, putting the scene on High Street far behind them.

But if she left Harriet without answers, what would her aunt do, then? Harriet would seek the truth one way or another. Inquiries around the village. Letters. Lord, what if she went so far as to call at Beaumont Manor?

Phoebe's stomach roiled, but she plastered on a smile, fishing the leftover coins from the haberdashery out of her reticule and dropping them into Emily's palm. "Margaret, Lady Emily was hoping to buy some sugar plums. Could you please go into the shop with her and ensure she finds what she wants?" She dug deeper into her reticule, retrieving the meager bit of pin money she possessed and handing it to her cousin. "Get some for yourself, too. I'll stay right here by the window where you can see me while I have a word with Aunt Harriet, and I'll come inside in a moment if you're still not finished."

Neither girl looked entirely convinced, but with their coins in hand and the promise of sweetmeats awaiting, they did as she suggested and disappeared through the door of the shop. Phoebe rushed over to the window, giving a little wave as they appeared behind the glass on their way to the counter. Then, with the smile still glued to her face—for it wouldn't do to disconcert Emily more than she already had—she turned to her aunt, inclining her head politely despite how her neck felt rigid enough to snap. "I don't have long. May I know why you wished to speak with me?"

"Don't play coy." Harriet hovered in front of her—although just to the side of the glass and out of Emily's view, fortunately—and pointed an accusing finger. "I want to know what you're still doing here when you left a note saying you were moving on. I took that to mean you'd thought better of your stubbornness and decided to accept Sir Ambrose."

Phoebe clenched her fingers, suppressing the urge to shudder. Thank God that hadn't been her path. As for the truth, she may as well get it out and be done with it. "I procured a governess position."

"A governess position ..." Harriet's eyes drifted to the shop's doorway. To the ornate carriage, adorned with the Rockliffe crest, that waited down the street. And then, back to Phoebe, where they once again grew large as understanding hit. "And how on earth did you do such a thing?" she hissed. "Does the marquess not have standards regarding whom he brings into his household?"

Phoebe could feel her brow tightening as her false cheer slipped away. She crossed her arms, waiting. Surely, her aunt didn't expect her to dignify the insult with an answer.

Harriet shook her head with a sigh, like she couldn't believe the appalling state to which the world had come. "Ah, well. Perhaps he cannot afford to, given the great scandal cast upon his own head."

Phoebe's heart gave a strange lurch. "I don't know what you're talking about."

"Truly?" Her aunt's remark was snide. Yet after a moment,

the derision melted away, her face lighting up in a way it only did when one of the village women called at the vicarage bearing a fresh piece of gossip. "You really don't, do you?"

Phoebe froze, sensing herself on a dangerous precipice. It wasn't too late to retrieve Emily from the shop and bolt to the carriage without hearing another word. She detested rumors, knew how crushing they could be. But at the same time, she couldn't help the spark of curiosity that flared within her.

Harriet took Phoebe's hesitance as an opportunity to lean close to her ear, lowering her voice to a furtive whisper. "You must at least know of the marquess's lengthy absence from England?"

Phoebe managed a brusque nod, her throat feeling tight.

"It was no holiday for pleasure," her aunt continued, her murmured words growing animated. "He was chasing after Lady Rockliffe, who'd absconded with their daughter. Apparently, the marchioness had taken a lover—a man from the East India Company, so they say—and thought she could run to the other side of the world with him."

Mr. Mowbray. The name Emily had mentioned while discussing her travels came rushing back to Phoebe, and she gasped, so many unknown pieces of the story beginning to fall into place.

"There are even rumors," Harriet said, taking care to shield her mouth with her palm, "that the marchioness was expecting her lover's child. However, there's no way to verify them now. Lord Rockliffe caught up to his wife in Saint Helena, where she'd been removed from the ship due to some sort of fever. Whatever the illness, it claimed her quickly, I hear, along with her lover. Lady Emily was the only one spared. But I suppose one could say that both mercy and punishment were given where due."

Phoebe couldn't speak, for what did one say in response to something so shocking? Something so horrible and tragic.

How details of a matter so intimate that happened half a world away had made their way back to Bowden, she couldn't say. She only knew that it felt terribly wrong to stand discussing them in the middle of High Street.

"Well." With a hum of annoyance, Harriet stiffened, drawing away from Phoebe's ear. "I tell you this not for the purposes of gossiping idly, of course, but to make you aware of the situation in which you've entangled yourself."

"Lady Emily is a *child*," Phoebe bit out, a surge of protectiveness rushing through her as she glanced through the window to where the girls stood waiting at the counter, Emily's dark braid trailing down her too-thin back. "After everything she's gone through, she doesn't deserve to become the subject of rumors. Likewise, the marchioness's actions are not Lord Rockliffe's fault."

"Perhaps." Harriet pursed her lips. "But where else is the scandal to fall?"

Phoebe stepped around her aunt, unable to listen to another word. "I have to go," she muttered, reaching for the door handle. The sooner she fetched Emily and got them both away from here, the better.

"Wait." Harriet's hand shot out, her nails sinking into Phoebe's sleeve to still her. "The dowager marchioness has not yet returned from London, and Lord Rockliffe's sister is newly married. Does that mean you and the marquess are living *alone*?"

Had Phoebe's chest not been knotted with tension, she nearly could have laughed at her aunt's sanctimonious expression of horror. "Hardly. He has a whole household of servants. I'm merely another of them."

"It's not the same thing, and you know it." Harriet's eyes became cold slits. "Have a care for your reputation, my girl. Talk travels quickly, and you could easily find yourself on the wrong side of a scandal. And if that happens, who knows what other information about you might come to light? I'm not sure if you appreciate how fortunate you've been to conceal your misdeeds thus far, but eventually, if you're not careful, that luck will run out. If I were you, I would wash my hands of the whole situation before it's too late. Especially when you've been offered a perfectly respectable alternative."

Phoebe wrenched her arm away, her stomach about to heave. Ambrose was *not* an alternative, however much Harriet tried to insist otherwise.

Her aunt had delivered a warning, the message clear. Yet, as Harriet herself frequently liked to say, Phoebe was a disobedient creature.

The warning only served to make her more determined to continue at Beaumont Manor.

It couldn't last forever; she knew that. The past would catch up to her, just as Harriet said.

In the meantime, though, Emily needed a supportive companion—a fact that had just become clearer than ever—and Phoebe was going to do everything in her power to fill that role.

As for the marquess—the brooding, stubborn, jaded, infuriating marquess who wouldn't get out of her head—well ... perhaps he needed a little compassion, too.

9

Now that Lady Emily's breathing had adopted the even rhythm of sleep, Phoebe lowered the book of poetry she'd been reading aloud, squinting at the timepiece on the mantel.

Ten o'clock. Perfect. Late enough that the household should be slowing down for the night. Not so late, based on the timing of their past confrontations, that *he* would be abed.

She set the book on the bedside table, rising noiselessly from the chair she'd pulled next to Emily's bedside. The girl didn't stir, her body remaining curled beneath the counterpane, her hand balled in a small fist that clutched the edge of her pillow. *Good.* Phoebe reached down, pushing away a wisp of black hair that had tumbled across Emily's cheek and bidding her a silent goodnight.

She was glad they'd managed to pass a pleasant day together despite the incident in the village. Even with Phoebe's best efforts to smile cheerily, Emily had been quiet during the carriage ride home, seemingly far too perceptive not to notice the shadow cast by the encounter with Harriet. However, after the two of them had enjoyed tea and an ample portion of sugar plums in the drawing room, and Marigold had come along to inspect their bonnet-trimming endeavors, trying to capture the yellow ribbon within her paws, Emily had brightened once more. There'd been no cause to speak of it.

But that didn't mean Phoebe neglected to think of it. No matter what she did, her aunt's gossip wouldn't stop turning through her mind. She ached for her young charge, gleaning a small bit of comfort from knowing that as long as they remained on the grounds of Beaumont Manor, she could keep her safe from the malicious rumors that Emily might not be able to avoid once she grew old enough to enter society. The marquess, though, had no such protection. What was she to do about him?

She tiptoed into the corridor, creeping through the dimness and down the stairs. All day, she'd remained on high alert, listening for any whispered words between servants about preparations for Lord Rockliffe's departure. However, she'd heard nothing, nor had she noticed signs of trunks getting packed or a carriage being made ready. Which meant that to discover the marquess's plans, she needed to go right to the source.

She continued her careful footsteps as she reached the ground floor, peering about to ensure no one else lingered in the corridor. Lord Rockliffe had been keeping himself so secluded from her that she had no way of knowing where he was or if he even remained at home this evening. She had few options but to check all the rooms he seemed most likely to frequent, assuming he was, in fact, in residence. His study. The library. The dining room. His bedchamber, if it came down to it.

Given the hour, she deemed the study the best—the *safest* —place to start. Down the main corridor and three doors to the right. She knew the route well after doing it in reverse the night she'd fled from his study with the salacious book in hand.

Tonight, the door was slightly ajar, and the subtle glow of flames shone from within. With a racing heart, she tapped gently against the wood, and when no answer came, she eased it open enough that she could slip inside.

Almost at once, her eyes fell on the impressive figure in the chair beside the fire, and her breath caught. She'd guessed right, then, finding him in the first place she looked.

She folded her legs into a curtsey, having performed the gesture enough times for it to become automatic. "Good evening, my ..." As she rose back to her full height, she trailed off, blinking in the low light. Lord Rockliffe was asleep.

For a moment, she stood unmoving, simply taking in the way his head rested against the back corner of his wing chair, tucked close to his shoulder, and his broad chest rose and fell. Perhaps him sleeping was her signal to go back to her bedchamber where she belonged. After all, he'd already given her sufficient chiding for her attempts at interference.

But she didn't retreat; she'd never been good at heeding caution. Holding her skirts tight to her body so the fabric wouldn't rustle, she crept across the carpet, a mouse entering a lion's den. A very foolish mouse who went all the way to the front of Lord Rockliffe's chair, positioning herself between him and the weakening fire.

Still, he didn't rouse, his closed eyelids displaying an even row of lashes that glinted auburn in the firelight. He looked so different like this—younger, for the lines that creased his forehead and mouth had melted away. She could detect little resemblance between him and his daughter, but in sleep, they had something in common. An expression of tranquility that came only when reality turned into dreams that proved far more pleasant.

Her foot began tapping silently against the rug. She

needed to speak with him, urgently, before he fled north and the opportunity no longer existed. But if he'd fallen asleep sitting up, he had to be exhausted, and she couldn't be the one to disturb his peace. Nor could she continue hovering above him, contemplating. Something about this felt highly intimate, bordering on invasive. Not unlike the day when she'd stumbled upon the sight of him propelling through the lake—

A hand shot out, clamping down around her wrist, and his head snapped upright, his eyes flying open to reveal two orbs of ice. "What's this?"

The air rushed from her lungs, and she gave a little jump, his iron grip the only thing preventing her from stumbling backward. "My ... my lord, I ..." She tried to remember titles, polite greetings, explanations, but her heart, having momentarily stopped, now pounded rapidly, and her tongue refused to cooperate.

"What are you doing, Miss Windham?" Lord Rockliffe's voice, while made of steel, also contained the huskiness of sleep. For a split second, his eyes wandered to reevaluate his surroundings. The low fire. The empty glass on the end table beside him. The book he'd left open next to it, the page displaying an illustration of some sort of corn.

But then, just as quickly, he brought his piercing gaze back to her. Waiting.

In her head, she'd gone through what she should say dozens of times. Her concern at him being so far away should Lady Emily experience a relapse with her health. Her steadfast conviction that his daughter shouldn't be left in the expansive house without a trusted family member nearby. That his daughter needed him, even if she refused to show it.

However, none of those grand speeches would come to her now. As she stared into his eyes in the dimness, all that remained was the essence of the matter. "Don't go." Her own voice was croaky, and she shook her head, making sure he understood. "Don't."

His fingers sank farther into her wrist, the touch searing through her sleeve to brand her skin. A sensation skirting the line between pleasure and discomfort. Did that mean she could touch him, too? She raised her unconstrained hand, bringing it toward his face inch by inch. Could she run her fingers over the sharp line of his jaw, a surface grown rough from the shadow of a beard? Could she push away the strand of hair—not quite red, not quite brown—that flopped onto his forehead?

If she dared.

And maybe she did, because if she captured him as he captured her, perhaps he would have no choice but to sit there and listen.

"Don't go," she repeated, a breathless whisper. So much less than what she should be saying, but all she had to give at present. "Stay here instead."

His chin jerked right before her fingers landed, and the deep crease returned to his brow. "Where is this coming from?"

She froze, her heart ready to beat out of her chest. *It comes from needing to make you understand but not knowing how. It comes from having too many feelings I don't know what to do with.* She bit her lip, fighting back the sudden sting of tears. The rumors of his past kept whirling through her head. How was she to tell him that she *knew*? That she wanted to make things better for his daughter. That she wanted to make things better for him, too.

"Lady Emily and I had an encounter in the village today." She paused, considering her next words carefully, for none seemed right. "It involved some ... talk ..."

Understanding washed over his features instantly, and his

lip curled, showing a flash of teeth. "If anyone *dared* utter an untoward word to my daughter—"

"They didn't," she rushed to say, her gaze darting to his twitching jaw. "Lady Emily was well out of earshot. Nonetheless ..."

"Nonetheless, *you* are now well informed." He released her wrist so quickly that she almost staggered, and he leaned against the chairback, folding rigid arms across his chest. "The talebearer didn't forget anything, I hope. Did you garner all the details of my wife's affair? Of her attempt to disappear to India with her lover? Of how her efforts left her and her unborn child dead in Saint Helena and nearly killed the daughter she already had?"

It hurt to give a nod of confirmation. "I'm sorry," she whispered, her stomach feeling like it had just received a blow. Listening to her aunt gossip about the marquess's tragic situation had been horrible enough. Hearing the details come from Lord Rockliffe's mouth, though, in a voice that rang cold and detached, made things so much more real, and so much worse. There was nothing she could say beyond repeating the useless words. "I'm so sorry."

"Stop." All at once, he was on his feet, his body towering above hers in a motion so fast that her breath whooshed away. "I don't want your pity."

She took a moment, making herself inhale and exhale. Behind her was the fireplace. In front of her, his chair. Their bodies occupied the limited space between with only a hint of a gap between them. "It's not pity." She closed the gap, letting her weight rest against his unyielding torso. "It's not."

Pity wasn't the right descriptor at all. This was understanding. Because she knew what it felt like to get a piece of one's heart ripped from one's chest, and she knew what it meant to lose.

"Regardless, Miss Windham." He tilted his head so their

foreheads nearly touched, his breath a heated stream against her cheek. "All that talk of scandal should make you run as fast as you can in the other direction. Not compel you to keep up with this misguided insistence that I remain at Beaumont."

She brought her hand up again, and this time, when she reached for him, he didn't shrink away. Her fingertips landed on the edge of his face, trailing down over his sturdy jawline. "I'm not running. You shouldn't, either. *Stay*." She locked eyes with him. Uttered words that had once made her forget reason in favor of rising to a challenge. "*I dare you*."

Silence, heavy enough to swoop down and crush them, filled the room, making time stop and their future hang in the balance. Until behind her, a flame popped in the grate, and in the next instant, his lips crashed into hers, hot and insistent.

Her body became as pliant as melting candle wax, sinking into him farther, and his arm shot out to encircle her waist. How many times had she imagined this? Had she allowed herself quick, forbidden moments in the dark when she thought of the way his hands—his mouth—would feel running over every part of her. Yet her mind's inventions couldn't compare to the reality of receiving his kiss, of the delicious pressure, of the way his tongue stroked and teased until her lips parted.

He tasted of brandy. A drink she'd never much imbibed, but when it came from his mouth, she couldn't get enough of it. The brandy was like fire. *Everything* was on fire, her skin pricking with warmth that didn't come from the grate behind her.

Her hand remained on his jaw, grazing the stubble, just as his stayed anchored at her lower back, his fingers making kneading motions that nearly caused her to moan. But it wasn't enough. She arched her back, experiencing another shower of sparks as her breasts pushed into the heat of his rigid chest and the erection tenting his breeches brushed along her abdomen.

Lord Rockliffe had far too solid a frame to be toppled by her weight. Yet suddenly, he collapsed into the wing chair, dragging her down on top of him.

Yes. Without missing a beat, he claimed her lips again, continuing the kiss as they sat in a tangled sprawl of limbs. Gripping his shoulders for support, she readjusted her body, swinging her leg to one side so she straddled his lap and the hardness she craved settled between her thighs. Only a suggestion of it, tantalizing her through too many thick folds of material, but enough that, this time, she couldn't contain her cry.

His hand went to her hair, clamping down on the thick knot near her nape and tugging so her head tipped back and exposed her throat. "So sweet." He leaned in, his breath teasing the sensitive spot just below her ear. "You torture me. You make me *want*." And then, his lips hit her neck, creating the most pleasurable suction, while his hand traveled to her neckline, toying with the fabric before slipping down the curve of her breast.

He was wrong; *she* was the one tortured. For his wicked fingers kept sliding over her, up and down, one side to the other, but never quite touching where she most wanted. Her desire spiraled, and she shifted in his lap, absorbing the quick burst of friction. "More," she murmured, her voice so breathless and needy that she hardly recognized it.

He wrenched his mouth away from her, a low growl rising in his throat. She began to form a protest from the loss of contact, but before she could make a sound, fabric split, and her dress was suddenly looser about the neck. His hands worked in a seamless flash of motion, shoving away the black bombazine, tugging down her stays, pushing aside her shift.

Until suddenly, her breasts were bared to him, and he came forward, capturing her nipple in his mouth.

His tongue flicked over her, first one side and then the other. So insistent and so assured, causing desire to pool between her legs. She could feel herself wriggling, hardly knowing what she was doing, only that he made her crave and *want*, just as he said she did to him.

"Lift your skirts." His guttural command fell upon the cleft between her breasts, and his eyes, dark with desire, shifted upward to lock with hers.

She didn't think; she simply acted, rising just enough so she could bunch the layers of bombazine around her waist and drop back onto his lap.

"Good." He set a hand upon her bare thigh, inching upward, and she sank her fingers back into his shoulder before anticipation caused her to wobble. "Is this what you want?"

His fingers were so close to her sex, to touching the parts of her that ached for him, that her reply sounded more like a moan. "*Yes.*"

He closed the distance, sweeping along her entrance and through her folds. Moving upward until he hit the bundle of nerves at the apex, and his fingertip lingered. Stroked.

The pleasure of it felt ready to consume her, each caress driving her closer to a peak. *But not without him. She wanted ... She* needed ...

She couldn't think straight, and her limbs were too unsteady to operate smoothly. Yet with clumsy fingers, she reached down, pulling at his fall. He jerked from the touch, a resulting shudder racing through her body. For despite her ungainliness, buttons were coming away, until at last, she managed to free him.

Her breath stopped as his fingers left her, as he took his rigid length in hand. She sidled forward, raising herself, antic-ipating—

But suddenly, two sturdy fingertips were inside her instead. "So impatient." He swirled through the wetness, bringing his lips back to the spot on her throat where he'd no doubt left a mark. Staying just long enough to run his tongue over the heated skin and rasp, "Let me see you come first."

He took hold of her hip, making her plunge the rest of the way onto his fingers, and then returned his hand to his shaft, guiding the tip to her pearl. Circling it over her, a combination of silk and steel that made her moan.

The sensation, his eyes upon her, his words—it was all too much. She shattered, her intimate muscles pulsing around his fingers as waves of pleasure overtook her.

"You need to tell me you're certain about this." His voice, not altogether steady, reached her as the strongest spasms faded away, although her body remained in a state of unrest. *Not done wanting*. "I need you to—"

Yes. Had she possessed all her faculties, she would have shouted the word. There was no question of certainty. She knew, beyond a doubt, how deeply she craved him. How she wished to sink onto the swollen length of him, have him fill her ...

But he was no longer speaking, nor was he looking at her. He angled his head, tilting an ear toward the doorway, his face stony and unmoving.

She hadn't heard anything beyond her own cries, hadn't been able to focus on a single thing besides her position on the marquess's lap and her burgeoning desire.

The world outside the study hadn't ceased to exist, though; she could recognize that now. Something thumped in the corridor, gradually getting louder. A rhythmic *tap, tap, tap*. Something approaching. Some*one* approaching. Her brain remained too foggy to put it all together.

But Lord Rockliffe understood. His expression shifted to

one of abject horror, his hand flying to haul her dress back onto her shoulders. To rapidly refasten his fall.

As he uttered a single word. "Goddamn."

10

F ew things could douse a cockstand faster than the imminent arrival of one's mother. A lesson Nicholas sorely wished he hadn't just learned from experience.

He gave his breeches a final tug to straighten them and shoved back the hair, now damp with perspiration, that had fallen onto his forehead. It was a wonder he could move at all when just seconds ago, he'd been locked in a pleasure-filled haze caused by Miss Windham straddling his lap, unfastening his fall, crying out her release, still wanting more.

Yet the ominous tap had made it all vanish. Somewhere in his desire-addled brain, which comprehended little beyond the concepts of *sweet* and *Phoebe* and *more*, the sound had loudened, assuring him of its reality. And then, its meaning had sunk in, making his stomach drop to his boots. The Dowager Marchioness of Rockliffe—who was supposed to be in London until the Season officially ended—was unquestionably not in London but at Beaumont Manor, her cane thumping against the corridor floorboards as she approached his study. *Damn my luck.*

He positioned himself in front of the fire, resting his palm against the mantelpiece as if he'd been idly enjoying its warmth, just as the door opened to reveal the figure he knew would stand there.

His mother wasn't large of stature, nor was she particularly spry now that her joints suffered the effects of rheumatism. However, something about her steely demeanor made her presence fill the room, and her slow, rhythmic steps, accompanied by the beat of her cane, only amplified the effect.

He gritted his teeth, waiting as she crossed the study, meeting her shrewd stare head-on.

"Rockliffe." She arrived at the fireside, giving him only the barest nod before shifting her gaze to where Miss Windham stood beside his wing chair, her hand resting primly atop the back. "Who's this?"

"This is the vicar's niece and Emily's new governess." He cleared his throat, the sounds of her breathy cries still ringing through his ears. "Miss Phoebe Windham."

"My lady." Miss Windham's ability to bob into a seamless curtsey didn't fail her even now, although her skin remained flushed, and her formerly severe hair knot had the audacity to droop.

His mother looked her up and down, quirking a silver brow. "Governess, you say?"

"Yes," he nigh on snarled, his fingers tightening around the edge of the mantel. He could think of a great many obscenities he wished to shout, but while dramatic scenes were certainly no anomaly in the Prescott household, he refused to start one in front of Miss Windham.

"A pleasure." His mother pursed her lips in a gesture that couldn't have shown less pleasure if she tried. "Rockliffe, I need to speak with you privately. I presume you won't mind leaving us, Miss Windham, for it looks as though you need to busy yourself with gown repair."

His knuckles cracked against the mantelpiece as he shot a

glance at Miss Windham's neckline. That blasted high, too-concealing neckline, which he'd grown overzealous about removing. Even in his fervor, he'd only left a small tear near the right shoulder, hardly noticeable. His mother noticed, though. The Dowager Marchioness of Rockliffe, damn her, noticed everything.

"Not at all." To Miss Windham's credit, she spoke as coolly as the dowager did, tilting her head with almost exaggerated politeness. "Goodnight, my lady. Lord Rockliffe."

Don't go. He wrenched his hand away from the mantelpiece, pressing his fingers to his aching temple. Fingers that smelled of her arousal. He wanted her back in his arms, writhing beneath his touch, putting her hands on his fall—

Except that moment had been soundly crushed.

He could only stand in silence and watch her depart, as if the whole encounter had never happened, until he was left in the dim study with solely his mother for company. And that was *not* a pleasant position.

He scarcely waited until the door closed to turn to the dowager and bite out his frustration. "Why are you here and what do you want?"

His mother was so prone to exhibiting churlishness that receiving it didn't faze her in the least. "Why do you think?" she asked mildly. "First, Amelia left London for her honeymoon, and then, you disappeared without a word to anyone after I specifically explained why doing so was a foolhardy venture. But I suppose I should hardly be surprised. In any case, the Season is nearing its end, and it was time for me to depart London as well. Especially as you seem in want of company and guidance."

"I am not." Each word fell from his tongue like a cold weight. "And why are you traipsing into my study at whatever hour it is and not residing in the dower house?"

"Because." His mother looked at him as if he were a child

who'd asked something incredibly absurd. "During your absence, I relocated here. As such, the dower house has experienced a period of disuse, and it will take time to get it sufficiently aired and back in order. It certainly wouldn't do for the guest we are about to receive."

"The *what*?" A muscle in his jaw gave a painful twitch. Had he somehow misunderstood, or had he truly just entered a new circle of hell?

"That's right." She hobbled the short distance to his wing chair, lowering herself to the seat—no doubt still warm from the heat of his and Miss Windham's bodies—and surveying him like a queen upon her throne. "I invited Lady Letitia Burville to spend a month with us here at Beaumont. Are you familiar with her?"

"No." He could barely choke out that single word, let alone muster the wherewithal to remember an expansive list of society ladies.

"Lady Burville is the daughter of a viscount and widow of an earl. Not only does she come from good breeding, but as a woman of five-and-forty, she possesses the maturity and good sense that one finds lacking in those of the younger generation. I admit, she isn't exceptionally wealthy—rumor has it old Burville played too freely at the hazard table—but we can hardly fault her for that. Had all gone according to plan, I would have had her here by dinnertime to make introductions, but a broken wheel on her carriage necessitated us making an unexpected stop at The Rose and Thistle. I had no great desire to dine there, but in the time it took us to do so, the repair was completed, and we were fortunate to have the skies clear so we could complete the journey by moonlight. Lady Burville's carriage departed the inn just a short time after mine and should be arriving any minute."

Fortunate? This was a fucking disaster.

"I don't want introductions, and I don't want visitors!"

He balled his hand into a fist and abruptly released it, although instead of ridding him of tension, the action only made it grow. "What scheme have you concocted in arranging all this?"

She smirked, her fingers tapping against the silver tip of her cane. "*Scheme* is an unfavorable word. I'm *assisting*. Because Letitia Burville is a respectable lady who would make a suitable wife—"

"No." He hadn't really needed to ask in order to realize the direction of his mother's plans. However, that word—*wife*—dropped the truth on him like a knife twisting in his gut, making his anger flare. "How dare you try that with me? *Again*. Do you never learn your bloody lesson?"

The dowager gave an indignant sniff. "Let go of the past, Rockliffe. This isn't the same situation at all. I do not know what sort of marriage Lady Burville desires, but she's of an age where she would have no expectations of expanding her family, and the topic need never even come up—"

"Stop." The brandy in his stomach roiled to the point he felt in danger of vomiting upon the Aubusson rug. How could he let go of the past when it seemed perilously close to repeating itself? His head continued pounding, an inner voice shouting at him to extricate himself from this nightmare without delay. And in that regard, he did have a weak shred of something to which he could cling. He folded his arms, fixing his mother, the bestower of an infamous glower, with a glare of his own. "There's no purpose in speaking about any of this, for it will all come to naught. I'm leaving for Foxhill in the morning."

She instantly stiffened in her chair—*his* chair—and raised her cane several inches off the floor, slamming it back down with a decided thump. "No, you damn well are not."

He clenched his jaw, his face rigid enough to splinter. The unbelievable gall of the woman! Always interfering, speaking to him as if he were still a boy to command when he was the blasted *marquess*, for Christ's sake—

"Enough, Rockliffe." Blue eyes—a mixture of ice and fire —bore into him, cutting him off before he could manage a word. "Haven't you already spent enough of the past decade wallowing at that musty old lodge? And to what purpose? It's macabre, this strange fixation you have, and I think you well know that you'll never change what happened there."

Shut up, cease this, don't dare say another thing. He intended to shout all those words and more; anything to put this at an end. Yet her speech delivered another stab to his chest, and the breath to voice his outrage rushed from his lungs. Leaving his mother free to barrel ahead.

"You've been through an ordeal. Now, you can have another chance." Her voice softened around the edges, and the detestable nuance it contained—*pity*—was far worse than anything they could yell at one another. "Don't you understand? The right marchioness will bolster your position in society instead of diminishing it, along with negating some of the gossip. Take a wife, and enjoy the benefits she brings. Use the opportunity to reestablish yourself in London next Season. Go back to the Lords. To White's. Become reacquainted with your peers. Act as the Marquess of Rockliffe because that is your birthright, no matter what damnable circumstances befall you. It is high time you stopped shrinking from the role."

She made it sound so easy, this woman who careened over everyone and everything, thinking she could make the world bend to her will. Even after going through countless experiences in which the world proved itself unbending.

If only the power to press on while ignoring inconvenient truths came naturally to him, too. But it didn't. On the contrary, these things followed him everywhere he went, reminding him of his detrimental failure. Something that couldn't be erased despite his mother's best efforts; in fact, her interference in the matter had caused no end of devastation.

The dowager, not prone to patience, gave an irritated huff at his silence. "If you refuse to entertain the idea for your own benefit, then do it for Emily," she said, eyeing him levelly. Prodding at the chink in his armor. "God knows she could use some stability after everything she's gone through. I'm sure it hasn't escaped your notice that the child is ailing. Perhaps having a mother figure back in her life will set her right again."

A mother figure. *Like Miss Phoebe Windham.* Why was all he could envision changeable eyes of blue, green, and gray and a face he'd been a fool to ever think of as nondescript?

Except Miss Windham was a governess. A woman who could leave his employ within a matter of weeks with the hefty sum he'd promised. And even if she didn't ... the position would end at some point or another. There was no alternative; he had nothing else to offer her. And then, where would Emily be? Time might strengthen her body and lessen her grief, but what if it never erased her disdain for him? She needed someone else. Someone who wasn't lacking.

He pressed his mouth closed, a bitter taste flooding his throat. Something alarming was happening. He was beginning to think his mother's proposition held a modicum of sense.

What a goddamn mess. This wasn't the sort of thing that should be sprung on a man when his body and brain still reeled with the aftereffects of interrupted desire. He needed another brandy, needed to go to his bedchamber alone—

But there was no time. The faint sound of the front door creaking open reached his study, followed by a hum of voices echoing in the entrance hall.

"Ah. That must be Lady Burville." The dowager gripped the arms of the wing chair, pushing herself upright and taking her cane back into her grasp so she could pivot in the direction of the door. She turned her head over her shoulder, toward the fireplace where he stood gawking like a clodpate. "Well, are you coming? It would be unthinkably rude if you didn't greet your guest."

A guest I didn't ask for! A guest I don't want.

A guest I would be remiss in discounting without at least considering what advantages an association between us could bring.

He pulled himself away from the heat of the fire, his legs like lead. His heartbeat a dull thud. "Indeed." He frowned at the sudden brightness that flashed in her eyes. "You've given me little choice. I'll not thank you for this."

Her cane tapped against the floor, assisting her in moving to the doorway with surprising swiftness. "Not to worry, Rockliffe. I don't require your thanks."

And with that, she was gone, not pausing or looking behind her to ensure he followed. No doubt she'd already made up her mind that he would.

Hell and damnation. He did. He followed her, silently cursing himself every step of the way.

Whether he chose wisely or would live to regret this remained to be seen.

11

"Tomorrow, I'll arrange for us to dine al fresco," the dowager marchioness announced as footmen swept in to clear the remaining dinner dishes and whisk away the tablecloth. "A lakeside luncheon would provide the perfect opportunity for us to show our guest the grounds, would it not, Rockliffe? And afterward, you can give her a tour of the estate. Do you ride, Lady Burville?"

Nicholas took a hefty swallow from his wine goblet, his eyes roaming toward the window where heavy raindrops continued beating against the glass, just as they had all day. The grounds would be wet tomorrow, and the deluge may have no inclination of stopping. Now that his mother had decided on a picnic, though, the mere consideration of weather conditions that proved less than ideal would be akin to sacrilege.

"I do." The lady to his right took a sip of wine as well, peering at him over the edge of her goblet. "My father had a particular interest in horses, and his country seat, Sanford, has an expansive park where I learned ..."

She continued speaking, telling a tale of her prized mare

from girlhood. However, her words began to blend, becoming an indistinct whir of chatter that floated around him. All that stood out was the woman herself, filling a seat that yesterday had been empty.

His mother was right: Lady Burville was no simpering society miss. On the contrary, her voice contained a note of measured elegance, her mannerisms courteous and dignified. She was a tall woman—a trait amplified by her perfect posture —with a set of flawlessly arched dark brows, a slender but sharp jawline, and strong shoulders set off by a subdued green gown. Not pretty—that seemed too juvenile a word—but striking, with an air of quiet confidence.

Despite the rain, he'd spent most of the day finding reasons to keep occupied outside of the house and *not* associate with the dowager and Lady Burville. However, now that they'd passed dinner in each other's company, he could see the truth in his mother's postulations, as much as he'd rather walk through fire and brimstone than admit it. Lady Burville gave the distinct impression she'd make a model wife. Even-tempered. Sensible. Respectable.

Except when he considered the possibility, nothing stirred within him but coldness.

"I believe we have a mare in our stables who will suit you. Persephone, a dapple gray. Do you think her fitting for Lady Burville's use, Rockliffe?"

His mother's question pulled him back to the dining table, where footmen were beginning to reenter with the dessert course.

"Mm." He gave a half-nod to the lady who sat peering at him serenely, straightening himself against his chairback. In reality, his mind remained far from the suitability of the horse-flesh in Beaumont's stables. Nor could it focus on the endless array of cakes, sweetmeats, and fruits the footmen piled upon the table, causing Lady Burville to utter a polite remark of appreciation.

"As for this evening," his mother said, plucking a custard tart off a silver tray, "some music in the drawing room would be just the thing. I hope you can indulge us, Lady Burville."

The lady agreed at once, launching into a speech about her enjoyment of the pianoforte. But once again, the words didn't sink into his awareness.

Someone was murmuring in the corridor. In fact, multiple low voices talked over one another, and then, something thumped against the floor.

He leaned toward the table to take a meringue he didn't want, trying to focus as Lady Burville expressed her fondness for Haydn's English Canzonettas.

Whatever had just thumped now scraped, making a dull screeching noise as it traveled across the floorboards. His mother's brow creased momentarily, and she tilted her head. She heard it, too, and was undoubtedly planning the lecture she would deliver to the servants later for their disruption. Yet her expression of ire vanished as quickly as it arose, her face becoming placid once more as she nodded in agreement at Lady Burville, whose speech hadn't missed a beat.

The voices sounded again, augmenting and then fading, followed by another thump.

"Careful! *Quiet*." That was Barrington, issuing commands in a perturbed whisper, his boots making rapid taps that echoed down the corridor.

Nicholas threw aside his meringue, shoving back his chair and pushing to his feet. "If you'll excuse me a moment."

He didn't wait to see if his mother took issue with his sudden departure but marched out of the dining room, following the direction of the commotion.

He arrived just in time to see two footmen—ones whose presence in the dining room had no longer been required—

disappearing up the servant's stairs while hefting the sturdy library ladder between them, Barrington supervising from the bottom stair with a frown.

"What's going on?" He approached the butler, feeling his brow quirk.

"My lord!" Barrington pivoted instantly, bringing his stocky shoulders upward so he stood at full attention. "I sincerely apologize for the disruption. There's a slight problem in the attic."

"A leak?"

"No, nothing like that, my lord." Barrington hesitated, his throat bobbing as he swallowed. "This problem is of the ... *feline* variety."

"Oh, for Christ's sake." Nicholas's jaw tightened so severely that it was a wonder he didn't crack a tooth. "And what does a *feline problem* entail, exactly?" *I may well be sorry I asked.*

Barrington smoothed a nonexistent wrinkle from his flawless black coat before pressing his hands to his sides, appearing the very picture of dignity. "It seems Miss Windham's cat slipped into the attic and climbed up to the rafters but is now afraid to come down."

And *that* was why his servants were in an uproar? Nicholas folded his arms across his chest, forcing his teeth to unclench. "Good. Leave the damn thing up there." *Give me a night where I don't have to worry about entering my bedchamber to the sight of a fur-covered mass using my pillow as a throne.* "It will jump down when it gets hungry enough."

Barrington pressed his lips together, a deep vee forming at the bridge of his nose. "I'm afraid Lady Emily is rather upset by the incident. Apparently, she was the one who opened the attic door and is blaming herself for the cat's predicament. Mrs. Connelly located a ladder in the attic itself, but it wasn't high enough to reach the rafters, even when the tallest of the footmen attempted it. Therefore, I hope you have no objection, but I took the liberty of allowing the library ladder to be brought up so the footmen can make another retrieval attempt. Unfortunately, the cat doesn't seem particularly inclined to cooperate."

"Imagine that," Nicholas muttered under his breath, his nails digging into his coat sleeve. There was no peace in this house. No safe space where he could be left to his own devices.

There was also no question of how he needed to proceed.

"I'll take care of it, Barrington." He ascended the first step, giving the butler a brisk nod. "You'd best get back to the dining room before the dowager has cause to breathe fire."

Then, he continued the trek up the servant's stairs, all the way to the attic.

He'd considered making a similar journey earlier today. Not to the attic, specifically, but to Emily's rooms below it. After all, if he was to determine whether Emily would take to Lady Burville, the first step was for them to meet. However, Mrs. Connelly had informed him over breakfast that Lady Emily was indisposed and wouldn't be up to the task. Nothing serious, she'd rushed to say, somewhat red-faced, but the young lady had adamantly expressed that she didn't wish for visitors of any kind. In other words, Emily wanted nothing to do with him, her grandmother, or the new houseguest.

And so, he'd left well enough alone, not willing to start a battle in which there would be no winning. Truthfully, he couldn't blame his daughter's reaction to yet another disruption; in fact, he rather wished he'd used the same excuse himself. And if Lady Burville was to remain for the month—assuming the dowager didn't terrorize her in the meantime—they'd have plenty of time for introductions another day.

Of course, Emily wasn't the only one with whom he had unfinished business. Miss Windham had remained shut away upstairs, too, not showing her face since last night in his study.

That didn't stop the incident from circling through his mind in everything he did. The soft weight of her on his lap. The press of her lips. Her wetness and heat.

And the moment the ominous cane had begun thumping against the floor, sending it all to hell.

He would give a small fortune not to have it end that way. But as undoing that damnable misfortune proved impossible, he needed to see her again, to say ... he didn't know. He would think on it more clearly once he dealt with the *feline problem*.

A hum of voices floated down as he reached the final set of narrow stairs. More talking over each other, it sounded like, accompanied by another loud groan against the floorboards.

He entered the attic to the sight of the two footmen who'd gone up before him dragging the ladder to the far side of the space and attempting to steady it alongside one of the rafters.

"It's your turn to go up there," one hissed, "seeing how I already attempted it."

"But cats make me sneeze," the other protested in an over-loud whisper, eyeing the rafter with a grimace.

Their spat continued, their efforts at staying quiet lessening with each word. However, Nicholas no longer heard what they said, for his attention transferred to a shadow in the corner. Emily, sitting upon the floor with her knees hugged to her chest, Miss Windham beside her with an arm wrapped around her shoulder. Both made gentle calling noises, tapping at a saucer of cream they'd positioned in front of them.

Except then, Emily's gaze shifted from the rafters to him, her face ashen in the low light, her eyes wide and troubled. He stayed unmoving, waiting for the cut direct. But this time—perhaps because she found herself too stricken—it didn't come.

He pushed forward, dodging trunks and old pieces of furniture to approach the ladder. "Stop bickering. I'll do it."

Both footmen whirled around, their mouths dropping open in unison. "I apologize, my lord, we—"

"Never mind. I said I'll do it." He stopped at the ladder's base, peering up to survey the rafter where, sure enough, an obscenely furry orange lump sat perched on the edge. What combination of neglected items the creature had used to jump that high, he couldn't say. Only that it seemed to feel itself lacking an equally acceptable way down.

"I beg your pardon, my lord, but I'm not certain that's wise." The footman who'd professed himself ill-affected by cats stepped forward, lowering his voice back to a murmur. "That cat is the devil's own spawn. She hisses and growls like nothing else, and the instant anyone gets near her, she runs out of reach."

Devil spawn. An apt description if ever he'd heard one. But as matters stood, he couldn't let that stop him. "Hold the ladder. Both of you."

"My lord ..." The footman who'd already made a rescue attempt gave the ladder another slight tug so the top skirted the rafter, and he glanced upward uncertainly. "I'm not sure how steady this is. It's still not quite tall enough to reach, and—"

"I'll trust you to hold it tightly, then." Nicholas wiped his palms against his breeches, then grabbed hold of one of the wooden rungs. Fortunately, Beaumont Manor footmen were of the trustworthy—and sturdy—sort, and they both obeyed in an instant, taking hold of the ladder so securely that it didn't make even the slightest wobble when he placed his foot atop the first rung. *Good.* If a time came in his life when he had to fall and crack his skull, he'd much rather it didn't happen in the name of a cantankerous feline named Marigold.

"I'll help." A female voice rang through the attic, and heavy skirts swished against the floor. Not just any voice, or any skirts. Miss Windham's.

He continued his upward climb, glancing down to see her slender fingers grasping the edge of the ladder alongside the footman's stocky ones. She was gazing up at him, her brow creased with concern, her eyes the same mixture of colors as a turbulent sea. "*Please* be careful, my lord."

He turned away, focusing his attention on lifting one foot after the other. He could still envision those eyes when they'd grown bright with desire. When her eyelids had fluttered closed and she'd cried out with her release. If he didn't turn his thoughts from that direction, he'd fall and break his head for sure.

The ladder grew more unsteady as he neared the top. Yet without looking down again, he knew everyone kept hold of it. The true challenge lay with what waited above him.

A warning growl sounded, alerting him that he advanced at his peril. He would have expected nothing less. Unfortunately for Marigold, he had no option but to proceed.

If there was any small mercy for which to feel thankful, it was that the cat didn't bolt, for he didn't especially relish the idea of having to crawl across the rafters. Instead, he came face-to-face with the massive orange abomination, and a pair of yellow eyes glared at him in contempt.

The thing hissed. Of course it did. He glowered back, his palms digging into the ladder's rails. "I don't like you, either." Then, before the creature could wreak any fresh havoc, he shot his hand out, securing it by the scruff of the neck.

A weight hit his chest, piercing him with a mass of tiny needles. He staggered, feeling the ladder wobble, hearing gasps from below.

"F—" He promptly clamped his mouth closed, his hands flying out to regain purchase on the rails and narrowly averting a disaster. His heart pounded far faster than he'd like to admit. Nonetheless, he supposed he deserved a small bit of credit. He'd managed to steady himself *and* avoid shouting a profanity in front of his daughter.

As for the cat, it remained attached to his coat like some parasitic vermin, holding tight by the strength of its claws.

He had no particular desire to hold the creature—doing so seemed a good way to lose a finger. Yet with its claws otherwise occupied, the cat accepted his arm when he cupped its ridiculously furry body, giving nothing more than a cursory low growl. Together, they went down the ladder, the attic below in perfect silence. The weight of numerous gazes fell upon him, though, something he could sense even without seeing.

Sure enough, everyone was waiting when his feet hit the floor, and it was difficult to say whose eyes were the widest. The footmen and Miss Windham, none of whom had yet released their grip on the ladder? Emily, rising to her feet, stepping out of her shadowed corner? Perhaps it was Mrs. Connelly, who at some point during the ordeal had appeared in the doorway, holding a dish that looked to contain the remnants of the fish course.

And here he was, a spectacle for them all, holding a bloody cat that refused to retract its razor-sharp claws.

"Go on," he grumbled under his breath, giving his torso an abrupt shake.

Surprisingly, he received neither hiss nor growl for his efforts. Indeed, the cat listened, the needles withdrawing from his chest as it jumped to the floorboards and sauntered over to Mrs. Connelly and her dish of sole. That was good to know: Marigold seemed to prefer fish to doing him bodily harm.

He smoothed his coat, scowling at the sight of the formerly pristine black wool marred by orange tufts. He would need to change if he was to go back down and listen to Lady Burville's musical performance. Perhaps fortify himself with a glass of port first, too.

But suddenly, his plan to make a hasty retreat to his

bedchamber vanished, for when he looked up, Emily was standing in front of him. Not staring daggers. Not turning her eyes to the floor. She simply gazed at him, and then, her lips parted, releasing words little more than a whisper. "Thank you, Papa."

At once, the tension in his body melted, and he allowed himself to sink downward until he crouched at her eye level. Not nearly so far a distance as the last occasion on which he'd done this, for it had been a long time. "Of course, Emmy." The long-ago nickname that she'd since deemed too childish slipped off his tongue before he could think better of it. How could he help it when, instead of peering at him with disdain, her face held the faintest hint of a half-smile, reminding him of the little girl who used to run to him and shriek with laughter as he swung her onto his shoulders? Had he realized just how fleeting those instances would be, he would have savored them more deeply. Dug himself out from beneath the heavy cloak of bitterness and made time for more of them.

She didn't recoil at the name, and for a moment, a future flashed before his eyes in which there came healing after loss. Closeness after division.

But with a plaintive meow from the cat, the vision evaporated, for Emily spun away, flitting over to where the demanding creature cried at Mrs. Connelly's feet. At least there was lightness in Emily's step. Another hint of the girl who used to traipse through the corridors of Beaumont Manor.

"Perhaps we'd best make Marigold wait to eat this in the kitchen," the housekeeper said, shooting him a knowing glance. "The last thing we'd want is for her to become so comfortable in the attic that she attempts another jump to the rafters."

"Yes, you're quite right. Let's go down at once." At last, Miss Windham released the ladder, leaving behind a subtle trace of wildflower perfume as she rushed toward the attic door.

"Miss Windham?" He pulled himself upright, finding the power to make her name project across the space, causing her to halt in her tracks. He still didn't know what to say, how they were to carry on. But given they were both here in the attic, it seemed as good a time as any to figure it out. "I'd like a private word."

The footmen needed no further cue to hoist the ladder between them and make a speedy exit, moving with far greater proficiency than they had on their way up. As for Mrs. Connelly, ever the efficient housekeeper, she smiled at his daughter, holding out a sturdy arm. "Why don't you come with me, Lady Emily? I imagine Marigold would far rather eat her dinner in your company, and I think Mrs. Hodges may just have a few sweetmeats left that you would enjoy."

Slowly, Miss Windham turned back to face him, her features set in an expressionless mask. "As you wish, my lord." The words were polite but distant, an acceptance born from duty and not any true inclination.

He took a step forward and then stilled, suddenly unsure where to go. Perhaps a private conversation up here in the dimness was a poor idea after all. Be that as it may, Mrs. Connelly and Emily departed the attic before he could utter another word, closing the door the instant the cat skulked out behind them.

Leaving him and Miss Windham well and truly alone.

"I apologize for all this." She started in at once, not allowing silence to linger between them. "When Lady Emily asked if we could come up to the attic to search for some dolls that had gone missing from her old nursery, I didn't see the harm in it. I'm afraid I didn't account for Marigold's jumping prowess."

He followed her gaze to a camphor trunk in the corner,

atop which lay a pair of ivory dolls, illuminated by the lamp that rested beside them. Perhaps they'd been brought up to the attic for safekeeping while his nephews—hellions, to hear the dowager tell it—were in residence last year. He could nearly smirk at the thought of the two boys he'd seen only in passing plaguing his mother with their antics, just as he and his younger brother, Samuel, used to when they were young. A very long time ago, for Samuel had estranged himself from the family upon his marriage to an *unsuitable woman* and, a decade later, had drunk himself to an early grave. He wouldn't have liked seeing his sons at Beaumont Manor. Would detest what the future had in store for them.

A sharp ache clutched Nicholas's chest, and he snapped his focus back to Miss Windham, willing it to dissipate. Even with his efforts, his skin continued to smart where the cat's needlelike claws had hooked him, and he had no doubt that when he removed his shirt later, he would find blood. Yet that much, he found he couldn't regret.

He pulled back his shoulder blades. Swallowed. "There's no harm done."

Miss Windham's lips parted, and one of her brunette brows twitched on her forehead. But just as quickly, she clamped her mouth closed, capturing her bottom lip between her teeth. *Hell and damnation, not that.* How was he to carry out a sensible conversation if all he could think of was Miss Windham doing wicked things with her mouth? And the wicked things he wished to do in return.

No. He'd asked her to stay so they could speak, and she was waiting, her foot poking out from beneath her hem to tap noiselessly against the floorboards. A gesture, he'd come to recognize, she performed when feeling anxious or uncertain.

"I assume you're aware of the new guest to Beaumont Manor, Lady Burville." Damn, what a bloody stupid way for him to begin. However, Miss Windham only inclined her head expressionlessly, waiting for him to continue.

"The dowager has invited her for a lengthy stay," he said, because now that he'd started, he may as well push through. "I'd like Emily to meet her. My mother, who believes the weather bends to her will, is planning an outdoor luncheon by the lake tomorrow. Assuming the skies clear as she commands them, will you both join us?"

The words still didn't feel like the right ones to say to her. However, hadn't he just offered the very thing she'd been so insistent upon? Time spent picnicking by the lake in his daughter's presence, in the hopes it wouldn't turn into a disaster.

"Certainly, my lord." She displayed perfect manners, but still, that hint of coldness wouldn't dissipate. "That is, assuming Lady Emily is agreeable and her health permits it. But I'll do everything in my power to encourage her attendance. Can I take that to mean you won't be leaving Beaumont Manor after all?"

"No, I'm not leaving. Not yet." He stiffened his spine, fighting against the heat that began creeping up his neck. The promise of Foxhill—free of disruptions and interfering mothers—still beckoned. Somehow, though, the satisfaction he derived from the thought felt hollow. *Because, maybe, escaping there was never the right choice.*

"I'm glad of it." She offered him a smile, and for a split second, his view of the attic became all brightness and warmth. But the smile didn't last, nor did it quite meet her eyes. Instead, her gaze darted to the attic door, and she clasped her hands in front of her, pale fingers against black skirts. "Is there anything else, my lord?"

So much else. The main reason he'd asked her to stay remained unspoken, and if he didn't take care, she'd be back down the stairs, shut away in her bedchamber before he uttered another word. *Out with it, then.* "We should discuss what happened last night."

Her cheeks paled, her fingers forming fists around the heavy bombazine. "Please, my lord, there's nothing to discuss. In fact, I think we'd best put the matter out of mind entirely."

A sick feeling settled in his stomach, and he found himself moving toward her and then stopping partway, suddenly unsure of the wisdom in getting too close. "If you have any regrets—"

"I have none." Her foot abruptly stilled against the floorboards. "And you can rest assured that I didn't view our liaison as anything it wasn't."

The pinpricks in his chest throbbed uncomfortably, his skin going cold beneath the layers of wool and linen. "You'd best explain to me what our *liaison* was and was not."

She held her chin high, assessing him with measured coolness. "It was but a careless moment. One that got out of hand. Not so far, however, that you need feel bound by any sense of honor or think that my reputation has suffered a stain. Unless your mother decides to make conjectures and spread gossip—which would not be to her benefit—our indiscretion need never be spoken of again, and we can place it behind us."

A careless moment. An indiscretion. Why did hearing her speak of it in so offhand a manner make his veins feel like they were filled with ice? She was correct, after all; that's exactly what it was. An instance where he'd let the fire in his blood get the better of him. It shouldn't have happened. Couldn't happen again.

But God, he wanted it to. Having her atop his lap, bringing her to release, had provided a mere hint of the pleasure they could give one another. He wanted to know how it would feel to have her naked body beneath him. How she would taste if he nestled his head between her thighs. What it would be like if she stroked him without the hindrance of his fall.

Except where would it lead in the end? *Nowhere*. He had nothing he could offer her.

He took a final step closer to her. *Still not close enough*. "As you say, Miss Windham."

She released an audible breath, her face remaining damnably unreadable. The only clue she gave was with her hands, still clutching tight to her skirts. "I should really be getting back to Lady Emily and Marigold."

What protest could he make to that? He'd said his piece. Not the maelstrom of half-formed thoughts and desires that rushed through his head, but the things he *could* say. There was nothing else left. "Goodnight, Miss Windham."

She released her skirts and curtseyed, as prompt and even as always, and for the first time, he found himself hating the formality of the gesture. "Goodnight, my lord." With that, she scurried over to the camphor trunk, making the briefest stop to take up Emily's dolls before rushing from the attic.

She left the lamp behind, doing him the courtesy of not plunging him into darkness. However, the flickering light only served to illuminate the fact that he was alone, and she hadn't looked back.

12

For a pristine summer day, on which the sun shone unobstructed by even a single cloud, a gentle breeze blew off the lake, and an endless array of refreshments lay spread out before them, none of the picnic-goers looked especially content. Lady Burville excepted, perhaps.

Phoebe took another sip of lemonade, peering over the rim of her glass at the formidable woman sitting at the wrought iron table placed lakeside for the occasion. This was no ordinary picnic involving a basket of sandwiches and a blanket spread across the grass. Rather, footmen had been traveling between the house and grounds all morning, setting up the table and chairs along with a large canopy to provide a shield from the sun. They'd carried on with their steady stream of activity once the picnic started, too, delivering dish after dish of hot, cold, sweet, and savory dishes alike.

Lady Burville's lips curved, and she uttered a comment about the excellent quality of the scones. A compliment she paid sincerely, in Phoebe's estimation, for each item upon the table truly was prepared to perfection. If only everything Phoebe tasted didn't seem to stick in her throat.

She set her glass down so she could replenish it from the pitcher, her eyes still not leaving Lady Burville. There was something about the woman—not unlike the dowager—that commanded attention. Whether it was her perfect posture, her rich dark hair, her evenly set features, her height, or a combination of all those things, she was unquestionably a lady of the ton, dignified in every regard. Visibly older than the marquess, but not in a way that made them appear ill-matched. In fact, they would be quite the impressive pair.

Phoebe took extra care not to let her gaze linger at Lady Burville's right, where the marquess had taken his seat and was silently drinking claret. She had enough trouble managing the visions of him that kept turning through her head without adding a live reminder. Even without looking at him, she could picture the shadows that had traveled across his face in the dim attic last night. His eyes upon her as she'd taken her pleasure in his study the night before. Most vivid of all, even after all these years, she could envision his body gliding through the lake beside them, his muscular torso breaking through the surface—

But it was all irrelevant. The images in her memory were no more conspicuous than the words she'd overheard upon going down to the kitchen yesterday to fetch more milk for Emily's tea. The two kitchen maids, busy at the worktable chopping an inordinate number of asparagus stalks, hadn't heard her come in, thus continuing their conversation without interruption.

A four-course luncheon all brought down to the lake? one of them had grumbled. *This Lady Burville must be someone special.*

The other had paused with her knife hovering above the asparagus, her voice growing animated. *The Dowager Lady Rockliffe is matchmaking again. I daresay we'll see the marquess married once more before the end of summer.*

Phoebe had hurried forward, then, making her footsteps heavy so they caught the maids' attention before she had to endure another word of gossip on the subject. She'd already heard enough. Already received a crushing reminder that she could desire all she wished, but the marquess would never be for her. Their *liaison*, as she'd called it, had driven her out of her head with longing, but it would lead nowhere in the end but trouble. She, of all people, should know that.

"How I wish I'd brought along my watercolors. It would be such a splendid day to capture the scene." Lady Burville's measured words cut into her thoughts, and Phoebe realized, to her horror, that the lady's gaze had turned upon her. "Do you paint, Miss Windham?"

Phoebe straightened in her seat, tilting her head in a way that made Lady Burville's hat block out her view of the lake. "A little." *Although if I were to paint the lake, I would have a difficult time not including an unclothed body emerging from it.*

"I see. Did you ever have instruction?" Lady Burville didn't miss a beat, her tone remaining as placid as ever. Why, then, did this feel somewhat like an interrogation?

"Not officially, no." It seemed a poor time to mention that during afternoons spent outdoors as a child, Phoebe had far preferred searching through the grass for insects than sitting at an easel. "My governess taught me a few things, but her painting skills were adequate, nothing more."

Lady Burville took a sip of lemonade, and the tables turned, for now she was the one peering at Phoebe over her glass, her dark eyes focusing unapologetically. "Windham," she murmured as she set down her glass, her brows drawing closer just a shade. "Are you a relation of Sir Ambrose Windham?"

As always, the name made Phoebe's stomach curdle, and the back of her neck grew cold despite the sun's persistent warmth. "He's my father's cousin," she managed to say without her voice turning frosty. "He inherited the baronetcy after my father's, Sir John Windham's, death."

"Indeed? Sir Ambrose was an acquaintance of my late husband. Pity that he's found himself a widower." Lady Burville's upper lip twitched, and Phoebe couldn't help but suspect she found the man distasteful as well. Who *wouldn't*? However, that was secondary to the intent way Lady Burville peered at her. Almost like she was calculating, digging through the far recesses of her brain.

Almost like she knows my secret.

Which was impossible. Ambrose and Eugenia both, for all their faults, had treated the situation with the utmost discretion. Phoebe pressed her clammy palms into her lap, trying to prevent them from shaking. In addition to being caught beneath Lady Burville's shrewd gaze, she could feel the dowager's eyes upon her. The marquess's eyes ...

"And you, Lady Emily?" All of a sudden, Lady Burville broke the stare, causing Phoebe to release a shuddering breath. How foolish she was to have such an overreaction, to let her imagination get carried away in creating unfounded fears. For Lady Burville was smiling upon Emily as if Ambrose's name had never been spoken. "Do you enjoy painting?"

Emily looked up from beneath the brim of her bonnet, the new sunny yellow ribbon doing nothing to mask the fact that her face looked like a thundercloud. "It's fine."

While Emily had made no protest to the initial revelation that her papa requested they join him for an outdoor luncheon, she'd appeared grim from the moment she learned it would also include her grandmother and the new guest, and that Marigold was to stay indoors. Her conduct as they all sat around the table left something to be desired, for she stared at her plate unless spoken to, and even then, she answered with only a clipped word or two. Phoebe could hardly fault her, though, when the marquess himself was only marginally more effusive.

Yet Lady Burville wasn't dissuaded by any of it. "Perhaps you prefer other pursuits." The lady's voice grew a note cheerier as if to compensate for Emily's sullenness. "Do you sing?"

"No."

"Do you play the harp or pianoforte, then?"

"No."

"What about needlework?"

"No." Emily folded her arms across her chest, leaning back in her chair in a manner that would have earned Phoebe censure from her own former governess.

"A pity." Lady Burville pursed her lips, and for a terrible moment, her attention returned to Phoebe, the disapproval in her expression no longer so veiled. But ultimately, she must have decided that the hostile girl and her incompetent governess weren't worth the trouble, for she snapped her head in the other direction, focusing on Lord Rockliffe. "Have you considered a ladies' seminary, my lord?" She waited until he looked up, then softened her features once more, reaching forward to daintily pick a strawberry from the dish in the center of the table. "I'm aware of one or two where the instruction is purported to be of the finest quality, and it would provide a wonderful opportunity for Lady Emily to garner the company of other suitable young ladies."

"An interesting proposition." It was the dowager marchioness, who'd acted as a surprisingly silent bystander during the exchange, who answered the question, her brow creasing in thought. "I hadn't considered it."

"I'd be happy to make inquiries." Lady Burville flashed an unnervingly pleasant smile, first to the dowager and then to the stony-faced marquess. "I could write some letters this very day, and the arrangements could be made and Lady Emily off within a matter of a fortnight—"

"Stop." Lord Rockliffe's voice, low and a little foreboding, cut into her speech, but it was overshadowed as the young lady in question scrambled to her feet so quickly that her chair toppled to the grass.

"What are you doing?" The dowager turned to her granddaughter with a frown. Phoebe had once heard Clara whisper about how the dowager marchioness's infamous expression of displeasure caused grown men to tremble in terror. Emily, on the other hand, gave her a split second of notice before spinning away, bestowing her with the cut direct and marching across the lawn.

"Where are your manners?" The dowager grabbed the cane that rested against her chair, giving it an indignant knock against the ground. "One does not simply bound from the table in the midst of a conversation. It's unseemly, and—"

She stopped mid-sentence, for with each word she spoke, Emily only got farther away, her strides increasing in speed as she hit the walking path, nearing the footbridge that crossed the lake.

Phoebe's heart sank, the lemonade she'd consumed suddenly burning the back of her throat. Once again, she could envision the breathless, tearstained girl she'd encountered in the field, only now, the nature of what troubled her was so much clearer.

She pushed back her chair and bolted to her feet, mumbling an excuse that she doubted anyone listened to. Frankly, she cared little if that made her ill-mannered as well.

"Really." From behind her, the dowager gave an incensed sniff. "What can Emily mean by such a display? My own children wouldn't have *dreamed* of exhibiting such behavior—"

"I assure you, Mother," the marquess cut in, his voice like ice, "we did."

And suddenly, more chair legs skidded across the grass, and heavy footfalls joined with her own as she started at a half-run toward the footbridge.

Lord Rockliffe gained on her quickly, the sound of his breaths loud enough to reach her ears above the swish of grass and her skirts, the heat of his approaching body something she could just *sense*. But instead of picking up speed, she maintained the pace she'd set from the beginning, turning to shoot him a warning glance. She had no intention of letting Emily out of her sight, but nor did she want to stop her and cause a scene while they still had Lady Burville and the dowager as an audience.

He must have understood, for he kept his position behind her, letting his daughter stay well in the lead. Emily made it across the bridge, veering off the walking path and dashing behind a showy purple rhododendron. For someone still experiencing the aftereffects of illness, she could run impressively fast when she set her mind to it. However, as she left the rhododendron and slipped around the oak tree behind it, her shoulders began to sag, and her steps grew shakier.

That's when Phoebe allowed herself to start sprinting, following Emily's route through the bushes and to the oak, where, thankfully, the girl had paused to catch her breath.

Phoebe halted as well, going just far enough to ensure the thick cover of branches and leaves would make her undetectable from the lakeside table. "Lady Emily?" She called her name softly, unsurprised when she received no response. This would require patience, and a great deal of finesse.

"Emily." One of the branches rustled, and Lord Rockliffe stepped within the giant tree's shade, moving toward the trunk. Yet, like Phoebe, he seemed to think better of it, stopping abruptly before he got too close. The marquess was so large, so commanding. In the shadow of the tree, though, he appeared dwarfed, and his features twisted into a look of obvious uncertainty. "Will you tell me what's wrong?" he asked in a murmur, seemingly as cognizant as she that a single wrong sound or motion would detonate this fragile moment of stillness.

Emily didn't run; at least they could say that much. However, her slender fingers tightened into fists, and when she finally looked up from staring at the ground, her eyes flashed with anger. "That woman is horrid. I despise her already. And you're going to let her send me away!"

"No." Lord Rockliffe gave his head a vehement shake. "That's not going to happen, Em. Not if you don't want it to."

He took a long step forward, halting again when Emily jerked her body away from the tree trunk, staggering backward to maintain the same level of distance between them. She appeared not unlike Marigold, warning him away, ready to reach out and attack the second he drew too close. Yet beneath the defensive facade, her chin began quivering, and her eyes developed a watery sheen.

The sight wrenched Phoebe's heart; it had to do the same for Lord Rockliffe. It lasted only an instant, though, before Emily pivoted away. "Oh, just leave me alone!" she shouted without looking back, resuming a half-hearted run deeper into the trees.

The marquess started forward and froze, the beginning of her name forming on his lips before dying off, replaced by a muttered curse.

"Give her a moment." Phoebe came up beside him, watching as Emily found the shelter of a yew tree not far away and tucked herself behind it. "She'll feel more even-tempered once she has a chance to catch her breath in private."

"I don't know what to do!" He careened to the side, slumping against the oak trunk where his daughter had just stood, his voice quieting so much that she scarcely heard the next words. "Nothing is right."

For a silent moment, she shifted her gaze between the two figures who found refuge in the trees. Perhaps they didn't realize how similar they were. Both determined to present a distant, impenetrable exterior to the world. Both vulnerable—and hurting—in ways she didn't think they liked to admit.

In fact, as he stood pushing back the hair that tumbled onto his forehead, watching the white ruffle of Emily's skirt—the lone part of her visible from behind the thick tree trunk—his vulnerability shone clearer than ever she'd seen it. He looked lost.

She inched her way over to him, keeping her slippers noiseless against the grass. After the intimacy they'd shared, could she not at least give him a comforting touch? A hand upon a hand, an arm around a shoulder ...

No, she couldn't. Not when another woman waited for him.

"Please, don't trouble yourself, my lord." She intertwined her fingers before they could get other ideas and made her best attempt at keeping her tone light. "I'll see to Lady Emily. You should return to the luncheon."

He let out a sound that nearly rang like a laugh except far too hollow. "God forbid I miss another second of that." Then, his body made a rapid turn, so fast and unsteady that it nearly collided with hers.

Surprise made her startle, not backward but forward, and a strong hand landed upon her arm to keep her from falling. They were far too close, her chest hovering alongside his, her skin burning beneath her sleeve from his touch.

And still, she didn't shrink from the position like she should have. Instead, she let him hold her wrist, let his blue eyes bore into her and his heat sear her, until he abruptly released his grasp.

"You're correct, Miss Windham, I should go." He pulled away like he was the one burned, giving his coat a few quick tugs to right it where it had wrinkled. "I'll not interfere any longer."

Time, which had slowed down as she experienced his touch, sped up again, for in little more than the blink of an eye, he was stalking away from the oak, around the rhododendron, back toward the walking path until all that remained of him was the fading stomp of his boots.

Leaving her to draw in a shaky breath and press her palm to the rough bark of the oak he'd just vacated, trying to rein in a pounding heart and a stomach twisted in knots.

He was doing just as she'd suggested and going back to the picnic. To his possible intended. *I daresay we'll see the marquess married once more before the end of summer.* The kitchen maid's careless words floated through her memory, causing an acerbic taste to creep up in the back of her mouth.

She sucked down the bitterness, her fingernails pressing into the bark. What right had she to mind? To form ill judgments of the lady's character or wish things were different?

None whatsoever.

But it didn't matter. She did mind, nevertheless.

13

Nicholas had the audacity to feel hopeful when the knock came upon his bedchamber door. In a moment of unthinkable idiocy, he envisioned changeable eyes, plump pink lips, and a measured voice assuring him that all was well again and everything would turn out just as it should.

Which made it all the more galling when he opened the door to his mother's frowning face and an irritated tap of her cane.

"What are you doing?" She eyed him up and down, his lack of coat and cravat causing the crease in her brow to deepen. "Barrington is going to announce dinner any minute, yet here you are, hiding away in a state of undress. I left you alone after you so discourteously abandoned the luncheon, but enough is enough."

He pressed his hand against the doorframe, barring the way before the dowager took it in her head to charge into his bedchamber and continue with the chastisement. One would think that reaching the age of six-and-thirty, not to mention inheriting a bloody marquessate, would exempt him from that sort of treatment, but no such luck, and frankly, he wasn't in the mood.

"I'm not going down to dinner tonight." He kept his tone deliberately mild, although tightness was beginning to set into his jaw. "Carry on without me. I'll get something sent up later."

His mother's eyes narrowed into slits. "If you tell me you've been taken ill, I won't believe you."

No, he wasn't ill. *Unsettled*, more like. After absconding from the damn disaster of a lakeside luncheon, he'd spent the afternoon riding about the estate, seeing to trivial tenant matters, to clear his head. He'd then received word from Mrs. Connelly upon returning that Emily and Miss Windham had passed some time picking wildflowers, had come in for tea and reading, and both seemed in good spirits. His solitary hours outdoors, combined with the housekeeper's favorable news, should have restored his equilibrium. Instead, he was more aware than ever that things at Beaumont Manor were *not* as he wanted them. That some things, quite desperately, needed to change.

"You look a fright, but you're not ill," the dowager so graciously informed him, giving her cane another impatient thump at his silence. "Now, get on your dinner attire and come down. Need I remind you that you have a guest?"

"No." He spit the word between clenched teeth, although as soon as it left him, a tiny chunk of the weight he shouldered melted away. "No," he repeated, the assertion equally as lightening, and suddenly, the decision he'd come to seemed more right than ever. "I'm done with entertaining. Should you wish Lady Burville to stay on, she will be *your* guest only, and I strongly suggest you see that the dower house is made ready without delay. In fact, I'll give both the chambermaids and footmen permission to make it their priority."

"Really, Rockliffe," she huffed. "You scarcely gave her a

chance. I hope you're not basing your decision on the theatrics of an incensed child, because—"

"Stop." He pushed a finger into the bridge of his nose, his forehead knotting with tension. "I'll not pursue Lady Burville. I'll not wed *anyone*. The sooner you can accept that, the better off we'll all be."

He narrowed his eyes as well, doing his own version of the Prescott glower. It had been stupid of him to consider any plan of his mother's—especially one pertaining to marriage—for even an instant. No, he *hadn't* given Lady Burville much of a chance. And no, he shouldn't make decisions because his temperamental daughter had had an outburst. Regardless, that didn't change what he intrinsically knew: were he to wed Letitia Burville, neither of them would make the other happy. More importantly, Emily wouldn't be happy.

The dowager could argue all she liked that he'd been too hasty, that these things could take time. Yet in his mind's eye, all he could see was the image of his runaway daughter sitting in the field with the blasted cat in her lap and Miss Windham at her side. Like old friends. Like they belonged.

If only the dowager were the type to be put off by adamant words and a caustic look. Instead, she seemed to take them as a challenge, staring right back at him. Not venomously, though. Instead, she looked ... *thoughtful*. Like she was looking through him and not at him. Contemplating. And that was damn dangerous.

"I mean it." Had he a walking stick handy, he would have pounded it against the floor, too. "Whatever you're thinking, whatever *scheme* you're drumming up because you believe you know better than the rest of us, stop. It won't work this time. You cannot orchestrate a compromising position when there's no one around to witness it, and even if you did, you do realize it would hardly have the same effect when both parties are widowed and over the age of five-and-thirty?"

She sniffed, having the nerve to appear affronted. "Why must you always assume the worst?"

"Because my assumptions are warranted." He folded his arms, his fingers digging into his sleeve.

She let out an audible sigh, readjusting herself against her cane as if, formidable force though she was, she began to grow weary. "Believe it or not, Rockliffe, I only want what's best for you."

"What's best for me," he snapped, "is for you to go down to dinner, leave me in peace, and forget all thoughts of match-making." God, he was weary as well, ready to sink into his armchair and not get up for a very long time.

"As you wish." Her words were complacent. Unusually so. "If you change your mind, you know where we'll be."

She stepped away from his door with far too little a fight. Doing just as he'd demanded but causing his stomach to roil, nonetheless. To the best of his knowledge, the dowager had never acquiesced easily in her life. He'd be a fool to think she felt inclined to start now.

He remained in the doorway until she disappeared from his sight and the thump of her cane faded, half-expecting to see the whole corridor go up in flames in her wake. But when it didn't, and he slammed the door on the scene, he found no resulting wave of relief.

He stalked across the room, not to his chair but to the window, tugging at the sash. He'd stake a large sum of money that this wouldn't be the last he'd hear on the subject of Lady Burville. Or if not her, then some other equally appropriate society lady whose presence stirred nothing within him but numbness.

But he couldn't fixate on that now. Didn't have the energy. He shoved the window up, sticking his head out for a blast of the cooling twilight breeze. However, the sinking sun brought no respite from the day's heat; indeed, the air had only grown hotter, thick enough to be cloying.

He inhaled it anyway, taking in the view of the sprawling park. Of the clusters of ancient trees, the more recently planted flowers and shrubs, the motionless water of the lake that sparkled like crystal. All grand and stately, worthy of envy. All *his*. Yet what good did it do when so much else had fallen apart and gone wrong? Could never be repaired.

He dropped his elbows to the sill, letting his weight rest against them. Whatever made the encroaching clouds feel heavy enough to burst seemed to exist within him, too. He was on edge, unsure of which way to turn, of how to make things right again before old misery crushed him and Emily both.

He was the Marquess of Rockliffe, supposed to be all-powerful and all-knowing. In this matter, though, he found himself at a loss. For as he stared at the darkening sky, trying to conjure a solution, only a single name—a single thing he could never keep—tumbled through his head.

Phoebe.

14

The sun had set upon the disaster of a day, but the night air only grew hotter, filled with a heavy sultriness that made Phoebe's face damp and her shift stick to her body. *Not unlike the first time I snuck onto the Rockliffe estate.*

She cast her lantern toward the lake, which had been rendered a glimmering black shadow. Were she to jump in and complete the dare from eight years prior, no one would see her in the darkness. She could shed her heavy gown, let the cool water rush over her body—

Yet it would do nothing to cure what truly afflicted her.

She kept walking, keeping her eyes on the gravel path that led around the lake. She'd already made it down from the house and across the bridge, coming to a section she hadn't traversed before. *Although a long time ago, I stood above it, peeking through the trees at the top of the slope ...* She fanned her face, a new wave of fire spreading across her cheeks. Not even a weak breeze blew off the water to counteract the overbearing humidity. Everything was too still. Too weighty.

Suddenly, though, a sound beyond her slippers crunching against gravel broke through the silent air. Only the faintest rustle, but given how restless she'd grown, it made her ears prick and her head dart upward.

She spotted him right away, even before she raised her lantern, for in the midst of the blackness came a tiny glow in the distance. Lord Rockliffe, her light revealed as she brought it upward, standing alongside a tree near the lake and smoking a cheroot.

She pulled the lantern back to her side at once, glancing behind her into the darkness. He'd have already seen her, of course, but was it too late to run back in the opposite direction and pretend this hadn't happened?

"Miss Windham." His call echoed through the night, his voice as heavy as the black, cloudy sky that seemed on the verge of breaking.

Too late, then. Her pulse throbbed unusually fast. Which was ridiculous. If she could live under his roof and sit at the same outdoor table as him and the woman he intended to marry, there was no reason she couldn't exchange a few innocuous words with him before she returned inside for the evening.

She drove her legs forward, pressing along until she reached his section of the pathway and could set the lantern upon the gravel. "Good evening, my lord." She folded herself into a curtsey, trying to ignore the fact that the man in front of her was devoid of coat, waistcoat, and cravat. Hardly surprising given the weather conditions and that he likely thought he'd remain unobserved. He hadn't known she would see the hollow of his throat or a hint of his bare chest, the surface smooth and muscled.

She brought her eyes up immediately, focusing on his face, and it became clear he'd been watching her. "Is the hour not late for a stroll?" he asked, and even in the dimness, she could tell his features were strained.

Her heart wouldn't stop racing, nor would her mind cease

turning in circles. Yet she clasped her hands neatly in front of her, trying to appear pleasant. "Lady Emily lost the new ribbon from her bonnet during the luncheon today. I thought I'd try finding it for her."

He arched a brow. "In the dark?"

"Yes. No." There suddenly seemed little point in prevaricating. "I may have minimal hope of locating the ribbon tonight, but I wanted the air."

"Beaumont Manor does grow stifling." He uttered the words more to the black expanse of lake than to her, taking a long draw from the cheroot before refocusing his attention. "And how is Emily?"

"She's well, my lord." Phoebe could assure him of that much, at least. "We had an agreeable dinner in her rooms, and she went to sleep easily, and ..." *and I have every reason to believe she will fully recover, and I'm certain she will let go of her anger in time, but if you were to render Lady Burville her new mother, you'd be making a mistake.*

She pressed her lips together, shocked at how quickly the exclamation tried pushing its way to the forefront. She would never overstep by voicing it, of course. It was based only on a brief encounter and an odd intuition. *And jealousy.*

"And I hope you don't let what happened today dissuade you from spending time with her," Phoebe continued, pushing down the thoughts that had no place, determined to express the ones that did, even though her throat felt thick. "Please, be patient with her, my lord. She's gone through so many upheavals, and the arrival of an unknown visitor provides yet another. I'm sure she'll adjust given time."

Lord Rockliffe stiffened, his eyes flaring dangerously in the darkness. "To what do you believe she needs to adjust, exactly?"

A weight dropped in Phoebe's stomach, the ground below her no longer feeling steady. "I mean if ..." Oh, *why* did she have to open her mouth? The last thing she wanted was to speak of it aloud, especially to him. But at the same time, if it was the truth, then why shy away from it? "I mean if your guest becomes a ... permanent resident here."

He made that sound of his that suggested a laugh but devoid of humor. "The speed at which gossip travels will never cease to amaze me. I'm not certain of exactly what you've heard, but because I can guess, let me make something clear." He flung the cheroot to the ground, extinguishing the faint light beneath his boot. "I'm not marrying goddamn Lady Burville!"

The impassioned words made her lean away, while simultaneously, a strange lightness cropped up inside her. *Not marrying ...*

She'd been wrong. The gossip was wrong.

The concept had no time to settle, for in the next instant, his body came forward, looming over hers with all the rigidity of a boulder, all the heat of a blistering flame. A sturdy palm cupped the back of her neck, making her breath catch, and then, most devastatingly of all, a finger traced along her jawline. Moved to follow the curve of her bottom lip.

This was the moment when she was supposed to pull away. To forget her desire to run her tongue over his fingertip and taste the salt of his skin. To forget how it felt to have that finger inside her, driving her longing.

But she didn't do that. She didn't move at all except for her lips, which managed to release two whispered words beneath his caress. "We shouldn't."

"No." His fingertip left her, leaving an instant void. "We decidedly should not."

"It would be ..." *wicked, wonderful, pleasureful, sinful ...* "Foolhardy," she managed, even as her heels rose off the ground. As her chin tilted upward.

"Yes." His face was so close, coming down to meet hers, his breath a hot trickle against her cheek. "Very much so."

A fat raindrop hit her forehead, fallen from a sky too heavy to hold it in. It was the last thing she absorbed before their lips collided, and everything ceased to exist but the searing press of his mouth.

The kiss was desperate, insistent, enough to make her legs wobble from the first moment. She twined her arms around his neck to anchor herself. Ran her hands through his hair, vaguely aware that the thick strands at his nape felt damp. Yet the realization flitted away as his fingers kneaded her lower back and familiar hardness pressed into her belly.

With each euphoric second they stayed that way, desire blossomed until all she could think of was *more. More of his mouth, more of his touch, more of the hardness.* She pressed her body tighter against his chest, releasing a muffled cry as his teeth sank gently into her bottom lip and he squeezed the globe of her bottom.

It was a wonder the low rumble in the sky caught her attention. Yet somewhere in the back of her pleasure-hazed mind, the concept registered. *Thunder.* Their lips drew apart in unison, and when she opened her eyes to peer at him, his face was wet. As was her own. She ran a finger over a soaked tendril of hair that stuck to the edge of her cheek, which emphasized what she'd somehow failed to notice. It was raining. Quite heavily, in fact, while a storm reverberated in the distance.

They would have to seek shelter. To go back to the house. She wasn't too far gone to recognize that, although she remained unmoving, far more preoccupied with the need to keep kissing him than to find refuge from the elements.

Lord Rockliffe regained his senses first, pulling away to retrieve the spluttering lantern near her feet. She nearly cried out again, this time in frustration, as his body left hers. But then, he offered her his hand just as a flash of light brightened the sky, illuminating his lips while he uttered three fateful words. "Come with me."

Thunder cracked the moment her fingers twined with his, the dampness of his skin doing nothing to diminish its overpowering heat. He took off at a sprint, her legs falling into step alongside his, fire spreading through her veins. For right away, she realized: he didn't guide them in the direction of the house.

Instead, they kept to the pathway on the far side of the lake, racing over gravel, veering off into the wet grass. The lantern's glow fell upon a stone structure up ahead. The Doric temple, its imposing columns blurred behind the curtain of rain.

His grip on her hand tightened, his footfalls growing more insistent. Once again, understanding glinted in her whirling head, and with the next flash of lightning, a jolt of longing surged through her core. They were running, nearly at the point of reaching shelter. Nearly at the point of reaching so much else, too.

He pulled her beneath the overhang, putting an end to the deluge that had already soaked them through. The rain, however, made little difference to her. She could focus on nothing but his hand, which released hers so he could jiggle the door latch. So he could push it open and take hold of her again, leading her inside.

A burst of cooler air hit her at once from the open, high-ceilinged space. The lantern flickered over a gleaming marble floor, over alcoves in the walls that held urns and statues. Everything was ornate and intricate, awe-inspiring—

And lasted only a second, for as the door slammed closed behind them, the flame sputtered and vanished, plunging them into blackness.

She gasped, blinking, trying to maintain her bearings.

Except then, lips slammed into hers once more, and his body came up against hers, pinning her to the door. She didn't need sight when they were like this. If anything, the dark only rendered his caresses more intense. Made her more aware when his fingers pulled at the tapes of her dress and the laces of her stays.

Despite the heat radiating through her, she shivered as fabric slid down her body and pooled at her feet. All that remained was her shift, sticking uncomfortably to her skin from the mixture of perspiration and rain. Until suddenly, the cotton tore and dropped, and his lips were no longer on her lips but on her breast, sucking her nipple into his mouth.

Her moan ripped through the darkness, her body awash in sensation from the wicked strokes of his tongue. His fingers joined, too, lavishing attention on the other side, turning her nipple into a hardened peak with a few flicks of his thumb.

She tossed her head back, fumbling in front of her until she located and clasped his shoulders. If he kept this up, her knees would grow weak, for each stroke he bestowed wound her more tightly, making desire flare into a blaze between her thighs.

He didn't keep it up, though. For a devastating moment, she found herself devoid of his mouth and fingers, and his shoulders dropped from within her grasp. Yet just as quickly, his hands connected with her hips, and she could detect the shadow of his body shifting, sinking to the floor, until he was on his knees in front of her. *Just like the scene in the book.*

Her breath rushed away in a tottering exhale, and she was unable to inhale again. The tip of his tongue skirted over her thigh just above the edge of her stocking. A teasing, featherlight caress that made her intimate muscles clench.

"I haven't stopped thinking about this." His words were hot against her bare skin, his tongue a fiery brand that traced a path upward, approaching the place where she ached with need. "Ever since the night you came on my fingers, I've been desperate to know how you taste."

She sucked in a gasping breath, the air barely hitting her lungs before his tongue swiped over her sex, and her breath turned into a cry. He gave an approving hum, the sound—the *sensation*—causing her legs to wobble. His grip on her tightened, holding her hips secure to the door while she steadied herself. Then, a strong hand slid down her thigh and to the back of her knee, coaxing it to rise until her leg lay sprawled over his shoulder. A position that left her completely exposed to him.

"You are even sweeter than I perceived." He licked along the seam of her thigh where arousal dampened her skin, and although the temple was pitch black, she *knew* he was peering up at her. "My one regret is that I cannot see your pretty quim. But I suppose I'll have to use my imagination."

She had just enough time to grip his hair before his tongue rediscovered her secret flesh. And this time, he didn't stop near her entrance but continued upward, exploring her folds. Coming to the bundle of nerves where she *needed* his touch, circling over it, taking it into his mouth.

This was the best sort of torture. This was *bliss*. Breathy sighs floated through the darkness as her desire built, and she was vaguely aware that they came from her. But what difference did it make? There was no one to hear, only the two of them in a deserted temple in a thunderstorm.

Her legs were quivering again, her muscles impossibly taut. She was nearing a precipice, each stroke of his tongue hurtling her closer until all at once, release crashed over her, and she let out a final cry, her body convulsing with jolt after jolt of pleasure.

His mouth stayed upon her, continuing to lightly tease and caress, until the last of her shudders died away. Only then did he unhook her leg from his shoulder and rise to his feet, pulling her into a fervent kiss.

His lips tasted of *her*. The thought sent a fresh shower of sparks flaring between her legs. He'd given her indescribable pleasure, brought it all to a peak, and still, her mind stayed focused on *more*. How could it do otherwise when his breaths were jagged and his arousal pressed against her heated skin?

Sightlessly, she reached for his fall, groping in the darkness for the buttons that would free him. He made a low noise in his throat, breaking the kiss so he could pull his wet shirt over his head and toss it away. The sound of the bunched-up linen hitting the floor came at the same moment she unhooked the final button, and suddenly, so many bare surfaces of him were hers.

She stepped forward and slowly pushed herself to her tiptoes, shivering as the dusting of hair across his chest abraded her sensitive nipples. Shivering again when the silky hardness of his erection brushed over her mound.

He hissed out a breath, his hands clamping around her waist, preventing her from moving any farther. "Phoebe." His voice sounded raw, her name coming out as part warning, part plea.

"Please, don't stop," she begged, her words beginning to crack. He'd never called her by her first name before—had never let his guard down enough to permit the intimacy—and the desperation he placed in it caused a new wave of desire to ignite in her core.

Yet he didn't move. Didn't say another word. The only sounds to fill the space were their heavy breaths, the rain beating on the roof, and the weakening thunder.

That's when, beneath the fog of anticipation, a glimmer of understanding hit her. He refused to rush. Wanted her to be certain. He'd said as much as she sat on his lap in the study, consumed by her spiraling need, just as she was now.

Tell him. A little voice cropped up in her head, fueled by a longing to render him as unhinged as he'd rendered her. *Fueled by proximity to the lake.* All these years, she'd shared her secret with Clara alone. However, the moment had come. She wanted him to understand the depth of her longing.

"I have a story for you," she murmured into the blackness. "About how, a long time ago, during an idle summer day at the vicarage, I accepted a dare. Would you like to know what it was?"

He gave no response beyond a heavy exhale, the rapid thrum of his heart echoing against her own. Which she knew, beyond a doubt, meant *yes*.

"*I dare you to go to Beaumont Manor and swim in Lord Rockliffe's lake.*" She repeated Clara's words as a whisper against his throat. Sensed a muscle tic in his jaw. "The day was hot, and I received assurances that the marquess was not in residence. And so, being a foolhardy girl of eighteen, I went.

"I stood in the trees and unfastened my gown"—she bit down sharply on her lip, suppressing a moan as his rigid manhood twitched against her—"and imagined how blissful the water would feel. It turns out, though, that I never got to experience it. My information, you see, was wrong. You *were* at home. And you were swimming."

This time, she got only silence in return. Not even the sound of a breath.

"I watched you," she said, a low, heated utterance that broke into the stillness. "I didn't mean to, but I couldn't look away. The sight of you moving through the water—it enthralled me. Made me feel heated and desperate, like I wished to place my hand between my legs and pretend it was yours—"

His mouth collided with hers, and words vanished, for they were whirling away from the door, stumbling toward ... she couldn't tell in the darkness. Didn't care, either, as long as their bodies remained entwined, his tongue teasing her, his erection pushing more demandingly against her thighs, promising so much pleasure to come.

Except suddenly, he halted, wrenching his mouth away from hers. "Jesus, Phoebe." His voice was strained, guttural, the hands that remained at her waist beginning to quake. "Do you know what you do to me?"

If it was anything like what he did to her, his body felt ready to combust. Nonetheless, he didn't move, and longing hung in the air between them, heavy and overwhelming. He was still uncertain, she realized with a jolt, about crossing a boundary with her that held consequences not able to be undone.

Tell him. The voice in her head returned, although this time, an icy flutter of nerves cut through the heat pooling in her stomach. The admission about the lake incident had glided off her tongue, the words natural and seamless. Driving her desire. This next subject, though, was different, something unspeakable that she'd always kept concealed. But if they were going to continue their intimacy, he should know the truth.

"I'm sure about this. I want you, I ..." The voice she'd found the power to use broke, and she paused to bite down on her lower lip, struggling with the words to keep going. There was no delicate way; she would just have to say it. "This isn't my first time," she burst out, her heartbeat a rapid thud. "You won't ruin me. I'm not a virgin."

She snapped her lips together, silence overtaking the temple once more. How infuriating not to have the ability to see his face, to be unaware how his features shifted upon hearing the revelation. Perhaps she'd shocked him. Perhaps he, too, believed the countless descriptors her relations had bestowed upon her. *Shameful. Immoral.*

"Good." All of a sudden, his mouth was by her ear, his

fingertips sinking deeper into her waist. "I don't want to go slowly."

And then, he grabbed her hand, and they began staggering once more, his footfalls rapid as they crossed the space. Everything was blackness, yet he seemed to know where he was going. Knew the exact moment to stop, guiding her hand to a cool stone surface.

She ran her fingertips over a flat edge and up to stone that was curved and dimpled, trying to make sense of the object beneath her touch. *A pedestal*, she registered, containing one of the urns she'd spotted before the faltering lantern made her surroundings vanish.

"Hold on to this." Lord Rockliffe's voice came from behind her, and he gave her a split second to obey before his hands went to her hips, tugging them backward.

She gasped, bracing herself with her elbows against the pedestal, the backs of her legs connecting with the wool of his gaping breeches and hardness that he guided between her thighs.

She'd seen this position in the book, too. The woman bent across the arm of a bench. The man entering her from behind. One of many images that had caused delicious tendrils of warmth to spread across her skin, that had caused her to lie restless under the bedclothes and *imagine*—

She let out a moan as his rigid length pushed into her, and all other thoughts darted away.

"Phoebe." He groaned along with her, leaning down so his lips hovered above her nape. "You feel so good."

Oh, so did he. He stretched and filled her in the best way possible. With a featherlight kiss to her neck, he eased back and pushed forward again, providing the first hint of friction. Just the tiniest taste of how wonderful it would feel to have him moving within her in a relentless rhythm.

Desire radiated through her body and surrounded her,

seeming to fill the air they breathed. Yet although it had turned nearly all-consuming, the tiniest spur of something else managed to push its way into the back of her mind. A warning. She may want nothing but him, now, but she wasn't quite so far gone to recognize how she'd be foolish not to have a care for the future.

"When we do this, my lord, we ..." She turned her head to face him despite how she could detect little more than blackness. "We cannot risk there being a child between us," she said, her words breathy and rushed. It was a wonder she'd managed them at all.

The sound of his brisk inhale filled her ears, and his hold on her hips tightened. "No. There will not be. It's ..." Now, he was the one struggling for what to say, leaving a heavy beat of silence between them. After an indeterminate number of seconds, she could sense rather than see his nod. Could feel his lips as they brushed along hers. "All right," he murmured, a low but determined rasp.

And then, he was thrusting into her with hurried, powerful strokes, making her inhibition sink like a stone cast into the ocean and her pleasure soar to the sky.

His hand traveled up the front of her body, capturing her breast, thumbing her nipple. She made a sound, trying to make it resemble *yes* or *more*, although it rang more like a nonsensical cry of desperation. Regardless, his fingers trailed back down, skimming her abdomen and navel, finding the peak that contained the heart of her yearning.

She couldn't hold on. It was too much; her muscles were tightening again, her limbs trembling.

"That's right, sweet." His thrusts deepened, his finger moving in insistent circles. "Come for me."

She shattered on command, her chest collapsing against the edge of the pedestal as blissful waves overtook her once more. Her muscles pulsed around him, drawing him in, but with a groan and a sudden rush of movement, he was gone, his seed spurting against her thigh.

She didn't know how long it took for the last of the spasms to fade or for the world to come drifting back. Only that after an unknown amount of time, she became aware of his chest sinking onto her back, draping over her like a shield, and that above them, the rain on the roof had diminished to a soft patter.

She was loath to move, unable to shake the sense that even one wrong twitch would take this satiated bubble they'd settled in and burst it. Yet when his weight shifted, and sturdy hands coaxed her to release the pedestal and turn around, she found her limbs didn't become any less pliant, nor did he retreat. She still couldn't see him, but she could sense him. Could detect him raising his arm, relishing the moment when his fingertip found the edge of her mouth and his lips followed, pulling her into a languid embrace. Her heart skittered in her chest, creating little fluttery sensations. *Dangerous* sensations.

She'd known all along that living at Beaumont Manor would only lead her to trouble. But in this moment, she couldn't regret it.

15

Given the choice, Nicholas would have stayed sequestered on the grounds of Beaumont Manor, huddled in the Temple of Athena with the heat of Phoebe's body beneath him, until the end of time. He didn't *want* to pull away from her to search for his discarded shirt upon the ground. Nor did he want to mutter words about the rain easing up and them returning to the house. The echoey stone structure, which smelled slightly of damp and had lacked any particular appeal to him until tonight, had become their sanctuary, and never again would he pass it without fire rising in his blood.

However, even beneath the cloak of darkness and the haze of satiety that overtook his body and mind, he could recognize the impracticality of remaining there overlong. The building contained not a stick of furniture. Nothing soft and inviting beyond *her*. Phoebe deserved silk sheets. Somewhere she could lie down while he explored her inch by inch.

And so, with another idea taking hold, he'd initiated their departure from the temple, throwing back on his wet shirt and assisting her with the fastenings of her dress.

When he opened the door, letting the outside world encroach on them once again, the air had both lightened and cooled, refreshed by the summer rain. A good thing, for even the act of touching her neck while helping her get dressed had caused a new wave of heat to spread through his veins.

The rain still hadn't stopped, although instead of a deluge, it fell in a sprinkle of misty droplets that dampened their faces as soon as they stepped under the sky. He couldn't resist pulling her in for an embrace. He wanted to taste the raindrops upon her kiss-swollen lips, to glean a final bit of sustenance before they left their sanctuary behind.

Her slender hand cupped his jawline. Traveled down to place her palm in his. And then, in an unspoken agreement, they began running, going back toward the distant glow of candlelight in Beaumont Manor's windows. This time, their pace was leisurely instead of frantic, for they were no longer rushing toward something they both needed but prolonging a moment he didn't want to end.

Be that as it may, they eventually reached the terrace doors, and he peered through the rain-dotted glass, ensuring the drawing room beyond lay empty before easing one open and leading her inside. The room was silent, lit by only a trickle of light from the corridor sconces. Yet it was enough for him to detect the blue-gray-green glimmer of her eyes and the bodice, which he hadn't quite fastened properly, clinging to her skin. Enough for him to see the settee in the corner that was large enough for her to lie down while he—

No. Not here. While the household was likely abed, Barrington would still be coming through to do his final rounds and lock all the doors for the night.

But that doesn't mean this needs to end.

He encircled her waist and drew her against him, pressing a kiss to the spot he loved where her jawline met her ear. "Come to my bed," he murmured, for although it was late, they had hours left until daybreak. Hours to continue the pleasure, to keep pretending that nothing else existed.

She shivered against him, her voice coming out on a wavering breath. "Yes."

He kissed the spot again before pulling away, his cock already beginning to stir. He remembered to exhibit discretion in creeping across the room and into the corridor, and out of an abundance of caution, he didn't bring them to the main staircase but to the servant's stairs, which wouldn't be in use at this time of night.

Beyond that, though, it was becoming increasingly difficult to move slowly. The fever had begun again. The escalating need. Darkness in the temple had made the sensations of touching her, tasting her, *entering* her so vivid that it was a wonder the pleasure of it hadn't finished him then and there. However, this time, he wanted his sense of sight. He would light every candle and then learn every one of her curves. Watch her face as he licked between her thighs. As he plunged into her. Perhaps he'd bring her in front of the mirror before the night was through so she could watch, too.

Thank Christ, they'd made it up the stairs, for his arousal pushed achingly against his breeches. He stumbled toward his door like he'd consumed too much brandy, her footsteps unsteady beside his as they hurried down the corridor. They were almost there, just a few more steps.

And he'd be goddamned if he could wait another second. He spun her toward him, claiming her lips as he shifted her to rest against the wall. She gave the most delicious little cry, part surprise and part pleasure, opening her mouth to allow him entry. She tasted so sweet; her body felt so warm and pliant beneath his touch. He kissed her deeply, his fingers twining in the wet strands at her nape and trailing forward to the column of her throat. His mouth wandered, too. Across her cheekbone. To the edge of her jawline.

"This time," he said against her ear, letting his finger trace over her bodice until he felt the hardened point of her nipple beneath, "I *will* go slowly. There is so much of you that warrants careful study, and I want my exploration to make you desperate."

She made a sound, incoherent beyond the fact that it was full of need. He swallowed it up with another kiss, blindly fumbling with the door latch beside him. He felt rather than saw it give, shoving the door with his palm and then backing his weight into it so it swung open the rest of the way and they could stagger inside.

All without breaking the embrace. He had no intention of taking his mouth from hers until he had her laid across his bed. Only then would he turn his attention to removing each article of her clothing one by one, and after that, his mouth would have numerous other places to keep it occupied.

The first gasp barely reached his awareness. It was low and came from far away, almost like a figment of his imagination that held no significance because it had nothing to do with *more* and *need* and *Phoebe*. The next gasp, though, was impossible to ignore. This one arose from Phoebe herself as a startled rush of air against his mouth, and in the span of an instant, her body became stiff in his arms, struggling to break away.

He released his grasp on her at once, his eyes flying open.

Jesus. His breath, too, caught in his throat, the fire that consumed him turning to ice.

Lady Burville sat upon his bed, the flickering light of his bedside candelabrum illuminating a face gone pale and a mouth that gaped in horror.

He stiffened his spine. Made a brisk attempt at smoothing his crumpled shirt. But damn, what was the point? Lady Burville seemed a shrewd woman, and even the biggest simpleton could discern the meaning of the scene he'd created. *Because I grew bloody careless.*

He stepped forward, his limbs feeling brittle enough to crack. "What are you doing here?"

Her mouth snapped closed, and she rose from his counterpane in a seamless motion, the filmy white hem of her dressing gown settling around her feet. The fabric was thin, nearing translucency, clinging tight to the contours of her body. Revealing she wore nothing underneath. *Oh, God. Of all the times—*

"I had it on good authority," she intoned, her voice tinged with steel, "that you were in want of companionship this evening. It seems, though, that you already found someone to fill the role."

A pit opened in his stomach, his muscles tightening under the vise of fury. "I can imagine who told you that," he bit out. "Regretfully, you've been misinformed."

"But you *did* want companionship. Just not mine." Her dark eyes flared, her glower falling first in his direction and then in Phoebe's, and he experienced an overbearing urge to step back to the door and shield Phoebe from the vitriol brought about by *his* recklessness. However, she stood as if made of stone, the grim set of her features a warning for him to keep away.

Lady Burville stalked toward him, stopping too close for comfort and pointing an accusing finger at his chest. "I thought we had an understanding, my lord."

"We didn't." That was the most damnably infuriating part about all of this. "Any understandings were between you and the dowager alone. To be clear, I'm aware of what she proposed. A new title and Rockliffe money for you. A respectable wife for me. That being said, I never agreed to any of it."

His voice rose on the last bit, and he found himself looking at Phoebe. Silently willing her to believe him.

"I see. I see a great many things more clearly now." Lady

Burville jabbed him in the sternum, forcing his attention back to her irate face. However, she wasn't gazing at him anymore but to the side. To Phoebe. "I did wonder at your incompetence as a governess, Miss Windham. But now, I understand you have other talents."

"Do *not* speak to her that way." His words became louder again, and of the two weights pushing into his chest, it was difficult to say which would crush him first: anger or regret. "Rage at me all you like, but do not—"

"Oh, good Lord!" A new voice cut through the air. An indignant rasp accompanied by the thump of a cane. He wanted nothing less than to lay eyes on the source, but his head betrayed him by turning anyway. Made him watch, motionless, as the dowager marchioness hobbled into the room, her gaze darting furiously among the three of them, all in various states of undress. She ground to a halt beside Lady Burville and stared up at him. Gave her cane another knock against the carpet. "What in *hell* is the meaning of this?"

He didn't take the time to feel horrified. His ire swelled and crested, fueled by the corrosive sting of betrayal. One that was all too familiar. "Why don't you tell me?" He spit out the words in a low hiss, his wrath on the verge of choking him. "You're the one who keeps bloody interfering. You're the one who took the exact thing I said just hours ago *not* to do and did it regardless."

"Do not get carried away with presumptions." Her mouth turned down, and although she tried to sound affronted, he didn't miss the slight falter in the words. "I may have suggested that you were alone and could use some ... encouragement. I didn't imply that it was to take place in your bedchamber without the benefit of suitable clothing. And I certainly didn't realize that you were not, indeed, alone."

For the first time in his memory, the dowager's cheeks took on a hint of pink that he could nearly believe came from discomfiture. Under different circumstances, the realization may have given him a paltry sort of satisfaction. Instead, all he felt was coldness.

"I don't give a goddamn about the exact wording you used. You brought this about, nonetheless. You didn't listen!" Perhaps he could have kept a more even head had he not had cause to shout such similar things in the past. Yet this was history repeating itself, and *God*, he was weary.

Three sets of eyes bore into him. One set icy and contemplative. One dark and furious.

And one, he couldn't see but feel, the intensity of the gaze pricking the back of his neck. *Hers* was the one that mattered.

He turned toward the door slowly, a dull ache tearing through his chest. She stood with her chin held high, her hands clamped against her wet skirts, not giving the slightest waver. However, he could see the hint of desperation in her eyes. The tension upon her ashen face.

"Phoebe ..." His throat felt raw. What was he to say in a situation where no words would suffice? He could apologize for being a selfish blackguard and dragging her into this mess, but what would it change? He couldn't take back how he'd placed her in a compromising position. Couldn't do the honorable thing without condemning her to another miserable fate.

Suddenly, even his worthless apology vanished from the tip of his tongue, for something rustled in the corridor, and a wisp of black hair flashed in the doorway before swiftly disappearing.

His body jerked as if he'd suffered a blow, and another torrent of dread flooded his insides. *Not this. Not now.* Yet he knew what he'd seen. Couldn't make it any less real than the other damnable things he wished hadn't come to pass.

He cleared his throat so his voice wouldn't sound altogether ragged. "Come in, Emmy."

He half-expected to hear her footfalls racing away the instant he uttered her name. Instead, she stepped to the middle of the doorway, a thin, pale figure in her too-large night rail, her eyes giant saucers as she peered in at the chaos.

"I ... I couldn't sleep." She took another wary step forward, glancing at the floor as if it might detonate beneath her feet. He could no longer guarantee it wouldn't. "I heard arguing."

He gave himself an instant to blink and indulge in a fleeting moment of oblivion. To swallow back the acridness coating his throat and attempt to make his expression mild and his words even. "I'm afraid Grandmother and I don't always see eye to eye. I apologize if our ... *disagreement* woke you. It's nothing you need trouble yourself over. All is well."

The last part was the biggest lie he'd ever told her. However, even if everything else ignited around him, he needed to make her believe it. All in her world had to be well.

Although that was the problem, wasn't it? In failing Phoebe Windham, he'd failed his daughter, too.

Emily folded her slender arms across her chest and tilted her chin to the side, giving him *the look*. This time, though, she didn't reserve it for him alone but brought her sharp gaze over each of them. Phoebe, who rapidly tapped her foot, her features twisting like she, too, sought the proper thing to say but didn't know where to find it. The dowager, who remained uncharacteristically silent. Lady Burville, whose face had only become flintier.

Emily had grown so quiet since the tragedy had befallen her, but he'd be a damn fool to underestimate her powers of observation. And eventually, instead of giving him the cut direct, she returned her observant stare to him, looking him square in the eye. "Why is everyone in your bedchamber, then?"

Lady Burville stormed forward in a flurry of sheer white

silk. "Never mind that," she snapped, her words bordering on shrill. "Get back to bed."

A growl rose in his throat. "Do *not* presume to order her—"

"Indeed, Letitia, that's where you should go as well." The dowager's cane slammed onto the carpet, the pinched line of her mouth sinking into a scowl. "Your *own* bed."

The lady paused only to deliver a last scathing glower. "I'm going there directly, and I'll be leaving this godforsaken house at first light. To hell with all of you." And then, she rushed from the room, her indignant footfalls stomping down the corridor.

His head reeled, but Phoebe didn't miss a beat. "Let's return to your bedchamber, Lady Emily." She extricated herself from her position against the wall, coming forward to place a gentle hand upon Emily's arm. "My discussion with your papa has concluded, and I'd be happy to read aloud until you feel tired again."

She spoke so mildly. Even managed a shadow of a smile. God, he didn't deserve her. Didn't want her to go until he could at least tell her that ... that ...

He had no bloody idea. Nothing he said would fix this. Nor could he place his daughter in the middle of his pitiable attempts.

Emily hesitated, shooting him another wary look. He didn't have the right words for her, either. Doubted she would want to hear them even if he did.

In the end, she spun away before he could make an effort, giving Phoebe a brisk nod. "Thank you, Miss Windham. I'd like that very much." Her voice sounded thin, brittle. Yet she placed her hand in Phoebe's and took off with a sudden burst of speed, making them both vanish in the span of a blink.

Wait. The imploration rose on his tongue, but he pushed

it back. For now, it was better to let them go. Even if everything about the way things had ended felt wrong.

"I'll see what I can do to quell the gossip." His mother's words rang out behind him, her tone strangely lacking its usual sharp edge. Not that it grated any less. "Lady Burville may be enticed to keep quiet if given suitable compensation."

He clenched his teeth, pressing his lips tightly closed. Why dignify that with an answer? They could pay Lady Burville a small fortune, but it wouldn't erase the damage already done.

Wood tapped against the carpet in a series of quiet thumps, and the dowager came around to face him, her weight shifting slightly so she leaned toward her cane. He wouldn't say she looked contrite—that word didn't exist in her vocabulary—but perhaps ... subdued. Which was infuriating in how grossly it proved too little too late.

"I won't plead ignorance of your dalliance with the governess." She pursed her lips, one of her silver brows giving an aggravating twitch. "But you had to know it couldn't last."

A knife plunged into his gut, ripping open an old and festering wound. *It couldn't last*. It never could where he was concerned. He had nothing to offer but disappointment and misery. The years of his marriage—the wife whose desperation to flee him in favor of someone whole had cost her her life—made that glaringly clear, and he'd be a fool to ever forget it.

That didn't make the reminder cut any less deeply.

"Get out," he muttered, slumping against the wall and gazing blankly toward the doorway. Hardly a retort worthy of the dowager's force, but weariness seeped through his bones, and he lacked the fight to offer anything more.

Something odd happened. His mother *listened*. After only a brief pause, the hem of her thick dressing gown rustled against the carpet, and her cane hit the floor in a series of slow, rhythmic taps, bringing her into the corridor.

"Goodnight, Rockliffe. We'll sort this in the morning."

Mercifully, they were the only words she uttered, although even that much proved more than he wanted to hear. He swung the door shut, stumbling to his bed with legs that felt leaden and dropping upon the counterpane.

Phoebe was supposed to be here, too. Lying beside him, beneath him, atop him as he reveled in her softness and warmth. But the counterpane beside him was cold and bare, containing none of her floral scent. Now, it never would.

He closed his eyes, remembering the sounds she made in the dark as he pleasured her. The feel of her intimate flesh beneath his fingers and tongue. Perhaps he was a selfish rogue—no, he *was* a selfish rogue—but he didn't want to take any of it back. The way it had all come abruptly crashing down he of course longed to change, but the act itself? That, he wished he could repeat every night for the rest of his life.

As for the future—all the long, solitary days ahead—he found his wishes didn't stop there. Visions flashed through his head, unbidden, of a dining table where the seat beside his was occupied. Of an arm resting in his as he strolled through the park. Of feminine laughter filling the corridors.

All because Phoebe was there, making the world brighter.

His eyes flew open, revealing nothing but his lonely, empty bed. Still, he wished. Wished things were different. Wished he were whole. Wished those visions could become a reality instead of slipping through his fingers.

But he'd learned a hard lesson many years ago. Wishing for something—even if you were the goddamn Marquess of Rockliffe—didn't make it so.

16

Neither Phoebe nor Emily spoke a word until they were safely back in Emily's rooms and the girl climbed into bed, shuffling her legs around Marigold's dozing, sprawled-out form. Phoebe had taken the few minutes of silence to try to regain some order in the chaos that pounded through her head. While half-numbed by the initial shock of what—*who*—awaited her in Lord Rockliffe's bedchamber, she'd at least possessed the wherewithal to extricate Emily from the ugly, acrimonious scene. But beyond that, she found herself at a loss.

She should think of some reassurance, something to make everything better. Except how was she to do that when, once again, her life was crumbling to pieces?

You have only yourself to blame. The admonition rang in her thoughts, voiced in unison by Aunt Harriet and Uncle Martin. Then by Ambrose. Even by departed Eugenia. They all jeered at her, the feckless girl who never learned her lesson. Who couldn't stop dragging disaster down on her own head.

She rummaged through the books on Emily's bedside table, a choking lump forming in her throat. *Read.* That's what she'd offered, and if she could manage nothing else, she needed to do at least that much. If she could only keep her voice from breaking.

"Miss Windham?" Emily pushed herself back up on her elbows, and Phoebe paused, turning to the wide amber eyes that peered at her in the candlelight. "You don't need to read aloud. But I wonder if … if you'd sit with me a few moments."

"I'd be happy to." Phoebe lowered herself onto the edge of the bed, and only when seated did she realize just how weary she'd become. Like she could lie down herself and not get up for a *very* long time. Yet she managed a thin smile as she reached for the candle snuffer to extinguish the bedside light. "Try to sleep now, all right?"

Emily gave a tiny nod, the faint flutter of her dark lashes against pale skin the last thing Phoebe saw before the room became dim. For some reason, the sight caused a pang in her chest. She'd known Emily only a short time but already felt an undeniable attachment to the girl. Wanted so much to give her reasons to smile again. The thought of not seeing her anymore … of Emily sitting in her bedchamber alone each night … Phoebe couldn't let her mind keep traveling that way or her shaky facade of calmness would dissolve in a shower of tears.

"Miss Windham?" Emily whispered her name again, her shadowed outline remaining upright, her eyes two huge, glimmering pools in the dark. "You're not leaving Beaumont, are you?"

Phoebe's aching chest constricted, causing another painful jolt. "Not until you and your papa wish it." She tried to sound light. Tried to ignore everything she'd sent crashing down around her and the regret that seeped to her core.

Emily hesitated, and while it was impossible to make out her exact expression, Phoebe could tell that she hadn't stopped looking. Assessing. Phoebe could give all the assurances she liked, but Emily was far too astute not to recognize that something was amiss elsewhere in Beaumont Manor.

In the end, though, her hand fell upon Phoebe's, and she dropped back onto her pillow, uttering nothing beyond a goodnight. For an indeterminate amount of time, Phoebe sat motionless, keeping hold of the slender fingers and listening to Emily's breathing become soft and regular.

Not until you and your papa wish it. She hadn't lied to Emily. Yet no matter how hard she tried, she couldn't forget how that time was coming all too soon.

As it turned out, *the end* arrived shortly before noon the next day. After remaining with Emily until long after the girl had drifted off, she'd then retreated to her own room, spending hours tossing and turning until sleep finally claimed her sometime around dawn. Consequently, she'd woken with a start to bright midday light and had leaped, disoriented, from bed and to Emily's rooms across the corridor. Only to find no one there but a chambermaid, who explained that Mrs. Connelly had taken Lady Emily to the village for the afternoon, and that Lord Rockliffe would like to see her in his study at her earliest convenience.

She'd expected as much. Not under those exact circumstances, perhaps, but she'd known a confrontation was coming. With a pounding heart, she fetched one of her high-necked black dresses—a relic of her half-hearted mourning that covered her like an ineffective shield—and pinned back her disheveled hair. The mirror revealed dark shadows beneath her eyes and a sickly cast to her skin, but what was she to do about it? The reflection was nothing but an accurate depiction of how she felt.

By the time she reached the study door, her pulse was out

of control, and blood rushed through her ears. Even so, she'd steeled herself for what was inevitably to come.

"Phoebe." He let out her name, low and guttural, the moment their eyes locked. He'd been in the midst of pacing, studying the floor as if it held answers, but her presence in the doorway—the small knock she hadn't dared delay in giving to the frame—caused him to halt in the middle of the room. He made a gesture with his hand, the motion strangely rigid. "Come in."

Despite the heaviness in her legs, she obeyed without hesitation, for again, what benefit would she find in prolonging the inevitable?

This room was where it all started. As she crossed the Aubusson rug, the burgundy and blue tones made so much richer in daylight, the thought niggled at her, creating an ache in the vicinity of her heart. This was where she'd signed the employment contract. Where she'd dropped the book upon the floor. Where their lips had first connected and they'd collapsed into his wing chair in a flurry of passion.

Well, it seemed this room would be where it all concluded, too. She stopped at a suitable distance from him—close enough that they could easily speak, far enough that she didn't imagine his heat radiating toward her or his crisp, masculine scent—and folded her hands upon her skirts. Waiting.

"Are you ..." He paused to glance toward the window and clear his throat, and as the sun streaked upon his features, it revealed them to be as shadowed and haggard as her own. "Are you well?"

"Quite well." Her words were both hollow and a terrible lie. Yet to voice anything else would be fruitless.

He made another indistinct sound in his throat. Motioned to his desk, where two leather chairs were placed to one side for those who sought an audience with the marquess. "Would you like to sit?"

"No, thank you." She held herself stiffly, willing her limbs not to waver. This shouldn't take long, and she didn't need the false comfort of a chair. Besides, it was best she stay positioned to make as hasty an exit as possible.

At her refusal, he didn't move to sit, either, but stayed where he was—both too close and too far away—with his arms pressed tightly to his sides. "First of all, I want to make something clear." He paused for agonizing seconds, his eyes flashing with something potent but unnameable, until all at once, words burst out, laced with fire. "I don't give a damn about what Letitia Burville has to say regarding her visit to Beaumont Manor."

She remained quiet, her memory flashing back to the affronted lady's shocked gasp. To her look of derision. To her acidic reproof. Phoebe didn't want to care about those things, either. Yet how could she do otherwise when last night's events had changed everything? Lord Rockliffe must recognize that as well as she did, must know what it all meant. And so, she waited again for what would inevitably come next, her heart beating with painful thumps.

"However ..." Sure enough, the word arrived after another beat of silence, and he drew in a breath, his fingers curling into the edge of his breeches, drumming up and down the wool. "My opinion on the subject isn't the only thing that matters." His tone quieted, grew brittle, and he stopped again, looking at the floor. The window. Back up at her. His body, of course, was as large and powerful as ever. Yet in his features, she could see uncertainty. Trepidation. That flash of vulnerability that made him appear less like an imposing marquess and more like an ordinary man who struggled.

Well, in that respect, she could lighten his burden and speed up the process for them both. "You don't need to continue, my lord. I'm not naive as to how the world works."

The lines of his face hardened into a look of suspicion, and a muscle twitched in his jaw. "In what regard?"

She could tread delicately around the subject. Say nothing else whatsoever and remain a passive listener, just as she'd done at the vicarage when her family's censure came hurtling her way. She didn't want to do that with him, though. Not now. Years of pent-up hurt and frustration rushed to the surface, and suddenly, she couldn't hold them in. "I'm the daughter of a deceased baronet. I no longer have a position in society. A home. Even a family on which to rely. I'm nothing but an accidental governess who behaved with impropriety. As a result, I'm dispensable. A regrettable dalliance, and a problem easily carted off—"

"Jesus, Phoebe, *stop* it." He took a rapid step toward her and then stilled, his fingers clenching into fists. "Do you really think so little of what I feel for you? That I planned to use you at my convenience and then send you on your way as if you meant nothing?"

He shuddered, his mouth twisting as if he were in agony. "You're not fucking dispensable! You're one of the only people on earth who can make my daughter smile. You *are* the only person who sets fire to my blood and makes me feel like maybe there's still a spot of brightness left beneath all the goddamn misery. I should have held that as sacred. Dealt with the longing that refuses to subside from afar. Instead, I was selfish and acted on it, knowing full well I could never do the honorable thing by you."

"Of course you couldn't, my lord. You needn't chasten yourself on that account, for I knew it from the beginning." She managed to speak softly, even as she inwardly trembled, fighting through shock to process his declaration. Her heart was foolish enough to flutter before the cold bite of reality set in. He could feel for her what he liked, and she could long for him in return. It wouldn't change one unavoidable fact. "You're a marquess and I'm a governess—"

"*No.*" He cut her off in a heartbeat, his blue eyes shining with a pained intensity unlike she'd ever seen. "*Never* because of that. The title follows me around like a damn curse. It means nothing. It doesn't make me worthy or change the ways I'm lacking. It cannot make me fit to wed you."

She sucked in a sharp burst of air, the room suddenly wobbling before her. *Wed you.* Impossible words, ones she hadn't been bold enough even to dream. *But why ...* Her eyes began stinging, her throat growing so tight that the question came out as a choked whisper. "Why would you say that?"

"Because," he shouted, his skin coloring, the cords of his neck growing exceptionally taut. The sunlight coming through the windows made his hair blaze like bronze, made each rigid contour of his face blaze along with it. Until suddenly, his gaze shifted to the floor, shadowing his features, and his shoulders drooped.

"Because," he repeated to the carpet, much lower this time. When he looked back up at her, it was as if all the vehemence had poured from his body, leaving only bone-weariness. "I cannot sire children."

17

Nicholas had gone through numerous stages ever since that fateful day all those years ago. First came denial. Then, when that was no longer an option, shock. Anger. Regret. All emotions that had raged inside him but he'd never put on display, refusing to acknowledge the truth aloud. Until now.

I cannot sire children.

It felt strange to utter the words. Raw and exposing, and even a little surreal. He *had* said them, though; the instant look of shock mixed with confusion upon Phoebe's face made that much clear.

I cannot sire children. The heaviness of the admission lingered in the air. Seemed to fill his lungs with each inhale and seep back into his veins until he had no choice but to confront it head-on.

"I ..." Phoebe's hushed voice broke the silence. "I don't understand."

He sighed, suddenly overcome by another torrent of exhaustion. There was still time to back away and pretend he'd never spoken on the subject, but to what purpose? What did he have to gain by concealing it any longer? At this point, it was just as well she know every ugly detail of the truth. So she'd comprehend why he could never offer her any of what she deserved.

He made a clipped gesture toward the chairs beside his desk. "Sit, *please*." She'd been adamant about standing, appearing before him with her squared shoulders and defiant chin. However, this was no quick, passing conversation to be held in the middle of the floor.

Fortunately, she didn't protest this time but approached the desk and sank into one of the leather seats, watching as he took not his commanding chair on the other side of the desk but the smaller one beside her. He didn't want the marquess's seat that allowed him to peer across the desk in a position of power. In this matter, *he* was the one defenseless. About to lay all the broken parts of himself at her feet.

"I was twenty years old when I inherited the title," he began, the words stiff but rolling off his tongue with surprising steadiness. "My father had been ill a long time, so it was expected. I'd been raised for the role. Knew it was my birthright."

He spared another glance for the vast mahogany desk, his mind flashing back to the first time he'd sat behind it with his father's signet ring upon his finger. Filled with eagerness. Self-importance. He quickly turned back to Phoebe, peering into gray-green-blue eyes that gave away nothing of her thoughts. She simply gazed in return, waiting for him to continue.

"My twenty-first birthday coincided with the end of my mourning period," he said, "and I celebrated the occasion with a party at my hunting box, Foxhill. Shooting season had just begun. My friends from Cambridge were all keen to attend." He swallowed, his fingers curling around the arm of his chair. Again, his thoughts wandered, taking him back to the revelry at Foxhill. The two successful days of fishing and shooting.

The nights filled with an endless array of spirits. The five-tier cake. The neighboring ladies they'd invited to join them for obscene parlor games.

"The day of the accident is a blur to me now." He paused, feeling beads of perspiration coat his nape. So many times, he'd run over the third, and what was to be final, day of shooting in his head. Trying to put it back together piece by piece, analyzing each move he could have made to result in a different outcome. Not that the knowledge would ever change anything. "We were in the wood, hunting partridge. I was always a good shot, but I remember missing. And when I fired again ..."

The tempo of his heart increased, warning him away from the memory. Yet Phoebe waited, and he'd come too far with it to back away now. He took a breath, his nose suddenly filling with the distant tang of gunpowder. "I remember the sound of the explosion. My hands burning. The jolt of pain as I fell to the ground. But after that, I remember nothing."

She gasped, her eyes becoming wide and horrified, and he didn't miss the way they darted to his hands and the thick scars that would never go away.

"When I awoke, my mother said I was lucky. Lucky to be alive. Lucky I hadn't disfigured my face." He gave a brisk, humorless laugh, having long wondered if she'd come to view that as a preferable option to the fate that had befallen him instead. "The dowager, who never does things in half-measures, had summoned a whole team of physicians, and they agreed with her. *Lord Rockliffe is lucky*. All except one. One fresh-faced physician from Edinburgh who dared to insinuate that the hit I'd taken as the rifle exploded, due to its location, could lead to difficulties ..."

Again, he trailed off, the weight of the past threatening to choke him. One step at a time, though, he *would* voice it. "The dowager is not the type to accept things that don't coincide with her will, and at that time, neither was I. My injuries appeared to heal, and after a period of recuperation, I *felt* well again. That lone dissenting physician was wrong, obviously, and I was determined to prove it."

He pressed his palms against the woolen knees of his breeches, taking a moment to regather his thoughts. He wouldn't subject her to the details of his nights that followed. The brothels. The lonely widows. The ladies with inattentive husbands. Yet at the same time, nor did he wish her to remain ignorant of any scrap of the truth. Of the man he was. "I cannot claim to be proud of my conduct back then," he said at last. "However, I viewed garnering a reputation as a rake as far preferable to allowing rumors of what the physician suggested to begin circulating."

He eyed her carefully, awaiting her comprehension and then repugnance, but the latter didn't come. Instead, she shifted forward in her chair, rapt by the words he somehow kept producing.

Carry on, then. Get it out. "The dowager was willing to tolerate my behavior for a while. However, after a few years went by, and my younger brother, Samuel—the spare—grew more distant from the family, her patience ran out." He shifted as well, his body tense against the seat. If only he'd paid more attention to his mother's ambitions at the time. If only he hadn't remained so caught up in his own affairs that he neglected to consider the lengths to which she'd go to turn things the way she wanted them.

"I met Lady Cecilia Burke at a soiree." He flipped the subject—temporarily—finding that instead of hostility, the name produced only a dull ache. Understanding glinted in Phoebe's eyes, but no part of her moved except her fingers, which curled into her black skirts. "I'd stayed well clear of young society belles until that point, but ... I enjoyed her company."

Phoebe's eyes flashed again, and his words, now uttered aloud, felt incredibly inane. Yet how else was he to state it? They were the truth, boiled down to its simplest form. He'd liked Cecilia, who immediately revealed herself to be no blushing young miss. For all that her demure white gowns suggested innocence, she'd never shied away from fluttering her golden lashes and leaning into him as he spoke. From placing a hand upon his shoulder, his arm, his back. From suggesting they slip away without the hindrance of chaperones.

"I shouldn't have gone into the Rockliffe House garden alone with her during my mother's ball." His admission fell like a cold weight, powerful even after all these years. He could still recall so much of that balmy, moonlit night. Could feel the softness of her lips and skin—a sensation that had once made his blood run hot and now left him icy. Could hear the horrified gasp that came from beyond their alcove in the hedge.

"The Countess of Merrick discovered us. One of the ton's most notorious gossips, naturally." He laughed once more, a sharp, hollow sound. "She had some other society matrons with her, although they mostly blended together. Only one other stood out." The woman who trailed slightly behind the others as if out for a leisurely stroll. The woman who, before or after that night, had never dreamed of leaving a ballroom to which she played hostess, especially for something as frivolous as a turn about the garden. The woman who'd ignored Lady Merrick's exclaiming and swooning and assessed him silently with shrewd eyes, knowing he and Cecilia were trapped where she wanted them. "The Dowager Marchioness of Rockliffe."

A shot of bitterness hit him as it always did at the recollection, but he pushed it aside, determined not to become entangled in it. "I did the honorable thing and offered for Cecilia, but she didn't agree to it at first, much to the dowager's shock and chagrin. Her heart, it turns out, already belonged to the Viscount Littleton, a man who'd turned his attentions else-where and she was trying to make jealous. It was only after Littleton announced his betrothal to another that she accepted my proposal, and we were married by special license shortly thereafter."

Phoebe's mouth twisted at that part, as if she were about to offer words of sympathy, but he stopped them with a small shake of his head. "I don't fault her for her reluctance. I didn't imagine myself in love with her, either, although once we were bound together, I wanted to make her happy. Especially when she announced, just weeks into our marriage, that she was increasing."

For a brief moment, he could picture her strolling out of this very room, her belly swollen with child, as he watched her from behind his desk, a marquess who was haughty once more. Because the physician's postulations about him were drivel. Because Prescotts always came out ahead.

"For a short time, all was well, until Cecilia woke up screaming one night. Her labor pains had begun far too soon." A night when circumstances flipped on him yet again, and every ounce of arrogance drained from his body, leaving only fear and helplessness in its wake. "A midwife was summoned, along with every physician within a twenty-mile radius. They all said the same thing: that a child born so early could never survive. That Cecilia herself could be in danger. But as it turns out, physicians, sometimes, are wrong."

He closed his eyes a moment, his heart thudding dully and his head knotting with tension. Just as they had on the night he'd paced the floor outside Cecilia's bedchamber until finally, a physician emerged, an odd, unreadable look on his face. *Congratulations, my lord, you have a daughter.* Words that should have been joyful. Words that made no sense.

"Cecilia made it through the birth without a single

complication." The image of her—sweat-stained and fatigued, but wearing a peculiar expression akin to the physician's—as he burst into the room flooded his memory, and he gripped the edge of his chair, forcing himself to look straight ahead. To Phoebe, who continued to listen. Who wanted to understand. "So did Emily. She was large for a baby newly born. Healthy. Perfect."

He saw Phoebe's lips part, registered the little sound of surprise she made, but his mind was drifting backward again, bringing him to steal across the floor of Cecilia's bedchamber to the cradle in the corner. To stare at the bundle that had been placed there and lift her into his arms. To stroke the spiky, dark hair. The round, rosy cheeks.

His heart had never felt that way before. *Full*. In awe. In love. While simultaneously splintering beneath the crushing weight of betrayal. The knowledge that every bit of confidence he'd regained, every moment he'd assured himself that he was whole, was based on a lie.

Sometimes, physicians are wrong. And other times, they're exactly right.

"We didn't much go out in society together after that. I couldn't abide the thought of rumors circulating. Of people gawking at us and *knowing*." It had been far easier to remain at Beaumont Manor, or better yet, Foxhill. To wander the grounds of the hunting box to prove he wouldn't be scared away from the place, even though inside, he felt vacant and wrecked.

Macabre, his mother had said of all the time he spent there, and his throat tightened as he grappled with the idea that her proclamation held merit. "The arrangement worked for a time," he said, swallowing back the tightness, pushing the thought away. "Emily spent her earliest years in the country, away from prying eyes, and Cecilia and I ... I won't go so far as to say we were happy, but we attempted to achieve some semblance of a reconciliation. To start over, to pretend that, maybe, our family would continue to grow in time. That's all it was, though. Pretending."

He glanced toward the sun-streaked window, remembering the occasions here at Beaumont when Emily had placed her chubby fist in his and toddled across the grass. When he'd held her in his arms, relishing her squeals of delight as she splashed in the lake. Those were the only pure moments of brightness, natural instead of forced.

With Cecilia, things had been bleaker. Trust didn't come. Passion didn't come. Their days together had been filled with stilted, formal conversation. His nights in her bed mechanical and emotionless. Always veiled by a truth he could no longer ignore.

He took a breath, his chest filled with a deep, grating ache that had never fully healed. "I think I sensed right from the beginning that I wouldn't be able to make that happen, and eventually, Cecilia didn't pretend anymore, either. Enough time had passed that she knew I couldn't provide her with the children she wanted. She expressed a desire to return to London, and who was I to interfere? I had nothing to offer her."

His shoulders threatened to sag, and he tensed his muscles, fighting against the encroaching weariness. A feeling left over from the first time he'd watched the coach containing Cecilia and Emily barrel away from Beaumont Manor, and everything had felt heavy and wrong. The solution to which had been his retreat to Foxhill.

"We both returned to the same household on occasion, for appearance's sake, never speaking of what we did with our time in the interim. If she had affairs, she was discreet, for news of them didn't reach the gossip rags. However, when she announced to me, after a few weeks we spent together at

Beaumont, that she was increasing ... I *knew*. I knew before she ever uttered the name Edmund Mowbray."

Phoebe's brows drew together at the revelation, although for his own part, he could conjure little more than a sense of detachment.

Which, consequently, had been his detrimental error. He'd failed to care enough until it proved too late.

"Her attempt at deception was short-lived, at least. She told me everything about Mr. Mowbray. How he was the third son of a baron. An employee of the East India Company who had recently returned to England. All details I didn't give a damn about until ... until ..."

He hated the sound of his voice, stammering and unsteady. This was the part of the story where detachment turned to a crushing mix of fear and fury. Where he flashed back to the day he'd run about the house, in and out of familiar rooms, only to find them vacant. The day his entire world had unraveled. "None of it mattered until suddenly, they were gone. Skulking off on a ship bound for India without a word to anyone, leaving behind nothing but rumors of Cecilia's pregnancy. Off to a place where she could start anew and erase every dismal year of our marriage, for she'd found someone else to give her what I could not."

He took a moment to inhale. To ground himself in the Beaumont Manor study before the emotions of that day, still so raw, spiraled back into existence and overtook him. "Had the situation involved only Cecilia and Mowbray, perhaps I would have done the merciful thing and let her go. But she took Emily. *My* daughter. Not mine by blood, but ... but *mine*. I couldn't allow that. If there was any cause to be grateful for the events of the preceding decade, any reason I could consider every fucking moment of misery and feel something besides regret, it was because of *her*. I couldn't allow her to be dragged from her home to God knows where. I couldn't condone a future in which I never saw her again."

Tears shone in Phoebe's eyes, and a single droplet slipped onto her cheek. Her pale, flawless cheek, down to the lips he hadn't stopped staring at since the day he'd met her in the field. He wanted to kiss it away. Wanted his future to be filled with her smiles. Yet it was because of how deeply he wished for her happiness—how deeply, damn him, he'd come to *care*—that he could never keep her for his own.

"When I found them in Saint Helena, laid out in a cottage and insensate with fever, I was *so* angry at Cecilia. Angry for what she'd stolen from me. Angry that she'd so blatantly disregarded Emily's wellbeing. Angry that my *child* looked so lifeless, and I knew I could lose her ..."

His voice broke, the air painful as it entered and exited his lungs. "But I was angry at myself, too." He let the ragged admission fall, giving it a moment to permeate the air between them. "*I* was the one lacking. *My* failings are what drove her away, killed her, and nearly cost Emily her life in the process. My inability to do the one goddamn job a marquess has and sire heirs—"

"No." Phoebe shook her head, slowly at first but then with vehemence. "*No.* You cannot blame yourself for their illness. Nor were the consequences of the hunting accident in any way your fault."

"I have no interest in debating blame." Finally, he let himself slump back in the chair, giving in to the exhaustion that riddled his aching shoulders. "The important thing is, I've learned my lesson, and I've accepted the truth. I cannot do my duty to the marquessate, nor can I do my duty as a husband. The first failing is mine alone to bear. The second, however, affects the woman bound to my side. I won't remarry only to inflict that sort of misery again." *Even though I cannot stop wanting you.*

For a moment, he thought her tears were going to keep flowing, and he clenched his fingers to prevent them from sweeping across her face and brushing the moisture away. However, she gave several rapid blinks, swiping at the corners of her eyes, and when she opened them again, they were drier. Harder. "And are you the only one who gets a say in your suitability as a husband?" She tilted her head, pressing her lips into a thin line.

"Yes." He didn't hesitate, even when his proclamation made her face grow flintier. "Because I'm the one who's seen the consequences that arise when I fill that role. You can placate me with words about how my deficiency doesn't matter. Perhaps you even mean them right now. However, you don't understand what it's like when disappointment has a chance to build. When with each passing year, you grow increasingly mournful about the children you'll never have, until instead of affection, all you feel is resentment."

That—a future in which he looked into her stormy sky eyes and saw nothing reflected back but his own shortcomings —was beyond what he could bear. She was still so young. Had a long life ahead of her where she deserved the chance for a proper family of her own. Babies with the same vibrant, changeable eyes whom she could cradle in her arms.

"Do not presume to tell me how I feel." Her voice loudened a notch, the ice in it enough to silence his next words. "Have you ever considered that not every woman wishes to bear children? That not every woman *can* bear children?"

Something pulled in his chest, tight and uncomfortable. Yet before he could begin to fathom it, a knock sounded against the door, accompanied by the butler's sturdy baritone. "My lord?"

"Not now, Barrington," he barked, his eyes staying fixed

on Phoebe, whose features appeared tenser by the second. "Leave us."

A moment of uncertain silence fell, in which there were neither words nor the sound of boots retreating down the corridor. Only a moment, though, and Barrington's voice rang out again. "My lord, there's a young lady—a Miss Buxton—here to see Miss Windham. She insists it's critical."

Phoebe got to her feet at once, her movements jerky, her gaze flashing between the door and where he remained in the chair. He didn't miss the strain in her neck as she swallowed, nor the tiny bob of her head in his direction.

Damn it. He swore under his breath, then pushed to his feet as well, every muscle rigid. "Send her in."

They stood beside one another, his head reeling with all the admissions he'd finally voiced aloud. And, even more significantly, with all the things that remained unsaid. The conversation wasn't supposed to end like this: unresolved, with a declaration of Phoebe's own that placed a pit in his stomach and led to yet more questions.

However, there wasn't time to address any of it, for no sooner did Barrington's footsteps fade than new ones appeared, light and hurried. A footman threw open the door, and a pink-faced, curly-headed girl, who couldn't be much older than Emily, burst inside.

"Margaret." Phoebe instantly rushed toward the girl—one of her numerous Buxton cousins, he inferred—with her brows drawn in concern. "What's happened?"

"Oh, Phoebe, it's—" The girl's breathless, animated speech halted as she caught sight of his presence in the room, and she folded herself into an awkward curtsey. "My lord."

He gave her a brisk nod before refocusing his attention on Phoebe, each fruitless second becoming an eternity.

"You need to come to the vicarage." Fortunately, the girl blurted out the information without further preamble.

"Mama bade me to fetch you and tell you to hurry, for you have a visitor."

He saw the color drain from Phoebe's cheeks. The little tremor of her clenched hand. "What sort of visitor?" Her question came out low, tentative.

The girl hesitated, long enough that he turned to see her feet shuffling against the floor, her finger winding in a strand of her unruly blond hair. "It's ... it's Sir Ambrose Windham." She paused again, continuing to twist the curl, her half-smile in response to Phoebe's sharp inhale speaking more of uncertainty than joy. "Wishing very much to see his betrothed."

18

Phoebe and Margaret spoke little on the carriage ride back to the vicarage. Her younger cousin burned with questions; that much was clear by her intent stare from the opposite bench. However, Phoebe silenced them with a single withering look.

"I'm sorry if I said anything wrong in front of the marquess," Margaret had exclaimed as soon as they stepped into the privacy of the Rockliffe carriage and started down the drive. "The vicarage is in such an uproar, and if I didn't reveal the truth then and there, I wasn't sure you'd see the urgency of the matter. Sir Ambrose arrived looking for you right when Papa was in the middle of writing his sermon, and you know how vexed he gets when interrupted. And then Mama, who was hosting a tea, worked herself into a frenzy, for Sir Ambrose grew quite insistent and loud. He doesn't have very fine manners, and he's rather malodorous. But is it true you're going to marry him?"

Phoebe had stopped the girl with a shake of her head and a few dismissive words, which nearly stuck in her throat. As much as her stomach churned, and she had an overwhelming urge to scream, she couldn't blame Margaret. Her cousin was merely a messenger doing as she'd been told. Withholding the information would have only led to an even worse possibility. Namely, that Ambrose, incensed by Phoebe's delayed response to his letter, would take the initiative to fetch her at Beaumont Manor himself. That Emily and Mrs. Connelly would return at the same time he did so. No, she couldn't allow that sordid aspect of her life to invade the marquess and Emily's home. She had far too much to regret as it was.

She peered dully out the window as the edge of Bowden came into view, reminding her that with each revolution of the carriage's wheels, the dreaded vicarage neared, whereas Beaumont Manor grew farther and farther away. Not that it mattered. An infinite distance could pass, and all she would envision was Lord Rockliffe's face as Margaret uttered the shattering words. *Sir Ambrose Windham. Wishing very much to see his betrothed.*

The air had rushed from Phoebe's lungs in an agonizing swoop, nearly making her buckle, and still, she'd observed the split second when his lips had parted and then curled into a look of ... she had no words to describe it properly. Outrage? Perhaps a little, but that didn't fully get at the heart of it. Shock, more like. Bewilderment, as though she'd just pulled the rug out from beneath his feet. *Vulnerability.*

Except, just as quickly, that unnamable flicker had vanished, the lines of his face hardening into an expressionless veneer.

No. It's wrong. This is all wrong. She'd wanted to cry, to shout, to cling to him. Such a thing couldn't be happening, not when he'd just bared his most safeguarded secrets to her and turned so much of what she believed on its head. His stubbornness during their conversation had incensed her, but it couldn't negate how her heart ached for him. For what he'd lost. For the assumptions he'd come to make of himself as a result.

However, before she could tell him any of that, he'd cast her with a cool glance, his blue irises sharp enough to cut through her. *Do you wish to go, Miss Windham?*

She'd wished it only marginally more than flinging herself off a cliff. But what other option was there? Margaret had stood waiting, throwing curious looks between her and Lord Rockliffe. Just as Ambrose waited at the vicarage, seeking the answer she hadn't taken time to write him, ready to wreak havoc that she couldn't allow to spread.

And so, she'd nodded, the action creating a sick, heavy feeling in her stomach as she'd uttered the most useless words: *I can explain later.*

Lord Rockliffe, to his credit, hadn't driven her out and slammed the door without a second thought. Instead, he'd offered—no, insisted—for her and Margaret to take the carriage, uttering a succinct farewell that proved maddeningly detached.

Which was what led her to this moment, with the familiar brown stone of the vicarage materializing outside the carriage window.

By the time she jumped to the ground, the deep, throbbing pain within her had become more a sense of numbness. Best not think too hard on what she was about to face and instead enjoy her last few seconds of freedom.

That's all it was: seconds. She took no more than a step up the path before the front door flew open and Harriet came bursting out into the sunshine.

"Phoebe." Her aunt called her name with false cheer, the highness of it betraying a note of hysteria. "How *lovely* that you've arrived. There's someone here to see you."

That someone appeared instantly, his large body coming up behind Harriet as a shadow in the doorway before he plodded into the light, the sunrays illuminating his smirk. Making every jarring detail about Ambrose Windham far too clear for comfort.

"Isn't this a surprise?" Harriet's saccharine voice grew shriller to the point she sounded like a poor actress on Drury Lane. "It's such a pleasant day, and Sir Ambrose has spent much of it confined to a carriage. Why not take him for a stroll in the garden so you can both enjoy some air?"

Dread hooked its claws in her belly once more, and she shot a desperate glance in her aunt's direction, her mouth forming a silent plea for help. But for what purpose? She abruptly shuttered her features, turning as emotionless as Lord Rockliffe when she'd left him. Harriet wouldn't help her. Why demean herself by pretending otherwise?

She drew in a steadying breath, the summer sun unable to prevent the ice that built in her chest. "Good day, Sir Ambrose." Even the simple greeting caused another wave of nausea to take hold, but she made herself look at him, willing her disconcertment to stay below the surface.

"Phoebe, my dear." He started toward her, stumbling like a man in his cups, but that mattered little to Harriet. Out of the corner of her eye, Phoebe spotted her aunt make a brusque summoning motion toward Margaret, and by the time Ambrose reached her, Margaret had flitted into the house, allowing Harriet to make a final insincere comment and slam the door. No one was there to see the moment when his sweaty fingers clamped around her arm, forcing her to tense her muscles so she didn't flinch, nor did anyone witness the cold, threatening sneer he bestowed. "It's been far too long."

Too *long*? On the contrary, another five decades of separation could pass and she'd consider the period insufficient.

She forwent reminding him of their encounter in Bath mere weeks ago at the time of Eugenia's death, instead leading him wordlessly toward the back garden, where perhaps one of her cousins would be playing, or someone at least might be looking out the window. However, the garden proved deserted, and the curtains of the back windows drawn.

It seemed the encounter would be hers alone to bear.

She brought him to the wooden bench beneath the apple tree, using the opportunity to shake free of his grip and lower herself to the seat. It came as little surprise when he sat, gracelessly, with his thigh skirting hers, but her lack of shock didn't make it any easier to suppress a shudder. Even in the short time since she'd last seen him, his teeth seemed to have yellowed further and his pale hair to have turned even oilier. Not to mention that he smelled, as strongly as ever, like he'd doused himself in a barrel of ale.

It doesn't matter. She shifted to the edge of the bench, looking through him instead of at him. If she could just endure a little longer, he'd leave her alone; this would be over.

"You've misbehaved, Phoebe." He began by flashing another self-satisfied smirk, hefting his weight to her side of the bench.

She tilted her head back, trying not to inhale the noxious air he breathed. "I'm sure I don't know what you mean."

His lips curved downward, and he made an obnoxious clucking noise. "Has no one ever told you it's exceptionally rude"—the word *exceptionally* slurred and staggered on his tongue—"to ignore your correspondence?"

Foolish. So foolish. She silently chided herself for putting off his letter as if the problem would disappear on its own. She should have known it wouldn't be that easy—although, to be fair, he'd given up on her easily enough eight years prior.

Well, enough was enough, and she would delay no longer. She ceased caring about the thin facade of politeness, wanting only to put an end to the encounter as quickly as possible. "I apologize for my tardiness and inconsideration in responding to your letter. Allow me to make amends immediately. Thank you for your proposal, but my answer remains unchanged from the first time you made it. No, I will not marry you. If that's the lone reason you came here, then our business has concluded, and I'll bid you good day."

His unkempt brows drew together, the frown deepening. "You always were a stubborn one. Thinking yourself high and mighty, even when you'd been cast down into the dirt. But what do you have to feel superior about now, hmm? Eugenia's gone, and you look about as welcome at the vicarage as a bad case of the pox. You should really reconsider my offer."

"Why?" She inched her body so far over that she was in danger of toppling off the bench, and still, he came closer, his unwelcome heat pressing against her, making her irritation flare. "Why do you want this union so much? You know as well as I that we wouldn't suit, and you've made no secret regarding your opinions of me. *Shameful. Of loose morals—*"

"A doxy. A ladybird. A *slut*," he supplied, the words creating a dull stab in her chest, one she'd never been able to shake no matter how many times she heard them. He fumbled in his pocket, retrieving a silver flask and grasping at the cap. "My thoughts on your character haven't changed. However, your time with Eugenia seemed to properly subdue you, and you're the only woman who will suit my purposes."

She gave herself a moment to stare at the grass and fight off the encroaching surge of nausea. She didn't want to ask. Didn't want to imagine. Yet her tongue moved anyway, her mouth acrid from the taste of bile. "What purposes?"

"Don't you already know?" She made herself look up just in time to see him take a gulp from the flask and pull it away, wiping the wetness from his lips with the back of his hand. "Sir John always made it known how little he thought of me. How much he loathed me being his heir. He was downright dish ... dish-re ... *dis*respectful. But now look. He's dead, and I have his house. His lands. His title. All I'm missing is his daughter."

"And that's one thing you will never get!" She sprang from the bench, glaring down at him as she waited for her trembling legs to accommodate her weight and flee.

Ambrose was wrong; her long, unhappy years with Eugenia hadn't left her demure and subdued. Instead, she was about to find herself scandal-ridden yet again. Even more lost and uncertain than the day she'd first encountered Lady Emily in the field.

She didn't know what to do. Where to go from here. She had no idea if she could still rely on the exorbitant sum Lord Rockliffe promised her, which had come to pale in comparison to everything else she'd gained at Beaumont Manor— everything she now stood to lose.

But of one thing, she remained stalwartly certain. "I won't marry you," she repeated, stomping her foot against the grass. "I *won't*. I'd sooner retreat to a workhouse. To sew in a dark garret until I go blind. To walk the streets like the harlot you say I am."

Ambrose blinked unsteadily, her heated words seeming to catch him off balance. Yes, she'd refused him once before, a long time ago, but she'd never raised her voice. Never returned the insults hurled her way. The novelty of it didn't appear to make sense in his drink-addled brain, and he tipped the flask to his mouth again, taking long swallows until all that remained were drops, which he shook into his throat.

When he lowered the flask this time, though, his mind must have reached a place of understanding, for his eyes narrowed, and his nostrils flared in anger. "You know what you are? Ungrateful." He clambered to his feet and hovered beside her, making the summer air she breathed develop the pungent staleness of a barroom. "You say you'd rather a workhouse? We *should* have sent you there after what you did. Left you to rot in a gutter somewhere. It's only because Genie was too soft for her own good, and I condoned it, that you escaped that fate."

A painful jolt seized her heart. Eugenia, soft? Eugenia, who'd begun her daily lectures on repentance and morality from the moment they'd departed for the cottage at the edge of the Suffolk fenlands. Eugenia, who hadn't relented—in fact, had only increased her efforts—when they'd relocated to Bath and Phoebe had dragged herself along, still shattered in both body and soul. Aching with a hurt so potent that she didn't think it could heal. Eugenia's actions had been more merciful than casting her onto the street, perhaps. But never soft.

"And still, you can't even say *thank you*." He hurled a thick, wavering finger toward her chest, and she stiffened her spine, refusing to let him see her cower. "I made you a good offer—far better than you deserve—and look at you! Saying *no*. Having the nerve to appear re- … *repulshed*. It's just the same as when you moped around after Genie with all the cheer of a Newgate convict. Couldn't even show grath- … grati- … *thanks* for how she took you in. How she hid your mish-takes and provided for your brat."

Phoebe's breath caught, and an odd flutter rippled through her chest. Ambrose, in addition to becoming insulted, was unquestionably foxed and, thus, apt to spew all manner of nonsense. Yet those last words he'd said … that he'd spluttered so maliciously but casually, as if they contained a well-known truth …

"What did you mean by that?" She stared at him hard, examining every detestable feature—the glassy eyes, the sallow skin, the deep grooves around his mouth—for the answer she sought.

Ambrose, blast him, said nothing. The dratted man

hiccupped, then busied himself with straightening his limp cravat, no longer meeting her eye.

"Ambrose!" Her voice turned too high, too sharp, unable to mask her rising panic. "*What* did you mean? When you claimed Eugenia provided for ... for my ..." She couldn't repeat it, the word that reflected nothing of her loss, her grief, her heartbreak.

Her memory flashed to the night she'd awoken in her cold, silent bed in the fenland cottage, her body battered, her eyelids so heavy it proved a struggle to pry them open. The space had felt eerily still and foreboding in those last few seconds of sleep-hazed ignorance. Those final uncertain moments before Eugenia's face, misty and out of focus, had appeared above her, the older woman's lips forming words that flickered at the edge of her awareness before sinking in to deliver a devastating blow. *The babe did not survive.*

Ambrose turned his attention to his pocket, pulling out the flask he apparently forgot he'd drained. Only after giving it a shake, and frowning from the disappointment of finding it empty, did he turn to her and shrug. He actually *shrugged*. "I mish-spoke."

"Tell me the truth." Her voice came out as a strangled whisper, and tears began stinging the corners of her eyes. *Why* would he have said that? That Eugenia provided for ... Even while drunk, why would he have blurted out such a thing unless ... unless ...

"Tell me the truth!" she repeated, only she screamed it this time, her fingers inches away from grabbing his waistcoat and giving him a good jostle. "I *heard* you. You said Eugenia provided for my ... my child. *How*, Ambrose? How, when she made something explicitly clear: *the babe did not survive.*"

Ambrose winced, pressing a palm to his sweat-stained brow. "Stop shouting. I don't know. What difference does it make now?"

"What *difference*?" Her mouth gaped, and her knees began trembling beneath her skirts, making her stagger backward before she could stop herself. If he were to heave a knife in her chest, it wouldn't hurt as much as those callous words.

He scowled, his bleary eyes traveling over her with distaste. "That babe was never yours to keep. You would have disgraced all of us—yourself included—but Genie stopped you. Did you a favor." He flung his arm out, pointing another accusatory finger toward her chest. "Like I said. You. Are. Ungrateful."

Her hands shook at her sides, itching with the urge to swing up and slap him. She wanted to scream even louder. To inundate him with her outrage. To force him to cooperate.

Except that would get her nowhere. If anything, it would render him even more uncommunicative and recalcitrant. If she wanted Ambrose—blast the soused, cold-hearted swine— to help her, she would need to exhibit delicacy.

"You're right." She swallowed back the acid her words created and took a breath, using every remaining bit of strength she possessed to keep her voice steady. Subdued. "Forgive me. I assure you, I would be very much obliged if you'd simply tell me where Eugenia sent the child she provided for."

For a long, uncertain moment, he studied her, his lips twitching as if the information lay on the tip of his tongue. Yet all of a sudden, he broke the gaze, and he jerked his shoulders into another detestable shrug, the gesture rife with annoyance. "I told you, I don't know, so cease nattering on about it. Genie's affairs were her own. Has nothing to do with me."

"Ambrose!" She shrieked his name in frustration as she staggered again, grasping the back of the bench so she didn't crumple to the ground. She was unable to look at him anymore, was going to be ill. Yet she couldn't lose her head when information so crucial hung in the balance.

She stared at the clipped blades of grass around her feet, trying to find purchase amidst her spinning thoughts. If Ambrose was too useless to assist—whether due to obstinacy or true ignorance—then she would need to sort this herself. However, nothing made sense. She'd long aided Eugenia with both her correspondence and household accounts—particularly in the last weeks when Eugenia had become bedridden—and had never seen anything that even hinted at such a deception.

How had the woman managed it? Holding in a secret—an untruth—of that magnitude for seven full years.

Phoebe's fingers curled and tightened around the bench, her nails digging into the wood as her mind flashed back to the days following Eugenia's death when she'd helped clear out their rented rooms in Bath. When assorted trinkets and papers had been deemed of no importance and thrown into the dustbin. The thought proved even more sickening than peering upon Ambrose in his smug-faced superiority.

Her grip on the bench abruptly loosened, and she stumbled backward, struggling to make her feet break into a run. Remaining here, shouting and talking in circles, was naught but a waste of time. She had to go, to search, to find—

"Wait." Ambrose's call made her footsteps freeze, and she whirled around to the sight of him lumbering toward her, an unsettling glint in his eye. "If you were an obedient wife, maybe I'd feel inclined to help you."

Her splintering heart lurched, grasping for a string of hope even as the rest of her recoiled at the prospect. What he proposed—the cruelness of it, the utter disgust it evoked in every fiber of her being—was no better than making a deal with the devil. But if that's what it took …

He ground to a halt in front of her, causing her nose to burn once more from the odor of ale mixed with sweat. His lips twisted into a cold sneer—even in his drunken stupor, he could obviously see her contemplating, could recognize how he'd cornered her—and in the blink of an eye, the flutter of hope within her broke into thousands of painful slivers.

She was desperate. He *knew* she was desperate. As such, she could see his words for what they were: a lie. Ambrose wouldn't help her. Even if he knew how—which was doubtful at best—he wouldn't. If she were his wife, he would never allow her to seek out the child whom he viewed as evidence of her shame.

She detected the clumsy motion of his hand approaching her wrist, and she darted away just in time, preventing herself from falling into his clutches. She peered into his too-red, perspiring face. Felt her teeth clench and loathing simmer within her as she spat a rejoinder. "My answer is no. It will always be no."

And then, she ran, finally finding the speed she required. Her legs flew over the grass and back around the vicarage, impervious to the affronted protests that rang out behind her. The front door creaked open as she passed, and Harriet's unpleasant voice joined the cacophony, but she ignored that, too. She would find no help from her aunt and would squander not a second of her time by futilely begging for it.

Perhaps there was no help to be had anywhere. There was, however, the Rockliffe carriage, which hadn't returned to Beaumont Manor but remained waiting for her in front of the house.

She couldn't be certain of her reception if she went back there. Nor could she think how she'd begin to explain ...

Yet, for better or worse, the Rockliffe carriage meant the one thing she needed first and foremost: escape. A place to sit, to calm her heaving breaths, to push through her shock to determine what she needed to do next.

And so, she ran toward the familiar black vehicle and the

pair of matched bays that stood exactly as she'd left them. As if naught had changed. A striking contrast to the cruel reality that nothing in her world would ever be the same.

19

Nicholas couldn't stop pacing. He walked past windows and furniture, over floorboards and carpet, around and around his study until it was a wonder the damn rug didn't get reduced to threads. Still, he kept up the useless circles, his head careening with all the things that had just come to pass, his chest clenching in knots.

He slowed by the chair where Phoebe had sat. Where they'd both sat, and he'd finally released the dark truths he'd never allowed to have a voice. Where she'd thrown out rejoinders he couldn't have expected. Where it had all been interrupted before they could glean any sort of finality from it because Phoebe had a visitor.

Sir Ambrose Windham. Her *betrothed*. A man he'd never met but despised with all the potency of an inferno.

He picked up the pace again, striding past the unlit fireplace. Past the wing chair where she'd fallen into his lap, and he'd first tasted her lips—

God. He would never occupy this room again without seeing the way her face lit up in pleasure. Without feeling her warmth and imagining the sweet scent of wildflowers.

Pity for him.

He traveled to the sun-streaked windows. The towering bookshelves. The doorway. Then began the loop again for possibly the hundredth time, and still, nothing made sense.

Phoebe Windham didn't have a betrothed. He'd first found her on the outskirts of Bowden, a woman still in mourning for her cousin and companion, seeking employment and a new place to live. A betrothed woman wouldn't have found herself in that predicament. Wouldn't have accepted a governess position.

Unless the sum he'd promised had proved too tempting. Unless there were aspects of herself she'd kept hidden and he'd never really known her. Unless she'd *lied*.

His lungs constricted, and when he reached his desk this time, he dropped his elbows to the surface, resting his forehead within his fingertips. He was no stranger to being deceived. Perhaps this was yet another example of it.

He screwed his eyelids shut, Cecilia's arresting face coming to him in the blankness. Twelve years had passed, and he could still envision the night so clearly. Could see her cheeks, still flushed from the exertion of giving birth, and the way she'd paced along the floor in front of him, even after he'd insisted she get back in bed.

You cannot blame me. I never set out to deceive you. This was forced upon us. I didn't choose it! The words she'd shouted as tears streamed down her face, and it was impossible to tell whether they came from remorse or fury.

He kept his eyes closed, remaining trapped back on the night he'd both lost and gained everything, and when the memory caused a cloying surge of emotion to rush up, he let it. He didn't fight back as it racked his body, making his arms shake against the desk and something snap within his chest.

It would have been so much easier to hate her. But in the end, Cecilia had been right: he couldn't blame her. She hadn't orchestrated the marriage or tried to trap him; the deception there was all his mother's. A grave miscalculation on the dowager's part.

Perhaps the deception hadn't been Phoebe's fault, either. Perhaps there was more to it than what appeared on the surface. At that, his eyes came open, a strange prickle shooting down the back of his neck.

The dowager had nothing to do with the situation this time. But *he* did. He'd insisted Phoebe come to Beaumont Manor, hadn't truly given her a choice. *He'd* been the orchestrater, bending things to his will. And, just like his mother, had gotten so much more than he bargained for.

Once again, he'd gained. And lost.

Something rustled in the doorway, and he jerked away from the desk, a name rising in his throat. *Phoebe.* Because this was all a mistake, a misunderstanding, and she'd come back so they could finish what they'd started.

But there was no one there.

He glanced around the empty space, expecting black skirts, a lip caught between teeth, a half-boot tapping against the floorboards. She didn't materialize, though. No one materialized, nothing—

Nothing but a streak of orange that scampered into the room, leaping onto his desktop and then sitting impassively, fixing him with its round yellow eyes.

Of course. Of course it would be the cat, inserting itself into places where it was least wanted.

He clenched his hands by his sides. Felt his mouth tighten and his forehead knot. "Get out." He tried to deepen the glower, but even he could admit that his effort lacked conviction. Quite frankly, he didn't possess the energy.

The cat, apparently, agreed, for it didn't so much as blink. For once, the blasted creature didn't even take the trouble to hiss.

"Get out," he repeated dully, although he didn't swing his arms or stomp his feet. In fact, he did nothing but stand there, for now that he'd stopped pacing, each of his limbs felt laden down by weights. "Go torment someone else."

Except who else was there? Emily and Mrs. Connelly hadn't returned from the village. And as for Phoebe ... who knew when she'd come back? *Would* she come back to provide the explanation she'd promised, to gather her meager things, to bid farewell to the girl who'd quickly come to adore her? Or had the final moment he would sit with her, alone, already passed them by?

The cat opened its mouth, the plaintive sound that emerged bordering on a yowl. For a moment, its large, ridiculous tail twitched, and then, it leaped gracefully to the floor, sidling up to his legs. Leaving an offensive clump of fur marring the side of his boot.

He should be incensed, cursing, yelling ... Yet all he could do was watch the damn thing as it weaved in and out between his feet.

Blasted nuisance of an animal, always causing trouble, interfering with his solitude when he only wanted peace. And the worst part was, he couldn't wish the cat away. Not when, for whatever godforsaken reason, *Marigold* made his daughter happy.

Worse still ... he couldn't wish Phoebe away, either. She'd disrupted his life. Challenged him. Made the most guarded parts of him crack into pieces. Even so, he couldn't think of her like a mistake that never should have been. Damn him, he couldn't stop *caring*.

Sir Ambrose Windham. Wishing very much to see his betrothed. The words persisted in racing through his head, their incongruity grating at his insides. Phoebe hadn't refuted them. She'd proceeded to depart for the vicarage of her own free will.

But that didn't mean the words were right. What if ... what if there was more to it than that? She'd spoken so little of her family that he found himself frustratingly ignorant, although she had made it clear that she couldn't remain with them in Bowden. What if something had happened that she wished to escape? What if she were in some sort of trouble?

The idea caused his ribs to tighten. He wouldn't have let her go had he thought for an instant that any harm would befall her.

And maybe it wouldn't; maybe that wasn't the case at all. Maybe she was simply returning to where she belonged. Where she'd always intended to go once she collected her salary. Back to her betrothed.

But could he leave the matter to rest on an assumption?

No. The answer sprang up immediately, and a tremor bolted down his rigid spine. He knew what it was to lose. To retreat. To spend day after day, year after year, at Foxhill because that was the easy option. *But never the right one.*

Old patterns didn't need to keep repeating themselves. With Phoebe Windham, he wouldn't retreat. Regardless of the situation—even if she revealed that things really were as clear-cut as they appeared and she'd lied to him all along—he needed to see her again. To find out what the bloody hell was transpiring at the vicarage with this so-called betrothed.

He gave his foot a shake, making the perturbed cat jump away and finally release the hiss it had been withholding. That was more like it. He took a single moment longer to peer at the mass of orange fur, the bared teeth, the intense yellow eyes.

And then, he was out the door.

20

Phoebe would survive if she could just keep moving. She clung tight to the carriage bench, absorbing each rattle, feeling each dip and bump in the road shoot to her roiling stomach.

Stillness would crush her. However, if the carriage's wheels continued turning, taking her away from the vicarage and Ambrose, she'd be back at Beaumont Manor where she could … she could …

Oh, she didn't know. Perhaps she needed to return to the village instead, to catch a stagecoach, to search every inch of Suffolk, and if that proved unsuccessful, then all of England.

But suddenly, she could do none of that, for the bile in her throat rose higher, her stomach heaved precariously, and she banged on the ceiling until the carriage did the one thing she desired least, though it had become dreadfully necessary: stopping.

She wrenched open the door, stumbling into the tall grass beside the road and sinking to her knees. At once, she found herself retching onto the ground, her stomach twisting, turning upside-down, until her insides became empty and raw.

The coachman's worried call came from behind her, and she could hear his body shift and jump down to the dirt, but she held up a hand, warning him not to come any closer.

She needed a minute. Just a few moments to gather herself and make her quivering legs rise. To climb back into the carriage and get moving again, to find what she'd lost, to make sense of a world where the last seven years had been a lie.

A sob tore from her throat before she could stop it. She pressed her palms to the ground in an effort to steady herself, trying to suck in a few deep breaths, but the air hit her lungs quickly, sharply, and another sob broke free. And another. They kept coming, overtaking her body at a relentless pace, until she was powerless to do anything but sit and watch her tears fall upon the long stalks of grass.

She became vaguely aware of more noises rising in the distance. *Hooves*, she registered, as the rhythmic beating against gravel drew nearer. However, the sound couldn't drown out the blood pounding through her head. Nor could it negate the frenzied drumming of her heart.

She didn't turn to look even when a cloud of dust wafted toward her and the hoofbeats abruptly halted, replaced by a horse's whinny close enough to ring in her ears. Only when boots thumped against the ground behind her, bounding over gravel and into the grass, hitting the periphery of her vision, did she tilt her head. She'd seen those boots before, recognized the polished black surface that now contained a film of dirt. Without looking the rest of the way up, she knew that Lord Rockliffe stood above her. That he'd come to find her.

Something inside her seized and broke, and whether the resultant emotion was despair or relief, she couldn't entirely say. She tried to push past it, to utter a greeting—some faint thread of normalcy—but when she opened her mouth, nothing emerged but another sob. Her elbows crumpled into the grass, and she faced the ground again, fighting for air that wouldn't come.

She caught the flash of motion when his boots shifted, and in the next moment, he was on the ground beside her, his large body leaning close as he settled on his knees.

"Phoebe." Strong hands cupped her face. Coaxed her chin upward until she was peering into steely blue eyes and a jaw that looked to be carved out of granite. "Did someone hurt you?" The words were dark, strangled, and even through the haze of her tears, she could see the thundercloud that washed over his features. The dangerous tic in his jaw.

She managed the tiniest shake of her head. Because no, Ambrose hadn't hurt her, not in the sense he meant. Aside from a few unwanted presses of his clammy palm upon her arm, he hadn't touched her.

The hurt came from what Ambrose had so carelessly revealed. As if the despicable ruse he and his sister had created made little difference. As if, with a few sloppy, drunken words, he hadn't changed the trajectory of her life.

But how was she to explain that all to Lord Rockliffe while sitting on the edge of a field with her breaths quaking and catching? How did she find the words to reveal the secret, long shuttered deep within her heart, that was now mixed with a lie?

It turned out that the marquess didn't await further explanations, for suddenly, his arms wrapped around her, and he lifted her off the ground.

Her body stiffened from the surprise change in position, and she knew she should protest, get back on her own two legs, resume the search that couldn't stop until she'd proved successful. Yet something about his sturdy chest felt so comforting. So *safe*. Shock had ravaged every one of her muscles and nerves, and instead of fighting the weariness, she succumbed to it, letting her head fall against his shoulder. Letting her tears flow and the miserable, choking sobs burst from her throat.

Lord Rockliffe marched back to the road as if she weighed nothing and uttered something to the coachman; the exact words, she couldn't distinguish. Whatever they were, the coachman nodded and turned to the carriage, whereas the marquess approached his impressive black gelding, easing her onto the animal's back.

She managed to twist her head, blinking at him as he vaulted up behind her.

"It will be faster this way," he murmured, pulling her close so her weight rested against his chest, taking the reins in hand.

And then, they were off at a gallop, over the familiar road that eventually led to a tree-lined drive. The stately facade of Beaumont Manor awaited them, no different from when she'd left it mere hours ago, providing another striking reminder that everything else in her world had since changed.

A groom stood waiting, ready to take the horse the instant Lord Rockliffe pulled to a stop beside the front portico, and the marquess was equally efficient at jumping to the ground and scooping her back into his arms.

During the short journey, she'd managed to get her sobs under control so all that remained were a few erratic gulps and shudders. She let him carry her nonetheless, resting limply against the protective heat of his chest as he bounded up the stone steps, spoke a few hurried words to the butler who greeted them in the entrance hall, and continued to the staircase.

She was so addled. So tired but nowhere near a point of being able to rest. So uncertain that if she did try to walk, her legs would hold her up and not buckle beneath her.

However, above it all, her mind hooked on a fresh spark of

unease, and she raised her head off his shoulder, trying to scan the corridor beyond. "Emily?"

"Shh." His breath hit her skin, a soothing stream of warmth, and his supportive arms tightened around her, his pace never faltering. "You needn't worry about that. She isn't due home yet, and Mrs. Connelly has instructions to see to her for the rest of the day."

Phoebe sank back again, the movement causing her breath to momentarily hitch and stutter. At least she could rest secure in the knowledge that on top of everything else, she wasn't involving Emily in the turmoil. Not today, at any rate. Not until she determined what to do. Where she needed to go …

It occurred to her that they were no longer climbing stairs but winding through a familiar corridor. The same hallway where she'd once scurried after him and he'd reached for her hand. The same doorway where he'd spun her around and claimed her lips.

He flicked the latch and pushed the heavy oak door open, bringing her into the quiet safety of his bedchamber. Setting her down atop the dark brocade counterpane that covered his bed.

She took in tiny gulps of the warm, still air—air that smelled faintly of him—watching as he lowered himself to his knees, setting to work on unlacing her half-boots until he could tug them free. The stockings beneath had become bunched, dusty, and damp, and he must have noticed, for he dealt with those next, pulling them off her aching feet. Not urgently, like when he'd removed her clothing while in the throes of passion. His movements now were slow. Careful. Gentle motions to rid her of the articles that had grown uncomfortable and disheveled.

She peered down at herself, to the horrible bombazine dress that had become caked in dirt and dotted with stray pieces of grass. The awful, somber dress that she'd kept plastered to her body as a sign of respect for her deceased cousin.

The woman who'd taken from her. Who'd *lied* to her.

Her hands flew to her back, her unsteady fingers tearing at the garment that suddenly threatened to constrict her lungs.

Lord Rockliffe came to his feet, leaning toward her on the bed. "I'll assist you—"

"I need to get it off." Her voice came out unnaturally high and frantic, but she couldn't calm it, couldn't stop her clumsy, desperate attempts to claw the dress away from her skin. "I cannot wear this detestable thing any longer."

He placed his sturdy hands upon her back, and in an instant, the material sagged, allowing her to push it down her body and shove it onto the floor. That was better—so much better—yet sobs threatened again, rising in her throat, choking her.

He grabbed at the laces of her stays, releasing her from the garment, allowing her chest to rise more freely as she sucked in a deep, trembling breath. But it was too late. Her tears poured to the surface and spilled over, despondency consuming her once more.

The bed dipped as he sank down beside her, and his arms enveloped her, nudging her into the protective embrace of his chest. Holding her as she cried.

She allowed herself a moment to simply rest her head there while her body shook. The broadcloth beneath her cheek quickly grew wet, but he didn't seem to mind; indeed, his grip on her tightened, and his fingers traced calming circles over her back. In a world where nothing else was right, his embrace felt comforting. *Safe.* Like one she never wanted to leave. Nonetheless, she didn't sink more deeply against him or let her tears intensify. Rather, she found the strength to push back the bitter lump in her throat and straighten her spine, for every second spent inundated by sorrow was another second spent without striving for answers. Without knowing her *child* was safe.

She blinked rapidly, trying to make her vision clear as she tilted her head to look at him.

"Phoebe." The way he said her name was tentative, soft. Yet in the next instant, his features became shadowed again, the dangerous lilt returning to his voice. "You may not feel ready to speak yet, nor do you need to. However, you can perhaps imagine the conclusions I'm beginning to draw, and if you give me even a single nod to confirm them, I will happily locate Sir Ambrose Windham and make this his final day on earth."

"No." She shook her head, her stomach giving an unpleasant lurch. As much as she never wanted to look upon Ambrose's detestable, smug, *lying* face again in her lifetime, she couldn't risk him coming to harm. Because what if there was a chance, however minuscule, that he *did* know something, and the information could somehow be cajoled out of him?

"I might need him ... he might know ..." Defending the man was vile business, and the words burned her chest. Yet it was all for a reason, one she could conceal from Lord Rockliffe no longer. "He might have information about the child. *My* child."

21

Phoebe waited for her revelation to sink in and the marquess's face to crease in repulsion as he realized the true nature of the governess he'd hired. For him to utter the same words she heard when she'd first announced her condition to Harriet all those years ago. *Disgraceful. Immoral.* However, the marquess stayed unexpectedly stoic, displaying naught beyond a slight twitch of his jaw.

He said nothing, allowing the room to fall into silence. Indeed, he was now the one waiting for her. Not angrily. Not judgingly. Simply giving her the space to continue.

She pressed her palms into the thin cotton of her shift, trying to keep herself steady, to prevent her voice from shaking. However, each tangled emotion from the vicarage bubbled and rose within her, and when she opened her mouth, everything came out at once. "For all the years I acted as her companion, my cousin Eugenia lied to me in the most egregious way. Ambrose, her drunkard of a brother, just let the truth slip, and—"

She paused for air, reining herself in. The words were too fast, would make little sense to him. She needed to start again and give him the full story, right from the beginning. To let loose all the events that had been tightly concealed as a shameful secret, locked away in her heart. And then, to tell him of the startling revelation that had come to light, which was still so new, so bewildering, that she struggled to comprehend it herself.

He'd opened up to her, giving her all the scarred, hidden parts of himself. Now, her turn had come to do the same. Whatever he chose to make of her admissions.

"Sir Ambrose Windham isn't my betrothed. He never has been." She started by allowing that crucial fact to land, detecting the faint rush of the marquess's exhale. "After Ambrose inherited my father's baronetcy close to nine years ago, he made me an offer of marriage, purely to spite the memory of the man who'd begrudged having him as an heir. Perhaps anyone looking in from outside would have thought it a favorable arrangement, for, by accepting, I would have kept the home and position I'd always enjoyed. However, I found Ambrose so unsavory a creature that I wasn't willing to pay that price. I declined and begged for my mother's family, the Buxtons, to take me in instead."

A decision she'd long questioned, frequently asking herself if she'd made a mistake and what, in her desperation, she could have done differently. But there was little purpose to pondering that now, especially when everything had changed. "I came to Bowden, and after my mourning period was through, I ..." *needed some fun in my life again, wished to feel like I belonged, wanted to forget the sight of you swimming in the lake ...* "I met a man."

She peered down at the flimsy fabric covering her lap, and for a moment, she could see her eighteen-year-old self adorned in fresh white muslin—the hated bombazine at last packed into a trunk—as she stepped into the local assembly hall for the first time. She could envision the way she'd flitted about, arm in arm with Clara, giggling and drinking too much ratafia. The way she'd participated in every quadrille, and she and her cousin had spent the time in between quietly conversing about which gentlemen they found most appealing, and how Clara had motioned toward a figure across the dance floor, whispering in Phoebe's ear: *I dare you to drop your glove right in front of that dashing soldier and see if he won't pick it up.*

"Major Berkley was handsome and charming. I liked him at once." She'd barely gotten started, and already, Lord Rockliffe's teeth clenched together, his hands forming tight fists at his sides. Yet she refused to shy away from the facts. If she was going to do this, she needed him to understand the whole story. Even the details she preferred to forget. "No one knew him well, beyond that he'd been invited, by some acquaintance or another, to a nearby house party. But *I* got to know him. In secret, mostly, during moments when we were both able to sneak away. Enough that I developed certain ... *expectations* and let myself get carried away with all manner of fancies. I didn't give them up even when the time came for him to leave Bowden and he issued no proposal. After all, he promised we could write, and I told myself I needed only to be patient."

The intensifying darkness overtaking the marquess's features confirmed his understanding of what she implied. Yet that part of the story wasn't the worst of it, the part that had truly twisted her heart and turned her life upside down. "He did write to me a single time. I tried so hard to pretend it was enough, that more letters would follow, that I just had to wait a little longer. But eventually, I couldn't wait. Not once I discovered I was increasing."

An icy shiver ran down her spine, inundating her with the same aching fear she'd experienced all those years ago upon realizing that unless he returned and did right by her, the seemingly innocuous dare she'd accepted—the drop of a glove

—would lead to her ruin. "I wrote to him. I wrote so many letters, and time went on, and not once did I receive a reply. I had no choice but to tell my aunt Harriet what had happened." *Because I've always placed far too much faith in Harriet's willingness to support me, haven't I?*

"I knew I'd been foolish, and I always suspected she'd be angry with me, but I couldn't have imagined ..." Phoebe pressed a hand to her forehead, as if the gesture could rid her of the echo of Harriet's horrified exclamations and angry reproofs. Of the revelation that had delivered a sickening blow to Phoebe's heart. "Major Berkley elicited curiosity during his appearances at the assembly hall, and Harriet loves nothing better than gossip. That's how, unbeknownst to me, she'd come to discover the man had a wife back in London."

Lord Rockliffe made a low, feral sound in his throat, and the quiet that followed felt unsettled, as if it might explode into turmoil at any moment.

"I didn't know! I swear, I never would have done such a thing willingly." She took a minute to squeeze her eyelids closed, refusing to let tears come to the surface again and get her off course.

"*You* are not the one at fault." The sharpness of his tone made her peer at him again, and the dark glint in his eyes made them look downright murderous. "This double-dealing bastard of a soldier, on the other hand—"

"There is little purpose in speaking of him now. Several years ago, I happened upon his name in *The Times* with the news he'd been killed at Alexandria." She studied the marquess's face, looking for a trace of grim satisfaction, but he remained as still and unyielding as stone. Which she supposed wasn't so different from her own reaction to learning the news, when she'd experienced neither gratification nor sorrow, only numbness.

She stiffened her shoulders, making herself unyielding,

too. Strong enough to keep going. "I'm not certain where he spent the years in the interim or if he ever came back to Bowden. Whatever the case, I was no longer here, for upon learning of what I'd done, Harriet and Martin sent me straight back to my former home at Birchby Park in Essex, telling me I could prevail upon Sir Ambrose's mercy."

Her stomach churned, still able to feel the swaying of that long carriage ride as she'd cradled her swelling abdomen, grappling with nausea that refused to abate. When she'd sat for hours with nothing to do but contemplate her desperation and helplessness. "I had no choice. My condition was beginning to show, and I didn't know where else to turn. Not surprisingly, Ambrose also found me disgraceful and put all thoughts of a union between us out of his head. He had an older sister, though. A widowed, childless sister. Eugenia."

Her throat tightened at the name. *Eugenia.* The woman who was part tormentor, part protector, and apparently, part deceiver. "She was also ashamed of me and wasted no opportunity to remind me of my misdeeds. All the same, she didn't cast me out as the others did. Rather, she appointed me as her companion, and then, she made arrangements. A secluded cottage in Suffolk where I could disappear for several months. She accompanied me. Stayed with me. Not happily, but she was always there. She was the one who went for help on the night the baby came."

The unsettledness in her stomach spread, creating a deep, turbulent ache in her chest. She'd never spoken of that night, had tried so hard to put the details out of her mind, although they always came back to her no matter how much time passed, continuing to startle her awake at night in a cold sweat. "There were complications. The labor went on too long, and …"

She folded her arms together, giving herself a light pinch. A reminder that she was here, safe, in Lord Rockliffe's bedchamber and not back in the cottage, her body ready to break from the unrelenting waves of agony, her voice worn out after hours of screaming. Not looking down and seeing blood upon the sheets, and hearing, in the newfound quiet, the worried murmurs exchanged between Eugenia and the midwife. "I didn't think I would live," she managed at last, hugging her arms a little tighter to her chest. "There was pain and exhaustion, and then, nothing. Only blackness that I didn't have the strength to fight."

She took a breath, bracing herself against the scraping in her chest as each tiny, hidden piece of her past broke free. "I'm still not certain for how many days I lay there. Only that when I opened my eyes in the cottage again, everything felt different, somehow. *Empty.* And then, Eugenia appeared above my bed, assuring me that I'd come through the ordeal, but that the baby ..."

She shook her head silently, knowing that repeating Eugenia's words would break her.

He understood. He had to, for his hand came out to touch her shoulder, and then, his arm went back around her in a protective embrace. A silent gesture of comfort that gave her the strength not to back away from the pain wrenching her heart.

"Eugenia provided so few details, insisted that my questions could serve no purpose. In the end, I gleaned only one small scrap of information: that the infant was a girl. But I never got to hold her or even see her. As soon as my health permitted, we relocated to Bath so Eugenia could take the waters, and I had to carry on as if everything that happened in the cottage had never existed. Even though my heart has always known otherwise."

She shifted in his arms, pressing a palm to her chest as it clenched with more painful memories that threatened to take her breath away. "I stayed with her for years, fighting back grief

I couldn't speak of, because when she labeled me immoral and said a woman like me would never find a position elsewhere, I believed her. When she led me to think that by proving my loyalty and obedience to her for as long as she lived, I would someday receive an inheritance, I believed her, too. I held an absurd idea that I'd be well-provided for, and that I'd take the funds to establish myself back in Suffolk, because that's the only way I could be close to what I'd lost ..."

She trailed off, the moroseness of her secret plan becoming especially apparent now that she'd spoken it aloud. However, if anyone could understand the desire to confront the location of one's deepest sorrow, perhaps it was Lord Rockliffe. The thought gave her a momentary pang of comfort, although it quickly dissipated as more memories pushed upward, wrestling themselves free.

She let her weight sink against his chest, her body suddenly becoming too taut, too heavy, to hold upright. "That was my failing. I was so ashamed of what I'd done that I put my head down and never asked questions, and when Eugenia told me things, I believed them. I always believed them."

Her voice was becoming shaky and rapid again, the shock she'd tamped down to a simmer flaring, ready to burst into emotions too powerful to name. "Why didn't I ask more questions? I *knew* Eugenia wanted to send the infant to another family. I *knew* she didn't like it when I tried to find out who that family was. I have so many missing hours following the birth, and I should have pushed harder in my questioning about them, but I didn't. I suppose I couldn't fathom anyone keeping a secret, telling a falsehood so grievous. But she did. She *lied*.

"I would have had no idea, would have gone my whole life without realizing"—her voice broke at the horrifying thought —"only for Ambrose coming back, thinking me sufficiently chastened that he would renew his offer of marriage. He was as abhorrent as ever. As callous and drunk, and when I refused him, his anger made him careless enough to reveal the truth. My daughter *did* survive, and Eugenia sent her somewhere, and for all these years, I never knew."

His body tensed, his arms tightening around her the instant she let out the shuddering words. The tight embrace was the only thing preventing her from dissolving into a mass of despair.

"Phoebe." His fingers cupped her chin. Lightly tilted it until she was looking up at him, peering into blue eyes that were gentle but simultaneously invited no protest. "You told me in no uncertain terms that I wasn't to place blame upon myself for things that happened in the past. Now, I'm demanding the same of you. This wasn't your fault."

Her chin quivered beneath his touch. "Please. I need to find her. Ambrose said that Eugenia had provided for her, but what if ..." She broke off, her hazy sense of unease expanding into inescapable fear. "What if, now that Eugenia's gone, the arrangement she made is no longer in place? If there's a chance my daughter is no longer being provided for, then what will become of her? Ambrose claims to know none of the details, and he's so unreliable, so *inebriated.*"

Her hands shook in her lap, her loathing for the repugnant man making her throat thicken with bitterness. Except now, she couldn't even wish him out of existence, for had he not shown up, intoxicated, at the vicarage, she never would have discovered the truth.

"Please," she repeated. "I don't know where to begin. How to find her. I just know that I cannot rest until I'm certain she's safe."

"Of course." He pulled out of the embrace, his rigid body rising from the bed, coming to stand above her. "I'm going to take care of this. Immediately."

Her eyes darted up to him as he straightened his wrinkled coat, his features unusually calm. *Unsettlingly* calm.

"There is little purpose in trying to force information out of Ambrose," she said, her stomach turning at the thought of Lord Rockliffe seeking out the detestable drunkard at the vicarage—or wherever he'd gone—and spending more aggravating moments talking in circles, getting nowhere. "What if he really does know nothing? Or if he leads us astray?"

He set his mouth in a hard line. "As much as I would take great pleasure in tearing Ambrose Windham limb from limb until he felt inclined to cooperate, I have no interest in reasoning with a man in his cups. There are other ways to procure the information you seek. We don't need him. Not now, at any rate."

Her anxiousness must have shown upon her face, for he reached out to cradle her jawline, his touch impeccably light. "Phoebe." He said her name commandingly. Reverently. That way of his that was soft but authoritative at the same time. "I'm going to make a few arrangements with my secretary. In the meantime, I need you to stay here and write down every detail you can think of regarding what you just told me." He motioned toward his small desk in the corner, atop which rested a stack of blank paper, along with an inkwell and quill. "Dates. Locations. Everything, no matter how small. Do you think you can do that?"

She gave a brisk nod, reaching for the hand that cupped her face and using it to pull herself upright. She'd managed to speak the whole story aloud, regardless of how much it hurt. Surely, she could put it on paper, too. Especially if it had the potential to help.

"Good." He set his hands—his strong, scarred, perfect hands—upon her shoulders. "I don't want to leave you alone, but it's imperative that I see to this as quickly as possible. Will you be all right until I return?"

"Yes." She nodded again, giving herself a final second to savor his touch before pulling away and stumbling to his desk, ready to pour the past out once more.

She sank onto the leather seat. Took the quill between her fingertips. "Please." She glanced over her shoulder as his steady footfalls began hitting the carpet, her voice little beyond a whisper. So quiet but filled with all the emotions she couldn't put into words. "Please, just—"

"I know." He paused in the doorway, peering over his shoulder, too, so their eyes connected. He didn't speak loudly, either, but his words contained certainty. Promise. Something she could trust. "I'm going to find her for you."

22

Nicholas moved mechanically—not thinking, simply doing—as he marched toward the last and, frankly, unlikeliest place he could have imagined going at a time like this: the dower house.

His urgent meeting with his secretary, Poole, had proved infuriatingly unproductive. What should have been a simple request to fulfill was met with stuttering apologies and vague non-explanations, until Nicholas had snarled his frustration and stormed from the room. Instead, he'd bellowed for the butler, Barrington, demanding the whereabouts of the woman who clearly had some explaining to do.

Only to be met with the news, as if it were the most natural thing in the world, that the Dowager Lady Rockliffe had relocated to the dower house that very morning.

He hadn't taken the opportunity to ask questions regarding the dowager's sudden compliance, as much as they pricked at the edge of his thoughts. All details were trivial until he found a means to set things right. Phoebe had received such a shock, had appeared so utterly broken, that every second he spent without fixing things for her was a damnable second too long.

At least the footman who responded to his pounding upon the door—newly covered in a coat of glossy black paint—didn't make him wait out in the twilight mist that had begun sprinkling down, nor did he voice any objections when Nicholas insisted he be permitted an audience with the dowager at once. The man, in his flawless blue livery, simply led him down the corridor and into the drawing room, where the dowager reclined upon a plush settee, a tray of pastries at her side.

"Rockliffe." She straightened the moment he appeared in the doorway, hurriedly smoothing her skirt and waving the footman away. "To what do I owe—"

"Why is Adolphus Clare no longer in our employ?" He rushed into the room, stalking across the freshly aired rug and coming to a halt beside the settee.

His mother blinked, a slight crease appearing between her silver brows. "Do you have need of a man of business? Because I've hired someone new, a Mr. Loxley, although I have doubts about his competency—"

"Not *a* man of business." He gritted his teeth, his exasperation ready to burst out loudly enough to rattle the delicate vases upon the mantelpiece. "I specifically require Adolphus Clare." The man who'd been with his family for over three decades. Who, for better or worse, understood all their inner workings and secrets, and would effectively fulfill any command, using any means necessary to do so. "Where is he?"

The dowager released a quick huff of breath. "He left, just as you surmised. Where he went, I do not know. I'm afraid there was some ... unpleasantness while you were abroad, and we haven't kept in contact."

Nicholas felt his forehead tighten, the tension creating a stab of discomfort between his eyes. *Unpleasantness.* Given his mother was involved, God knew what that entailed. He couldn't begin to contemplate it at present; it was significant only in that Clare's absence took his plans and annihilated them.

He spun away from her, a muttered curse flying from his lips. He'd have to go to London without knowing Clare was waiting for him, ready to jump into action, then. Perhaps hire a private detective instead. Yet finding someone both proficient and trustworthy would take extra time, and Phoebe deserved answers *now*.

"Wait, Rockliffe." His mother's voice stopped him just as he was about to burst back out the door and put the useless encounter to an end. He turned brusquely, peering at the small but domineering figure that sat upon the settee as regally as a queen. At the shrewd blue eyes that were unnervingly like his own. "You could ask Theodora."

He stared at her blankly, the stiffness in his forehead creeping down through his jaw. What in hell did she mean by bringing his brother Samuel's widow into this? A woman who'd also distanced herself far from the Rockliffe name, although, like it or not, the title would come for her eldest son eventually.

Nicholas had been away from England a long time and too preoccupied upon his return to delve deeply into family happenings—and what misdeeds the dowager had committed —during his absence. But suddenly, a spark of understanding tugged at the back of his mind. A recollection that while he was gone, Theodora had remarried a man by the name of Jeremy *Clare*.

"Jeremy Clare is Adolphus Clare's son," his mother explained in confirmation of his suspicions, reaching for her cane and placing her palm upon the curved silver handle. "I have reason to believe that Theodora and her father-in-law are not on amicable terms, but nonetheless, she and the younger

Mr. Clare may be able to inform you of the older Clare's whereabouts."

His fingers began drumming along his sleeve, a beat to accompany the pounding in his head. This whole situation was sounding more lurid by the second, and allowing himself to start pondering it would lead to nothing but aggravation. He would sort out the intricacies of what had transpired later. For now, he simply required a means to an end.

At his curt nod, his mother pushed herself off the settee, using her cane to shuffle to the escritoire in the corner. "I would ask what this entails, but I'm certain you won't tell me." She bent over the gilt-edged desktop, taking up a quill and scribbling down a few lines. After blotting the ink, she folded the page in half, holding it out for his perusal. "Whatever the case, that look on your face makes me believe it's important, and while I cannot guarantee that Theodora will prove cooperative or that Clare will do your bidding if you do find him, I sincerely hope your efforts are successful."

He came forward to accept the foolscap, stealing a quick glance at the London address contained within. His to take and run with. Yet despite his urgency, he couldn't help but pause at the uncharacteristic—dare he say?—*mildness* of her speech. Had she really provided aid and wished him well without demanding an explanation or trying to interfere? *Unfathomable.* However, the deceptive, unsettling gleam was absent from her eye, leaving only an expression of slight curiosity.

He had too many reasons not to trust her. Should have learned his lesson many times over. But, blast him for a fool, when he looked at her, he could see something in her crinkled features that he'd almost call motherly concern.

A trick of the dimming light, surely. Yet as he stayed, scrutinizing, the look didn't fade or harden. His force of a mother appeared ... *restrained.* Not only that, but she'd left Beaumont

Manor and returned to the dower house. No further excuses or delays. She'd simply done it.

What that meant, he didn't currently have the where-withal to say for certain. Mayhap some new scheme that she took extra pains to conceal. However, subtlety had never been the dowager's strong suit, and while he was perhaps being idiotically charitable in his assessment, he could once again imagine something unusual. Something his mother would never voice aloud, but maybe—just maybe—would express in other ways. An apology.

"Go, Rockliffe." The dowager flicked her wrist toward the doorway, putting an end to the weighted silence. "I know you didn't intend this as a social call, and you appear to be in a hurry."

He shoved the page into his coat pocket, giving himself a final moment to take in a quick, bracing inhale. She was right; he needed to make haste. There was just one matter left.

"Thank you." With a terse motion, he inclined his head, the word feeling strange on his tongue. For too many years to count, he and his mother had been far more inclined to shout at one another than to utter pleasantries. This once—when it mattered more than ever—he hoped the thanks were warranted.

She dipped her chin in response, standing as dignified as ever with the support of her cane. The idea that the accompanying twitch of her lips could be a smile was altogether too peculiar. Regardless, it was the final thought that struck him as he hurried from the room and back to Beaumont.

23

When Nicholas returned to his bedchamber, nothing awaited him but the rumpled counterpane upon his bed and two sheets of paper, covered with rows of sloping handwriting, folded upon his desk. Evidence of Phoebe's presence, although she was nowhere to be seen.

He ignored the supper tray sitting on his bedside table, racing back into the corridor and bounding up the stairs two at a time until he arrived on the floor above. A space that had become enveloped in silence.

Taking care to keep his footfalls quiet, he peeked into Emily's room, where the candles had been extinguished but her sleeping form remained visible. A slender lump beneath the covers with the enormous cat dozing beside her, its paws stretched out and its belly up in the air. That was a relief, at least. His daughter had returned home, contented enough to settle early for the night. But no Phoebe.

He quickly retreated from the doorway, his head beginning to hum. Surely, she wouldn't have grown so anxious that she left, without a word, to take matters into her own hands.

She couldn't go alone, not without anyone—without *him*—to help her when she was clearly still reeling from shock.

But then, he saw it. The flicker of light emerging from beneath the door to the other side of the schoolroom. Phoebe's room.

He crossed the corridor, dropping a few light taps upon the door. No response. He tried again, and at the continued stillness, he eased it open, his chest immediately tugging at the sight.

Phoebe was here, asleep. Not restfully like Emily, but rather as if she'd collapsed across her counterpane in exhaustion and hadn't gotten back up. Her hair remained partially in its pins, and while she'd changed into her nightclothes, she'd neglected to remove her dressing gown, leaving the garment to become tangled around her sprawled-out limbs.

He inched forward, studying her face in the light of the candelabrum she'd left burning on the bedside table. Even in sleep, her features remained tight with worry, and her cheeks were unusually pale.

"Phoebe." He murmured her name, allowing himself to sink to the edge of the bed beside her. He placed a hand atop her shoulder—a soft, bare patch of skin where her dressing gown had slid down—and gave her a gentle nudge. On one hand, it felt like doing wrong, for God knew she could use the rest after what she'd been through. But on the other, she looked so unsettled, so restless, and he wanted to take those burdens and make them go away.

It was alarming how much her troubles felt like his troubles. How he had an overwhelming urge to tear apart the world until everything became right for her again. He knew —Christ, did he know—the incomparable pain of having one's child stolen away, of thinking his daughter may be forever lost. He'd be damned if he let Phoebe live with that agony.

He curled his fingers lightly against her skin, and with the subtle motion, her eyes flew open, her expression glazed and uncertain. Until suddenly, she sucked in a sharp breath, bolting upright onto her elbows.

"I can't believe I fell asleep." She gave her head a terse shake, sitting up straighter and pushing back the errant clumps of hair that had come loose and clung to her face. "I was supposed to be up waiting, to be doing more—"

"There's no shame in it." He met her fingers as they ran over her crown, stilling her hand with his. Tracing back to her cheek and tucking another strand behind her ear. "You had a shock. Don't begrudge yourself a few moments of rest. I only woke you because I knew you'd be eager for news. I'm riding to London at first light. There's someone I plan to meet, a trusted, longtime employee who's known for his discretion and efficiency." Someone who, technically, was a former employee, but with any luck, he could be bought back for the right price.

"It will provide a good start, at any rate," he continued. "If need be, I'll hire a detective. Procure additional men to travel north and take up the search. Through whatever means, we *will* locate her." He found himself leaning toward Phoebe, a lightning-like surge coursing through him as his hands went down to clasp her shoulders. In this matter, he wasn't so different from the dowager: he refused to accept an outcome that didn't agree with the one he wanted.

"Thank you. I cannot begin to say how grateful I am for the assistance; I ..." She let out a long breath, her body loosening beneath his grasp. Her voice quieting. "Thank you."

As if there were any world in which he *wouldn't* help her.

For just a moment, he lowered his head, letting his lips brush against her temple. Her hair hung in disarray, not yet rid of all the dust from the field. And even so, she smelled faintly of wildflowers, sweet and fragrant and beautiful. "You should try to get some more rest now," he said. "I plan to leave a note for Emily in her bedchamber, if you could ensure that she gets it in the morning. But I shan't be gone long. A day, two at most, and we can determine where to go from there."

She nodded, and at that, he pulled away, raising himself off the bed. Away from her warmth. "Goodnight, Phoebe." He uttered the farewell without looking back at her. Because there were too many things left unsaid between them, too much temptation to hold her in his arms and simply be with her, and he couldn't afford to get distracted by any of it. She was depending on him; as such, this wasn't a moment for thinking but doing, and he needed to leave. He would write Emily's note, go to the stables to ensure Merlin was prepared for the early morning journey, return to his bedchamber to check that his small valise was packed as requested—

"Wait." Her breathy call came just as he turned to the doorway, making his boots halt against the floorboards. Making each item on his ordered list of what came next disintegrate and his body pivot back toward the bed. Toward her.

"Don't go yet. I cannot sleep again right now; I don't want to be alone. Please ..." She caught her bottom lip between her teeth. Released it with a quiet entreaty. "Stay."

Just like that, he was atop the counterpane once more. Sitting beside her on the edge of the bed with a feeling in his chest that proved frightening in its intensity. She was right there, his to reach out and embrace, caress. Yet before he could move another muscle, she shifted closer to him, her spine growing straighter, her expression intent.

"My lord, our conversation in your study ended far too abruptly, and there's something I need to say to you." She folded her hands upon her lap. Squeezed her eyes shut a moment, and when she reopened them, her blue-gray-green gaze shimmered, penetrating him with its raptness. "What you told me about the hunting accident. About Emily. It doesn't make you any less of a marquess, or of a father to the daughter you clearly love beyond measure." Her hands flew up, and suddenly, she was the one embracing him, squeezing tight to his shoulders. "You were never broken. Not to me."

"Phoebe." Her name came out cracked, guttural. She could say he wasn't, but with her words, something deep within him constricted and then smashed, each piece jagged and aching.

"I don't say this to placate you. I don't mean it as a passing fancy that will fade with time and disillusionment." She paused, her chest quivering as she took in a long breath. "After what happened in Suffolk ... I do not *want* to get with child again. The surgeon who came to see me afterward said it may no longer be possible, that I'd risk experiencing similar complications again even if it were. So, if that is the standard by which you judge a person deficient, then I suppose I'm broken, too."

"No." He cut her off before she could say another thing, his throat growing thick. He *hated* hearing those ugly words about her, even if they came from her own mouth. Phoebe wasn't deficient. She was strong, determined, compassionate, *passionate* ... She was everything good, everything in the world that made him hope, and he needed to make her understand. "I've never wanted you any way other than exactly as you are. That hasn't changed. That will not change."

"Nothing has changed for me, either." She tilted her chin upward. Drew her face closer as years of his pent-up self-loathing scraped between his ribs and tore free, leaving behind an odd sense of buoyancy. A momentary flash of a future where maybe he wasn't alone.

And then, her mouth fell upon his, the gentle press of her lips stealing the last of his reservations and enveloping him with a sense of rightness. He returned the kiss in kind. Not roughly and desperately, like in their previous encounters, but lightly, taking the time to truly absorb each sensation, to savor every motion. She tasted like the sweetness of summer. The salt of tears. She was soft, warm, and exquisite, and he cupped the back of her neck, wanting every last facet of her.

How long they remained with their lips joined, continuing their careful exploration, he didn't know. He recognized only that with each passing second, something was building within him, raw and powerful. A feeling akin to the lust that had become his frequent companion where she was concerned, but also so much more than that.

This was something startling. Something that made him vulnerable.

And even so, he didn't shy away from it. When she arched against his palm, making their lips draw apart, he didn't jump from the bed and bring the encounter to a swift end.

Instead, he stayed with her. Watched as she brought her fingers to his cravat, working to free the series of knots. As she took the loosened scrap of linen and cast it to the floor, then dragged her hand down the front of his waistcoat.

"My lord, I want ..."

He pressed a finger to her lips. Dragged it along her cheek and into her hair, where he located one of the confining pins. "It's Nicholas." He tugged the pin at the same moment he uttered his name—the name he so seldom heard, an intimacy he permitted few others—causing the thick lock to tumble down her back. "You should call me Nicholas."

"Nicholas." She whispered it back to him, slipping his buttons loose while he worked to release more pins, until his waistcoat gaped open and her hair hung around her like a shiny brown curtain.

"Phoebe," he returned in a rasp, letting her push his coat and waistcoat down his arms so all that remained was his shirt. Letting her take hold of that, too, and begin nudging it upward, and he finished the task, pulling it over his head.

Then, it was his turn to tend to her. He leaned in, shifting the shoulder of her dressing gown to expose the same patch of skin he'd seen when he happened upon her sleeping. He brought his lips to it, leaving a trail of kisses as his fingers unfastened her belt, and the dressing gown also came open, sliding down her body with his faint pull.

For a moment, he simply drank in the sight of her clad in nothing but her shift, noticing all the details there'd been no time or place to think of earlier. The way the tops of her breasts, as pale and smooth as cream, sloped above the neckline. The way the thin fabric clung to her body, revealing shadows that hinted at the beauty beneath.

A low sound emerged from his throat as he reached for his boots, and without looking away from her, he pulled them from his feet and sent them tumbling to the floor. As he worked, she drew her legs onto the bed, shuffling to the side to allow him room. Lowering herself until her head hit the pillow, her hair fanning out behind her.

He pulled his legs up as well, his breeches growing uncomfortably tight against his growing arousal. Her bed was far smaller than the one that stood in the marquess's chamber, but it proved big enough. The perfect size for him to lie alongside her and kiss her again. First, her lips. Then, her ear. Her jawline. Her neck.

She ran her fingers down his bare abdomen, skirting along the waist of his breeches in a way that caused need to surge in his veins. "Will you extinguish the candles?" she asked.

"No." He took hold of the ribbon securing her shift, and when she made no objection, he pulled it loose, watching the garment slacken. "This time, sweet, I'm going to look at you. I want you to look at me."

Her reply came in the form of a quivering exhale, and he placed his hands upon her thighs, gently easing them apart. Making just enough room that he could kneel between them and gaze at her from above. He took hold of the shift, easing it down with the same care, just until it rested below the curve of her breasts, revealing the two perfect globes. The deep pink nipples.

He wanted them in his mouth, to feel each bud grow taut from his ministrations, to hear her cry out in pleasure. At the same time, though, this felt like too significant a moment to be rushed. Finally, he was getting to see her. To have her all for his own, without interruptions. His to savor, to explore, to *know*.

And so, he took his time, resuming his kisses where he'd left off at her neck. Working across the length of her collarbone. Finding the place where her heartbeat echoed up to his lips. Traveling down to the valley between her breasts, her skin smooth and sweet. Only when he'd given sufficient attention to each flawless curve did he take her nipple into his mouth, suckling the rosy point. Rediscovering the taste of her, learning which motions of his tongue made her breath catch.

He licked and stroked, one side and then the other, and when her hips began writhing against the mattress, he grasped her shift again, sliding it lower until it hung slackly upon her hips. Then, he lay down in the space between her thighs, turning his cheek to rest lightly against the soft surface of her abdomen. His lips followed, creating a path that led to her navel. That veered to the side and halted where faint silver marks decorated her skin. Evidence of the life she'd once carried inside her.

"My l-lord," she stammered. "That is, Nicholas, I ..." Her head rose from the pillow, and her hands went to her belly, splaying wide like a shield.

"You're so beautiful." He entwined her fingers with his, guiding them back to rest atop the counterpane. "*So* beautiful."

He kissed the top of one of the marks. The middle. The end. Watching as the hesitation melted from her features and she dropped to the pillow once more. With his palm still pressed to hers, he kissed every wavy silver line that told the story of her past.

Just as his hands told the story of his. Each jagged scar a damnable symbol of how he'd been battered and cut down, how his life had changed. A fact he'd spent so long bemoaning. But in the end, he'd lived to rise above it, hadn't he?

Like Phoebe, he was marked, forever altered, but not broken. *Not broken.*

He eased her hips off the mattress so he could pull her shift the rest of the way down and cast it to the side. Then, he brought his mouth to the same thighs he'd explored in the dark, only this time, candlelight illuminated the pale skin beneath his lips. Illuminated the patch of curls between her legs, and the way her mouth fell open, releasing a sigh, when he at last brought his tongue there, licking down her seam. She was wet and hot and utterly alluring, and he drank her in, tracing over every fold. Finding the bundle of nerves that made her cry out, circling it until her nails dug into the back of his hand, and her eyes screwed shut.

"Watch," he murmured, letting his breath float over her sensitive flesh. Keeping his lips just above her until her eyelids fluttered open, her pupils bright with longing. When their gazes locked, he took hold of her legs and coaxed them to bend, nudging them even farther apart. Leaving every intimate surface of her bared to him.

She gave her hips a tiny thrust, fisting her hands in his hair. "Nicholas, I need—"

He answered by returning his tongue to her clitoris, the sound of his name on her lips like kindling to his own burning desire. He licked and caressed and sucked, observing each twitch that crossed her features as her body grew taut and quivering. Witnessed the moment when she bit down on her lip and abruptly released it with a moan, her muscles pulsing from her release.

He kissed her one more time—a lingering caress to sear the essence of her into his brain—before rising back to his knees and reaching for his fall.

And, just as he'd instructed, she watched. Her eyes widened, followed him as he slipped the buttons loose. As he shoved the breeches from his hips and freed his rigid cock. He placed a hand to each side of her head and stretched out above her, and suddenly, it was no longer just her eyes upon him but her fingers, the careful stroke down his arousal enough to tear a groan from his throat.

Her fingers curled, sending more shockwaves to his nerves as she guided him to her entrance. Her hips moved upward. His moved down. And with that, he was deep inside her, buried in tight, welcoming heat.

He said something. Her name, maybe, or words of praise for how damn good this felt. How *right* it felt. Frankly, he was having trouble forming a coherent thought. Everything had been reduced to sensation, need, and a deep pull in the vicinity of his heart.

Again, the fire in his veins caused his body to burn, making it demand *more, now, quickly*. And again, he held the urgency at bay, sinking into her with long, steady thrusts. Committing every detail of her to memory. All too soon, other responsibilities would beckon, and the day's struggles would come hurtling back. For as long as this moment lasted, though, it contained nothing but the two of them.

He heard himself utter more words. *Good girl. Beautiful. Sweet*. Felt the weight of her legs as they wrapped around him, saw her chest rise and fall as her breaths grew heavier. He stared into stormy ocean eyes, the yearning that coursed through him building like a tempest of its own. Building in her, too, if the soft sighs she emitted were any indication.

He raised a hand from the bed and slid it between their joined bodies, finding the center of her pleasure. Circling it with his forefinger. Allowing himself, just one time, to plunge into her faster, deeper.

Except one time wasn't enough. Already, her body was tightening, her hips moving more frantically, and all of a sudden, everything he'd held back inundated him at once. He allowed the feverish pace to take over, his need restrained only by a thread that seemed perilously close to snapping.

"Phoebe." He called out to her, a heated sound of both reverence and desperation. A sound accompanied by her cry as she shattered around him, her intimate muscles clenching him tight. He gave one more thrust, and release hit him, hard, his body thrumming with unraveled desire as he spilled his seed deep inside her.

Bracing his weight on his forearms, he dropped his chest to hers and buried his face in the crook of her neck. Waited until his heart rate slowed, his breaths were no longer so ragged, and he could find the strength to withdraw from her and collapse to the side.

Even then, a strange sensation tugged at his chest long after the pleasure-filled waves faded away. It had never been like this with anyone before: a need that went beyond physical pleasure. A desire for closeness. A feeling like he never wanted to let her go.

He held tight to her on the narrow bed, drawing her to her side so her back reclined against his chest. He'd stay just a little longer, until he was certain she could rest again.

"Try to sleep, sweet." He stroked her hair. Her shoulders. Traced patterns along the places he'd kissed on her abdomen.

It took a long time, but eventually, her breathing became even, and when he shifted up onto his elbow so he could steal a glance at her face, her eyes were closed.

The odd sensation within him grew, squeezing like a vise

against his heart. He inched away, untangling his body from hers with painstaking slowness, careful not to disturb what was no doubt her fragile state of rest.

"I'll return soon," he said under his breath, far too quietly for the words to reach her awareness. He supposed he must have uttered them as a reassurance to himself.

Because he *would* get Phoebe the answers she sought.

He *would* see her happy.

And then ...

Maybe he'd dare to think that he'd have her in his arms, his bed—his heart—again, and that happiness would include him and Emily, too.

24

Nicholas rode to London with such haste the next morning that he didn't stop to consider what would happen when he arrived at the address on Buckingham Street. He therefore couldn't have anticipated, upon knocking at the front door of the tidy brick terrace house, that he would set off a cacophony akin to what one might find at the Royal Circus.

A gravelly bark emanated from within, followed by the sound of pounding footsteps—a swarm of them, to be precise—and a flurry of childlike voices, which gradually grew louder and more heated.

Until suddenly, the door flew open, and a stocky bulldog sprang out, its hefty paws colliding with Nicholas's breeches as it emitted another series of barks.

"Oh." From behind the overzealous dog, a small face fringed by an unruly mop of russet hair peered up at him, the boyish features creasing with disappointment. "You're not the deliverer from Gunter's."

Nicholas blinked, placing a tentative hand atop the dog's massive white and brown head. The creature looked more like a resident of a blood sport arena than a family pet. Yet it wagged its tail enthusiastically and gave his clothing a few sniffs, its tongue lolling to the side of its thick jowls.

"Uncle." Another face—this one adorned by dark hair and a pair of wire-rimmed spectacles—regarded him with suspicion, although the boy did do him the courtesy of pulling the dog's collar and commanding the animal to sit.

Benedict. The boy's identity hit him at once, even though Nicholas had only ever seen him in passing. This was his brother Samuel's eldest son. The boy Samuel had always kept far away from Rockliffe House, although it didn't change Benedict's fate as the next Marquess of Rockliffe. Just as Alexander, the younger of the pair—and the very image of Samuel—was destined to be the spare.

After a morning of hurrying, Nicholas found himself staring, motionless, with a strange ache tugging at his gut.

However, Benedict rapidly broke the gaze, giving his brother a subtle jab between the ribs and stiffly inclining his head. "I mean, good day, my lord."

"My lord." Alexander followed suit, bowing with exaggerated politeness and nearly tripping over his feet in the process. However, he quickly righted himself, and when he brought his eyes back to assess the near-stranger looming in the doorway, the bright blue—Samuel's blue—shone with eagerness, not mistrust. "Sorry about Achilles. He was just a bit too excited from the knock on the door. We're all excited because we're having a party tonight, and Mama has ordered a tray from Gunter's filled with sweetmeats *and* cakes. It's because Jeremy —he's our new papa—has just published another novel that's already sold over one *thousand* copies, and—"

"Be quiet, Alex," Benedict hissed, shoving another elbow into his side.

Alexander scowled at his brother, jostling him back but then giving a resigned sigh. "You're right. It's bad manners to talk about the tray after Mama said we couldn't have anything from it until later." He looked down at his boots a moment, his forehead rumpling, before his head keenly popped back up, and he flashed a hopeful half-smile in Nicholas's direction. "But if it arrives in time, perhaps she'll reconsider and allow us all to try a sweetmeat, seeing as how you're a guest *and* a marquess."

"Boys?" A female voice rang out from the top of the stairs before he could reply, and a figure—Theodora—came forward, starting down the steps before abruptly stilling. Her hand tightened around the bannister as she took him in, her features settling into a sharp glare. "What are you doing here?"

"Mama, have you forgotten?" Alexander turned to her, shielding his mouth with a hand and speaking in an overloud whisper. "You're supposed to curtsey and call him *my lord*."

"There's no need to stand on ceremony." Nicholas chanced a step forward, landing just short of the doorway. The reception he'd received from his nephews—and the dog—had placed him half in a stupor, and he squared his jaw, forcing himself to focus. "I require only a moment to speak with you, Theodora, or your husband, if he's about."

She resumed her descent down the stairs at twice the speed, inserting herself into the space between her sons and throwing a protective arm around each boy's shoulder. "Why?" Her voice contained all the warmth of an icehouse.

He may as well reveal the truth without delay. "Regarding the whereabouts of Adolphus Clare. I have urgent need of his assistance."

Although the movement was slight, he could have sworn he saw her shoulders drop with unknotting tension. In the next instant, though, a storm cloud passed over her features, and her fingers clenched in the folds of her skirts. "I cannot help you, *my lord*."

He quirked a brow. "Cannot, or will not?" He had no desire to start a conflict with a woman who clearly wanted nothing to do with him, but nor was he in a position to give up so easily.

"Ben, Alex." She shifted her attention to her sons as if he hadn't spoken, her tone brightening as she gave each boy's shoulder a squeeze. However, her eyes continued flitting in Nicholas's direction as if he were a marauder whose every move required scrutiny. "I think Achilles would appreciate a walk. Why don't you take him with you and see if Jeremy is on his way back from Hatchards yet? And please, when you find Jeremy, tell him to hurry home, for we have a visitor."

The boys frowned in unison, and Alexander rocked back and forth from his heels to his tiptoes, folding his arms across his slender chest. "But what if the tray from Gunter's comes and we miss it?"

"All the more reason to make haste." She managed a small smile, giving her younger son's curls a ruffle and motioning down the street.

Benedict's eyebrows remained drawn together, and although his features bore far greater resemblance to Theodora's than Samuel's, Nicholas couldn't help but think that if the boy felt so inclined, he'd accomplish an impressive imitation of the Prescott glower. Whether that should make Nicholas proud or alarmed, he couldn't say. Whatever the case, the expression vanished as Benedict shoved his spectacles in his pocket and whistled to the dog, who immediately stood at attention.

"Come on, I'll race you." He spared his brother the pithiest glance before bolting onto the pavement, setting off another blast of raucousness as both boys vied for speed, the dog trotting happily behind them.

Theodora watched them, calling a cheerful farewell that got drowned out by their loudening exchange over who was going to win. But as soon as the boys turned the corner and disappeared, she stepped to the side of the doorway with an expression like stone, making a rigid gesture toward the entry-way. "You may as well come in. I'd prefer not to draw the neighbors' attention."

It was hardly the most enthusiastic invitation he'd ever received, but he accepted it, following her up the stairs and into a small but comfortable sitting room with sunlit windows that overlooked the street.

Rather than take a seat, she strode to the large desk that was positioned against the farthest window, gripping the edge and staring down at the surface as if the array of paper, water-colors, and brushes it contained were of the utmost interest. He didn't sit, either, but stopped in the middle of the floor, placing distance between them that she unquestionably wanted. Even from afar, he could see the way her knuckles turned white as her fingertips sank deeper against the wood.

Which sent his own fingers drumming rapidly along his coat sleeve and his mind grasping for something that had never been his strong suit: patience. She didn't *want* to talk to him. Was apt to shut him out entirely if he pushed too hard.

And so, he waited. Waited for each heavy, lingering second to tick by, until at last, she released her grasp on the desk and spun back in his direction, her expression notably cooler. More subdued. "I confess," she said, "your reason for being here is far different from what I anticipated."

He cocked his head, letting the words sink in. Prescotts may be especially good at glowering, but Theodora had a talent for displaying a whole range of emotions in the depths of her intense dark eyes. As such, he could see the contrasting mixture of trepidation and relief. Caution and concession.

All at once, understanding hit him like a blow to the gut. Due to his lengthy estrangement from the family, Samuel had never been aware of the consequences of Nicholas's accident at Foxhill. As for Theodora ... she *knew*. At some point after Samuel's death, when copious debts had forced her and the boys into the dowager's household, the dowager must have told her. She knew that, someday, her son was going to be forced into a life that Samuel had tried desperately to escape. And as such, she'd assumed that the current marquess had come to claim his heir.

He felt a sharp pinch at the bridge of his nose. "I wouldn't—"

"Yes, I know. I hope I don't come to regret it, but I'm going to attempt to trust you on that matter. In honor of the times Samuel forgot his bitterness and spoke fondly of you." Her eyes shot to the floor, her lips giving a small downward twitch as if she'd just experienced the same pinprick of grief he had. However, it lasted only a moment before she faced him once more, drawing her spine tall. "Regardless, I don't think it wise to send the elder Mr. Clare back into your clutches. Not after the fiasco in which he entangled himself out of duty to the Prescotts. The *crime* he was willing to commit—"

"For God's sake," he exclaimed, "I wasn't here. I don't *know* what he did." *I'm not in a position to let it matter right now.*

Her mouth became a flinty slash. "In that case, I suggest you have a conversation with your mother."

He gritted his teeth, the reminder of the dowager and her antics—whatever the hell they were on this occasion—sticking like a thorn in his side.

Had this visit been nothing but a mistake and a waste of time? Perhaps he'd be better off finding a detective agency after all, with the hope that the person he hired possessed the same competency as the former Rockliffe man of business.

Except, somehow, he couldn't abandon his current path just yet. Not without giving one last attempt.

"I intend to," he said, forcing his jaw to unclench. "But for now … I wouldn't be here if it weren't important. Not to the dowager, but to me. Rather, to someone I know. Someone I …

care about, very deeply. A mother who's been wronged." The significance of the words shot through him, the constricting sensation in his chest inundating him with the knowledge of just how genuine they were. He *cared*. Although, in truth, *care* seemed too insignificant a word to describe the feeling that radiated from the center of him and spread through his veins.

"I see." Theodora's eyes widened a touch, the spark in them suggesting that she did indeed understand. For a long, uncertain moment, she gazed at him, her lips pressed into an indecipherable line. Until suddenly, she released a sigh, and with it, the hard set to her features softened. "Jeremy and I have not kept in contact with his father. However ... he's written to us. We have his address. But you understand, of course, that I cannot divulge it without consulting Jeremy first."

Nicholas tensed his muscles, willing his face to show nothing of the hurricane raging within him. The answer should have incensed him. He was tired of bloody waiting, wanted the information *now*. Yet at the same time, she'd given a conciliation. A chance that, maybe, he would get what he came for after all if he could just be patient a little longer. And if Mr. Jeremy Clare—who no doubt had a bad taste in his mouth from the Rockliffe name—felt inclined to cooperate.

"I'll await his return," he uttered stiffly, taking a few steps toward the closest window. Retreating. Heading back to the window again.

Theodora, at least, voiced no objection to his continued presence. Instead, she remained where she was beside the desk, resuming her study of its contents. Alternating with glances out the window that shifted to occasional glances at him.

He followed suit—distracting himself by peering through the glass at the bustling street below. Except his eyes kept drifting to her, too. They'd never really been acquainted with one another, not after the dowager's disapproval of the *lowborn, unsuitable woman* had caused Samuel to cut ties with the entirety of his family and marry as he pleased. Nicholas knew her only from afar as the poet's daughter with whom his brother had fallen in love. The woman who'd been by Samuel's side, forced to watch as alcohol and opium progressively consumed him, until one day, she'd become a debt-ridden widow. The woman who'd carried on, fighting above every shred of adversity she'd experienced, and was a devoted mother to the next marquess. Nicholas's heir.

He sucked in a breath, his lungs feeling raw. There were certain phrases that he, as a marquess, had little cause to say. That truthfully, he couldn't recall ever crossing his lips. Yet an odd lump was rising in his throat, fighting to break free. If ever there was a time …

"I'm sorry, Theodora." The words burst out, low and not entirely even. Because he was so damn sorry for things too numerous and difficult to name. Sorry for the estrangement, that he hadn't done more to rectify it. Sorry that just as he'd lost a brother, she'd lost a husband. Sorry for whatever hell she'd gone through when Samuel's debts had forced her to turn to the dowager for help. And most of all—the matter that plagued him with guilt, that prodded at him as one of his largest failings … "About Benedict."

She cast him an incredulous look. "Sorry …" She mumbled the word back to herself as if she didn't fully comprehend its meaning. After a beat of silence, though, she gave her head a quick shake. "I don't expect an apology for something beyond your control."

She turned abruptly back to the window, her brow creasing in contemplation. He didn't speak, didn't move, letting more moments of silence settle between them before, at last, she blew out a long exhale. "Samuel wouldn't have wanted it," she said quietly, and although she peered down at the street, her expression was much farther away. "But I look at

Ben—his studiousness, his determination, his sense of right and wrong—and I think ... I think that perhaps, someday, he could be very good at the role."

The words hit him sharply, penetrating far below the surface. But not like the point of a dagger or the weight of a boulder. This felt rather like ... lightness. *Relief.*

In response, another phrase, which perhaps he too seldom found the opportunity to utter, was rising on his tongue. *Thank you.*

However, before he could say a thing, she pressed a finger to the glass, her face illuminating. "Look, that's them now."

Sure enough, the same two curly heads that had disappeared down the street just a short time ago came around the corner at a sprint, the enthusiastic dog bounding behind them. This time, a man—whom Nicholas had only encountered once, briefly, but long enough for recognition to now set in—accompanied them, his footfalls just as hurried but decidedly grimmer.

Assuming the younger Mr. Clare could be persuaded, Nicholas was so close to getting the information he needed, after which he'd be riding to the address in question like he had flames at his heels. However, in these final moments he had alone with Theodora, there was one more thing that required saying.

"I'd like to know him." He stared through the window as Benedict raced along, watching as the boy shoved a wind-blown piece of hair out of his eyes and called something to his brother—the small copy of Samuel. "And Alexander. If you'd let me."

He turned to find Theodora eyeing him levelly, her arms folded across her chest. "You'll forgive me for not wholeheartedly throwing my sons back into the arms of the Prescott family."

Yes. He could hardly blame her on that account. Wouldn't

try forcing her to change her mind. Even if the loss—the lack —forever left him with the sting of regret.

Yet in the next instant, she let out another sigh, her shoulders loosening. "I'll think on it. I do only want what's best for my boys, and maybe ... well, as I said, I'll think on it."

All at once, heaviness became lightness, and he could feel his lips twitch. His jaw slacken. "Thank you." This time, the words made it to the surface, and he brusquely dipped his chin. Watched as she did the same. The ensuing silence between them didn't feel weighty but ... conciliatory. Hopeful.

It lasted but a moment, though, before the front door creaked open, and numerous pairs of feet—and paws—barreled inside.

Nicholas pivoted toward the doorway, giving his coat a few curt tugs as the footsteps started up the stairs. Now, it was time to make amends with another, and it was crucial he succeed.

For Phoebe.

25

Nicholas scarcely noticed the driving rain that soaked him through as he made his way back to Rockliffe House in Mayfair. The fact that his wool coat had become waterlogged didn't matter, nor did the mud that splashed onto his boots.

It didn't matter because his journey had been successful. With a moderate amount of reluctance, Jeremy Clare had divulged the location of the London solicitor's office where his father had become employed in an unassuming clerk's position. And with significantly less reluctance, Adolphus Clare had agreed to undertake the task presented to him. Clare, after all, was nothing if not loyal, and while he may have intended to distance himself from the Prescott family, old habits died hard. Not to mention that the compensation Nicholas offered involved a sum that proved difficult to refuse.

After effectively seeing this assignment to completion, Adolphus Clare would never have to work another day in his life. For the time being, though, the man was on horseback barreling toward Suffolk—hopefully, ahead of the rain—with instructions to send word the moment he uncovered even the slightest detail.

And because Clare was known for his efficiency, he would find Phoebe's daughter. He *would*. Nicholas repeated the thought back to himself in a steady cycle, refusing to contemplate any other option.

By the time he approached the front door of Rockliffe House—his unannounced arrival requiring him to stand on the step and knock—he couldn't say he felt easy about the situation, precisely. He missed Phoebe already. Missed his own daughter. He realized how wrong—how empty—it felt to be away from them both and cursed the downpour that necessitated him waiting until the morrow to head home to Beaumont Manor. However, he could at least derive satisfaction from knowing that he'd achieved what he set out to do that day and matters moved in the right direction. *That everything would work out exactly as it should.*

The greeting he received when the door swung open, though, did little to add to his optimism. Flynt, the family's longtime butler in London, had always been stern-faced, but the look he gave Nicholas upon offering a half-hearted greeting and moving aside to allow him entry proved nothing less than miserable.

"Not to worry, Flynt." Nicholas removed his sodden top hat and coat, giving his head a shake that sent droplets flying to the marble floor of the entrance hall. "I require nothing more than my bed made up for the night. I'll be gone again in the morning, so I'll put you and the other servants to little trouble."

"My lord." Flynt stiffened, the appeasement only making him look grimmer. "A gentleman—although I hesitate to employ the term—was here seeking an audience with you earlier today. I informed him that you were not in residence, but he insisted on leaving a note nevertheless, claiming it was of the utmost importance."

Flynt tilted his head toward the side table, where an untidily folded piece of paper rested atop a silver tray. Nicholas arrived at the table to seize the page in three brisk strides, disregarding the wet squelches his boots made against the tiles.

It was far too early to receive any news from Clare. Even so, he tore open the note, his stomach swiftly plummeting as his eyes flew over the untidy scrawl.

Lord Rockliffe,
You have paid me a grave insult and besmirched the honor of my betrothed. I cannot allow such an affront to stand. As such, I demand satisfaction. We will settle this like gentlemen, with pistols, at a time and date to be determined. Name your second, and have him visit ...

He skimmed over the details pertaining to the name and address of the aggrieved party's second, not giving a damn about any of it beyond the signature scribbled in an uneven line across the bottom of the page. *Sir Ambrose Windham, Bt.*

"My lord?"

Nicholas was semi-cognizant that Flynt called out to him, although his gaze wouldn't lift from the letter. A potent heat rose within him and burned behind his eyes, until it was a wonder the page before him didn't burst into flames.

"My lord, is something the matter?"

He turned without answering, not trusting his throat to form words. Not trusting himself to do anything but move into the corridor, one rigid step after another, and seek out the refuge of his study. His mind was no longer forming logical thoughts but inundated by blazing, omnipotent fury.

He slammed the study door behind him, rushing over to the empty grate and letting his body sag against the mantelpiece, his hand forming a fist around the paper and rendering it a crumpled ball. If only a fire roared so he could toss it away and watch it turn into ash.

Of course, that wouldn't prevent the sloppily—*drunkenly*—penned words from continuing to sear into his head, making his ire explode like fireworks. *Insult. Betrothed. Satisfaction. Pistols.*

The man was a bloody swine, not worthy of gentlemanly conduct. Nicholas would far rather snap Sir Ambrose in two with his bare hands and be done with it.

Except he couldn't. Phoebe didn't want any harm to befall her cousin just in case, somewhere in his drink-addled brain, he held information.

Damn the man, having the audacity to believe that *he'd* been the one wronged. Furthermore, how could he even know about the private happenings at Beaumont Manor? Nicholas squeezed the paper tighter within his fist, his vision beginning to fill with sharp bursts of light. He'd best not ponder the question too thoroughly or he may be led to tear apart the city until he and Sir Ambrose came face-to-face, after which he couldn't be held responsible for his actions. Besides, the matter of *how* was secondary to the fact that Ambrose Windham was parading around, thinking he had a claim on Phoebe—

A sudden knock at the door tore Nicholas from his thoughts, although his blood remained just as heated, the force of it pounding through his ears. "Go away, Flynt," he bit out between clenched teeth, his jaw nigh on vibrating.

The door creaked open regardless, and a couple of heavy footfalls connected with the study floorboards. "Rockliffe?"

At the unfamiliar male voice, he pivoted abruptly, blinking as he took in the identity of the intruder. "Branscombe?" Through the gloom in the study, the features of the man hovering near the doorway became recognizable as belonging to the Duke of Branscombe, his sister Amelia's new husband. Unexpected, as after delaying their honeymoon on account of Nicholas and Emily's surprise return home on their wedding day, they'd finally departed so they could enjoy some time alone at the ducal estate.

Nicholas managed to tip his head in a semblance of a greeting, although he could make no guarantees that his expression didn't appear murderous. "Aren't you and my sister supposed to be sojourning in the country?"

"I'm afraid Amelia and I don't have the best of luck when it comes to escaping the city." The duke's eyes lit up at the mere mention of his wife's name, and his lips twitched, almost as if he'd uttered a private joke. "No sooner did we arrive at Edgecote Hall than I received word that my butler here in London had taken seriously ill, and certain arrangements had to be made. We could have done it through correspondence, but Amelia said she'd feel better about overseeing the matter in person. We had to return to London soon at any rate, as I plan to address Parliament before it adjourns for the year."

Nicholas nodded, although his head throbbed far too fiercely to return the answer with any sort of pleasantry.

"Amelia was hoping to retrieve a few books she left behind in the Rockliffe House library." Branscombe took an additional step forward, letting another beat of silence fall before continuing the explanation. "I told her I would fetch them and save her a trip out in the rain. We didn't know, of course, that you were in residence or I'm sure she would have come along. Although I begin to wonder if this is a bad time."

"No. Go to the library and take the books. Whatever she wants." *I'll hardly have use for them if I find myself at the wrong end of a pistol.*

He stiffened at the morbid thought, his brow tightening as if to squeeze it away. What purpose was there to allowing his mind to travel down that road? From what he'd discerned,

Ambrose Windham was too much of a drunkard to manage a straight shot, and Nicholas had excellent aim. At least, he used to. The challenge would lie with firing the pistol to the side and not succumbing to the temptation to point it somewhere fatal.

Ire rose again as a choking mass in his throat, and the sentiment must have emerged in his features, for Branscombe was gaping, not daring to come too close but looking like he wished to say a great number of things. Ultimately, though, the duke abandoned them all, retreating to the corridor with nothing more than a slight incline of his head.

"Wait, Branscombe." Nicholas pulled the words from his raw throat, fighting to keep them collected. "I don't suppose I could prevail upon you to act as my second."

The duke halted in his tracks before turning in one slow, rigid motion to peer at Nicholas as if he'd grown another head. "Y-you'll need to repeat that. I'm not certain I heard you correctly."

Nicholas stalked away from the mantelpiece and collapsed into his wing chair, motioning for Branscombe to take the seat next to it. He didn't *want* to ask such a thing of his new brother-in-law. However, the Duke of Branscombe, and no other, had shown up in his study at the opportune—or perhaps inopportune—moment, and Nicholas could garner little enthusiasm for the thought of traveling to his former club and attempting to find someone else for the task.

The duke was quick to accept the proffered chair, although his face had become awash with more questions than ever.

Nicholas didn't keep him waiting. He provided the pertinent information in as succinct a manner as possible, then unclenched his fist and handed over the page containing the details of Ambrose's challenge.

"It's complete horse shit," he muttered as Branscombe

perused the letter, his brows drawing together as he took in the chaotically written words. "The man is demented. I want this over and done with as quickly as possible so I no longer have to waste my attention on someone so abhorrent." *Especially because I do not* have *time to waste. Not when Phoebe is relying on me.*

"Indeed." Branscombe lowered the page to his lap, letting out a shallow sigh. "I'll do as you require. However, are you sure the conflict cannot be solved in some other fashion? If Sir Ambrose is as inebriated as you suspect, he may not even remember the challenge come morning."

Nicholas took great pains to prevent his voice from turning into a roar, although he couldn't keep the venom out of his speech. "He asked, in writing, for a duel, and that's what he'll get. I'll be damned if I let that liar and blackguard question my honor. Nor will I back away and give him any cause to feel like his false claims have merit. Not when they involve Phoe—my daughter's governess." *A woman who is so much more than that to me.*

"I understand." Branscombe shot him a knowing look not unlike the one he'd received from Theodora upon alluding to Phoebe's plight. Almost like he comprehended the words that Nicholas hadn't given voice. *Because perhaps people who were acquainted with falling in love knew how to spot the sentiment in others.*

The thought gave him a knock in the chest, temporarily robbing him of breath. It was both heavy and freeing, a flame that shot higher than the others blazing inside him.

Yet before it could proliferate, Branscombe rose to his feet, giving the note a final glance before stuffing it into his pocket. "I'll seek out this Mr. Philpot"—he named the second Sir Ambrose had appointed in his letter—"and see what arrangements need to be made."

"Thank you." The word still sounded clipped when

coming from Nicholas's tongue, although he was becoming better practiced with it. He drummed his fingers along the arm of his chair, trying to muster a moment of calm amidst the lingering haze of indignation. After all, for the second time that day, he'd gotten the assistance he required. Clare would find Phoebe's daughter. Branscombe would see that the duel took place without delay. In an abysmal situation, matters were going as well as they could. Nicholas just had one final thing to ask. "Is there any chance you would refrain from telling Amelia about this?"

Branscombe moved his head in a single horizontal line. "None."

Well, it was worth an attempt. Yet if Nicholas's meetings today with both his siblings-in-law had taught him anything, it was that love made people loyal.

Again, a muscle in his chest gave an insistent tug, and he sank his fingers into the upholstery, waiting for the feeling to pass. He didn't have time to think on it now, nor would he waste valuable seconds arguing that a man as clearly besotted as the duke should keep secrets from his wife. Nicholas could only hope this would all be over with before the dowager caught wind of it.

"Very well." For an instant, he let his head rest against the chairback before stiffening his shoulders once more and shooting a pointed look toward the doorway. "Don't let me delay you any longer, then."

"I'll return as soon as I have news." Branscombe took a final moment to peer at him, his dark eyes glinting with concern and his mouth set in a compressed line. Yet whatever his sentiments, he left without another word, his boots echoing rapidly down the corridor and his voice mingling with Flynt's as he arrived in the entrance hall.

At that, Nicholas let his posture slump again, and this time, he made no effort to correct it. He took a long breath, eyeing the empty crystal decanter on the end table next to him. Surely, the out-of-sorts Flynt wouldn't find it too great an inconvenience to fill it.

Then again, while Nicholas's throat had gone dry, he found he had little thirst for brandy. Yes, the drink was warming. Numbing. Except suddenly, he didn't want whatever swirled within him to be muted.

The flame that had burst to life in his ribcage—the one ignited by thoughts of love and loyalty—had never quite died out, unable to be subdued even by his simmering ire. That was the thing about it, though: it didn't bring with it the tight, agonizing burn of indignation. Not that he held any illusions it wasn't dangerous. Be that as it may, the sensation also felt ... right.

He stared into the fireplace, heat spiraling through him despite how the grate remained empty and dark. When this duel business was over, he was going to have a great many feelings to sort.

26

I shan't be gone long. A day. Two at most.

Phoebe tried her hardest to force the marquess's reassurances to remain in mind; if she didn't, she may well go mad. However, a third afternoon had now arrived with no sign of him, and the fragile scraps of equanimity she'd summoned were rapidly beginning to disintegrate.

She paced along the drive that conveyed travelers to and from Beaumont Manor's front facade, her hands twisting in her skirts. Up until this point, she'd made the wait tolerable by keeping herself occupied, pouring everything she had into distracting Emily from the week's upsets, including her newly absent papa. After several days, though, of as many walks, teas, picnics, and lessons as Phoebe thought prudent, Emily had gone to her bed after today's luncheon, whereupon she'd promptly fallen asleep, and Phoebe didn't have the heart to disturb her. For, try as she might to pretend nothing was amiss for Emily's sake, she suspected the girl knew as well as she the exhaustion caused by acting like all was well when it truly wasn't.

Phoebe increased the speed of her footfalls, her slippers

crunching against the same gravel she'd trod upon near a dozen times now on the endless trek between the front steps and the gate. Striding up and down, shooting frequent glances to the empty road beyond the iron bars, was an exercise in futility. Nonetheless, she couldn't seem to stay still, every nerve ending remaining on high alert.

Perhaps that's why her ears pricked at the faintest rumble. Why her eyes immediately fell upon the flash that materialized in the distance. For a moment, her heart soared, daring to drum up hope. But just as quickly, it vanished like a doused flame.

Yes, the rumble indeed came from hooves. However, as she squinted to bring the sight into focus, it became clear this was no rider on horseback but a pair of white horses pulling a gleaming black post chaise. Not one belonging to the marquess, either, for although the vehicle thundering closer to Beaumont Manor had some sort of emblem upon the door, the colorful blur lacked the vibrant red found in the Rockliffe crest.

Her body jerked in a clumsy motion, backing away from the gate as if the bars had grown spikes. *It isn't him.* Disappointment formed a pit in her stomach, creating an ache with each step she took back toward the house. Returning indoors, with nothing to do and being no closer to the answers she desperately sought, would prove nothing short of agonizing, yet she couldn't remain on the drive gawking at the unknown carriage.

She walked quickly with her gaze fixed on the gravel, a mild curiosity rising as to the identity of the person within. A peer, judging by the crest on the door, who'd come to call on the marquess, or perhaps a visitor for the dowager. Either way, the rapidly approaching conveyance had nothing to do with Phoebe, and she didn't look back, even when hooves beat and wheels rattled behind her.

Except suddenly, the postilion was calling to the horses, and the post chaise rolled to an abrupt halt right beside the section of path she traversed.

The wheels had barely stopped turning before the door flew open and a woman's tense, wide-eyed face peered out at her. "Miss Phoebe Windham?"

Phoebe blinked, a fresh spur of apprehension churning within her knotted stomach. "Yes?" Something about the woman, with her pale eyes and cropped red-gold hair, rang familiar, although no memories sprang to mind of a meeting between them.

Nonetheless, the woman seemed to know her, and in an instant, she'd leaped to the ground, not bothering to wait for the accompanying footman's assistance. "Oh, thank heavens, it *is* you." She rushed to Phoebe's side, her voice breathless, as if she'd been running rather than sitting in a carriage. "Allow me to introduce myself. I'm Amelia Prescott. Well, Amelia Astley as of late. That is, I'm Nicholas's sister."

Yes, it all made sense now. Had Phoebe's mind not reeled so violently, she likely would have recognized the woman at once from her girlhood portrait that hung in the gallery. "Your Grace." Phoebe had the presence of mind to curtsey—remembering Mrs. Connelly's mention of the former Lady Amelia recently marrying a duke—although her limbs felt stiff and slow to function.

"No, please, none of that. It's simply Amelia." The duchess spoke rapidly, breathlessly, and although her words were kind, the tension didn't leave the corners of her mouth. "I need to speak to you about Nicholas. Urgently." She cast a hesitant glance toward the house, and despite the front steps remaining a good distance away, she shielded the edge of her lips with her hand and lowered her voice. "Do you know if my mother is at home? And where is Emily?"

Phoebe's heart began rapidly thumping, and she had to

swallow back tautness before she could manage speech. "I couldn't say about the dowager marchioness, for she's recently moved to the dower house. As for Lady Emily, she's in her bedchamber resting."

"Oh. Oh, good." The duchess—Amelia—paused a moment, conjuring a tight smile, but it was impossible to miss the apprehension behind it. "Would you like to go to the drawing room? To sit, or perhaps call for tea if you first require sustenance ..."

Phoebe shook her head, uncertain her legs could even carry her that far. "I'd far prefer you just told me now."

"Very well." Amelia squared her slender shoulders, but not quickly enough that Phoebe missed the small shudder she gave. "I won't mince words. Nicholas has been challenged to a duel."

The statement made Phoebe's stomach do a strange flip, although the echo of it was hazy, as if she couldn't quite be sure the words were real.

"He asked my husband to stand as his second," Amelia rushed to continue, "and while Jonathan made every attempt to negotiate a more peaceful resolution to the conflict, they could settle on nothing but pistols. In case you haven't noticed, my brother is aggravatingly stubborn, and Sir Ambrose remains insistent on how grievously he's been wronged."

A sharp pang sliced through Phoebe's abdomen and stole the breath from her lungs. The idea of a duel was horrifying, sickening, and the name that had just crossed Amelia's lips made Phoebe's throat fill with bile, even as her mind fought against it. Insisting she'd misheard, that there had to be some mistake. "Did you say—"

"Sir Ambrose Windham. Yes." Amelia's brow crumpled, the blue of her irises like shards of ice. "He claims that Nicholas has compromised his betrothed. Whom, I believe you're aware, he says is you."

"He's a liar!" Phoebe burst out, a surge of incensed heat rushing to her face. "I was never his betrothed, never gave him even the slightest bit of encouragement—"

"I don't doubt you, Miss Windham. The reason I've come isn't to question your integrity." Amelia took a step closer, her fingers curling into fists at her sides. "It's because I need you to prevent this duel from happening."

Phoebe struggled to take a breath, her thoughts racing at too dizzying a pace to keep up with. Why did Ambrose make such an accusation? How could he have known of her intimacy with the marquess? Why did he think he had any claim to her when she'd refused him countless times?

Yet above the relentless questions, one thought stood out, blaring at her louder than any of the rest: *this is all your fault.*

"Please." Amelia's chin quivered, and there was a crack in the word. "My brother just returned home. I cannot lose him again. Nor can Emily. *Especially* not Emily."

"No. She cannot." Phoebe's voice came out as a rasp, for her throat was raw, her chest throbbing from the mere suggestion of something too terrible to contemplate.

Amelia pressed her lips together a moment, although it didn't stop them from trembling. "I went to Rockliffe House and tried to reason with him," she said, barely above a whisper, "but my efforts proved ineffective. If *you* were to speak with him, though ..."

Her voice faded to nothing, and in the silence, a jolt of understanding arose, making Phoebe's heart lurch. The marquess's sister believed that *she*—the friendless, scandalous governess—held influence with him. Her mind raced, taking her back to every touch, every heated word, every deep-rooted secret she and Nicholas had shared. She wanted it to be true. Wanted to be a helpmeet, someone he esteemed, someone he could trust. Yet did he really feel that way? Especially now, after the calamity she'd brought upon him.

"Please," Amelia repeated, and although her speech remained quiet, a torrent of force appeared behind the word. "Nicholas allows few people to get close to him, and it's very seldom, if ever, that I've heard him voice what he's feeling. However, in deciphering what *isn't* being said, I've reason to believe he cares about you, so deeply—"

"I'll speak to him and do everything in my power to stop this. Of course I will." A fist closed around Phoebe's heart, and she pressed at the corners of her eyes, refusing to let the burn behind them turn into tears. Later, she could spend all the hours she liked pondering Nicholas's sentiments toward her. Now, she hadn't a second to waste. If there was even the slightest chance he would listen, she had to see him right away. She had to because ... because ... "I cannot bear losing him, either," she choked out.

Amelia released an audible breath, the tension in her tall frame loosening. However, no sooner did her posture slacken than she drew herself up again, fixing Phoebe with a determined gaze. "You'll need to hurry. The duel is to take place at dawn tomorrow."

Dawn. Tomorrow. The revelation hit like a blow, making the horrifying situation so much more real. That was mere hours away. How was she to get to London in time, to find him, to convince him ...

"You can take the Rockliffe coach, of course," Amelia said as if reading the direction of Phoebe's thoughts and anxieties. "Let's go inside so I can ask that it be made ready immediately. If you hurry, you'll arrive in London by nightfall. I'll stay here with Emily, so you needn't worry in that regard. To the extent such a thing is possible, I'll also attempt to handle my mother."

Phoebe managed to nod, although her head continued

reeling at an even faster pace than her thundering heart. There was so much that needed doing and so little time, and she couldn't fail. Not when Nicholas's life was at stake.

And so, without another thought beyond that, she followed Amelia's clipped gesture and jumped after her into the ducal post chaise.

Less than an hour later, Phoebe sat in the Rockliffe traveling coach, on the road to London with every bit of speed the horses could muster. The journey would be relatively short—four hours or perhaps less, Amelia had assured her—yet each revolution of the wheels seemed to take an eternity, each second bringing her closer to tomorrow's dawn.

She peered through the window without taking in anything of the passing scenery, her foot tapping briskly against the carpeted floor. If nothing else, she could use these moments to focus on what she should say when she and Nicholas reunited. What combination of words would convince him not to go through with the duel.

He had to understand: Sir Ambrose Windham was a drunkard and a miscreant, and if they could both see that as plain as day, other members of the ton must realize it, too. If Ambrose went about slandering the marquess or disparaging him for not accepting the asinine challenge, would anyone even pay him any heed? Surely, the off chance that a gentleman or two might gossip wasn't reason enough for Nicholas to risk his *life*.

By the time the countryside faded away and they entered the crowded streets of London, just as the sun was sinking low in the sky, she had at least a semblance of a speech planned—although it may be difficult to deliver it without tumbling into the marquess's arms and not letting go.

However, when at last the carriage stopped in front of an elegant Mayfair town house, allowing Phoebe to burst from its confines and pound upon the front door, the butler who admitted her delivered the worst news. "Lord Rockliffe is not at home."

She stood motionless at the edge of the entrance hall, her stomach sinking to her boots. "Where is he? When did he leave? When will he return?"

The austere-looking butler—Flynt, he'd supplied during their brief introduction—furrowed his brows in a way that made him appear especially somber. "I'm afraid I don't know. He was in the study with his secretary for much of the afternoon but left about a half hour ago, saying only that he wanted no dinner prepared tonight."

Phoebe pressed her lips together, stifling a curse. Those countless minutes in the carriage had indeed taken too long, and she and Nicholas had just missed each other. *Blast.* What was she to do now: go out and search the maze of unfamiliar London streets and hope she happened upon him? But what if, in the near impossible pursuit, he returned home and their paths failed to cross once again?

"May I come in and wait?" She made the decision in a heartbeat, aggravatingly uncertain as to whether it would prove the right one.

Flynt's brows flickered again, just a shade, although he wordlessly turned, leading her down a corridor and into a drawing room near the back of the house. Only one of the lamps was lit, but it was enough to show that, just as at Beaumont Manor, every piece of furniture, every decoration and accessory, was immaculate. However, once Phoebe's gaze fell upon the gilded escritoire near the window, she could notice little else.

"Is there anything I can bring you, miss?" Flynt remained hovering in the doorway, his mouth a tight line.

"No, thank you." She tapped her fingers against her skirts, already envisioning the words that would flow from her quill. "However, if someone could deliver a note for me in a few minutes, I would be much obliged."

She waited just long enough to detect his nod of acknowledgment, then flew to the escritoire, her hands shaking as she tore open her reticule and removed the papers she'd stuffed within. Fortunately, the one she needed—on which Amelia had written an address for her husband and Nicholas's second, the Duke of Branscombe—appeared on top, and she penned a hasty note imploring his help in locating the marquess.

Once Flynt came to collect it, placing the note in a footman's hands for immediate delivery, she dared to summon the faintest strand of optimism. Yet the more time that stretched on, leaving her alone to pace the silent drawing room, the harder it became to hold onto it.

Sometime later, after the hands of the mantelpiece clock had inched forward too many times to count, Flynt returned with a letter in hand, his sudden appearance nearly causing Phoebe to jump out of her skin. However, after tearing open the page, marked by the Duke of Branscombe's seal, she ascertained nothing beyond that the duke was unaware of Lord Rockliffe's whereabouts but would begin searching the gentlemen's clubs right away.

Which was a start, Phoebe supposed, although so far away from the news she yearned to hear.

She resumed her turn about the room, her eyes returning to the ticking clock, to the windows that showcased the dusky back garden. The sun had dipped below the horizon and would reappear all too soon. She *had* to see Nicholas before then. And he *would* return home and speak with her. Wouldn't he?

Sometime after the clock struck eleven, Flynt returned once more, although his hands were woefully devoid of any letters. "Miss Windham?" His weathered features remained stern, although beneath the rigidity, there was also something in the way he looked at her that suggested gentleness. Concern. "If you'd like to continue waiting for Lord Rockliffe's return, may I offer you a bedchamber for the night? Or perhaps a tea tray?"

"No, thank you," she said stiffly, wishing she could summon even the tiniest flicker of pleasantness upon her face but certain she looked despondent. As much as she appreciated the offer, the idea of sleep or food was unthinkable. "I'll remain here in the drawing room, if you don't mind."

Flynt pursed his lips, but ultimately, he left without another word, leaving her alone to watch the clock once more.

When midnight came, she returned to the escritoire, her heartbeat a rapid thud in her ears. Another note had traveled with her to London. A piece of paper she'd pulled from her reticule with the others and tossed onto the desktop, scarcely wanting to look at it for the way it made her stomach roil. Be that as it may, too many hours had passed, and simply waiting for Nicholas was no longer an option.

She forced her eyes to the page, to the familiar messy scrawl that filled her with loathing. Amelia had given her Ambrose's letter—the one in which he'd issued the detestable challenge. The one containing the name and address of his second, in case she had need of communicating with Sir Ambrose. Which, it turned out, she did.

She retrieved her reticule once more, withdrawing the final item Amelia had given her for the journey: one hundred pounds in banknotes should she require funds.

Even combined with the fifty pounds she was to receive for her salary, it wasn't a life-altering sum for a baronet who owned productive lands. But perhaps there was a chance that profits at Birchby had declined under Ambrose's management —or mismanagement, more like—or that his dissolute lifestyle would leave him eager for more coin. Enough so that he would accept a bribe.

She took up a quill and a blank piece of paper, copying down the name of the second denoted in Ambrose's letter and following it with a few hasty lines.

Before she abruptly threw down the quill and crumpled the paper in her fist, tossing it to the side.

Her plan wouldn't work. Ambrose wasn't after money. He wanted to feel like he'd won. And to do that, he needed *her*.

She clenched her teeth, fighting back the urge to retch. All these years, she'd turned him down, preferring displacement, poverty, ruination, *anything* above living as Sir Ambrose Windham's wife. Yet what if, by accepting his proposal, she could put an end to all this? Nicholas wouldn't have to fight the duel. Emily wouldn't run the risk of losing her father. If she could give them nothing else, she owed them that much.

Only ... what of Phoebe's daughter, whom Ambrose had concealed from her for seven long years? At this very moment, someone was out searching for her, could be so close to succeeding. And then what? Would Ambrose allow Phoebe, as his wife, to have anything to do with the child?

No. She sank to the dainty seat beside the escritoire, her legs unable to hold her any longer. No, she'd be a fool to imagine for one moment that she'd ever hear tell of her daughter again.

The possibility, still so new, of a reunion with the girl would be wrenched away from her as quickly as it had arisen. How was she to bear that? How was she to carry on when everyone who meant anything to her was gone and her heart had been torn into slivers?

She glowered at the letter that had once passed through Ambrose's hands, bitterness wrapping around her chest like a tightening band. *Damn* the man. Damn him for inheriting her father's title, for making her a stranger in her childhood home, for trying to spite her father's memory by marrying her. Damn him for making her feel worthless and immoral when *he* was the one who drank to excess, who kept secrets, who fabricated insults and defended his nonexistent honor by insisting on something illegal—

Her hand froze in midair. She'd taken the abhorrent sheet of paper into her fist, ready to crush it, rip it to shreds, and stomp on the tattered remains as she cried out every modicum of her outrage and sorrow. Except suddenly, rather than do any of those things, she stared at it. Her eyes darted over each despicable word all the way to the signature at the bottom, her mind whirling, sharpening, as if through the dark haze, a spark had ignited tinder.

She jumped to her feet, rushing out of the drawing room and into the lowly lit corridor. "Flynt?" She was too frantic to call his name with any sort of delicacy.

Fortunately, the butler appeared from the shadows at once, upright and attentive.

"I require the carriage immediately for a matter pertaining to Lord Rockliffe," she said, hardly able to utter the words fast enough. "The Duchess of Branscombe said I could have it at my disposal."

Flynt inclined his head, his dark gaze falling to the paper clasped between her shaking fingers. "As you wish, Miss Windham. Although if you're looking to send another letter, are you certain I cannot have a footman deliver it for you?"

"No." She shook her head, her feet already shuffling, desperate to travel into the entrance hall, out to the street, into the carriage. "Thank you, but I need to do this myself."

He hesitated, and she could fully anticipate the protests hovering on his lips. It was dark, late, not a suitable time for an unaccompanied young woman to be out on the streets of London. Were she to reveal her intended destination, his objections would only increase tenfold, and she knew he wasn't wrong. Yet none of that mattered. Nothing signified beyond that she had somewhere to go and not a moment to lose.

Did her desperation and urgency show upon her face? Or did Flynt also suspect the danger posed to the marquess? Whatever the case, he relented with a barely perceptible sigh. "A minute, then. I'll ask for the carriage to be hitched and brought around at once."

Thank the stars. She waited just until Flynt had disappeared down the corridor before slumping against the wall, fighting to catch her breath. This was it. The only strand of hope she had left, and she couldn't fail.

She tugged open her reticule, carefully inserting the letter she'd planned to tear to pieces but now guarded like a priceless gem. With the page tucked away, she pushed herself up again, running to the entrance hall so she'd hear the horses the moment they approached the front steps.

The street beyond the window remained shadowed by complete blackness—for now. Yet dawn wouldn't stay away forever.

She only prayed she wouldn't be too late.

27

The day would be clear, Nicholas observed dully upon arriving at Primrose Hill just as faint streaks of light appeared on the horizon. If the weather were as fine back in Kent, perhaps Emily would spend her day by the lake as Phoebe looked on.

He jumped down from Merlin's back, ignoring the uncomfortable tug in his chest that the thought conjured. After a sleepless night during which he'd pondered far more than was good for him, he needed to make himself emotionless. Focused. Or his aim focused, in any case.

The field was empty, quiet, the only noise coming from birdsong in the surrounding trees. Which was perhaps why the faraway sound of hooves pounding against gravel instantly caught his attention. He turned toward the road and waited, motionless, as the galloping horse drew nearer and nearer, until all of a sudden, the Duke of Branscombe burst through the trees, his face flushed and severe in the dim light.

Branscombe caught sight of him at once, and he rushed to the center of the field, vaulting from his horse and rushing to Nicholas's side. "Jesus, Rockliffe." He bent forward, pressing his palms to his knees as he drew in a few rapid, gasping breaths. "W-where were you all night?"

Nicholas eyed him in silence, watching the duke's chest heave up and down. There was really no succinct way to answer that question. After spending much of the day discussing arrangements with both his secretary and solicitor —because only a simpleton would go into a duel without having his affairs in order, even if he had no intention of being bested by a raging sot—he'd gone to his club. After all, what did a gentleman do on the eve of such an occasion other than eating, drinking, and making merry to excess?

Except nothing about that arrangement had felt right. Instead, Nicholas had departed after the first splash of brandy hit his tongue, thinking to pass a mindless hour or two at a gaming hell, and when that proved unappealing, to return home for the limited time before dawn. Yet he'd found he couldn't do that, either. Couldn't stomach the thought of sitting alone in the study where earlier that day, he'd penned a letter to his daughter—just in case—and arranged for Miss Phoebe Windham to receive both her year's salary and the funds to keep Mr. Adolphus Clare, or another investigator, in her employ as long as required.

With nowhere else to go, he'd wandered the streets and deserted parks—his head tangling with things he couldn't quite decipher—until the time came to collect Merlin from the mews by White's and ride north to Primrose Hill.

The duke, of course, didn't need to know all that. And so, Nicholas stiffened his spine, keeping his features shuttered. "I was ... out," he supplied unhelpfully.

Branscombe let out a sound that was part guffaw, part huff. "Someone arrived at Rockliffe House with a pressing need to speak with you." His eyes narrowed, focusing on Nicholas with an intensity that was bloody unnerving. "A Miss Phoebe Windham."

Nicholas's ears pricked, every inch of him going on high alert. "*What* did you say?"

"She sent me a note last night, imploring me to help find you, and I assure you, I made every effort. However, after searching with no success, I went to Rockliffe House myself, only to discover that you had never come home, and Miss Windham had left in the middle of the night without revealing her destination."

"*What?*" Nicholas all but snarled. This wasn't right. Phoebe couldn't be here, couldn't be involved in this. And if she was no longer at Rockliffe House, then where had she gone? London under the cloak of darkness was no place for her to travel alone, damn it, and if she'd dared put herself in harm's way ...

A potent mixture of fire and ice filled his veins, and his head pounded with a splitting, frantic beat. Except it wasn't just his head. Additional hooves thundered into the grass, and a horse whinnied as it came to a halt, followed by the heavy thud of boots hitting the ground.

"Ah. Rockliffe, I presume."

He didn't need to turn around to realize to whom the lilting, spiteful voice belonged. For it to fill him to the brim with venom.

He pivoted sharply, his jaw rigid enough to splinter. A reddened, thickset face peered back at him, the glassy eyes glinting with malice. Nicholas didn't want the revolting man's name defiling his tongue in return, and so, he did nothing but move his chin a fraction of an inch, using every bit of restraint he possessed not to bound forward and plant a fist in Ambrose's throat.

At the edge of the trees, a spindly, whey-faced man—Sir Ambrose's second, Philpot, apparently—beckoned to Branscombe, and the duke took the horses and hurried over to him, the two entering into a tersely murmured conversation.

Allowing Ambrose the unimpeded space to take a step closer, filling Nicholas's nose with the stench of sweat and sour ale. "I trust I need no introduction." His tongue moved thickly, and his body swayed as he regained his footing. God, he really was drunk as a swine, even at this hour of the day. "In any case, you know my intended well enough. *Too* well."

Nicholas snapped his teeth together, leaning closer into the repugnant miasma surrounding Ambrose Windham, hovering near his detestably smug face. "You're fortunate I don't shoot you between the ribs here and now," he hissed, deathly quiet, "and return to Mayfair with your blood smearing my boots."

Ambrose bristled, pointing his chin in the air as if to compensate for the fact that Nicholas held the advantage in height. "That's not very gent—gentle-man-ly of you," he slurred. "Though I'm not sh-urprised. A *gentleman* wouldn't make free with another man's betrothed, even if the chit is a trollop."

A growl tore from Nicholas's throat, his vision filling with bright, angry streaks. Had his pistol not still been in Branscombe's keeping, he would have made good on his threat and been done with it, consequences be damned. Why could the man not get it through his thick skull: Phoebe wasn't his fucking betrothed! Nicholas would *not* stand by and hear her degraded. Least of all by a ridiculous, rambling toss pot.

Which begged a question. "What in *hell*," he bit out, "makes you think yourself justified in casting about these accusations?"

"Because they're true!" Ambrose's voice loudened, his puffy cheeks becoming mottled. "I know all about what happened at your estate with your so-called gover-nesh. Letitia Burville told me everything."

The name cracked through Nicholas's head like thunder, rendering him momentarily speechless.

"That's right," Ambrose sneered, a burst of spittle landing on his chin. "You thought you could keep it a secret. Well, imagine my surprise when on my way home from Kent, I encountered a lady known to me who was so aggrieved, so *aghast*, by what she'd seen you and your little harlot doing—"

"Enough." Nicholas stormed past him and toward the trees. He'd be damned if he spent another second looking at that smug, perspiring face. Nor was this the moment to begin cursing the consequences of having Lady Burville as a house guest. He had no more patience for waiting. No more patience for contemplating. Dawn was breaking, and this needed to end. *Now.*

He made a harsh, snarling sound to draw Branscombe's attention. "I require my pistol."

The duke ceased his conversation instantly, looking up in mild alarm. Nicholas half-expected for Ambrose's string of jeers to continue behind him, making him all the more eager to get his finger on the trigger. Yet the only words that came were a surprisingly steady, "As do I."

Good. Despite Branscombe's obvious reluctance, he was efficient in producing the box containing the pair of flintlocks, and Nicholas rushed to take his, the smooth wood and metal a welcome weight in his hand.

"Rockliffe." When Ambrose, accompanied by Philpot, staggered to the middle of the field with his pistol, Branscombe murmured his name, the syllables containing an unmistakable note of warning.

Nicholas couldn't blame the man for his hesitancy, not after the way Amelia had shown up at Rockliffe House denouncing everything about the duel and her brother's participation in it. He didn't wish to create trouble for his newlywed sister and her husband. Yet surely, Branscombe must see: a man too inebriated to walk straight was even less likely to have good aim.

He cleared his throat, trying for a bit of levity. "When this is over, Branscombe, remind me that I owe you and Amelia a generous wedding gift."

"The gift is for you to stay alive," Branscombe muttered under his breath, snapping the box closed and setting his sights on the field beyond.

That settled it, then. Nicholas wasted no time in taking his position in the grass, careful not to let the abhorrent sight of Sir Ambrose cloud his vision as they lined up back to back. The next time Nicholas deigned to look at him, he would have his finger upon the trigger.

"Fifteen paces," Philpot announced, repeating the instructions that Branscombe had already discussed with Nicholas more than once, "after which I'll give the call to fire."

The seconds moved to the side, and Branscombe gave him a subtle nod, his face like stone.

It was time.

One, two—

Would Phoebe mind *very* much if he pointed his pistol more accurately than he'd intended? If not to the center of Ambrose's chest as he so desired, then mayhap to a leg or shoulder. If the bastard was indeed withholding information, perhaps the fever that was likely to follow the bullet wound would render him delirious enough to reveal it.

Nine, ten—

"Nicholas!"

His name soared through the air from far away, a high, panicked shriek.

The measured rhythm of his footfalls stuttered, his boot jerking against the grass. *Phoebe.* The voice couldn't be hers, perhaps wasn't even real—

"Stop!"

The voice sounded again, nearer, louder. *Hers.* His gaze darted toward the trees, his eyes searching wildly until they detected a flicker of motion. A dark, swishing skirt. A flash of pale skin. A strand of flowing hair. Then, a horrified face—*her* face—burst through the leaves, lips parting. "St—"

A sharp crack obliterated her scream.

And then, there was nothing but silence. Darkness.

I was too slow. Too slow. Too slow.

The thought haunted Phoebe, pounding through her head relentlessly during every long hour she spent hovering by Nicholas's bedside. Silently beseeching him to wake up.

She laced her fingers with his and squeezed, his skin cool beneath her touch, his large hand limp atop the counterpane. The same way it had been for the past four days, ever since the bullet had grazed him and he'd toppled, striking his head against a rock nestled in the grass.

She shuddered, the horrific scene replaying in her mind as clear as the morning it happened. The blast of gunfire ringing in her ears every bit as loudly. If only she'd arrived before Nicholas and Ambrose turned away from each other and began marching to their positions. Or perhaps before they each took a pistol in hand. In truth, she didn't know the exact moment when fate could have been reversed. Only that her frantic arrival at Primrose Hill, with a Bow Street runner in tow, had proved too late.

Yes, her scream had made them both falter. Had caused

Ambrose to clumsily pivot and cast a disoriented glance to where she bounded through the trees. For a fraction of a second, she'd thought there was a chance, that with the help of the runner—who possessed written proof of Sir Ambrose Windham's illegal intention to duel—the scene could end without bloodshed.

But she'd been wrong. For when she'd let out another desperate scream, Ambrose had fired.

She leaned closer to the bed, resting her cheek against Nicholas's fingertips. A thousand lifetimes wouldn't be enough to negate her regret over what happened.

Had the marquess's path in the field been even marginally different, one might almost label him as lucky. The bullet wound in his shoulder had been stitched and was healing nicely. No sign of inflammation or fever. In the end, it was likely to be naught but another scar, just like the ones upon his hands.

If only the bullet hadn't knocked him off his feet. If only that small slab of stone hadn't been buried in the grass where he'd fallen ...

"Miss Windham?"

She raised her head abruptly, Flynt's voice pulling her out of the spiral of despair before it could consume her. Over the past days, she and the butler had come to know each other well. Not so much by exchanging words but by simply being in each other's presence in the painfully still house. A house where Phoebe, in the absence of any Prescotts—for Amelia, while clearly frantic, had remained in Kent with her mother and Emily in hopes she could conceal the accident until there was better news to report—had become a makeshift mistress.

The physician visited daily, of course, as did the Duke of Branscombe. Servants entered the room occasionally to see to the marquess's care. However, for all the other agonizing, uncertain minutes of the day, Phoebe kept vigil alone. After making it clear that she didn't *want* to leave Lord Rockliffe's bedside—for she needed to be there to drip water across his lips, to bathe his brow when the room grew warm, to examine every flutter of his eyelids and slight twitch of his limbs that gave her hope—she suspected it was Flynt who'd begun ordering trays to be sent up to her. In fact, he sometimes even delivered them himself.

At the moment, though, he was empty-handed, his creased face unreadable. "There's someone here who wishes to speak with you."

With *her*? Something in her stomach quivered and then seized. "Do you know the caller's name?"

"Yes. Mr. Adolphus Clare." Flynt's brows lifted a shade, betraying the faintest note of curiosity. "Lord Rockliffe's former man of business. He said that the marquess had recently brought him back into his employ, and that in Lord Rockliffe's absence, he urgently needed to see you."

The morning Nicholas left for London, he mentioned something about his man of business ...

Her gaze shot from Flynt back to Nicholas, her grip on his hand tightening. Was this the news she'd so desperately been waiting for—the other matter that occupied her thoughts relentlessly?

From the doorway, Flynt cleared his throat. "I've taken the liberty of sending Mr. Clare to the drawing room. Should you wish to go down, I'll ensure that Lord Rockliffe has someone to sit with him."

She took a quick breath, the quiver within her escalating into a whirlwind. She didn't want to leave Nicholas, not even for a minute. Yet if the purpose of this visit was truly for what she suspected ...

"I'll return soon," she whispered, gently releasing her grip on his fingers and straightening the counterpane atop him.

Were he awake, she had every confidence he would encourage her. That he would stay by her side and support her no matter what she learned.

She used that knowledge to draw strength as she murmured a few words of thanks to Flynt and exited the bedchamber, alone, with a final glance back.

After all the hours of sitting, her legs felt stiff and ungainly, her footsteps too loud as she headed toward the staircase. Yet by the time she reached the bottom of the stairs and approached the drawing room, the sound of her slippers connecting with floorboards was nothing compared to the rapid heartbeat thundering in her ears.

She paused outside the door, using a tremulous hand to smooth her bedraggled hair and creased skirts. Forced herself to inhale slowly.

And then, she burst into the room, where a middle-aged gentleman was perched in an armchair near the back window, his head turned to the garden beyond. Even from this angle, she could see that his thinning hair was windblown, his apparel rumpled and dust-stained. As if he'd just come in from a long journey.

She let out the breath she'd been holding, willing her voice not to shake. "Mr. Clare?"

He whirled around and pushed to his feet, surveying her from beneath a pair of sharp graying brows. "Miss Windham." He gestured to the chair beside him, his face devoid of any warmth—although there was no malice in it, either. Rather, he looked like he took the *business* part of his title seriously and wished to waste no time. "Do you know why I'm here?"

She rushed forward to take the seat, although she had little hope of sitting still. She didn't want to skirt around the subject, either, but with a matter such as this, there was no easy way to begin. "I ..."

"Lord Rockliffe asked me to travel to Suffolk and investigate the whereabouts of a child born to you seven years prior," Mr. Clare supplied without preamble.

Hearing the truth spoken aloud so bluntly, after all the years it had been concealed, was enough to steal the air from her lungs. But at the same time, there was comfort in not having to prevaricate any longer.

She managed a small motion with her chin. "Yes."

He nodded in return, his green-gray eyes fixing on her with resolve. "The parish register in Redgrave, ten miles west from where you made your home, has record of a baptism that took place on the second of June, 1799. Mother, Phoebe Cole, deceased. Father, unknown."

She'd promised herself she would remain stoic until Mr. Clare revealed every part of the story, but the information came at her so fast that she couldn't stop the gasp before it escaped her lips. *Phoebe Cole*—the false name Eugenia had attached to her in Suffolk. The name she'd used until, at the earliest possible moment, Eugenia had insisted they flee, pretending their months in the lonesome cottage had never happened. Leaving behind nothing of themselves but a fabrication.

"The infant was called Mary Anne," he continued in his matter-of-fact way. "Sent to live with a childless couple, as I discerned in my travels. A Henry and Judith Miller."

Mary Anne. Her daughter's name was Mary Anne. Had the Millers chosen it for her? Had they cared for her since that day? Did they love her like their own? Phoebe had no greater wish.

Well ... no greater wish than that *she'd* been the one allowed those privileges. That the heart-wrenching lie hadn't been told, that the separation had never happened.

She clung to the edge of the armchair, fighting against the burning sensation in her eyes and throat. The past couldn't be changed. All she could do was find a way to endure it and look to the future. Which first meant she had to be very clear she understood.

She opened her mouth to let a few shaky words emerge. "So she's ... she's been with a family in Suffolk all this time?"

He shifted in his chair, giving his head a quick shake. "No, not any longer. Three winters ago, the Miller family contracted fever."

Suddenly, the room whirled before her, and she clamped her eyes shut as a searing ache twisted her heart. *No.* That couldn't be where the story ended. Not after they'd come this far, after she'd dared to summon hope. How was she to accept having it so soundly dashed? Having her heart shatter all over again.

"Forgive me, Miss Windham. Perhaps I've led you to misunderstand." For the first time, Mr. Clare spoke with a note of hesitancy, and when she wrenched open her eyes, he was running a hand over his travel-weary brow. "Burial dates were recorded for Henry and Judith Miller. Not Mary Anne. After making some additional inquiries, I discovered that she was sent to a school for young ladies in Bury St Edmunds."

A ... a school? Which meant ... she'd survived?

She'd survived.

Phoebe stared, openmouthed, unsure whether she wanted to yell at the man or wrap him in an embrace. The tight knots in her chest began unraveling, making her body looser, lighter, and she was aware that her limbs were quaking. However, she wouldn't get ahead of herself this time. Wouldn't assume a single thing until confirmation came from Adolphus Clare's lips.

She clasped her trembling hands in her lap, trying not to let hope flicker. "And does she remain there now?"

"Yes."

Yes. The best word on earth. Her palm flew to her mouth, and whether she was about to weep or laugh, she couldn't entirely say.

"A respectable and well-managed establishment, from what I could determine," he rushed to add, clearly not one to waste time in silence—especially if silence ran the risk of giving way to tears. "Her fees, it seems, are paid yearly by an anonymous benefactor. In my haste, I didn't stay to uncover further details. Should you wish for clarity regarding the person's identity, I can make another journey north. Although perhaps that's unnecessary?"

Eugenia. It had to be. Mr. Clare's mild expression suggested that he believed so, too.

Phoebe would never think warmly of the woman after her atrocious deceit, but if nothing else, Eugenia had at least seen that Mary Anne was provided for. That she hadn't been cast out into the world with nothing.

"You can think on it first, of course," he said. "For the time being, I've written down the pertinent information should you plan to travel there yourself." He reached into his coat pocket to retrieve a folded sheet of paper, and she nearly tripped over her feet in her haste to accept it from him.

She skimmed the page, quickly taking in the name of the school. Proof it was real. A place where she *did* intend to travel. Where, perhaps, horrible wrongs could be made right.

"Thank you." Her voice came out low and unsteady, and she didn't trust herself to add anything else. Indeed, how could mere words express the depth of her gratitude?

He put a hand up, sparing her the need to make an attempt. "Merely doing my duty." Then, he pushed himself from his chair and came to stand beside her, although his gaze had shifted toward the doorway. "If there's nothing else you require at present, I'll take my leave."

She had too many questions to count—had he seen Mary

Anne himself? Had she smiled? What was her hair color? Did she enjoy her lessons?—but she let them go, setting them aside for a day, very soon, when she hoped to call him back and plan the next steps. When, God willing, she would be free to travel with nothing else weighing heavy on her mind. For now, though, Mr. Clare looked in need of a washbasin and bed after his travels, and she wasn't in a position to linger, either.

They said a brief farewell, although as for the exact words they exchanged, she wasn't entirely cognizant. Her mind had already traveled back upstairs, and as soon as Mr. Clare stepped into the entrance hall to be escorted out by a footman, her feet followed, going to the staircase and taking the steps two at a time.

When she arrived back in the marquess's bedchamber, the person sitting in the bedside chair was none other than Flynt himself, although he rose when he spotted her, his ever-staid expression revealing that nothing had changed in her absence.

She thanked him quietly for keeping watch and turned down his offer of a tray, assuring him that she needed nothing and was quite well to sit with Lord Rockliffe for the rest of the afternoon. In truth, a large lump was rising in her throat, and she didn't know how much longer she could contain it. Didn't want an audience when it emerged.

Her knees shook beneath her skirts, but she held herself stiffly as he took his leave, waiting until his footfalls faded down the corridor and then vanished.

Leaving her alone with Nicholas once more, the bedside chair ready so she could resume her position. However, she didn't stop at the chair this time but went right to the edge of the bed, dropping onto the counterpane beside him.

"He found her," she murmured, reaching to connect their hands again, scarcely able to believe she was uttering the words aloud. That they were true.

"He found her," she repeated, cementing the fact within her heart. "He found her."

A droplet of water fell upon the counterpane. Then another. She pressed a fingertip to her cheek, only to find it wet. It seemed she was crying, tears running down her cheeks like tiny rivers.

With that, a wave crashed through her body, inundating her with every bottled emotion at once, and she collapsed upon his pillow, the lump in her throat bursting out as a sob.

She stretched out alongside him, allowing the fervent mixture of sorrow and joy, regret and relief, to course through her veins until her tears ran dry. Was there any chance he knew she was there? That he could hear her? She had no way of knowing. Nonetheless, there was something she needed to say to him.

"Thank you." She pressed down on his fingers, then raised her palm to rest over his beating heart. "*Thank you*. You arranged this for me. You gave me the most precious gift. I owe you a debt I can never repay."

She peered at him, envisioning the intensity of his blue eyes that was now masked behind closed lids. "And yet, I'm not finished asking favors of you."

She huddled closer to his motionless body, positioning her mouth so her breath caressed his ear. "I need you to wake up. To be well again. In fact, I must insist upon it. For if you do not ..."

She bit down on her lip, her ensuing exhale coming out ragged. *If you do not, my heart will never recover.*

Her mind flashed back to the day, all those summers ago, when she'd first spotted him galloping down the road. When, as a girl of eighteen, she'd become instantly captivated. The allure hadn't faded a full eight years later when, against all odds, she'd been thrown into his household as a governess. On the contrary, the passion had intensified, grown, and although she should have known better, she just couldn't bring herself to deny it. Instead, she'd given in to her desire, and he'd taken it beyond her wildest dreams. She cherished every kiss, every touch, every murmured, heated word they'd shared.

But that was only part of it. What she'd come to feel for him went so much deeper than surface-level attraction.

Because yes, he was grumbly and impatient and infuriatingly stubborn. Yet beneath it all, there was vulnerability. A deep-rooted hurt that he'd trusted her enough to share, that she understood, that had forged a connection between them too profound to be severed.

She loved him *for* those reasons, not in spite of them.

I love him.

The feeling twisted in her chest, providing an acute pang of clarity. She thought of sparkling lake water, illicit books, strawberry preserves, whispers in her ear. Envisioned a strong body pinning her to the wall, climbing the attic ladder, moving inside her, picking her up when grief made her fall.

And she knew, without a doubt. *I love him.*

"Please, Nicholas." She increased the pressure of her fingertips, his heartbeat a steady thrum beneath them. The rest of him still unmoving.

She'd suddenly been granted a chance at a future that had long seemed impossible: one involving her daughter. A chance for the missing piece of her—the hole in her heart—to mend. There could be no greater joy.

Except ... his absence, too, would leave a hole. A gaping, unfillable chasm.

She remained with her head on the pillow beside him, watching the sunrays that streaked through the window and illuminated the bronze in his hair. How many minutes passed, she didn't know, only that the light gradually retreated as the sun's angle shifted. Other than that, nothing in the room changed.

Eventually, footsteps echoed in the corridor once more, which came as no surprise. Flynt didn't like waiting too long between visits to the marquess's bedchamber in case either of them needed anything. However, something about the footfalls didn't sound like the butler's measured, heavy gait.

She pushed herself up on an elbow, tilting her head toward the doorway. These footsteps were lighter, hurried, and mixed with a distinctive sort of thumping. Too cacophonous to come from just one pair of shoes.

She slid from the bed, futilely smoothing the old gray skirt that she'd already wrinkled beyond repair. The physician and the duke had both paid their calls for the day. The housemaids would never dare run in such a fashion. Which could only mean—

An intricately carved walking stick crossed the threshold of the bedchamber, putting an end to her speculation. For bursting in alongside it was the unmistakable figure of the Dowager Marchioness of Rockliffe, her blue eyes flashing like an ice storm.

And the dowager wasn't alone. Behind her, a full head taller, came Amelia with her unmistakable cropped copper-gold hair, and behind the duchess came a flash of a smaller, familiar white skirt. *Emily.* Accompanied by Marigold, who slunk into the room with the brisk but noiseless strides of one with a purpose.

They were all here, crowding into the room, taking in the terrible truth that, until this moment, had only existed to them from afar: Nicholas was unconscious.

After a beat of silence, the dowager began speaking, her tone clipped and censorious, although there was no mistaking the apprehension behind it. However, Phoebe didn't hear the exact words. Her attention focused in on Emily, and she ran forward, wrapping the girl in a tight hug. She'd missed her terribly and worried for her beyond measure. Yet at the same time, she wished so much that Emily wasn't here. That she didn't have to see her father like this.

"I'm sorry." Amelia rushed over to Phoebe, bending close to her ear so she could speak in an indistinct murmur. "Mother found out, and there was no stopping her from coming. Emily overheard our argument, and there was no dissuading her, either. I didn't know what else to do. I was hoping we might arrive to find some improvement in Nicholas's condition."

Phoebe pressed her lips together, giving her head a slight shake. But as she did, Emily jerked within her arms, pointing wide-eyed toward the bed. "Look! Papa's trying to speak."

Phoebe whipped her head around, her gaze flashing back to Nicholas's sleeping form. But while Marigold had jumped onto the bed and was sniffing him with alacrity—*oh, he really wouldn't like that*—Nicholas himself remained stationary.

She took a moment to clear the tightness in her throat. It would no doubt be jarring for Emily to experience what had become Phoebe's new normal over the past few days. The way Nicholas stirred in bed, almost like he was going to open his eyes and be back to his old self, only for deep sleep to drag him under once more. How was she to find the right words to explain that to a twelve-year-old child? To ensure they came out as gently as possible.

"*Look*." Emily let out an exasperated huff, tugging on Phoebe's arm to drag her back to the bedside and gesturing emphatically toward her father.

Nicholas's hands twitched. Just a little at first, a motion that was barely there. But then, it happened again, his fingers stretching across the brocade counterpane. His feet shifting beneath it.

Phoebe had experienced enough false alarms that she should have known better than to anticipate, but even so, she froze, not daring to make even the slightest movement. Her eyes, though, traveled up his body, racing past his broad chest and stubbled throat to rest upon his face.

The breath she'd been holding shot out as a shuddering exhale. Her heart seized and then soared.

His mouth moved as if forming silent words, and his eyelids came open. And this time, they didn't close again.

29

Nicholas's eyelids had become impossibly heavy, and when he accomplished the feat of prying them open ... his vision had turned orange.

He took a moment to blink, trying to bring a hazy world back into focus. Yet that only served to make the orange in front of his face sharper and ... *furry*.

Oh, for the love of Christ. *That cat* was sitting atop his chest.

"Get off," he croaked, shifting his body against his mattress. For that's where he seemed to be: in his familiar bed at Rockliffe House, tucked beneath the counterpane.

Unfortunately for him, the weak motion—why in hell were his muscles so useless?—did nothing but make the cat reassert its position by sinking its claws deeper into the counterpane. A contented rumble began vibrating in the creature's throat, and he scowled, acutely aware of a dull ache in both his temple and shoulder.

Marigold kept purring, untroubled by any of it, and although the animal's intense yellow eyes drifted closed, he couldn't shake the feeling of being watched.

He blinked again, forcing his stiff neck up from his pillow. Only to find four faces staring down at him from the side of the bed. His mother. His sister. Emily. Phoebe.

He heard a low gasp—Amelia's, he thought. Detected the unmistakable thump of a cane.

And then, the room erupted into a chaotic flurry of noise and motion. Emily's white skirts fluttered as she made an abrupt movement backward. Phoebe turned and began whispering to her. Amelia and his mother were exclaiming something to one another, the dowager using her cane for emphasis. As meanwhile, the cat continued its gravelly purr, pressing its paws into the counterpane as if it were kneading bread dough.

In the end, the first sound to rise above the others was the dowager's voice, a steely timbre that hovered above his head. "You're awake, Rockliffe."

The obvious statement cheered him about as much as the mound of fur that refused to vacate his chest. "Of course I'm awake," he grumbled, his throat so dry that it felt filled with sand. "How would a person sleep amidst this kind of uproar?"

She let out a sharp breath, her cane pounding into the carpet. "It's been four *days* since you last opened your eyes. Do you have any idea of the alarm I felt? And for Amelia to try keeping the truth from me ..."

His mother continued with her diatribe, casting an incensed look at her apparently errant daughter, although Amelia ignored it, her gaze only on him. "Do you remember what happened?"

He dropped his head back to the pillow, closing his eyes as he tried to sort through the haze. He was in his bed at Rockliffe House, in the daylight; that much, he'd already established. However ... he hadn't climbed into bed to sleep the day away of his own volition, had he?

No, because ... because the last he remembered, he'd been

at Primrose Hill in the first light of dawn, preparing to fight a duel with Sir Ambrose Windham.

Except then ... Phoebe's voice had rung out. And a gunshot ...

He struggled upward, mustering enough power this time to displace the cat and get himself into a semi-sitting position. *Phoebe.* He craned his neck, desperate to catch her eye. The blasted duel was supposed to be but a hitch before he could rush back to her at Beaumont Manor and concentrate on the search for her child. He'd promised her; she was counting on him. Yet if he'd truly been lying here at his town house, insensate, for a full four days—

"It's all right." Suddenly, their eyes locked, and in the next instant, she was at his side, tipping a cup of water to his lips. The wetness acted as such a salve to his parched throat that, as anxious as he was to question her, he accepted it without protest. In turn, she brought her face close to his, gifting him with the brightest smile. Shooting him a knowing look that made her blue-gray-green eyes sparkle. "Everything is well."

Did that mean ... had Adolphus Clare returned with news? *Good* news? They had so much to discuss the minute they could be alone. But first ...

From behind Phoebe, the weight of another gaze fell upon him. Emily's. Her amber eyes were as astute as ever, staring at him like she could see below the surface. It was the sharp but unreadable look she always gave before turning as if he didn't exist, and he couldn't say what emotions it concealed.

"Emily." He managed her name, the water he'd swallowed helping him do so without rasping. Instead, it emerged almost like a question, and truthfully, he didn't know what to say next. His attempt to provide stability for her had failed miserably, and above all, he yearned to know if she was well. However, recent experience had taught him that he was always one wrong word or gesture away from receiving the cut direct, and he wasn't sure how he would bear lying in bed uselessly as she ran from him.

The moment stretched on as she stood, peering at him, her body unmoving besides a slight quiver in her chin.

Until all of a sudden, she flung herself onto the bed, throwing her arms about his chest in a firm embrace. "Papa," she exclaimed, burying her face in the counterpane beside him, the brocade covering muffling her next words. Not so much, though, that they didn't shoot straight to his heart. "I was so afraid for you."

He lifted a hand, chancing to lay it atop her back, and when she didn't shrug him away, he let it settle. "You needn't be any longer, Emmy. I'm well." His head hurt, and his counterpane was covered with more cat fur than he'd like, but those things aside, he truly meant it. In fact, having her close—a feeling he'd thought he might never know again—brought a type of contentment he hadn't experienced in a long time.

She burrowed against his side, her grip on him refusing to slacken.

"Mother?" Amelia's gentle voice drew his attention up from the sight that still felt somewhat illusory, and she flashed him a quick smile before turning to face the dowager. "I believe we should call for the physician now."

The dowager gave a brusque nod. "Yes, quite right. Go ask Flynt to see to it straightaway."

"I require your assistance." Amelia traipsed to the doorway, standing at the threshold of the room while fixing a pointed look upon their mother.

The dowager's silver brows shot up and then drew together, her mouth twisting into a frown. "For heaven's sake," she muttered. However, the complaint faded out at the end, and with a terse sigh, she started forward with her cane, giving in to Amelia's not-so-subtle efforts to grant him a moment alone with his daughter.

Phoebe stirred as well, her skirts—gray, for a change—sweeping along the floor as she began to turn. He stopped her, though, with a glance at the bedside chair. Emily trusted her, seemed to thrive in her presence. And for that matter, so did he. It felt right for her to stay.

She nodded her understanding, and as his mother and sister retreated into the corridor, she took a seat. Keeping silent but giving him a grin that lit her eyes as she peered upon the scene in his bed.

After the lengthy period of detachment, he was willing to stay like this—simply reflecting on his gratitude—for as long as Emily needed. God help him, he was even willing to tolerate Marigold, who'd settled on his other side. But after another minute, a choked sound emerged from the counterpane, and his daughter's narrow back shuddered beneath his palm.

"Em?" He tipped his head downward, and sure enough, the sound came again, an unmistakable sniffle followed by a gasp.

"Don't cry." He rubbed her back, wishing the gesture somehow had the power to take her tears away. "Everything's going to be all right now. I promise."

Phoebe reached for her, too, giving her shoulder a soft squeeze. Nevertheless, Emily's thin body continued to shake with the force of her sobs.

"It's all right," he repeated helplessly. "Everything is all r—"

"I'm sorry, Papa!" At last, her tear-stained face popped up, the words bursting out from her trembling lips. "I'm sorry I was so horrid to you for all this time. I didn't mean it. It's just that I thought ... I thought you wouldn't want me anymore. Not after ..."

She buried her face once more, leaving him to stare at Phoebe in horror, her open-mouthed shock mirroring his own. Emily believed he wouldn't *want* her? The suggestion cut like a blade. How could such a misconception have come about? How could he have *allowed* it to come about and then linger?

Very gently, he slid his fingers under her chin, coaxing her to look at him. "That could never be true, sweetheart. *Ever.*" He shook his head vehemently, not giving a damn for the ache. "What made you think such a thing?"

She blinked, her lashes spiky and wet against her pale skin, and took in a deep, wavering breath. "I overheard Mama talking to Mr. Mowbray when we were getting ready to board the ship. He asked if she was certain there wouldn't be trouble with you if she took me to India, and she said no because ... because I wasn't really your child."

The knife in his chest twisted deeper, the sheen in her eyes doing damn unnerving things behind his own eyelids. A fiery pit blasted open in his stomach. How could Cecilia have been so bloody careless with her words when she *knew* Emily always listened? How could she have led their daughter to believe something so untrue? How could she herself have believed it?

Yet Cecilia was gone, and there was little purpose to hurling his anger at her. As much as it may sting, perhaps he also needed to look at himself. To consider the portion of the blame that lay on his shoulders, for all the times he'd run off to Foxhill alone, consumed by his misery.

Well, that ended here. He couldn't erase his mistakes from the past, but he could spend his future making up for them. Starting by vanquishing Emily's misbelief and ingraining the truth so she never doubted it again for as long as she lived.

He held the sharp outline of her face within his palms. The face that made every bit of deceit and unhappiness in his marriage worth it. "You've been mine since the day you were born. Mine under the law, but, more importantly, mine in my heart. I love you, Emmy. Nothing in the world could change that."

He realized that he was breathing harder, that his pulse had become a beat in his head. When was the last time he'd made a declaration like that? *Never.* He should really do it more often. Because yes, it left him defenseless, but there was also something freeing about taking what he held bottled inside and letting it out. In giving her the truth she deserved to hear.

She pressed her mouth closed, and when she opened it to speak, her voice was low. Hesitant. "Do you truly mean it?"

"*Yes,*" he said emphatically, leaning forward to press a kiss to the wispy dark hair at her crown. "Always."

For a moment, the bedchamber was silent, for she gave him nothing but her shrewd amber stare. And then, the best thing happened. She smiled. A small, lopsided grin before she flopped back to the counterpane and snuggled against him once more. "I love you, too, Papa."

He wasn't quite prepared for how the words would hit. For how his throat would tighten and his chest ache, and still, he would recognize the feeling as joy.

He turned to the bedside chair to find that Phoebe's eyes had begun shining, and she gave them a brisk wipe before carefully rising to her feet. "I'm going to give you a moment," she murmured, reaching for the pitcher on his bedside table. Her lips curving upward. "Let me go refill this. I'll return soon."

The look she gave them as she departed said everything— that she understood his happiness. Emily's happiness. That she felt it, too.

He watched as the last bit of her hem disappeared into the corridor, his mind turning with all the things they needed to discuss. First, an assurance that she had hope of a happy outcome with her daughter as well. And then ... perhaps he and Emily could also share in her joy. Like a family ...

A nudge against his elbow drew his attention downward, and funnily enough, Marigold's nose pressing into his sleeve didn't provoke him to flinch or curse. For once, the creature's presence seemed—dare he say?—tolerable, and he let her be, instead focusing back on Emily, whose eyelids had grown heavy.

Make no wonder with everything she'd gone through today. The news she'd overheard at Beaumont Manor, the journey she'd taken, the matters they'd discussed. The resolution they'd reached.

He stroked her hair, watching as her eyelids closed fully. Feeling the months of distance and animosity melt away until all that remained was truth. Trust. Love. Perhaps someday, she would seek a deeper conversation regarding her parentage. However, his message would remain just the same as right now: she was his daughter in every way that mattered.

"Papa?" Her quiet question seemed to come from afar, making him vaguely aware that exhaustion was closing in on him, too. "Are you in love with Miss Windham?"

His drooping eyelids flew open, leading him to discover that, yet again, he'd become the subject of her scrutinizing gaze. And here he thought she'd fallen asleep.

"You're too clever for your own good," he mumbled, the words nearly tripping over each other, and Christ, why had he gotten so hot all of a sudden?

She pushed herself up on an elbow, arching a quizzical brow. "Does that mean yes?"

He gave a half-grin in spite of himself, sinking deeper against his pillows with a long exhale. It was no easy feat to conceal anything from someone so observant, so why attempt it? Why deny what became plainer to him with each passing day? "Yes, I believe it does."

Emily paused. Nodded once. Then dropped her head back to the counterpane as if she hadn't just posed a question of monumental importance. "Good. I'm very fond of her as well. Will you get married?"

He swallowed, refusing to let his response tangle this time. However, there was little he could do about the fact that his heart was fluttering. *Fluttering*, like he was a ridiculous love-struck boy fraught with nerves.

He supposed there was naught to do but embrace it. To answer the question with the same bluntness Emily had used to deliver it. With the truth. "Perhaps. If she'll have me."

Emily's eyes had closed again. Her slight smile, though, didn't fade. "She will."

30

After being jostled awake for a thorough prodding by the physician, Nicholas couldn't list a confrontation with his mother as an activity he wished to undertake. Nonetheless, as the physician departed his bedchamber, pronouncing him in seemingly good health and instructing him to take nourishing broths until his strength returned, the figure who appeared in the doorway after mere seconds elapsed was none other than the dowager marchioness herself.

"Yes?" Nicholas sat up straighter in bed, unable to keep the irritation from his voice. He wanted Phoebe. *Alone.* Between the repose he'd taken with Emily and the doctor's visit, he still hadn't been able to speak with her, and the anticipation was beginning to make his skin prick.

The dowager either didn't notice his impatience or didn't care—the latter, most likely—for she held tight to her cane, using it to cross the floor to his bedside.

"You needn't get yourself in a huff." She shot him a wry look, lowering herself into the chair where Phoebe had sat—which, consequently, was the very thing to increase his huffiness. "I don't plan to stay long."

"I'll hold you to that," he grumbled, watching as she took an absurd amount of time positioning her cane against his bedside table and then smoothing her skirts. He folded his arms across his chest, waiting—not patiently—in stony silence for her to say what she intended and be done with it.

"I …" She paused in a rare moment of tentativeness. Cleared her throat. Opened her mouth to speak and then closed it again before finally saying, "I wanted to ensure that you are suffering no ill effects after what happened."

For someone grazed by a bullet and struck in the head, I feel bloody wonderful. His jaw tightened, and he couldn't help but glance at the doorway. "I am not."

She nodded. Brought her gaze to the window. Turned back to him with her lips curled in distaste. "I still cannot believe the gall of that Ambrose Windham. We'll see if he feels so confident once he stands trial."

Nicholas's shoulder gave an answering throb. "Trial?"

"Why, of course." Her features darkened, her gnarled fingers clenching as if they closed around the man in question's neck. "Not only was he fool enough to put his challenge in writing, but he fired his pistol early in full view of a duke and a Bow Street runner. A conviction of attempted murder would be the least he deserves."

Fragments of the morning on Primrose Hill flashed through his head. The rustle in the trees. Phoebe's scream. The gunshot. *She hadn't been alone.*

He shifted against the pillows behind his back, letting the news settle. If his mother expected him to rejoice in the revelation, she'd find herself disappointed, for it paled in comparison to, say, *not* having the blight of Ambrose Windham cast upon him in the first place. Yet given the circumstances, he supposed it was as good an outcome as any. And Phoebe had helped bring it about. She'd wanted to protect him.

"As for Letitia Burville." The dowager scowled, uttering

the name venomously and then hesitating again. Putting to rest any question he had over whether she was aware of Lady Burville's involvement in Sir Ambrose's challenge. "There's another creature who possesses too much nerve for her own good."

"Yes," he agreed, his tone dry as sandpaper, "one would hate to associate with a lady possessing such deficiency of character."

The quip gave her pause but only for an instant, for it seemed that she'd suddenly regained her voice. "One gentleman enjoys associating with her, in any case. You'll not believe what I read in *The Times* this morning."

The dowager didn't often trouble herself with mundane gossip, but judging by the way she tilted toward him, her eyes widening intently, she was about to make an exception. "Lady Letitia Burville wed Charles Drummond, the Baron Copley, just yesterday by special license. Can you believe? A whirlwind courtship if ever there was one. No doubt the baron's vast estate in Derbyshire played a role."

Nicholas pursed his lips, unable to drum up any larger of a reaction. Frankly, he didn't care where Lady Burville made her home or with whom. His association with her was over and the resultant damage done. Behind him. Another woman filled his head, and this inane chatter was doing nothing but keeping him from her.

Again, his mother remained oblivious to his indifference, for she kept going, her voice lowering a shade and her mouth twisting into a sneer. "That's not the full story, though. I've heard rumors the baron's wealth is merely a facade. That his lands haven't turned a profit in close to a decade and his list of debts is a mile long. If that's the case, *dear* Letitia may find herself regretting her haste. But I suppose some lessons must be learned the hard way."

"Indeed." Nicholas arched a brow. *Such as the pitfalls of playing matchmaker when one's interference isn't wanted.*

His mother, who'd promised to make her visit brief, was doing no end of skirting around the issue at hand. Like she had something in mind to say but wouldn't voice it.

Well, he was tired of discussing people who wasted space in his thoughts, and if she wouldn't come out with it, he'd take the lead instead. After suffering the consequences of her meddling, he was now going to use the situation to his advantage.

"On that note," he said, "I'm ready to put the matter of Letitia Burville, Ambrose Windham, and that asinine duel behind me." *Which includes* your *role in bringing Lady Burville into the house and giving her false expectations.* He didn't speak the words aloud but narrowed his eyes to indicate as much. "I have other things on which to focus. Namely, I'm going to ask Miss Windham to marry me."

His mother's spine snapped upright, and a pinkish hue spread over her face. The quiet that followed was heavy, tentative, for the cords in her throat tightened, giving a slight quiver as she readied herself to release an irate deluge.

"*And*," he added before that happened, "you are not going to utter a single word of protest."

Her parted lips snapped closed, although her eyes flashed in a way that could make one think hell was covered in ice, not fire.

Lucky for him, he'd seen so many of her glowers over the years that the look didn't even cause him to blink. All that mattered was the silence, which gave him the freedom to lay out everything he intended to make clear. "I will not expect a jubilant celebration on your part. *However*, should Miss Windham do me the honor of becoming my wife, you are going to treat her with the courtesy befitting of the new

Marchioness of Rockliffe. It may happen that certain things come to pass that you do not agree with. There's apt to be gossip amongst the ton, and we'd best anticipate another scandal involving our family name. Be that as it may, you are going to accept the marriage, and should you ever feel the urge to do otherwise, you will kindly keep the sentiments concealed while reminding yourself of the detriments that arise when you interfere."

The dowager, to her credit, didn't shout or argue. She *listened*, her blue eyes wide and fixed upon him, the ice in them melting away. And when at last she spoke, it was only to pose a question. "You're very certain this is what you want?"

"Yes." *Unequivocally.*

Her jaw twitched, and a strange flicker passed over her features—no doubt from the myriad opinions she struggled to keep contained. In the end, though, the only thing to emerge was a long, resigned sigh. "There's nothing further to discuss, then. I'm not of a mind to argue with such obstinacy."

He clenched his teeth to hold back a bark of laughter. What was that saying regarding a pot and a kettle?

Ultimately, it didn't matter. As he'd long recognized, his mother wasn't the sort to admit fault or to do anything so uncouth as apologize; indeed, he'd end up in the grave before receiving her words of remorse. Yet in making this concession —however offhandedly and begrudgingly—she'd given just that: an apology.

Should he take that to mean she wouldn't involve herself in his choice of bride for once? Trust remained a shaky entity between them. However, his thoughts trickled back to the Beaumont dower house when she'd given him the clue, without question, to Adolphus Clare's whereabouts. The day when he'd looked at her and hadn't seen cunning but ... softness.

Come to think of it, a shadow of the same expression had

returned to her face now. The lines around her mouth and eyes as she peered at him stayed a shade tight, perhaps, but not hard. The look was familiar, akin to one that, God knew, had creased his own features too many times to count. A look of a parent concerned for their child.

Hmm. Perhaps she did only want what was best for her family—the thought poked at his chest—even if she had a damn awful way of showing it sometimes.

As the situation drew parallels to that in the dower house sitting room, the same response suddenly felt appropriate. A word he'd articulated to her once so could surely utter again. "Thank you."

She sat up a little straighter, extending her arm, and for a moment, he thought she was going to reach for him. Ultimately, though, her hand stopped at her cane, her fingers curling around the silver tip. "As promised, Rockliffe, I'm keeping my visit brief." She pushed herself upward, drawing her spine tall in a picture of perfect, composed elegance. "There's someone else eager to come in and see you, and it seems the feeling is mutual."

Was ... was that another *concession*? The realization caused him to gape. He could feel his mouth hanging, knew he looked ridiculous, but there was nothing he could do to prevent it.

She stood looking down on him, as regal and unapproachable as a queen. However, against the backdrop of the over-sized furniture that graced the marquess's chamber, she also appeared ... small. Still subdued. Enough that, when he looked at her, he didn't see only an adversary. He saw his *mother*. The bane of his existence. The cause of his existence.

"Thank you," he repeated under his breath as she began hobbling across the carpet and toward the doorway. Too low to reach her, but it felt right to say it, nonetheless.

Perhaps she intended for her muttered words to remain

out of his earshot as well. Be that as it may, they traveled back to him, a quiet hum he could just decipher before she disappeared into the corridor and nothing remained but the echo of her cane. "I'm glad you're well, Nicholas."

31

The seconds for which Phoebe was forced to wait before returning to Nicholas's bedchamber stretched by like an eternity. First, the physician arrived, his visit lasting longer than she knew an examination could take. Then, the dowager insisted on a private word, and no one, Phoebe included, had felt the inclination to gainsay her. Instead, Phoebe paced the drawing room in anticipation—an activity she was becoming regrettably familiar with of late.

When, at last, word came from Flynt that Lord Rockliffe was alone and wished to speak with her, she sprinted nearly the entire way upstairs, ladylike footsteps and reserve be hanged. However, in the final few paces leading to his bedchamber door, she slowed, all the long seconds suddenly seeming to speed up and race by.

Although perhaps the racing was actually the rapid thrum of her heart. The frenzied pulse in her head as she tried to sort everything she needed to say to him. As she thought of what she hoped for. And of what she feared.

She took a breath as she stepped into the doorway. Placed a hand on the skirt she'd been wearing far too long.

Nicholas was sitting on the edge of the bed waiting, a light flashing through his eyes as they fell upon her.

And in that moment, every inhibition melted away. She ran, crashing onto the bed beside him, casting her arms about his neck. It felt so good to bury her face against his shoulder, to breathe him in, to have his quiet exhale brush through her hair.

And then, when his arms reached out to encircle her waist, drawing her close—she couldn't describe that feeling as good. It was *heaven*.

"Phoebe." He murmured her name in the shell of her ear. The best sound, the best sensation. However, it lasted only a moment before he pulled back, and although he kept his voice low, urgency crept into his tone. "You need to tell me everything that happened over the past four days. Am I correct in thinking that my man of business sent you news?"

She nodded hurriedly, trying to shake the feeling of his touch long enough to focus. After her days of sitting in this room in agonizing silence, waiting for things that may or may not come to pass, so much was happening all at once, overwhelming yet wonderful. "Mr. Clare returned from Suffolk and came to me here at Rockliffe House earlier today."

He sucked in an audible breath, his fingers sinking into her shoulder. "And?"

"He found her." She repeated the words she'd sobbed to him while he lay unconscious. Words that had since had a little more time to percolate, although the feeling they evoked in her chest remained airy enough to seem surreal. "She remained in Suffolk this whole time. First with a family and then, at a school in Bury St Edmunds, where it seems Eugenia was paying her tuition. She's in good health, he said, and ..." She stuttered, a familiar lump rising in her throat. "Her name is Mary Anne."

"Phoebe." Again, he murmured the sound that did

strange things to her insides. He pulled her into another embrace, and when he drew away this time, he gifted her with something she'd so seldom seen upon his features, that transformed his whole countenance: a smile. "You can go to her, then."

"Yes." She smiled in return, even as tears threatened from the powerful surge of emotion shooting through her veins. The joyful anticipation of reuniting with her daughter grew all the time. She couldn't stop envisioning the first moment she laid eyes on her, the moment she held the girl in her arms. But even so, it didn't negate the ache that came when she thought of leaving Beaumont Manor permanently and never seeing Nicholas or Emily again.

"Whatever assistance you need—whenever you need it—is yours." He pushed a tangled strand of hair behind her ear, then hesitated, a small vee forming between his brows as he studied her. "Only ... don't travel to Suffolk as Miss Phoebe Windham. Go as the Marchioness of Rockliffe instead."

Phoebe's mouth dropped open, all the air in her lungs escaping in a single short gasp. "But ..." She clenched her fingers against the counterpane, refusing to let her heart soar beyond the depths of reality. Beyond the awful facts she couldn't ignore. "I've brought nothing but trouble upon you. Your association with me could have cost you your li—"

"Listen to me." His strong hand cupped her jaw, and he leaned in, forcing their gazes to lock. "My life before you was rife with trouble. *You* are the one who made it bright again. *You* are the one who made me realize what it is to fall in love. A duel is a small price to pay, and I would do it a thousand times over if, in the end, I had you at my side."

Love. He ... he *loved* her? If only he could see how the admission filled her heart, how every word he spoke was what she dreamed of, too. Having Nicholas not as someone she longed for from afar but as the man—the husband—beside her. The person for whom she would go to the ends of the earth. Whom she would love for all eternity.

"But ... I cannot be a proper marchioness." Again, doubts churned in her stomach like a pestilence. Everything she wished for was in front of her, dangling on a string. However, the words that had become ingrained in her over the past years held her captive, clamping tight to her chest and swirling through her head until she couldn't hold them in. "I'm scandalous and shameful and—"

"No." The set of his jaw turned hard, his blue eyes ready to pierce her. "I never want to hear those words spoken about you again, even if they come from your own mouth. Anyone who ever made you think that is both wrong and insignificant, as is anyone who chances to voice that opinion in the future. To me, you're perfect, and I don't want you any way other than exactly as you are. For that's the essence of it: I *want* you, Phoebe. As a wife. As a mother to my daughter. Just as I hope you want Emily and me to be family to you. *And* to Mary Anne."

With that came her undoing. A moment when something inside her broke loose and the concealed tears began slipping through her lashes. "I want that, too," she whispered, making the thumb he used to wipe moisture from her cheek suddenly halt.

The admission was frightening, like she still reached for something she wasn't supposed to have. Yet perhaps it was time to let go of the trepidation and believe in second chances. To believe in herself. To believe in love.

Hope rose within her, a blossoming swell, and this time, she didn't try to tamp it down. It grew, the buoyant sensation spreading through her limbs until she felt like she could float to the ceiling. Until her chest unknotted, and all that remained was the truth, ready to burst free. "I want *you*. I've thought of you ever since I took that silly dare to swim in the Beaumont lake, never imagining an association between us would be possible. Now that it *has* been possible ... I love you, Nicholas. For your strength and loyalty. For making me feel desired, accepted, supported. For staying with me in my darkest moment and finding a way to make the world right again."

More droplets ran down her face, and his hands stayed there, holding her close, brushing the tears away. He looked as though he scarcely dared to breathe.

"I want to do that for you as well," she said. "To make you always feel like the world is good and full and forgiving. Like you're supported and loved. Because while you can be remarkably aggravating at times"—she couldn't resist throwing in the playful jab, giving him a light tap on the nape of his neck—"I, too, think you're perfect just as you are, and I have no greater wish than to become your wife. Emily's mother. For—the *four* of us to be a family."

How wonderful it felt to say that. To let herself well and truly imagine without inhibition. To believe that all her dreams really could come true.

And then, he sealed it with a kiss, his mouth falling against hers with a pressure that made her dizzy.

Was it possible to expire from too much happiness? Warmth and lightness inundated her senses, a stream of bliss she never wanted to end. She reveled in the embrace, savoring each caress of his fingers, each motion of his lips.

It was no easy feat to eventually pull away. Yet as much as she lamented the loss of his mouth on hers, she was greeted with the sight of peerless blue eyes boring into her as if she were the stars and moon. With another smile that was hers alone to claim.

This was her future: passion, and joy, and love more potent than she'd known could exist.

The kiss was only the beginning of their happiness.

Epilogue

Two months later

For an evening in September, when the sun had already set and given way to a sliver of moon, the air in the Beaumont Manor garden stayed particularly warm. Then again, Phoebe couldn't imagine ever feeling cold while walking arm-in-arm with her husband.

Without breaking the leisurely pace they'd established as they meandered down the gravel path, she cast a glance his way, her heart giving its usual flutter. Nicholas's features were shadowed, lit only by starlight and the faint glow of the lantern he held at his side. Nonetheless, the mere outline of him—the suggestion of broad shoulders, of a strong jaw, of hair that had the slightest hints of bronze—was enough to evoke memories that made her pulse quicken.

She pressed her fingers a little tighter against his coat sleeve, relishing the feel of the heat, of the rigid muscles beneath. Sometimes, she still needed to do this—to take an especially thorough look at her surroundings, to press her hand or lips to his—to remind herself she hadn't imagined the whole thing. However, the dusky figure next to her squeezed back, meeting her gaze with a languid half-smile.

He was, unequivocally, real. *Hers.* Her husband.

With a slight increase in speed, he led her across the foot-bridge and continued along the path at the other side of the lake. They hadn't come this way in a long time—not since the night of the storm when they'd fled to the temple and let desire consume them. A shock of heat pooled between her legs at the memory. That passion still ignited each evening when the house fell quiet at last and they could close themselves into his bedchamber. However, opportunities to go beyond the manor's walls, alone and unhurried, had proved rare of late.

The past two months had indeed been a whirlwind, filled with life-changing things. Wonderful things. Their marriage by special license in the Rockliffe House drawing room. Her journey to the young ladies' seminary in Bury. And then, the moment she'd been introduced to the girl with the blond braid and eyes of the same color Phoebe saw when she looked in the mirror—*changeable eyes*, Nicholas called them—and recognized her as her own.

Eyes, on Phoebe's part, that had filled with tears that spilled over in a steady trickle, despite how she'd sworn to herself that she would remain composed until after saying everything she needed to.

Are you sad, my lady? They were the first words Mary Anne had spoken to her in her bell-like voice, watching intently as Phoebe crouched at her level.

Words that had made Phoebe's tears flow harder, although her smile had become so wide, it felt like her cheeks might split. *No, darling.* She'd shaken her head. Let her fingertip run along the edge of her daughter's soft, wispy braid. *I've never been so happy in my entire life.*

The schoolmistress had placed them together in a quiet sitting room, leaving Phoebe to explain to Mary Anne the purpose for her visit as she saw fit. An endeavor that could have taken hours had she recounted every detail from the past eight years, but that she also needed to make suitable for a young child to hear. And so, she'd simply come out with it, peering into the face that had instantly captured her heart. *I'm your mama.*

The declaration had understandably made the little girl's features pucker in confusion, although instead of shying away, she'd come closer, as if to whisper a secret in Phoebe's ear. *But … I don't have a mama.*

You do. And I love you all the way to the stars. Phoebe had held out her arms, knowing she was a stranger to the girl, that she had no right to expect anything. Closeness would take time. Except then, Mary Anne had walked right into her embrace, burying her face against Phoebe's shoulder as if she'd always belonged there.

Phoebe didn't have words to describe what she'd felt in that moment as the two of them clung to each other. Only that those precious seconds would be forever etched in her memory as the time when all facets of her heart had finally become whole.

She'd departed the school with Mary Anne shortly thereafter, passing the hours in the carriage by asking her questions about her likes and dislikes, about all the little details she wished to learn. By telling her, in return, of the father and sister who awaited her back in Kent.

Arriving at Beaumont, where everyone Phoebe loved was under the same roof at last, proved another monumental occasion that evoked emotions too powerful to name. It marked both a new beginning and the start of an adjustment period. The time in which the four of them learned to be a family.

The change hadn't happened seamlessly overnight. After all, each one of them had been placed in a role they never could have anticipated. After a few days, though, of wandering around the house in quiet wonder, Mary Anne—Anna, they'd taken to calling her—had begun conversing more and more, showing herself quick to laugh and eager to ask questions. She especially enjoyed frolicking in the garden throughout the day, bestowed them all with the biggest hugs before bedtime each night—a privilege Phoebe would never take for granted—and held a particular fondness for Emily, the distinguished lady five years her senior.

Emily deserved commendation, for she'd adapted to the position of older sister splendidly. She was both thoughtful and patient with Anna's questions, was generous with gifting her old playthings, and never complained—much—when the younger girl wouldn't cease following her around.

The two had spent many hours together on a picnic blanket by the lake, laughing at Marigold's antics and reading aloud from Emily's favorite books. And as the summer days slipped by, Emily's face grew less gaunt. Her limbs sturdier. Her body slower to tire.

The result of good country air, surely. Although Phoebe liked to think that perhaps the company in which she found herself also played a part.

As for Nicholas—she stole another glance at him, grinning at the strand of hair that had toppled roguishly onto his forehead—the summer had brought some subtle changes to his countenance as well. He'd recovered his strength in short order —fortunate, as the period directly after the injury, in which he'd been forced to slow down and rest, had irritated him to no end. The recent news that Ambrose had been sentenced to Newgate made them both go about with a little more lightness in their steps. However, she knew that wasn't the true reason for why he no longer held his shoulders so stiffly. Why the lines around his mouth had softened. Why his smiles had become more frequent.

The reason for those changes could only be love. An elusive happiness that had finally settled.

She'd witnessed it in the simple moments. The times he and Emily walked side by side in the garden, pushing themselves to go a little farther each day. The times he swung Anna atop her first pony, leading her out of the stables as she squealed with delight. The times—twice, now—that she'd caught him asleep in his study with Marigold in his lap, his fingertips buried in her mass of orange fur. Not that he'd ever admit to it.

They were all moments that pulled at her heart, too, filling her with bright, unsurpassable joy. A joy she and Nicholas couldn't always discuss at length—truthfully, the days were often too busy, and the nights too impassioned—but that they expressed with glances across the breakfast table. With the brushing of fingers whenever they drew near one another. With quick, stolen kisses beneath the trees.

Tonight, however, was different. After close to a week of rain, the four of them had taken advantage of the returning sun by staying outdoors until dusk, rendering Anna tired enough to sleep early for a change. With the drawing room silent, devoid of the girls' usual poetry recitations and songs upon the pianoforte that proved endearingly ... *creative*, Nicholas had suggested a walk. A proposition Phoebe had accepted wholeheartedly.

She cherished every second spent in her girls' company, had relished the entire carefree summer, and was already lamenting the arrival of October, when they'd agreed they would hire a governess specifically trained for the role.

Nonetheless, it felt nice to have Nicholas alone for a spell. To saunter instead of run, to rest her arm upon his indefinitely, to know that if she leaned in for a kiss, they wouldn't have to rush it.

She was about to tell him so—and perhaps demonstrate

the kiss part—when their surroundings gave her pause. They'd veered off the path and were starting down a gentle slope, the grass tall and soft beneath her slipper-clad feet. Why, he was leading her toward the lakeshore, although the lake beyond was little more than a black expanse, catching only a tiny glimmer of light from the lantern in his hand and the stars above.

He trod carefully, holding tight to her so she didn't stumble, and he seemed to recognize the exact place to stop and set down the lantern despite the darkness. After which he whirled her around, his fingers deftly locating the row of buttons that fastened her new sapphire silk evening gown.

Blood rushed to her head from the sudden spin, from the feel of his bare fingertips against her back. "What are you doing?" The words came out fluttery and breathless.

He kept going, working down the entire row until the dress gaped, and he pushed it from her arms. "Something that is long overdue."

She gasped as the dress hit the ground and the warm breeze rustled through her shift. He got to his knees, his hand falling squarely upon her thigh. Eliciting a husky moan from her throat. However, instead of traveling upward, stroking and circling the places that always made her shatter, he slid his hand to the ribbon that held up her stocking and unfastened the bow. Repeated the process on the other side.

Night air danced against more unclothed skin, and her head whirled at a dizzying pace. He seemed so determined, rising back to his feet and ridding her of her stays before taking hold of the final ribbon upon her person—the one securing her shift. Yet here he remained fully clothed, not lingering and caressing like he usually did but giving her only the barest of touches.

She grabbed hold of his shoulders, stepping sideways and pulling him along with her so their faces both fell under the lantern's glow. She parted her lips but didn't attempt speech, shooting him a look of silent curiosity.

The corners of his mouth twitched in response, and he gave his chin a pointed nudge toward the stretch of blackness beside them, distinguishable as water from the soft lapping sounds that hit the bank. "You once had aspirations of swimming in this lake, did you not?"

She felt her brows shift and her eyes go large. "Yes, but—"

"Your chance has come, wife. The night is warm. We're alone."

Oh, Lord. How did he manage to make such seemingly innocuous words sound so deliciously sinful? They shot through her with a thrilling little jolt, causing gooseflesh to appear on her skin and need to pulse between her legs.

He didn't say the phrase that, nearly a decade prior, had set all this in motion: *I dare you.* It felt like a challenge nonetheless, and, as was the case with Clara at the vicarage eight years ago, a challenge was something from which she wouldn't back down. Especially when it contained such wicked promise.

She peered at him through her lashes, running her tongue over her bottom lip. "Will you join me, husband?"

A stifled noise rose from his throat, and his fingers jerked where they hovered above her neckline. Nonetheless, he shook his head. "Not yet." He retrieved the lantern with his free hand, his body remaining vexingly beyond the point of brushing against hers. "You got to observe me as I swam. Now, I'm inclined to watch you."

The words curled low in her belly like a caress. He had a valid point, and she supposed it was only fair that she obliged. But more importantly ... she *wanted* to oblige. To feel his gaze upon her, worshiping her like a water nymph. A goddess.

He glanced down at the ribbon securing her shift and back

up to her face, his eyes two gleaming, desirous pools that voicelessly posed a question: *May I?*

Yes. Any brief thought she had of making him wait, of filling him with the same maddening anticipation he'd evoked with his brief, featherlight touches, vanished in the blink of an eye. Rather, vanished in the span of her brisk nod, which came of its own volition. She couldn't wait any longer, for her body had grown too hot, and she wanted, *needed*—

He wrenched the ribbon loose, and in a single fluid motion, the fine lawn garment slipped away and puddled at her feet. Leaving every inch of her exposed to the whispering breeze. To his heated stare.

She shivered, her skin tingling and nipples pebbling, although certainly not from cold. He made another sound, low and ragged, and for one charged, anticipatory moment, it looked like he would finally grant her the pleasure of his lips.

In the end, though, she got only his breath, which skirted along the shell of her ear as he leaned in. His exhales had become unsteady. His voice a rasp. "Go on. The water's deep here. You can jump." He shifted abruptly, holding out the lantern to illuminate the place where shore became water.

This was it, then. If she stayed on land any longer, she may very well attempt to pull him down to the grass with her and forget a lake existed.

She turned to the dimly lit stretch of water, taking a step to the edge of the shore. She briefly entertained the thought of easing her foot below the surface to test the temperature. But no. If she was to fulfill the dare, she would do nothing by half measures.

She closed her eyes, envisioning sunlight. Swaying trees. His powerful limbs pushing through the water.

And then, she jumped, plunging below the inky surface.

The sudden blast of water shocked her nerve endings, for

the air above had been too warm, too heavy, but the lake was cold, bracing ... *exhilarating*.

The numbness evaporated, leaving her senses sharper, and she began kicking through the depths, hurtling upward in a euphoric rush. During a handful of the summer's hottest days, she and the girls had sat on the shore and dipped their toes in the water, sending up gentle splashes as they moved their feet. However, that feeling couldn't compare to the bliss of being submerged in it, to having the coolness inundate her over-heated skin, to hearing it roar past her ears as she made her ascent.

She broke through the surface and threw her head back, releasing a giggle. She hadn't felt this way—so free, so alive—since ... well, ever.

The scrap of moon shone directly above her, surrounded by a plethora of twinkling stars. As for the lantern—she began treading water, reorienting herself with the direction of the shore—it was no longer in Nicholas's grip but on the grass beside him. Illuminating the fact that he'd bent over and was hastily tugging off his boots.

With a grin, she dove back under the surface, basking in the water's invigorating embrace. If only the girl of eighteen who'd stared through the trees at the lake—at the man *in* the lake, and felt her heart race—could have seen ahead to this moment. Could have watched all her desires come to fruition.

The feeling went beyond elation, and it wouldn't stop spiraling. For when Phoebe's head popped out of the water this time, Nicholas was there beside her, capturing her by the waist. Claiming her lips.

Their bodies collided as they bobbed in the water, his taut, slippery chest rubbing against the tips of her breasts. His manhood brushing temptingly against her sex.

The kiss quickly grew deep, urgent, a melding of tongues that sent need ricocheting to her core. She didn't consciously decide to swim back to land, but regardless, it seemed that's where they were floating, their rotating legs propelling them the short distance back to shore.

Which, suddenly, was precisely where she wanted to be. The water and his lips continued to shroud her, perfect and vitalizing. However, it was no longer enough, for she needed …

She needed him to break out of the water and vault back onto the shore, to pull her along with him, to lie with her on the grass in a tangle of limbs.

Which was exactly what he did. He stretched his dripping body atop her, nudging his swelling cock between her thighs. Pressing his wet lips to her ear, her throat, to each of her hardened nipples.

Until all at once, everything spun, and she was no longer beneath him but atop him, peering down into eyes dark with longing.

With her body aflame, she leaned into him, kissing away the droplets that dotted his left shoulder. The place that, not so long ago, had contained an injury but now bore only a small scar as a memento of his resilience. Despite her escalating need, she lingered to breathe him in, to kiss every part of the ridged surface until the only moisture remaining on his skin came from the tip of her tongue.

Only then did she raise her spine, gasping as he took hold of her hips and shifted them upward. Positioning her in the place they both desired most: directly above his arousal.

Her mind flashed back to one of their earliest nights in the marquess's bedchamber as man and wife. A night when she'd retrieved the pilfered book that had been stashed away in her clothespress and they'd lain in bed, flipping through the pages together. When he'd asked what illustrations best pleased her, and, with her pulse beating between her legs, she'd pointed to a woman sitting astride a man like one might sit on a horse. After which he'd dragged her atop him, guiding her onto his cock while issuing a guttural command: *ride me, wife*.

She repeated the motion now, plunging downward until his rigid length filled her to the hilt, causing the same shower of sparks to flare. In fact, the fire seemed even more potent this time, ready to burn to the stars above.

She established a rhythm, moving her hips up and sinking back down in a relentless cycle, each stroke bringing her closer to the edge of a dizzying height. The gentle breeze continued to sway over her wet skin, but she felt nothing except heat. How could cold exist when he fixed her with his stare, rapt and smoldering beneath the lantern's glow, like she truly was a creature to be revered?

Her limbs grew tight and quivering, the sound of her needy cries floating through her ears as if they came from afar. And then, as yearning began to feel like it would drive her mad, his fingers joined his eyes in the veneration, tracing along her breasts, down her abdomen, to her mound. Finding the pearl that contained the heart of her pleasure and circling, stroking—

Release crashed over her like a flood, making the stars come down from the sky to dance before her eyes. Her intimate muscles pulsed around him with sharp, blissful spasms, and he thrust his hips upward with a groan, a burst of warmth shooting deep inside her as he found his own release.

She collapsed onto his chest, embracing the lingering pleasure-filled waves, inhaling the crisp scents of grass and leaves, the heady scent of arousal. He held her tight, his fingers sinking into the curve of her bottom as they waited for their heart rates to slow and the world to stop spinning.

Eventually, her breath returned to a normal tempo, and his chest went from heaving with exertion to subtly rising and falling beneath her cheek.

That was the moment he bent his head so he could

whisper in her ear. "Tell me, sweet. Was your swim in the Beaumont lake everything you hoped it would be?"

She'd thought herself sated, but that low hum, that kiss of breath, didn't fail to elicit its usual twinge between her thighs. And a caress upon her heart.

She turned her neck, resting her chin upon his chest so she could gaze at him. The man she'd once desired from afar as an impossible dream, but who now, against all odds, was *hers*. Her partner. Her strength. Her true love, now and forever.

"It was *everything*, husband." She let the final word linger on her tongue, never tiring of the chance to use it, to remind herself of her remarkable good fortune. "Everything, and so much more."

~

THE END

Bonus Content

Sign up for Jane's monthly newsletter to get access to free bonus content, including a subscriber-exclusive epilogue for *The Marquess Returns*. You will also be the first to know about new releases, giveaways, special promotions, and more. Join now at: www.janemaguireauthor.com/newsletter

About the Author

Jane Maguire is a Canadian author whose lifelong passions for history, writing, and love stories inevitably led her to begin penning historical romance novels. While her love of historical fiction spans all eras, she focuses her writing on high society in the regency period. She enjoys crafting stories with lots of angst, which makes giving her characters their happily ever afters all the more satisfying.

When she isn't at her computer writing and researching, you can find her vacationing in the Rocky Mountains, playing classical music on the piano, or simply curling up with a cup of tea and a good book. She lives with her husband, two kids, and a very floofy cat.

You can find Jane online at www.janemaguireauthor.com.

www.ingramcontent.com/pod-product-compliance
Lightning Source LLC
Chambersburg PA
CBHW050926220726
48290CB00018B/1602